Orphans

of the

Carnival

———

Orphans

of the

Carnival

A NOVEL

CAROL BIRCH

DOUBLEDAY

NEW YORK LONDON TORONTO

SYDNEY AUCKLAND

All rights reserved. Published in the United States by Doubleday, a division of Penguin Random House LLC, New York. Originally published in hardcover in Great Britain by Canongate Books Ltd., Edinburgh, in 2016.

www.doubleday.com

DOUBLEDAY and the portrayal of an anchor with a dolphin are registered trademarks of Penguin Random House LLC.

Book design by Pei Loi Koay
Jacket design by Janet Hansen and Emily Mahon
Jacket illustration © Culver Pictures / The Art Archive at Art Resource, NY

LIBRARY OF CONGRESS CATALOGING-IN-PUBLICATION DATA
Names: Birch, Carol, 1951– author.
Title: Orphans of the carnival : a novel / by Carol Birch.
Description: First edition. | New York : Doubleday, [2016]
Identifiers: LCCN 2016002398 | ISBN 9780385541527 (hardcover) |
ISBN 9780385541534 (ebook)
Classification: LCC PR6052.I785 O77 2016 | DDC 823/.914—dc23
LC record available at http://lccn.loc.gov/2016002398

MANUFACTURED IN THE UNITED STATES OF AMERICA

1 3 5 7 9 10 8 6 4 2

First United States Edition

For Martin

PART I

New World

T his is where your lost toys went, the one the dog chewed, the one your mother threw out without asking when you left home, the ones you always wondered about.

The island says: bring me your lost, your scorned, forgotten masses, bring me your maimed and ridiculous, bring me so much as a finger or a toe and I'll take you in. Be you ever so grotesque or beauty sublime, it's all the same to me. Everyone's allowed in. Doesn't matter who you were or what your story, doesn't matter what state you're in. You could've been smashed to smithereens, even your broken bits are welcome here.

————————

There's nothing to the island. The Aztecs made it, many moons ago, long before the white men came. Trees, a stream, a few shacks, an old wooden landing stage. White butterflies hover over red flowers. From time to time a bird whistles, high and thin and querulous. A stream of water makes no sound. The dolls are legion. Strange fruit, they hang on every tree, and the trees crowd close. They hang like bunting on rusty wires running between the trees. They have covered all the walls, inside and out, filled every crack and cranny. The oldest has been here for more than fifty years; the youngest just arrived. The filth is proud.

In the center of the island, at the center of a shrine in the middle of a moldy old shack with the word MUSEO over the door, a solemn black-haired, blue-eyed girl doll sits like Buddha under a framed color photograph of the hermit of the island, now dead. She is decked with

beads and thin curled ribbons, some faded, some less so, surrounded
by the gifts people bring to her, a strange trove of jewelry and holy
pictures, sweets and candles, coins and finger puppets, small toys, a
Rubik's Cube, a troll, a worn set of Pokemon cards and a pink-haired
white pony with large mascaraed eyes. This little girl will want for
nothing. She is the little girl who drowned here so long ago, whoever
she was. No one knows. It doesn't matter. Little girls are loved and they
drown, and there must be comfort for what can't be cured. There must
be dolls and shrines and remembrance in the company of a host of faces.
Under the corrugated roof, dolls and their parts dangle from the rafters.
From ceiling to dirt floor they hang on the flaking whitewashed walls.
Spiders have woven furry gray curtains between them, veiling the faces
of a few. There is a blunt-faced boy, made by the cobwebs into a strange
smudged apparition. Flies hum. Silky eyes, whitened as if by cataracts,
peer through trailing gray lianas. Baby dolls, sexy dolls, rag dolls, teen
queens, ugly dolls, demon dolls, elvish dolls, dolls in the national cos-
tumes of various countries, naked and clothed, suspended, flying like
angels. A strung-up baby in a blue romper suit hangs broken-necked,
half-faced, dirt-encrusted. A gangster's moll in a silk dress is losing her
hectic red curls. A tiny face sleeps in the rafters, the underlip tucked in.
The closed eyes have the authentic, ancient look of the newborn.

The smell of long-established mold was thick and warm on the air.

Outside, a slight breeze scarcely moved the long leaves and whiplike
branches. You could walk 'round the island in a couple of minutes, but
no one did. The endless diversity of decay slowed you down, variations
on dollskin: poxed, blistered, burned black, bleached white, patterned
elaborately, sometimes geometrically, by weather and the passage of
time. Flies crawled on the dolls, gathering like mud in the creases of
their clothes. Their eyes spewed bugs. Crazed with a million cracks,
mud-splattered, twined with leaves, they grinned with filth-clotted
mouths, reached out for a hug, beseeched, pondered, smiled serenely.
Most of them were babies.

An obscene pink knob poked out of a headless torso. A girl with mud-
bedraggled hair and the left leg of another leaned down in greeting, her
face a moving black mask of bugs. An old lamp lay in a thicket, a head
with black-rimmed eyes poking out of it. A single strand of hair hung
down to its chin, and its large blue eyes were innocent and interested.

It seemed about to speak. A fat white leg hung on a line. In the root of a tree, a tangle of limbs clung to each other. A clown wore a bonnet. Naked Barbies with hair gone wild had colonized a thin tree, one of them sensibly wearing her sunglasses.

It was a sky burial in slow motion.

· *1854* ·

The train shook, her brain shook. She flew into the future, dreaming she was lost in a big white house that went on forever, the windows dusty like the windows of the diligence taking her on the first stretch of her journey, from Culiacán to Los Mochis, to get over the mountains and out of Mexico. She saw glimpses of far mountains and miles of scrub, and occasionally a poor peon tramping in rags. Then she was back in her bunk, listening to the sound that had woken her up: a baby crying, far along the train toward New Orleans, a lost thin bleating like a lamb.

Needing privacy, she'd paid a few extra dollars to get a berth for the night. The sleeper was dark and cramped, the passage very narrow, people walking up and down it constantly, brushing against the thick hessian curtain she'd pulled across in front of her bed. A man in the bunk across the passage snored and snorted and tossed, so close it was indecent, and the clanking and screeching, the jolting and swaying, the dusty coal smell kept her awake. At least she had sheets and they were clean. She huddled down into them with old Yatzi, thinking about the great city, every great promised city, New York, Chicago, Boston, and the people she'd meet tomorrow in New Orleans. Yatzi's bald wooden head was tucked under her chin.

The whistle was a soul in distress. God, but this land was flat and endless. Miles and miles of spreading green, some trees, occasionally a crossroads. The flatness had become a dream verging on nightmare. No one lived here. That there were flat places in the world she'd known, but the enormity of it scared her even more than crossing the mountains. She'd been afraid all the way from Culiacán. The first couple of days she kept thinking she'd get off at the next stop and go back home. She thought she'd be discovered. They'd be attacked by bandits, robbed. Killed. Two more weeks, slogging higher and higher into her mother's mountains in a smelly wagon she couldn't even get out of to stretch her legs, not till everyone else was asleep, and then only for a brief interlude of wide cool darkness, a quick look up at the frosty stars. The driver and all the passengers thought she was a young girl traveling alone to meet her guardian, veiled because of a vow she'd made to Our Lady. Respecting her silence, they left her alone and were kind and helpful whenever they made a stop. Up the mountains, down the mountains, going mad with boredom, sleeping and drifting, jerking awake a hundred times, and with every mile that jolted by feeling more and more unreal, losing all sense of distance, the world a giant carpet unfolding endlessly.

In the morning they pulled into a depot. She was up and dressed and veiled, sitting by one of the small windows. The porter came with bread and coffee. New Orleans was no more than a couple of hours away, he said. The coffee was appalling. She was sick to death of this veil. She'd never had to wear it so much at home. It didn't matter. All these new people she'd have to meet, she'd be famous, Rates said. She would perform. They'd flock in their millions. And they'd pay. After New Orleans, New York. Let them goggle. You show them, you show them what you can do, how proud you are, you go out there and let them see you. Can't do it, she thought. *Scared. Scared.* Have to. Come this far. Who is this Rates anyway? *Mamá, I'm lost.* She sipped the bitter muck. He could be a crook or a madman for all she knew. All she remembered was a suave pudgy little man, well spoken. In New Orleans, Mr. Rates said, there'd be a big rehearsal room where she could practice on a real stage. What if he wasn't there? Alone in New Orleans. Never get back home.

The conductor was calling all aboard. The place filled up. She watched the country roll by again, flat as ever still, but broken up now with vast stretches of water and acres of sugarcane, and people sprinkled out like black corn, working the flatness. The long car was packed, boys passed up and down the aisle selling candy and papers, and the heat was terrible. Off in the distance from time to time a cluster of slave cabins would appear, and sometimes a great white house. The windows didn't open. The air was ripe with sweaty people. A stove at one end leaked smoke.

At the station she stood with her grip on the ground beside her. The place swarmed, the same as all the other way stations they'd stopped at along the road, only bigger and noisier. She didn't see Mr. Rates and didn't know what to do, where to wait. Everyone was shouting, shunting luggage around. She tried to get out of the way, close to tears. And then he loomed in front of her, the portly man from the night of Marta's wedding, with his thin-lipped smile and small pale eyes. At the wedding he'd been dressed like a gentleman, but here he wore a loud checked jacket and carried a black cane with a silver tip.

"My dear Miss Julia," he said in an oily way.

"Mr. Rates," she said, "I was just wondering what to do if you hadn't been here."

"Of course I'm here."

A thin pockmarked boy whose nose turned up extremely appeared at Mr. Rates's side. He looked straight at her veiled face, then away.

"And on time, you see," Rates said. "Is this all you have?"

She looked down. Her stuff looked paltry. "This is all," she said.

"Excellent. Michael!"

The boy picked up her grip and her guitar and set off briskly, weaving through the crowd. Mr. Rates offered Julia his arm and led her after him. "You must be tired," he said. "Terrible journey, terrible, I've done it myself. All went well, I take it?"

"Yes."

"Excellent."

Outside, the horses hung down their long brown heads, nostrils steaming. Their carriage smelled of dung and lemons. All the books she'd read in Don Pedro's house had not prepared her for the excitement of New Orleans. "But it's too big!" she said with a nervous laugh. "It goes on and on." It was a city of long streets and tall terraces, big houses with gardens, Spanish courtyards that put her in mind of Culiacán, and everywhere people teeming, loitering, meeting and parting, more people than she'd ever seen. Music flashed by, the high whistling peal of a street organ. Trying to see, she carefully lifted her veil, and was aware of a tightening in Rates's attention. But she held it slantwise, cleverly, so that it was like looking out of a tunnel. No one could see her.

"Careful," Rates said very softly by her ear.

She had never felt so buried yet so alive, and she dropped the veil.

"I'm scared about meeting all the new people," she said too quickly.

Rates leaned back. "Of course," he said, "it's only natural. But there's nothing to be afraid of." He smiled and, putting on his grand stage voice declaimed, "You were born to entertain!"

"I'm sick, sick of this veil!"

"Not long now," he said, "you can take it off soon," patting her gloved hand and leaning close so that she could smell a slight odor from his breath. "You're not shy, Julia," he said. "It's what I noticed first about you. How calmly you faced the world with that stupendous, utterly unnatural face of yours, and of course—you know the spirit in which I say that, it's merely a stated fact—I knew then you were a natural. No, no, there's no doubt in my mind, no doubt at all, but that you'll thrive."

The carriage swerved to get by a crowd spilling into the road.

"Tell her about the St. Charles Theatre, Mikey," he said.

"It's grand," Michael said, bored, looking out of the window on the other side, where a horse pulling a big dray was blocked by a lopsided cart. The man driving the dray started shouting in an accent she couldn't make out.

"Wait until you see New York," said Rates.

"I can't believe I will."

"Oh, you will," he said, "you will."

"Wish I could go to New York," said Michael grumpily.

"It's not as pretty as New Orleans," said Rates, and the boy gave a crude snort as if prettiness was overrated. "It's like an old whore," he said, "all paint and dirty underneath."

Mr. Rates's sister-in-law ran a rooming place in one of the faubourgs, an area where shuttered cottages mingled with low terraces and over-hanging roofs. On shady wrought-iron balconies, on steps, porches, people, people everywhere, all kinds, Spanish, black, white, every mixture. They pulled up beside a high fence in a busy street, not far from a corner where women hovered seriously over baskets of fruit outside an oddly shaped store. A tall middle-aged woman in a dark blue dress opened the gate immediately as if she'd been watching for them, and peered into the carriage eagerly before they'd even had a chance to get out. "Well, the new girl," she said and giggled like a giddy girl. Her face, vivacious and fleshily wrinkled, was heavily powdered white and wafted a scent of flowers into the airless carriage. "Can't wait to see what you got under there," she said cheerfully.

"Julia, this is Madame Soulie," Rates said, "my sister-in-law."

"Terrible journey, I dare say." Madame Soulie stood down so the driver could open the carriage door. Rates descended heavily, turned and gave his hand to Julia. "It was such a long journey," she said breathlessly, stepping down.

"Hellish, I'm sure." Madame Soulie aimed a kick at a wiry gray dog rooting in the trash that bloomed along the bottom of the fence, snarling and unleashing a stream of furious French at it before snapping back startlingly into her practiced smile.

"Please," she said, "this way. What a tiny little thing you are!"

They followed her through the yard to the house, while Michael came along behind with her luggage. Pink azaleas blazed along the sides of the path. On either side of the cottage a shingle roof hung down low, and a pomegranate tree shaded the walkway to the back. Somewhere inside a piano plink-plonked lazily.

Madame Soulie jumped up the step with a girlish bob unsuited to her bulk and called, "Charlotte!" She held her hand out behind her to Julia, who took it and stepped into a wide yellow-walled room with a door on either side and a gallery above. She got an impression of faded, leaf-patterned divans. "Charlotte," Madame Soulie called again. "Where are you? Oh, there you are."

A bony mulatto girl of about twelve appeared silently.

"Charlotte, take Miss Julia across." Madame Soulie wore five or six very long strings of beads that she fiddled with constantly. "Are you hungry, dear?"

"Not at all," said Julia, "only very thirsty."

"Rest a while," Rates said genially, flinging himself down in an extravagantly exhausted way on one of the divans as if he himself had just come all that way. His belly was a dome of worn white linen. "The girl will bring you hot chocolate. Time enough to meet the others."

Michael shuffled in, dumped Julia's grip and guitar in the middle of the floor and stood looking down at them, breathing heavily.

"Well, don't just leave them there," said Madame Soulie, "take them across." She clapped her hands, and as Michael picked up the grip and

Charlotte the guitar, turned the clapping into a Spanish dance in their wake, urging Julia after them.

"We are all one big happy family here, madame!" she called after them as they emerged into the backyard. It was large, with three two-room shacks opening onto it. Curtains hung over the windows. A table and benches were pushed against the side of a brick kitchen, and half a dozen chickens pecked between weed-grown stones in front of it. A swing had been fixed to the bough of a very old apple tree. She was aware of figures, one in a doorway, one peering out of a tiny crisscross window, but she felt scared and didn't look at them. Halfway across the yard a little stooping goblin came running out from the kitchen, sudden and utterly impossible. She screamed.

"It's only Cato," Michael said.

He was all face and not enough head. What there was of his head was dark brown and exaggeratedly egg-shaped, bald and tapering to a point like a dunce's cap.

Seizing her hand in his little stick fingers, he spoke urgently in a high voice that broke and stuck and skidded nasally, drowning any words.

"So tiny," she said.

His fingers were hot and squirmy. His face pushed itself avidly at her with a massive width of smile. A fat black woman in a guinea blue skirt and white blouse appeared in the doorway of the kitchen, a wooden spoon steaming in her hand. "Come on now, Cato," she said patiently, "you get back now."

"He likes people," Michael said, looking back over his shoulder. "You never saw a pinhead before?"

"Never."

She stared into the shiny crinkling eyes, wanting unaccountably to unveil.

"He's just a big baby," Michael said.

"Cato!" the cook called.

Mewing excitedly, Cato ran back to the kitchen. His breeches were cut off at the knee. His legs were thin, bent sticks and his feet were too big. He put his head very far back and smiled up at the cook as if he were trying to break his face.

"Here we are." Michael was lugging her grip through an open door.

Charlotte, a frail thin-faced girl, stood back and waved her on in, staring at the veil as if trying to see through.

"Thank you," Julia said. *Wouldn't you just love to know what's under here?* She looked around. It was plain but comfortable. Someone had tried to make it nice with blue flowers in a jug and a clean yellow tablecloth. A game of solitaire was abandoned on a side table. Two narrow beds were neatly turned down, and a pink curtain was half drawn back on a rail of wide, brightly colored skirts. Michael put her grip down. Charlotte drew back another curtain, heavy gray linen. "You in here," she said. "You sleep here and put your things in there. You want chocolate?"

"I'd love some," said Julia.

"Look," the girl said. "You got a window."

It was open for the air but covered with a net. Another net was 'round her bed. Veil on veil on veil.

"I'll bring you some chocolate," said Charlotte, staring blatantly. "You'll want hot water too, I guess."

The boy didn't look at her at all.

When they'd gone, she tore off the veil and tossed it onto the bed. She was dazed. Three weeks and she'd be on a real stage in a theater. What have I done? She got under the net and lay down on the narrow bed with her hands over her face, moaning softly. I should have gone back to the mountains, she thought. When she was little she thought the mountains were full of people like her, that there was a place up there where all the women were hairy and had more teeth. And it had occurred to her to just set off, take that path she clearly remembered, along which her mother had walked away. The path rose first gently and then, in the distance where everything turned blue, very steeply.

Where was the girl with the chocolate and the hot water? She jumped up again and stood at the window, listening to the sounds beyond the end of the street, a muffled hum, a whistle, a rumble and a call. The Mississippi, how far away she didn't know, not far, she'd seen it from the train, the big steamboats paddling up and down with people on the upper decks with hats and parasols. I am a woman who's been on a train, she told herself. I'm in a great city. I'm going to New York. I could go anywhere.

A baby cried somewhere, out along the back alley.

She'd met Rates the day of the wedding. She'd been called from the kitchen to sing and play her guitar. All the doors and shutters were thrown open to the patio. Everyone was there, all the bright sparkling crowd of them, the boys, the young men and their wives, Doña Inés, her mouth held in the tight way she had when she was pretending not to be drunk, all the young bucks and flowery girls, and the children, some of whom had not seen her before. This was a particular treat for them. But it was nothing. She'd been stared at since she'd come into the world. She wore her red dress, a red flower in her hair, stood before the bank of paper flowers and strummed on her guitar, the same old thing she'd learned on, red and scratched. She sang "La Llorona" and "La Chaparrita," then laid the guitar aside, took up her harmonica and played for Doña Inés, "A La Nanita Nana," and everyone sang along. Afterward Don Pedro came forward, kissed her hand and held it and stood smiling before the crowd. "My dear friends, Señorita Julia Pastrana!" he said, and they cheered and laughed and some gave her sweets and little gifts. Listen to her! That *voice* coming out of that *face*! One lady gave her a necklace made of blue stones. "I think you're miraculous," the lady said. The *mamás* brought their babies in their arms to look at her, and she smiled and smiled. One child was afraid and screamed and was carried away by his scolding sister, saying "Oh, Enzo, making such a fuss. Señorita Pastrana will think you're very rude."

"Not at all," said Julia, but the girl did not hear. Poor little boy, she thought, will he wake screaming, with a great jerk, seeing me in the dark?

"Who taught her to sing?" someone asked.

Will he try and try to put my face from his mind and be unable, and wish he'd never seen me? Will I have him waking in a sweat still when he's a man grown up with his own babies?

"I did," said Marta, who'd changed out of her wedding gown and put on a green-and-white dress over several layers of frothy lilac petticoat. She had not taught Julia to sing. Julia had always sung. She'd sung around the Palace as a child, sung as she worked, sung as she fixed a hem. She never showed herself unless she was called, and these days she was not called upon so much, usually only when Don Pedro had a visit from some important somebody with silk lining in his cuffs. And if that important somebody or that important somebody's wife had heard of her and wanted to see her, she'd come out when they were sitting with their cigars and brandy, all ready and waiting and agog, in her red dress with a red flower in her hair. That had been Don Pedro's idea, but she liked it. Red flower, black hair. Or purple bougainvillea from the vine growing along the boys' balcony. *Hool*ya! *Hool*ya! Calling her to the patio. *Hool*ya! *Hool*ya! Summoning her to entertain them.

Rates had appeared in front of her, a round-faced man in late middle age with a prissy little mouth and the plump chin of a great baby. He was in company with an intense boy, one she remembered, one of those who got the pull, whose eyes got stuck on her in a troubled way.

"Señorita Julia," the boy said, "you did not dance."

She wasn't at her best; she was tired. She'd been up long before light with the other servants. It had been a horrible day. She'd been crying because of the blue dress. If she was very careful, she could cry without anyone knowing, letting the tears hide one by one, strictly controlled, in the hair beneath her eyes. This was useful.

"Not tonight," she replied.

"I saw you dance once before."

She smiled politely.

"I wish you would have danced," he said stubbornly, his eyes steady.

"Shall I dance for you now?" She smiled, picked up her skirts and did a couple of swirls, backward and forward, side to side, stamping her feet and finishing with arms akimbo. A cheer went up from those close by who saw. The older man applauded.

"You have talent," he said with a slight bow of the head. A Yank, by his accent.

"Thank you, señor."

"Didn't I tell you?" The boy spoke with an air of great seriousness. "She's remarkable. She speaks English, Uncle. And you ought to see her dance. The way she points the toe."

"Indeed." The man held her gaze. "Miss Pastrana," he said in English, "you really ought to go on the stage."

Julia smiled, looked down.

"She exceeded all expectations," Don Pedro said jovially, appearing at her side and putting one arm about her shoulders. "I taught her to read myself. She can speak French too, if it's called for. Can't you, Julia?"

"Mais bien sûr, monsieur," said Julia, raising a laugh.

"Miss Pastrana," the man said, as the band struck up once more and Don Pedro was dragged away to the dance floor by one of his daughters-in-law, "have you ever been in New Orleans?"

"I have never been anywhere, señor."

In English he replied, "Should you decide to make your fortune, señorita, come and see me in New Orleans. My card, *señorita*." Which he presented with another small bow.

"My uncle is in the entertainment business in New Orleans," said the boy importantly.

The name on the card was Matthew Rates.

"New Orleans," he said, "New York."

The outer door opened, Charlotte coming in with the chocolate.

"Charlotte," she called, "I've taken my veil off. You can bring the chocolate in here if you like, or leave it on the table and I'll get it when you've gone."

Julia set about unpacking her grip, putting things in the small cupboard next to the window. A moment later a voice said, "Miss Julia, there's some pecans too," and when she turned Charlotte was standing by the curtain with a bowl of hot chocolate and a dish of pecans on a tray. For a long moment she held Julia's eyes, devoid of expression, then she set down the tray. "Mr. Rates say he'll come by for you when you're rested," she said.

"Thank you, Charlotte."

Then she was gone. To tell. She was used to freaks, of course, but still. The chocolate was dark and wonderfully rich, and Julia drank it by the window, eating pecans and looking out at the twining plant on the back wall of the yard, thinking about Cato. He doesn't know he's a pinhead, she thought. He lives in that face like I do, but it's different because he doesn't think about it.

I do.

And there were more to meet. She'd be a difference among differences. It was a peculiar feeling.

Later Mr. Rates came across with Madame Soulie. "At last!" she said, walking straight over to Julia and peering down eagerly into her face, "I can see you! Oh my, oh my, you really are the strangest person I have ever seen." Her eyes bugged out. "And believe me, I've seen a few." She reached down and touched the hair on Julia's cheek with one finger. "You are quite unique."

"So I'm told," Julia said. There were no freaks among freaks, but it was dawning that she really did surpass the lot.

"You didn't exaggerate, Matt," Madame Soulie said.

"What did you expect?" Rates looked smug. "When have I ever exaggerated? She'll slay them in New York."

"Ooh, it's lovely and soft!"

Madame Soulie's hand was light and cautious. She stepped back. "You are so like an ape it's scarcely credible," she said. "You just don't *look* human. And yet you do. And you speak so nicely."

"I can't be an ape because they don't talk," Julia said in French, smiling, "but I know how I look."

"Absolutely!" Madame Soulie laughed. "An ape doesn't talk!"

"*I* talk," said Julia. "I speak French and English and Spanish. An ape doesn't speak French and English and Spanish."

Madame Soulie goggled with delight.

"Mr. Rates," said Julia, "Whom am I sharing with?"

"Myrtle and Delia," Madame Soulie said. "You'll get along fine."

"Of course you will," said Rates. "Come and meet them."

They were in the next-door shack, which had big shutters opening out onto the yard and served as a communal parlor. The room smelled heavily of citrus and was crowded with fraying armchairs. Rates led her in by the hand through the open door. They'd been told about her and knew what to expect. There was a White Negro, a Rubber-Skinned Man, a Girl with No Arms and a Girl with No Legs. Michael sat scratching his pockmarked face on a piano stool. Seeing her for the first time, he smiled slowly.

"Jonsy," Mr. Rates said, gesturing at the yellow-haired paint-white Negro, whose cochineal-colored suit matched his pink eyes. He stared at her, aghast. "And this—" indicating a dark, heavy-jawed girl in a calico dress, who ended at the waist and appeared to be growing out of the florid roses on the rug "—this is Delia." Delia twitched a corner of her mouth and one eyebrow. "And Myrtle." A plump blonde woman in an orange kimono and red shawl half reclined in an uncomfortable-looking, overstuffed green armchair, drinking from a tin cup.

"Pleased to meet you," she said.

"And this is Ted." Ted sat beside a small card table knitting a black stocking very nimbly. The Rubber-Skinned Man, she assumed, but he just looked ordinary.

"And here," said Rates, grandly, "is Julia."

She smiled. She was terrified.

"Sit here, Julia, next to me," said Myrtle. "Want a drink?" She flourished an opened bottle of brandy.

The chair was scratchy, the smell of perfume overpowering. Myrtle handed her a tin cup with brandy in the bottom. It warmed her and went straight to her head. So this is how it's to be, she thought. No return.

After that, though she remembered talking to Myrtle about the journey, and realizing that the hand raising the cup to Myrtle's reddened lips was actually a very supple, long-toed foot rising gracefully from layers of skirt, she was so tired it all became dreamlike, and she said she really must go to bed or she'd fall asleep where she was.

In bed with a swimmy head from the brandy, she thought of old Solana back home. Her voice calling, high and thready. Lying there bedridden now, peevish thing worn-out from nursing them all, the young men and boys, Marta, Julia too when they brought her in from the orphanage. Julia was the one in and out all day dealing with the dribble and phlegm, the smell of piss, the feeding and washing and wiping of mess. The night of the wedding she'd shown Solana the man's card. "Look." In the process of emptying the old woman's bedpan. "This man thinks I could make a lot of money on the stage."

"Don't be ridiculous!" Solana had just finished a coughing fit. Her eyes streamed and her nose ran clear water. Her face was like the picture of a brain in a book in Don Pedro's study.

"Why is it so ridiculous?"

Solana's breath came in long icy shards. "What man anyway?"

"I don't know. Just a man. Sit up." Wiping the old woman's nose.

Solana squinted knowingly. "What's the matter with you? Someone upset you?"

"No."

"I don't know why you still let things upset you, Julia," she said, irritated, "I've told you enough: God loves you, that's all you need to remember."

"I know."

"*Do* you know?"—cough, cough—"*Do* you? I don't think so."

"I'll fetch your broth," said Julia.

And later, in spite of the tiredness pinching her bones, she hadn't been able to sleep. *You have talent.* She'd got up and gone down to the inner patio, drunk water from the pump and sat on the steps with her head leaning against the dusty pink wall. *Indeed. You really ought to go on the stage.* Her feet ached and she wanted to cry for no good reason. They were still at it in the salon, but it was peaceful here. Yes, I am a very lucky girl. I know.

And you, Julia—Solana's voice when she was younger. *You've done well. This lovely house. You started off in a cave and now look! You can read! That day he came for you, that day was your lucky day.*

Solana came from Zacatecas and had two lost sons, one killed by Santy Anna's soldiers, the other gone away with them to Texas and never come back. Died at the Alamo because he'd have returned if not, God knows he surely would have returned. Santy Anna was a fat little devil, Solana said. That good man Don Pedro, a great man, a kind man, took me in, and was fair from the first day. While Julia scoured pots and cleaned the sink, Solana told her how it was.

"He took you in too with your curse, and he wouldn't have any of us say a thing against it. Got you from the orphanage. And all I know is your mother went out walking in the dark of the moon, and that's not your fault, and there's no more to it than that."

"Why?"

"Only God knows."

"There may be more people like me."

"Not where you came from. They wouldn't have put you out if you'd been the same as them. You're from the Diggers, way up there," pointing a finger up as if to heaven. "It's a terrible hard life up there, poor as dirt, but they're not like you. There's no more. You're one of a kind, my love. Your mother wasn't like you, no one was. Doesn't make you worse than anyone else. You're what you are. You've still got a soul. Now, wash those radishes."

The courtyard was softly shaded. There was that old iguana Federico on the vine watching her, a wily old beast who'd lived with the family for as long as anyone could remember. It had all been so pretty, the *carretelas* departing, the *padrino* escorting the bride, the horses' manes white, threaded with scarlet. And all the lovely dresses, the orange, the pink, the blue one Marta screamed over. She should have given it to me, Julia thought. She's got so many, she'd never have missed it. I could have altered it, it would have fit. She stood up, the blue dress falling around her in imagination, Rates's words in her head as she climbed to the gallery: *Should you decide to make your fortune, señorita, come and see me in New Orleans.* She leaned out, pretending she was behind the footlights in a theater. A cheering crowd threw roses. The men tossed their hats in the air. Such tiny fine feet, they said.

Yo soy como el chile verde, Llorona, picante pero sabroso . . .

Still. Not a single one of them would ever love her. Solana had made that clear. "I'll be honest with you," she'd said, a long time ago, "you can be as good as anyone, and you can be proud and always stick up for yourself and get respect, but there's one thing you won't get, *nena*, and that's a man. Not with your face so far gone. Don't expect it."

"I know."

Hadn't she always?

"The world's a cruel place, and there's nothing fair about it."

Julia had been about nine or ten, and even then Solana had been very old. She'd taken Julia's face between her hands and looked fiercely into her eyes and said, "Listen, you. It's not your fault. None of it's your fault. And you won't get a man but it doesn't matter. What's a man? Same as a woman. Nothing. It all goes anyway. God loves you, and Solana loves you, and your mother loved you, and that's all that matters. She did it for the best, your *mamá*. Of course she didn't look back. That would have made it harder for you. She gave you to the *vaqueros* because she wanted you to have a good life."

She remembered the *vaqueros*, big men with wide sunburned faces, high on their soft-eyed brown horses. They drove three black-spotted cows with twisted horns before them. She'd never seen horses and cattle and men before. They put her on a horse, wrapped up like a bundle, strapped safe to the ripe poncho of a fat *vaquero*, and her mother walked away. She could say "Mamá" by the time she reached the orphanage, that much she knew because they told her so. Mamá was in the big mountains. Mamá was a kind, surrounding feeling that could bring tears to her eyes if she let it. And Mamá was a sharp clear picture, the first memory, her mother's back walking away from her, with resolution. She'd cried out, "Mamá!" But her mother never turned around. Mother's shawl was sad and frayed. Her pigtail curled at the end under a battered straw hat. Water ran nearby, and the mountains glowed with a light that seemed to flicker faintly at the edge of vision.

Julia had ancient dreams. From the very beginning they were there, before any articulation—dreams that had little of substance, but friendly oceans of feeling. In the dreams Julia was full and warm, and darkness was above and all around, safe. And there were places of great light, where the ground fell away and birds with forked tails flew below her. But it had all gone, whatever it was. The Sanchez household had its own little chapel. When the priest told them about the Garden of Eden, she thought that was it, those mountains into which her first clear memory, the memory of her mother's back, retreated. The fat *vaquero* made kind clucking noises at Julia as they rode down into Culiacán, speaking a language she'd yet to learn. The men stared at her, big brown bloodshot eyes all over her face. One of them dabbed himself here and there, thick fingers to the shoulders, the forehead, again and again as they babbled and jabbered, she as strange to them as they to her. She looked back with her thumb in her mouth, clutching her doll and crying. You, Yatzi. They took her away to a place where a woman looked at her and screamed. They tried to give her a proper doll with a painted face, but she didn't want it, she wanted Yatzi that had come with her out of the mountains, and she screamed when they tried to take him away. They said her mother said she wasn't her mother. Then again, said the nun, the man said she wept as she handed the child over, and kissed her, and prayed over her. Julia didn't remember that. Only the pigtail. Then the shadows in the orphanage, the smell of beans and garlic, a wide white staircase rising up to a shady corridor in the Palace, arcaded and tiled in blue and white, and two boys playing a game of cards in their Sunday suits. Their iguana, the one there on the vine, sitting patiently watching from the top of a balustrade. These things were so far away they inhabited a space from which also rose dreams and fairy stories and the things you saw halfway between waking and sleeping.

Ay de mí,
Llorona, Llorona— Llorona—
llévame al río—
tápame con tu rebozo, Llorona
porque me muero de frío.

I could get paid for this, she thought.

That's when she'd known she was going away. But not yet.

Oh, St. Jude, she'd prayed, holy apostle, worker of miracles, close kinsman to Jesus Christ, hear me again, dear Jude, come now to my aid in my great need, bring the consolation and succur of heaven in all my necessities, tribulations and sufferings, and let me be loved like other girls, let me be loved like a human, and I promise to forever remember your great favor and always love and honor you as my special patron and do my best forever to increase devotion to you wherever I go. Thank you, St. Jude. Amen.

———

Solana died six months later, and then she was free. She left early one morning, before it was light. Federico the iguana was sitting on the fountain with his face pointing at the moon. No one else was about. The old patio, there it was as it had always been. They were all sleeping. She'd said no real good-byes, just slipped away. She didn't think anyone else would miss her very much. Maybe a little. After all, what was she? A servant, moving on. She took a small grip, her harmonica, her guitar, a half round of white cheese, Solana's old rosary beads and her doll Yatzi.

You and me, Yatzi. You and me.

She heard the lonesome baby cry again, out there somewhere toward the Mississippi. Julia opened her eyes. Myrtle and Delia must have woken her, coming in with whispers and a smothered giggle. They bumped about in the dark, trying not to disturb her. How strange. Far away under this sky it's all still there. The patio, the stone bench, the fig tree, the shadow of the fountain. She saw it in moonlight, full of broken paper flowers, as it was that night.

H ot night, summer 1983. These were not nights for sleep, too febrile, too sweaty. Rose, walking home from some eternal flop-out, some smoky mustering in Camberwell, twoish, threeish, singing sotto voce the Heart Sutra to lighten the road (still the length of Coldharbour Lane to go) stopped still when the sky growled. A cosmic dog, big one with teeth. She was drunk enough to look up and laugh out loud. What the hell, there was no one around. A change of pressure, a flicker of lightning, then the first high murmur of rain.

Rose had sad brown eyes with tired hollows beneath, a wide big-lipped mouth and hair that stood out all around her head, thick, black and wiry. A scar sliced through her right eyebrow, giving that eye a slight droop at the outer corner. The years had rolled her into her thirties, thin and rakish, somewhat tousled and rough around the edges, and it was OK. The fear was at bay. As the rain set in, she turned her face up. It was good to be drunk. Simply wonderful sometimes to fray the edges, crank up the contrast. All she had on was a loose silky top and some old jeans, and she was getting soaked, but it was nice. She walked on, savoring the dark empty street and the way the soft hissing of late-night traffic from Denmark Hill, and the lights shining on the wet pavement, made everything romantic.

Ahead of her, halfway down Love Walk, was a large garbage bin piled high with rubbish. She never could resist a garbage bin, particularly one full of the dregs and leavings of a house clearance. Whenever she came upon one, and London was awash with them, she stopped and had a good rummage and rescued anything that moved her. Many things did. When she was small, she'd bestowed consciousness on the things around her. Not just dolls and soft toys, but books, clothes, crockery, chairs, teapots and hairbrushes, rugs and pencils, even the corners of rooms and the turns of staircases, the gentle purring sound her bedroom window made when a car's engine idled in the street outside, or the feathery stroking sensation in her chest when she was nervous with someone. All these things she'd named and given personalities.

She didn't do it now, of course. But still—

Oh! Poor piece of paper, she'd think, passing a torn scrap in the street. Poor grape, last on the stalk, missing its friends and wondering why no one wants it.

This bin was nothing special, a pile of rags and rubble. She walked 'round it. A drop of rain hung on one eyelash, quivering in the edge of sight. Askew on the heap was a scattering of debris, shadowy nothings, in their very nothingness as heart-wrenching as anything, she thought, but you couldn't stop for everything. The doll's remains lay half in, half out of a doorless microwave oven near the top of the mound. She had to clamber aboard and scramble a bit to reach him. He was naked and limbless, with brown leathery skin, and a big head so damaged that his face resembled an untreated burn victim, the mouth a raised gash, the nose and ears pockmarked craters. One eye, made of glass, was sunk deep in his skull. The other was a black hollow.

"Poor baby," she said, picking him up, cradling him sentimentally in her arms for a long moment before shifting him to her shoulder and patting his back. "Poor, poor baby," swaying happily in the rain.

She took him back to the ridiculous rambling old tip of a house on Coldharbour Lane where she lived, four enormous floors filled with escapees from small crap towns the length and breadth of the land. The air was an essence of all the people who'd ever passed through, and even though it was the middle of the night, the house had a faint hum of people doing things behind closed doors.

Rose went up to her flat at the top of the house. A waft of incense and dope greeted her when she opened the door. Inside was like an Arabian souk, all colored hangings and cushions, mirrors, embroidery, long-fingered plants tumbling down deep purple walls. The room was full of stuff she'd brought home from garbage bins and gutters and pavements, shelves full of things she felt sorry for. Old matchboxes and broken jewelry, bits of paper, sticks, fragments, remnants, residues, boxes, knickknacks, broken things, the teeming leavings of the world.

"Poor thing," she said, putting the maimed doll among her Indian cushions as if it were a cuddly toy, sitting back on her heels and looking into its round black face. The empty holes of the eyes and mouth conveyed an impression of sweetness.

"Tattoo," she said.

Next morning Julia dressed quickly, drew back the curtain and crept silently through the room where the two girls were still asleep. A cockerel crowed in the dark, not too near. Another, closer, answered. Finding the latch, she lifted it silently and went out into the yard. Voices passed on the street. A light burned in the house. There was a movement over by the vegetable patch, and when she looked she saw the tall thin figure of a man walking backward. With no hesitation, he passed along the side wall, turned and crossed the back of the house, momentarily dimming the light from the window, then disappeared 'round the corner into the leaf-hung walkway that led to the front. Though the light was coming, nothing but his shape and peculiar swift locomotion was clear. *Diablo.* There was no sound. He's come for wicked children who won't go to sleep. *You don't have to worry about that, Julia,* the Sanchez boys used to joke, *one look at you and he'll run! Like the devil!* When she was sure he wasn't coming back, she walked down and used the privy, and by the time she was back Delia was up, sitting on her bed smoking a small cigar.

"So," she said in a blunt throaty way, "your big show." Thick black pigtails hung on either side of her face, and a red shawl was wrapped 'round her shoulders. Emerging from it, her forearms were tawny and muscled, thick-veined as a fighter's.

"The first," Julia said.

"How long's it been? Since you went on the road?"

"I'm losing track. Two or three months."

"Ooh! So new. So how's it all getting along with you?" She waved one brown arm. "All this."

"Sometimes wonderful," said Julia, "sometimes frightening."

"Rates said you lived in a palace. Down in Mexico."

"A long time ago. My guardian was governor in Sinaloa, but I hardly remember it. Then we moved to the house I grew up in."

"He decent? Your guardian? Why you wanna leave?"

"I was looking after an old lady," said Julia, "but then she died."

"An old lady?"

"Old nurse lady."

"So was he decent?"

Don Pedro had always been fond of her in a distant way, as if she were a good old dog that had been with the family a long time. Sixteen years. "He was decent," Julia said.

Delia blew out a cloud of thick blue smoke, put her head back and gazed pensively at her. "Has Rates given you any money yet?" she asked.

"I have some money," said Julia, "a little. My guardian gave me some before I left. But Mr. Rates has been buying everything, I haven't had to . . ."

"You made a deal?"

"Of course. There'll be money when we've done the shows."

"No, I mean a deal," said Delia impatiently, "a deal in writing."

"I haven't signed anything."

"Oh, but you must, you must." Delia jumped down from the bed onto her hands, cigar in mouth. "Don't go a step further till you've got something in writing," she said, loping across the floor with strong arms and poking Myrtle in the backside. "Wake up, Myrt." Sinking down, the cigar wagging on her lip. "Listen to this, she hasn't got a contract."

Julia hated thinking about money. There'd always been enough. Other people provided, but she had to work. She could sweep and wash and light fires, or she could sing and dance and let them look. Singing and dancing won all, hands down. Money made her head ache.

"Myrt!"

Myrtle mumbled, then turned over. When her eyes opened they were glazed for a while, unfocused, but suddenly they registered Julia and shot open. A brief hysterical indrawing of breath, quickly controlled, and she jerked up. "Sorry, sorry," she said, laughing awkwardly at herself.

"She hasn't got a contract!"

Myrtle closed her eyes again. "You should have had a lie-in," she said to Julia, "you're supposed to."

"I always wake early."

"It can be a curse." Myrtle opened her eyes again but closed them immediately. Last night's eye paint had bruised her pillow and lay encrusted across the top part of her cheeks. She looked both older and younger than the night before.

"You have to get a contract." Delia sprang back onto the bed. "No word of mouth. Today. Before you sing another note. Tell him."

Myrtle clenched her eyes and yawned till she shook. The sound of Cato's swerving stumbling voice came in from the yard along with a faint, drainy smell of sewage.

"Who is that?" Julia asked. "That Cato. Where's he from?"

"He come from Alabama," said Delia.

"With a banjo on his knee," said Myrtle, and they laughed.

"True enough," Myrtle said, "he comes from Alabama. Off of a big plantation."

"Does he live here all the time?"

"No one lives here all the time."

"He's not with us," said Delia. "He's with this kid Ezra."

"What does he do?"

"Cato? Oh, people just like to see Cato. He don't *do* much."

"He dances," Myrtle said. "Kind of."

"Yeah. Kind of. But mostly he just runs around."

Myrtle burst out of bed in a flurry of white and went behind the screen. The sound of peeing trickled through the room.

"Myrt, have you got my comb?" Delia raised her voice. "The one with the fans?"

"I saw it," came Myrtle's voice from behind the screen, "but I can't remember where."

"What about you," said Julia, "how long have you been doing this?"

"For always," said Delia, relighting her cigar, which had gone out. "We used to be with a showman. Separate acts, this was, a long time ago, and we got along so we figured we'd try and make a go of it together and cut him out. He was slippery. Nothing written down. Got to get it written down. We get good rates now. We negotiate. This man Rates now." She lounged back against the pillow. "We all started out on the right foot."

"So you remember," Myrtle called from behind the screen, "you tell him, you want a contract, numbers, security."

"I will."

"Don't underestimate it, Julia," Delia said. "All this. It's hard work. Always on the move, God, you can die of boredom. You got to get paid. You make sure."

"I will. I'll talk to him."

———

Charlotte was sweeping the yard outside the back door. A fat white cat with a smug expression watched from the step. Ted and Jonsy were eating pancakes and eggs on a bench outside the kitchen, and Cato was on the swing, thin legs kicking, head thrown back.

"Sit down, Julia," Myrtle said, "you want some eggs?" She sauntered toward the kitchen door. "Morning, Cass," she said, leaning in, "any coffee?"

Julia sat down at the table nervously, nodding at Ted and Jonsy. Ted nodded back. "Sleep well?" he asked, shoveling egg with his fork. By daylight, he was cadaverous.

"Not so well," she replied, "I kept waking up and wondering where I was. But I've been doing that ever since I left home."

Jonsy was still wearing the pink suit.

"That's a nice color," she said, nodding at it.

Jonsy's mouth and eyes widened at her.

"He doesn't speak," Myrtle said.

Ted ate food like a man filling a hole in a hurry. "You've come a long way," he said, emptying his plate and sitting back with a satisfied shifting of the shoulders.

"I have," she said, "and I'm going a long way more." The strangest feeling, sitting out here with strangers, bare-faced. What do you want? she asked herself. Just this, out in the world, free, unafraid. Don't spoil it by being afraid, fool. Pretend. Shake inside but never let it show.

Ted put his plate down next to him on the bench, picked up his can of coffee and slurped loudly. "I can tell fortunes," he said dryly.

"Can you really?" Julia leaned forward eagerly. "Is that what you do? I'd love to have my fortune told."

He drew the makings of a pipe from a pocket. "Anyone can tell your fortune," he said with a dolorous air. "Your face. I been doing the rounds these fifteen, sixteen years, and I never in all that time seen nothing like your face. Oh, they'll pay to see you. They'll pay, all right."

Myrtle sat down across the table. She'd cleaned herself up and was puffy 'round the eyes. "You're no fortune-teller," she told Ted.

"Aren't you?" asked Julia, disappointed.

"No." Ted looked mildly amused but didn't bother to smile.

All this time her eyes had been straying to Cato, trying to take him in.

"Do you want to see what I do?" asked Ted.

"Of course I do."

"This."

He gripped the skin at the side of his neck and pulled it away from his body about four or five inches till it stretched into a thin membrane. Julia screamed, then laughed. Hearing her, Cato jumped down from the swing and came running. Ted let go of the great flap of skin and let it slap back into place.

"How do you do that?" she asked, delighted and appalled. "It looks as if it hurts."

"Doesn't hurt at all." Ted swilled the coffee grounds 'round in his can. Cato crouched next to him on the bench and set about picking fingerfuls of his neck and face, pulling them out as far as they'd go and letting them snap back. Unperturbed, Ted puffed away. When the cook brought coffee and eggs and more pancakes, Cato let go of Ted's skin and lurched toward her along the bench babbling excitedly, but he was so gangly and badly coordinated that he knocked Jonsy's cold coffee flying. "You bad Cato!" the cook yelled, striking the table with the flat of her palm. "I'll tell your master on you."

Cato wheedled up to her, stroking her apron. She put her hand on the slope of his head and her eyes connected with Julia's, snagged and stared. Julia smiled. The cook nodded.

"Cato, you have to be careful," said Myrtle. "You know you're clumsy so you have to be careful.

"Anyhow," Myrtle said, "where's Ezra? How come we always get to do the babysitting? Ezra!" She threw her voice clear to the other side of the yard. "Ezra!"

"Why is everyone always shouting around here?" said Delia, swinging herself onto the table. "Is this pancake anyone's?"

"Hoo-hah." Cato pointed at Julia. "Hoo-hah."

"Yes!" she said, "Hoo-oo-lya!" Rates and everyone else called her Julia with a J, and it was nice to hear the old pronunciation, even if it were unintentional. "That's how they say my name in Mexico."

Cato came 'round to her side of the table and put a child's hand up to stroke the hair on her cheek. "Yes, Cato," she said, smiling, "I'm hairy."

"Cato," said a high man's voice. "You behave yourself."

A big round-shouldered boy with curly black hair was coming slowly across the yard, giving himself plenty of time to get used to Julia before speaking. "You should ask," he said nasally, "don't bother the lady."

"I don't mind him," Julia said.

"Ezra Porter, ma'am." He offered a large fleshy hand. "Just you tell him if he's in the way, he won't mind. Come on now, Cato, you leave the lady alone."

"But I really don't mind."

Fascinated, she and Cato stared at each other.

"Listen," Ezra Porter said, "if you're sure you don't mind . . ."

Breakfast was over and people were dispersing. The girls went off to the rehearsal room and everyone else drifted away, till there was just Julia and Cato smiling at each other, and Ezra Porter shuffling about with the look of a giant well-fed toddler, saying nervously in his irritating voice, "You know I—I have one or two things I really need to do. If you really don't mind watching him for a while I'd be obliged. . . . But don't let him go out in the street."

"We'll play on the swing," she said, "won't we, Cato?"

Cato dashed for the swing, and Ezra Porter nipped smartly away.

"Ready?" she said. "How high do you like to go?"

But of course she couldn't understand a word he said.

The back of his head was like a coconut, and his hands on the ropes were clenched and eager. She started pushing him, but as soon as his feet lifted from the ground he shrieked so loudly she had to stop.

"Ssh! It's all right. You're on the ground."

He wouldn't get off the swing and started shaking the ropes.

"I'm not pushing you if you're going to scream," she said.

She tried again but it was hopeless.

"Come, you can play my guitar," she said, but as she led him across the yard he became distracted by the white cat, and followed it 'round to the front of the house, hooting excitedly. She ran after him. The front yard was cool and shady and Madame Soulie was bending over, watering her azaleas.

"Why are you up front, Cato?" she said, getting up. "You go back now. Go on. Good boy."

"He's after the cat," Julia said.

Madame Soulie put down her can. The cat leapt up the fence and dropped down into the street. "Go back now, Cato. Are you looking after him?"

"Yes."

"What? He's left you in charge, has he?"

"Yes."

"Don't let Ezra take advantage."

"I don't mind," she said.

"Well, perhaps you should. Anyway, keep him back there. Gate's closed but they look through the fence. Go on, boy. Best you stay back there too, Julia."

"Yes."

"He was taken for the devil baby once," Madame Soulie said, "and it could've turned nasty."

"The devil baby?"

"The devil baby." Madame Soulie brushed her apron down, advancing on them with her bulky height, sweeping them back down the walkway and following after. "Did you never hear about that?"

"I never did."

"It was this woman across the lake who had too many girl babies and she wanted a boy. She got so sick of all these girls she said, goddamn I'd rather the devil than another girl. Well, she got what she asked for. A big bouncing boy with horns and a tail and hooves and teeth, standing upright and talking right away."

She made sure they were well shepherded as far as the benches outside the kitchen. Cato ran back to the swing.

"Poor mother died of fear when she saw him," said Madame Soulie, "and he ran away down into the street and up over the roofs. They tried to kill him, but he won't be killed."

"I heard a baby crying last night," Julia said.

"Oh, you'd know it if you'd heard him. I heard him once. Never saw him, wouldn't want to, but I heard him." She shuddered. "Dreadful sound. Never leaves you."

"What was it like?"

"Not like any ordinary baby. Not even like a cat." She shuddered again, more visibly this time. "Anyway, this boy here gets out one day and walks down the street and someone screams: the devil baby! Look! Ezra had to run out, good job he's so big, Ezra. You've got to be careful, believe me. Look, you want me to go get Ezra?"

"Oh, no. We'll stay in back," said Julia, "won't we, Cato?"

Madame Soulie returned to her watering, and they went back to Julia's cabin. He was hopeless trying to play the guitar and soon lost interest. "You dance then," she said, "I know you can dance."

She played her guitar and he danced, with knees cracking and no vestige of grace, his smile eerily oversized, till he grew tired very suddenly and fell asleep on Myrtle's bed with a look of surprise on his face. Strangest face she'd ever seen.

Poor devil baby, she thought, playing on. Crying for Mamá. Because Mamá took one look at him, screamed her head off and died.

———

Brady Childer's grocery and coal yard stood on the corner past a shoemaker's and a couple more cottages. Upstairs was a room, oddly shaped because of the way the store had been built at an oblique angle on the corner, with a piano and a couple of old sofas pushed up against the walls, and a balcony running along two sides. Long windows were open for the air, but they were always covered by several gauzy layers of drapes. Couldn't have the people across the way getting a free show. When Julia arrived with Mr. Rates, Michael was playing a jaunty "Rose of Alabama" at the piano while the girls danced. What a sight! Delia danced on her hands, strong square shoulders and lean hips wiggling in time. She wore a plain gray dress and a red *tignon,* and her eyes were closed. Myrtle hoofed it energetically by her side, the frills of her sleeves flapping up and down and occasionally revealing smooth pink stumps.

Perfectly in time, the girls sidestepped each other, changing places. Julia threw back her veil. When they finished, she clapped her hands and shouted "Bravo!"

"Water!" Myrtle said, "I'm dying."

"You're so clever!" Julia took off her shawl and threw it on one of the sofas.

"*Merci,*" said Delia, swinging herself across the floor and jumping up onto the sofa. She lay back in one corner with her arms thrown over her head.

"We've been doing it a long time," said Myrtle, swigging from a bottle. A fine sheen of sweat shone on her forehead.

"Has Michael got my music?" Julia asked.

"I should hope so." Rates was fanning himself in the heavy air seeping in through a gap in the gauze.

"I'm out of practice," Julia said, nervous, stepping into the center of the room.

"Poor old Michael," said Michael, "he doesn't get a break."

"Soon enough," Rates said.

Michael bent low over the keyboard.

"So much space to dance," she said. The girls sat side by side waiting for her to begin. She wanted to run. Fool. Nowhere to practice on the journey. You've come this far, she told herself sternly.

"You ready?" he asked.

You've done it a million times. She nodded.

It was horrible at first. He played her Spanish tunes clumsily but with gusto, too fast, and she lost the rhythm a couple of times. But then she did what she always did at home, danced as if no one was there. It was the only way. Once she got into her stride and he'd slowed down a bit, they were fine. In fact it began to be fun, and she sensed appreciation but didn't dare look at anyone in case the luck broke. She'd been doing this from childhood. The story went that Don Pedro had noticed her sitting still as a stone to listen in the doorway as he played the piano one day. "Hello, little Julia," he'd said. "Do you like the music? Is it pretty?"

Doña Inés happened to be passing at that moment.

"She should learn the violin," she'd said, "I should like that."

The violin didn't work, but the old red guitar that was lying out on the stone bench on the gallery had become hers, and someone must have given her the green harmonica, she couldn't remember, and the boys' music teacher showed her how to sing scales and tap out rhythms. She'd learned the schottische, the polka and the highland fling. Songs came in with Solana, in her old cloak coming in from the marketplace, in her good cloak coming back from Mass. Most of them were desperately sad because sadness made better songs. These days she danced more ballet. It was hard but she was getting better, and when she was tired she could slip back so easily into the old Spanish steps, turning, stamping, clapping her hands. In the lovely wide space of the room above Brady Childer's, she began to whirl.

"Olé!" cried the girls, jumping to their two hands and two feet, and when it was over, everyone cheered. I did the right thing, she thought.

Everything was exactly as it should be.

Madame Soulie was in the yard when they got back. "Marvelous, aren't they?" she said, emptying the contents of a box of handbills fresh from the printer onto the wooden table and spreading them out in a fan shape. Human Curiosities, they cried, the words elaborately leaf-twined. The most remarkable and unimaginable abnormalities known to man, living testimony to the infinite variety of nature. There they all were, Jonsy the White Negro, Edward Pitcairn the Elastic Man, Myrtle Dexter and Delia Mounier, Armless and Legless Dancing Wonders. And there at the top of the bill—Julia Pastrana, The Marvelous Hybrid Bear Woman.

The only one whose humanity was in doubt.

"Is that your name?" asked Charlotte. "That big one there?"

"It is," said Julia.

"You're at the top!" said Charlotte.

Mr. Rates came out of the house. "We've been mentioned in the *Picayune*," he said, waving a newspaper in one hand and a playbill in the other. "Look. I don't think the words 'Bear Woman' are big enough. What do you think, Ede? And don't you think they should be a fraction higher?"

Madame Soulie put her head on one side and frowned.

"I think we should seize the current," he said, "strike while the iron's hot. What we need for you, Julia, is a good picture."

"A photograph?" Julia sounded amazed.

"No, no. Get someone in to draw you. Pen and ink perhaps." Rates smiled. "You'd better get used to this, Julia. They'll be standing in line to draw you, you know. We need a new pamphlet, a separate one, The Life of Miss Julia Pastrana. Same nice ivy design 'round the letters."

"Acanthus, Matt," said Madame Soulie, "they're acanthus."

"Mr. Rates," said Julia, "I need my costume for the show."

"Of course you do. I've been thinking about that," he said.

He'd promised to buy her a new dress. She'd never worn a dress from a shop before. Solana had made all her clothes till she was old enough to do it for herself.

"Would it not make sense for me to wear it when I sit for the picture?" she asked.

"Very good idea." Rates looked surprised. "One second." He held up one finger, turned and went back into the house.

"Let's get out of this heat." Myrtle moved away toward the shack. "Come on, Julia." Inside was scarcely cooler than the yard. Myrtle picked up a palm fan and got onto her bed, settling cross-legged in front of her toilet box.

"Don't let him tell you what to wear," Delia said, coming in behind. "He will if you let him."

"He wanted to put me in this downright vulgar thing," said Myrtle. "Skirt up to here like a whore."

"And have you asked about your contract?"

"Oh, no," said Julia, "I forgot."

"No good," said Delia, "no good at all. You have to look after yourself."

"She's right," said Myrtle. "You can't afford to be silly about money. That's the only thing I learned from my mother."

"I remember your mother," Delia said. "She didn't know the first thing about money." She unwrapped her *tignon* and her long hair fell down.

"That's what I mean." Myrtle opened her box and looked at her face in the mirror. "She was about as stupid with money as it's possible to be, my mother, so I said, *I'm* never going to be like that and I never have." She looked at Julia and smiled. "She drank, my mother." She took out her tweezers, leaned forward and curled her white-bloomered leg up easily to pluck one raised eyebrow. Rates knocked sharply and came in with a red dress lying over his arms. "Try this on for size," he said to Julia. "We can get it cut down a bit."

Julia took it and held it at arm's length. Low-cut and short-sleeved, it had a cheap look about it. "It's wrong," she said.

"What do you mean, wrong?"

"It wouldn't suit me," she said.

Rates laughed, an impatient whicker down his nose.

"It's better if I choose my own clothes," Julia said.

"What's wrong with it?" said Rates, looking huffy. "It's a nice dress."

"Well, you know a woman usually knows best what suits her," Myrtle said, licking her toe and stroking her eyebrow. She picked up a jar from her box of pastes and powders with her foot, passed it to the other foot and started unscrewing the lid carefully. Her toes had the deftness of fingers.

"It should be in your contract," Delia said, head on one side, combing out her hair.

"What would you like to wear?" asked Rates.

She knew exactly. "I'll write down the measurements," she said. "We could have it made up. But I'd need to see some cloth."

"Hm." Rates looked puzzled. "I thought we could just go into town and . . ."

"Oh," she said, "I've been making clothes all my life. It's much cheaper. The dress must be right or the dance won't work, and I know how it should be."

Rates stuck out his chest and looked sideways, making chewing motions with his thin line of a mouth. "Well, I suppose I can get some samples sent over," he said, "I'll ask Madame Soulie to arrange it."

"I'd rather go shopping," said Julia. "I don't want the cloth brought here, I want to go out and see the shops and the market."

"She'll know what to buy," said Myrtle, rubbing Creme Celeste into her face.

Charlotte stuck her head 'round the door. "Aunt Soulie wants Julia," she said.

"Julia's tired." Delia threw down the comb and began plaiting her hair down one side.

"That's all right," said Julia, "I'll come."

C ould have been a doll that got burned, hard to tell. Sitting against an elephant-embroidered cushion, Tattoo, Rose thought, was like a stray dog brought in from the cold.

She heard the messy banging of a piano downstairs, went out onto the landing and called down. "Adam!" Her deep voice echoed in the stairwell. When she called again, the piano stopped and he came out on the landing below, covered in paint, a pinch-faced twitchy kind of a person with spiky hair and a crooked jaw that he held in a stiff, unnatural way. "What?" he said irritably.

"You know exactly what."

"Oh, Rose!"

Rose sat down on the top step, imperturbable, smoking a cigarette. "No skin off my nose," she said, "but he's not going to let you live here rent-free forever."

Adam hunched his shoulders and kicked the wall sulkily as if he were twenty years younger. "End of the month," he said. "You know that."

"End of which month, Ad?" She smiled. "You know Laurie. He's getting cranky."

"Ah, but you, Rose, you can always get 'round him." He looked up, a sour twist to his mouth. "Use your influence."

"Ha." She picked a fleck of tobacco from the tip of her tongue. "It only goes so far, my dear."

She'd been an artist's model, sold pizzas, tried to get by making embroidered skirts, but now she was here, collecting rent for Laurie and passing on messages about leaky taps and blocked toilets, living a whole year now rent-free herself in return for that and her haphazard cleaning services. Fallen on my feet, she sometimes told herself, with a sense of having found a safe berth on a heaving sea.

"Make a brew, Rosie," Adam said, continuing to kick the wall.

She got up, flicking ash into her hand. A shapeless garment the color of wet sand hung loosely down past her knees, and her legs were bare and brown. "Come on then," she said.

He followed her up and stood frowning on the rug in front of the fireplace watching her make tea. A door stood open to her bedroom, through which could be seen her unmade bed trailing a thin Indian coverlet, bare boards painted blue, long shelves jumbled with beads and glass and spools of colored threads. She made frames, ornate creations. Now and again she sold one or two through some craft shop or other.

"What the hell is that?"

Adam was staring at Tattoo with an affronted, almost angry intensity.

"That's Tattoo," she said, pouring boiling water into the teapot and frowning at the steam billowing up in her face.

Adam picked up the doll and turned it 'round in his hands. His top lip rose at one side like a nervous dog's.

"Don't you like him?" she asked, stirring the pot. She put the tea cozy on it, turned and stood with folded arms looking over at Adam. God love him, she thought. Sweet. Not the type to get involved with though. Tough front, inside all mush. They smother you, those kind. Mind you, I suppose they all do in the end. Unless they're married like Laurie, and even he—

"That's horrible," he said.

"It's just an old burned doll," she said, pushing her hair back, pushing it about with her hands. "I was coming home and there he was on top of a garbage bin. How could you resist that little face?"

"It's horrible," he said again. "Looks like a hoodoo doll."

"No, no, no." Closing her bedroom door on the mess within as she passed—too intimate a display for him—she came and plucked the doll from his hands. "You leave him alone," she said, "I have to find him a home," and bore the thing, like a great treasure, to the mantelpiece above the blocked-up fireplace. The mantelpiece was already crammed, but she moved things about with deft precision. Three-legged brown plastic horse with a hole in its back. Torn Chinese fan. Pink candle with teeth marks. Disgruntled Moomin, lacking an arm. "There!" she said, propping Tattoo against the wall in the middle and standing back. "He's happy there. Don't you think he looks good?"

"Good?" Adam shoved his fists deep in his pockets and the skin between his eyebrows turned square. "It's just a trunk," he said. "It's got no arms and legs." But in a way, he thought, it did look good, hacked-out, primal. Kind of an artwork. "Why d'you call it Tattoo?" he asked.

Rose shrugged. "You pour the tea," she said, crossed the room and stretched out on the sofa, closing her eyes. She heard the rattle of cups, the clink of a spoon. She remembered the original Tattoo, could see him now with his smudgy gray eyes and thin smile of a mouth, his face young and friendly and shy, standing with his arms down by his sides on his scuffed blue shoe base, blue trousers, red coat, tall black hat. The paint was rubbing thin all over him, specially his hat. He was six inches high and lived in her pocket and she'd always had him.

Adam plonked a mug of tea down next to her head.

She opened her eyes. "I named him after a wooden soldier I had when I was little," she said, sitting up. "My grandmother got him from a jumble sale. He was very old. Homemade."

"The way you remember these things," said Adam, taking a seat at a respectful distance and blowing on his tea.

"He was lovely," she said. "Had the face of a holy fool. My mother threw him out when we moved house when I was nine. I called her a murdering bastard."

"Did you? When you were nine?"

"Probably not," said Rose, putting her mug down and lazily plaiting her hair. "Should have done though."

It began to rain unexpectedly, hot rain from a heavy summer sky, wildly drumming on the windowpane.

"Names are important," she said. "When a thing has a name, that's when it really counts."

M adame Soulie was in the parlor with three ugly dresses laid out on one of the divans. "Oh, Julia," she said, "I thought some of these might suit you. Much too big, of course, but we can make adjustments."

She was sick of castoffs. "Mr. Rates is taking me shopping," she said.

"Julia," said Madame Soulie, coming briskly toward her with something lilac and old-fashioned held out in front of her as if she were dancing with it, "never look a gift horse in the mouth. Of course he will still take you shopping. But these are gifts from me."

"Of course. Thank you so much, Madame Soulie."

Always the dull ones. Old, unworn, unwanted. Never again. This time she'd get a dress better than the blue dress, just for her.

"You're very kind, Madame Soulie."

"See," she said, "it fits you very well about the shoulders. Why don't you try it on?"

"Now?"

"Why not? In there, see, you can put it on in there and I'll pin it for you."

"Oh no, really . . ."

Madame Soulie was not the sort to argue. Julia went into a dark musky room almost filled by a vast bed. It had a vague redness about it and a slightly moldy smell, and the curtains were closed. The lilac dress fell around her like a sack, smelling of stale perfume. She remembered the way the blue dress had felt on the day of the wedding, settling onto her as she shook herself into it. Madness to try it on. Those wicked boys. Oh, play up, Julia. Say we made you do it. We did, didn't we, Clem? We did, we made you. Look, we'll go out and you put the nice dress on and the shawl over your arms, and we'll find you a veil. The veiled lady! Lady of mystery! Dress up as Marta, go stand on the balcony, fool the guests, whip off the veil at the last second, revealing all. Of course she'd had no intention of showing herself out there. She just wanted a chance to wear the dress for five minutes. It was much too long, of course—she was child-sized—and tight across the bosom, but so perfect, peacock blue with lighter blue flowers 'round the low neckline, short puffed sleeves and three layers of skirt. But then Marta had come running in and screamed that her wedding day was ruined and she hated everyone, everyone, *and you've used my tortoiseshell comb too, oh, that's just too much,* bursting into tears and hitting Elisio hard on the side of his head. *Get out! Get out, all of you! Get out, get out, get out! You'll have to wash it. The comb too.*

Nothing would ever change.

Julia drew back the curtain in Madame Soulie's room and observed her face in a large oval mirror. There'd been a day, it must have been before her fifth birthday, when she looked into the cradle at a chubby brown baby with lips like a flower and a cheek as ripe as a peach. She saw her own dark hand moving toward the round bald head, startling against the white cloths. Elisio. Doña Inés somewhere high above her and smelling faintly of flowers drew in her breath with a high sharp sound, the air changed, and some knowledge of profound difference was finally born. Solana, then still strong and quick, had grabbed her arm quite roughly and said, No!—as if she'd done something wrong. She'd cried. Later Solana gave her a pear. Don't touch baby.

If I could just— Would it be possible, she wondered habitually, if I could just shave— But no, she'd tried and it was not possible, she'd have to shave fifty times a day for it to work. And there'd still be everything else. She remembered a moment, looking into her own eyes in another mirror, razor in hand. The horrible pale flap of skin suddenly nude above her upper lip showed all the more clearly the jut and thrust of it. She'd burst into tears. She never bothered now. Best just keep her hair nice, comb it gracefully toward the temples, down into her beard, keep it as nice as she could. You couldn't hold back the sea. Her face in the mirror was calm, the hair a bit of a mess. A pain burned in her chest. Am I human? Am I actually human? And if I'm not, what does it mean? Ape woman, bear woman, human. Thing. Still me, still the Julia creature. Hush, silly girl, said Solana's voice. The good Lord made you, that's all that matters. And she followed the thought till it billowed and swooped into a mighty chasm where she was afraid to go.

Madame Soulie opened the door and caught her crying, looking at herself in the mirror. Julia dropped the curtain.

"What's this?" said Madame Soulie, striding into the room. "Crying? Oh, no, no, we mustn't cry."

"If it's the mothers that have done wrong," said Julia, pulling herself together, "why does the curse fall on the children?"

Madame Soulie took her by the arm and led her back to the parlor. "I've often wondered about that," she said, "and I'm afraid to say I have no idea. The dress is wonderful on you. Stand here in the light and let me pin the hem. And"—she darted away, rummaged behind a pile of clothes that completely obliterated one of the armchairs—"I've got some lovely little boots that might fit. Where are they? Much too small for me."

Julia wiped her nose and gazed at the pomegranate leaves hanging down outside the window. Wouldn't make any difference what she wore.

"Now!" said Madame Soulie in a tone dripping promise.

"Should I stand here?" asked Julia. A bird landed among the leaves and stared at her with tiny black bead eyes.

"Julia."

She turned. The boots were dark red with black trim and pointed toes, old but well cared for, the leather soft and clean.

"They're beautiful," Julia said. "Whose were they?"

"A child." Madame Soulie held them at arm's length. "Grew out of them. Her mother was in a show at the Charles. Try them on."

Julia sat down and put them on. Her feet slipped into them as if they'd always belonged to her.

"Walk up and down," said Madame Soulie. "Oh, look at your tiny foot! It's like a child's foot."

"They're perfect. Thank you!"

"And they fit?"

"Perfectly. Can I keep them on?"

"Of course you can. Now stand still." Madame Soulie knelt to gather up the hem of the lilac dress. "Sometimes," she said, "a curse can be lifted."

"Someone tried once," Julia said sadly. Remembering Solana burning something smelly, bathing her in salt.

Madame Soulie stuck three or four pins into her mouth. "It has to be someone with the power," she said through narrowed lips, "not just anyone." She shook the material. "There's a man I know."

Julia looked down on the crown of Madame Soulie's head. She'd put something on it for the color but the gray was coming through. "He couldn't help me," Julia said.

"Probably not, *chéri.*" Madame Soulie looked up, drawing a pin out of her mouth.

"This man," said Julia a little later. "What else can he do?"

"Gris-gris, fortunes. You know."

"He tells fortunes?"

"He does." Madame Soulie rose heavily to her feet. "Would you like to go and see him? I can take you."

"Really?"

Madame Soulie smiled. "Leave it to me."

Rates took her to the French market, then to a big store on the Rue des Grands Hommes. They went next morning early, she in her new red boots, walking with her gloved hand resting on his arm, watching the streets through the mesh of her veil. Women with baskets on their heads walked ahead of them. They passed an oyster stand and she wanted to stop, a man was playing a harp, another an accordion. Rates hurried her on nervously to the market on the levee, but when they got there her nerve faltered. It was the noise, a clicking of bones, a plucking of strings, the yelling of wares and cackling of hens, the grumbling of wheels on stone. A massive press of people jostled in the aisles, slaves and sailors, rough men and ladies of quality. Someone knocked into her and she tightened her grip on Rates's arm. "The colors!" she said, sticking close. "The flowers!"

"Yes, of course." He hurried her on. "We'll buy some flowers later if there's time."

But it was all such a rush so of course they didn't. In the clothes market she chose ribbons, then it was on to the Rue des Grands Hommes without a break, where Rates told the woman in the shop she was his granddaughter who'd been ill and was sensitive to light. She picked out a yellow and white corset and some rose pink fabric and they were back in no time. It was as if someone had opened a door and she'd got just one glimpse of something wild and exotic before it closed again. Sitting at the table in the yard, she drew a plan of how she would have her costume. Pearl buttons. Six tucks on the skirt. For her hair, feathers and a single white gardenia. She wrote it all down, listing every measurement.

It wasn't ready in time for the portrait. For that she borrowed a plain cream-colored gown from Myrtle. Delia helped her pin it into place. "Lord Almighty," she said, doing up the buttons down the back, "look at you. Never seen nothing like this in my life. You could be at the American Museum. Do you mind?" She stroked her hands across Julia's shoulders, then down her back, following the hairy downward-pointing arrow.

"I don't mind," said Julia. Solana used to stroke her when she was small, but stopped when she got bigger.

"It's like stroking a bear," said Delia.

The portrait was to be done in the front parlor of the house. The artist was no more than a boy, frail and smooth-faced. "Oh, my saints," he whispered, gazing, "oh, my saints and angels," as Julia settled herself in the overstuffed button-back armchair. After this, the boy remained silent, working diligently away with his pencils and pens and inks. The clock ticked loudly. She went into a trance, gazing straight ahead. From here she could see the sideboard, with its bowl of jasmine and the framed daguerreotype of a dignified militiaman with sad eyes. That must be Monsieur Soulie, she thought. I wonder what happened to him. She wondered what the precise state of things was between Mr. Rates and Madame Soulie. Rates was too smug and bloated, and he had no lips. I wouldn't have him, she thought, and couldn't help smiling. Poor man, rejected by the bear woman. The bear woman's choosy.

"Don't smile, please," the boy said softly.

"Sorry." For the rest of the sitting she contemplated the darting eyes of the young artist, whose gaze was now fierce but remote. She scared him and it couldn't be helped. Some never got through it, some did. And more to meet. Soon, rehearsal at the New St. Charles, onstage, with a band. People at the theater. You chose this, girl, she told herself. You could have stayed home. She worked herself up for the rest of that sitting, and the one after, with so much time to do nothing but sit still and think. She'd fail, she'd fall over, be sick. But the time came closer and she didn't run, and suddenly she was there in the peculiar backstage land of stairs and doors and voices, and soon there was the stage, and the band below her, all staring up. And it was all right. These musicians had seen everything and adjusted quickly. Even so, they were quietly shocked in those first moments. No escape. They struck up a polka. She danced, forgetting all about them and pretending she was alone. She was dancing on the patio after everyone else had gone to bed. Like before, they cheered when she finished. Relief flooded her, and she smiled and ran to the front of the stage. I'll give them a good look, she thought, leaning down, saying, "Thank you! I've never sung with a band before."

The musicians beamed and gawked, knowing they were getting a treat.

Then the violin played the sighing first notes of "I Dreamt I Dwelt in Marble Halls," and she sang. It poured like cream, perfect.

"Take a bow," said the leader.

———

Madame Soulie, big bust heaving contentedly, played on the air with her fingers. "He's got *power*. You look in that man's eyes and he *sees* you."

"But to turn *me*," said Julia, "would be a miracle."

"Well, of course, one mustn't expect too much." The carriage rumbled onto Bayou Road. "But I don't see the harm in trying. We only live once."

"I agree." Julia looked out of the window.

"He knows about you anyway," Madame Soulie said. "I've told him some. Oh, here we are!" She was jolly, as if they were on a jaunt.

There were some fine big houses on Bayou Road. Dr. John Montanee's was low and set back a little. A muted red glow came from the windows. There was a lantern on the porch and red dust on the threshold.

"We're lucky he could fit us in at such short notice," Madame Soulie whispered, rapping on the door and adjusting Julia's collar as if she were a child, "he's so busy. They all go to him, everybody. I've seen it when they're standing in line a mile away."

A woman with tired eyes and a long oval face opened the door and motioned them in, placing one hand on Madame Soulie's sleeve in a familiar way as she did so. *"Bonsoir, chérie,"* she said, her eyes sliding toward Julia. *"Bonsoir, madame."*

"Here we are." Madame Soulie swept grandly into the room, "and here is *she*. Julia dear, come in, come in. Marie, how are you?"

"Seen many a better day," said the woman wearily, "and a few worse."

The room was warm and dim and cluttered with furniture. Lizards sat about on the backs of sofas and arms of chairs, and the walls were hung with desiccated things, toads, scorpions, chickens' feet. Skulls grinned from the top of a high cupboard. A fire burned low. Two girls lounged almost vertically in easy chairs, drinking wine and looking at Julia with no apparent interest. Deep in the room, standing in front of a red curtain was the Doctor himself, a tall gray-bearded African man in an expensive black suit with a frilly white shirt front. She'd never seen a rich black man before. His cheeks were slashed, three big gashes on each side. A python coiled around his waist and neck, its face hovering peacefully in front of his chest. "Miss Julia," he said, his voice deep and heavily accented, "come on in," indicating that she should follow him behind the curtain.

"Go with the Doctor," said Madame Soulie. "I'll be right here. Go on."

The Doctor adjusted his snake as if it were a scarf. "Come on in here," he said. "Come on now, nothing here to be scared of."

Behind the curtain was a short passage, another door, a small dark room with a picture of the Virgin Mary on the wall and an elephant's tusk in the corner. Bunches of herbs hung from the ceiling, white candles burned tall and straight on an altar, and the air was smoky and rich, heavy with a dark soporific perfume she could not place. He motioned for her to sit in one of two chairs drawn up close beside a small table spread with shells and straws, sat down himself in the other, took the snake's thin head gently between the fingers of his right hand and settled its brown and yellow coils more comfortably. It turned its face to look up at him. Behind him on the shelf was the skull of something small and delicate.

"He's beautiful," Julia said.

"This here's a lady," said the Doctor, smiling.

The snake's round black eye was still.

"What do you want?" the Doctor asked.

"Madame Soulie said she told you about me."

He nodded.

"I might be cursed," she said.

He nodded again.

"My nurse said it was because my mother walked out in the dark of the moon. My guardian said that was nonsense. But no one has ever told me what I am."

He sat rubbing his beard for a long time.

"How old are you?" he asked.

"I'm twenty-one," she said.

"Let me see you."

She took off her veil, and he sat looking at her without any movement for so long she wondered if he was trancing her. His eyes were soft and bloodshot but very penetrating. He winked suddenly, and she smiled. "Answer my question," he said. "What do you want from me?"

"I don't know."

"You want me to make you like everybody else?"

"Yes."

"No," he said, leaning forward and speaking sharply, "that's not what you want. Think again."

She thought he was scolding her and spoke too loudly in self-defense. "Can you lift the curse?"

"Ha." His smile was sudden and brilliant. "Can't do a thing for you." He reached across and took her hand. "That's no curse. I can give you some gris-gris though. What you want? A man?"

She was shocked.

"I pray to St. Jude," she said.

"What's he say?"

"Nothing."

"Take off your glove."

She did. His two big hands closed around her cold hand. "Close your eyes," he said.

They sat in the dark, which darkened more, as if the candles were going out one by one. It was like falling half asleep. He took his hands away. He was burning herbs, moving around, shaking something that whispered, saying softly: Papa Legba, Papa Legba, Papa Legba, over and over again. She thought she could hear someone else nearby singing along, a woman's voice or maybe more than one, but it seemed unlikely and she didn't want to think about where it was coming from.

"Will I ever be loved?" she asked.

The Doctor gave her a drink, straight into her mouth, his big warm hand on top of her head. "You'll be loved," he said, "Within a year."

He moved away. Through her eyelids she could see the flickering of candlelight and heard the rattle of shells and bones falling.

"Open your eyes," he said.

Two bowls, white powder and dust.

"Someone's watching out for you," he said, sitting across from her, studying the bones. "Your mamá's watching."

"She gave me away," said Julia. Her voice came out double, vibrating. Her eyes fell upon the small neat skull on the shelf. A cat, she decided, and her eyes filled up. Poor puss.

"She's watching over you anyway," he said. "And she's not the only one."

"You said I wasn't cursed." He wasn't going to help her, it was obvious. How could she ever have thought it? "Can't you tell me anything?" she said. "I wanted you to tell me what I am. I don't know."

"No curse to lift," he said. "And what you are? You're a strange girl, that's all. Hush." He closed his eyes and sat silent for a while. "You're going across the sea," he said, "you'll keep moving."

"Me?"

"Just moving, always." He opened his eyes and looked at her. "Something's coming," he said, "big something."

"Bad or good?"

"Both."

She laughed. "That means nothing."

"No," he said seriously, "that means everything."

"I don't know what you mean."

"No matter."

What did you expect, she thought. Wave his arms? Say the right words? Lo! A miracle. "But there *are* curses," she said, pulling on one of her gloves.

"Listen," he said, "I can fix a curse. I can lift a curse. Whole lot I can do, but I can't lift a curse that isn't there. Can make you feel better though."

"What about what my nurse said? How my mother walked out in the dark of the moon and that's why I'm like I am."

"Your nurse don't know what she's talking about," he said. "Your mama can walk out any old moon she likes long as she's careful."

He was back there in the chair opposite her, leaning on one elbow, frowning, his snake advancing from his left shoulder into the air before him.

"I've been thinking," she said, "it just seemed wrong. Why the baby gets the curse for what the mother did. And maybe she didn't even know she was doing it." She looked down at her hands, one gloved, one hairy. "Madame Soulie says there's a devil baby running about on the roofs. I was so scared. I couldn't get to sleep that night for thinking about him." She pulled on the other glove. "Poor thing. Running about all night across the roofs and down the alleys all on his own and everybody running away from him and all because of something his mother did."

The Doctor's face was serious. He looked at her for a long time without blinking or saying anything, putting his hand beneath the head of his snake. His eyes were full, as if he'd seen a whole world of sorrow. She couldn't tell how old he was. Old. Poor eyes seen it all. "You know I knew that devil baby," he said, and a chill ran through her. "For sure."

"Is he real?" she whispered. "Is it true?"

"True as anything."

"And he cries in the alleys?"

"I never heard him."

"What was he?"

"Born red. Scales, like this." He ran a finger along the snake's body. "Born screaming. Nothing anyone could do. Mama couldn't look at him. Friend of mine tried to raise him but he ran away. Don't know where he went."

"Ran away? A baby?"

"Six months old, up and ran. Little bumps here"—he touched his brow—"little horns. No hooves, never had hooves."

"But what was he?"

"A baby."

"A baby what?"

"Who knows? I knew his father. And he said his wife never said that thing about the devil anyway, people just made that up."

"And you saw him? The baby? What was he like?"

"Oh, a very bad thing. Couldn't get near him. Terrible thing. Woman I knew tried with him but he grew too quick."

"But what *was* he?"

"A bad baby. And when people started seeing him here and there his whole family took off. He's around, they say."

He took from under the table a small bottle and a tiny red bag and slid them across the table to her, and she understood that their time was up. "What is this big thing that's coming?" she asked.

"Love," he said, "up the road."

"Within a year, you said."

"Within a year. For sure."

They stood.

"Did he have a name?" she asked as he held the door for her, "the baby?"

"Valentine," the Doctor said. "His name was Valentine."

Madame Soulie paid one of the women fifteen dollars on the way out.

"He's marvelous, isn't he?" Madame Soulie said as they got into the carriage. She was tipsy from drinking wine in the front room.

"Is he not a slave?" Julia turned the red gris-gris bag in her fingers. It was sewn shut. She had no idea what was in it, only that it felt like tiny chips of bark and would draw fortune. The love potion was in her pocket. "What is he? How can he have so much money? That good house."

"A free man," said Madame Soulie and laughed. "Came as a slave from Africa and now look. Free, rich and black. He *must* have power."

———

The night of the show, Julia dusted herself with orris root and combed herself very carefully, arms, breasts, shoulders. Her head hair, adorned with gardenias and feathers, was done up in curls. Rose pink silk flounced about her short full figure on a froth of white petticoats. From the carriage she saw the posters all along St. Charles Avenue for the show, her name at the top and bigger than all the rest. She saw the crowds on the steps and all along the block, the flowers above the great doors in front of the theater, and all the lights from the chandeliers shining out from the foyer. The carriage took them 'round the back. Rates, in a frilly white shirt, his sparse gray hair pomaded, handed her down and led her in through a warren of scurrying forms only dimly seen through the veil to a small room with mirrors and chairs, a table with glasses and a bottle of brandy.

There was some time. The walls were flimsy. Next door, Ted and Jonsy and Michael were laughing about something. Myrtle, brush between her toes, painted Indian ink around her eyes. Delia blew a kiss to her reflection. Julia fiddled with her gardenias, flicking an imaginary speck of dust from her rose-colored stocking, inspecting the pearl buttons on her tight white shoes.

Her nerves were jiggling.

She felt better sitting in the wings, watching, waiting her turn, drinking water and wine. Funny how different people were when they performed. Jonsy, the stone-faced and silent, laughed and grinned, cakewalking across the stage, the whiteness of his skin and hair against the pinkness of his eyes and suit. Ted curled his hands into claws when he picked at his flesh, his face turned into something unearthly and slightly wicked. He pulled the skin under his chin up over his face till it covered his nose completely and his eyes glaring out above looked mad. Then it was Myrtle and Delia's turn. They played a Jew's harp. Myrtle's lips were waxed and carmined 'round the frame. Delia, balancing on a pedestal by her side, plucked the reed.

The world stopped at the footlights.

Rates came and stood at her shoulder. "What a marvelous place this is," he murmured suavely. "Think of this, Julia. Only three years ago the great Jenny Lind, the Swedish Nightingale, was up on that very stage. And now here you are. Julia Pastrana. Top of the bill!"

Till the last minute she thought she'd turn and run, just turn and run, think later.

It was time. No different from singing at home at a party, lowering the veil across her face, blood beating in her ears. She took her place in the center of the stage and breathed deeply behind the shiny purple curtain. My God, but the stage was wider than she remembered. The others, who'd all gone before and could now rest, were watching from the wings. The auditorium rustled. She heard Rates walk out in front of the curtain. He spoke in a voice she'd never heard before, basso profundo, declaiming, "Ladies and gentlemen! Mesdames! Messieurs! I am proud to announce! The world debut! Of the most remarkable woman in the world! The greatest wonder of nature! From the wild mountains of Mexico! Perhaps—even—the Missing Link!"

A long breathless pause.

"I give you! The only one of her kind, the truly incomparable—Julia! Pastrana!"

The curtain rose.

The theater was a great gold cavern with a thrilling echo. The lights lit up faces, row after row after row, every one fixed on her. She smiled beneath her veil. Her lips had dried up so she tried to lick them but her tongue, too big at the best of times, had dried up too and seemed to have doubled in size. She swallowed. Sing to the people at the back, Rates had told her. The back was miles away. But first the band struck up the Minute Waltz. A little run on the tips of her toes then into the dance, keeping time with all the changes, twirl, pirouette, pique, turn. Slow down. Glissade, then into the Hungarian Dance, and from there to flamenco, swishing her skirts and stamping. The crowd cheered. When she stopped and curtseyed, they cheered more. Then Rates walked out and took her hand, holding it high to his lips and bowing to her as if she were a great lady.

"Wonderful, Julia," he said quietly to her, then turned to face the audience. "And now it is time!" he cried, "to reveal to you—one of the *great* wonders of our time, the *only* one of her kind—the *non*pareil—the most remarkable being known to mankind—la-*dees* and *gent*lemen—mesdames—messieurs—I give you—"

They had rehearsed it time after time above Brady Childer's grocery shop. She held herself ready, arranging her face into an easy yet dignified smile that would become more animated as the audience relaxed—and after all, as Delia had said, what more was this than what she'd been doing all her life one way or another?

"—the one and only!—"

She stepped away from him and lifted one elegant white-gloved hand to the end of her veil.

"—Miss JULIA PASTRANA!"

She unveiled.

There was a moment of absolute silence, a second or two at most, then a collective sucking like a hurricane drawing in its breath to blow. A few people shrieked. Julia walked toward the front of the stage. She heard a wag in the audience say, "It's a chimpanzee in a dress!"

Someone shouted, *"Loup-garou!"* She laughed. Her eyes twinkled, her smile was genuine. Now that she was on, she didn't feel so bad. I'm looking at you, she thought. You are looking at me. And you're paying. The band played "La Llorona." She'd sung it hundreds of times, it's what she'd always done, and she sang it tonight with a certain lightness and spring that somehow accentuated its tragedy, walking up and down the front of the stage and peeling off her long white gloves, discarding them as she looked out into the sea of faces, meeting eyes boldly, as fascinated by them as they were by her. The crowd roared and waved its handkerchiefs, and it was such a glorious moment she thought she might faint.

⸻

The night before they left for New York there was cold ham and figs and a jug of wine, laid out on the table in the yard. Cato and Ezra Porter were heading for Knoxville in two more days, and other people were coming to stay in the shacks 'round the yard.

"Going on a big train, Cato," Delia said, wafting the air with a palm fan.

Cato was sitting on the henhouse.

"You and Cato," Julia asked Ezra, sipping her wine, "how did you come by each other?"

"Found him near Pittsville, Alabama," Ezra said. "In a bar. Was with a man called Flynn who had fleas he used to feed on a big special vein he had running down the inside of his arm."

Cato's bare heels drummed the side of the henhouse.

"Cato, get down from there," said Ezra. "Poor stuff, it all was—you know—not even the midway, back of the midway, out of the midway, box on the sidewalk, tent thrown over three sticks, you know?" He got up and traipsed over to the henhouse. "Someone brought Cato in the bar. This kid kind of pushed him in. Was scared, not like he is now. Me and Flynn sitting there and the bartender just staring, says, Jesus Christ, it's some fucking freak. What the hell, get it out of here. And Flynn just about filling his pants. Didn't bother me. They used to bring the freaks through every year where I grew up. I knew what he was."

He took Cato's hand. Cato pulled it away and walked along the ridge of the henhouse, arms outstretched.

"Kid said he'd been following him about like a lost dog and he didn't know what to do. He's been walking up and down all day just up the road, they shooed him away, and now he's following me, he says, and I don't know what to do. Look, he's giving me the creeps. From the plantation most like, bartender says. Better take him to the sheriff. They don't want him up there, the boy says. They put him out."

Julia took her drink over to the swing, sat down and swung gently.

"And I said, no," Ezra said, "people'd pay money to see him. And Flynn says, I ain't going anywhere with that thing."

Loose-jointed, Cato jumped down and moved with his peculiar bent-kneed gait over to where Julia swayed under the apple tree.

"So after that," said Ezra, "it was just me and Cato."

"Hoo-hah!" Cato said, holding up his arms as if wanting to be picked up.

"You want to swing?" she said. "Shall I push you? You won't scream, will you?"

He shook his head.

"Come on then." She got down and put her drink on the ground and he clambered on with sounds of gobbled delight. As she pushed, he howled with joy and his thin bare feet kicked wildly.

"Cato!" she said, "You promised!"

Madame Soulie came out of the house carrying a banjo and sat down with the rest. "It'll be very quiet around here tomorrow when you're all gone," she said.

"The new batch'll be here before you know it," Rates said, peeling a fig.

Madame Soulie played "Rose of Alabamy," slow at first.

"I'm not pushing you, you're too noisy," Julia said.

Cato got down.

"I could play this once," Madame Soulie said, playing a little faster.

Cato lifted up his long skinny arms and swayed.

"I will miss you, Cato," Julia said.

Duende, she thought. Goblin. I'm the loup-garou. Jonsy's a ghost. Arm in arm against a full moon sky, walking with the devil baby. "Dear little *duende,*" she said, and was struck with a momentary sense of belonging.

Rose was reading about an island in Mexico, the last resting place of hundreds of dolls.

"Trouble is," said Laurie, "for you it'd be like going to Battersea Dogs' Home. You'd want to bring them all home with you."

Adam, hovering uneasily about with a slightly sneery look on his face, was wondering if he should leave. He'd been drinking tea and talking to her about M. R. James when Laurie just walked in and slobbed down with her on the sofa, taking over. Laurie wore an emerald green velvet waistcoat over a naked brown torso, and his shoulders and arms, packed with veiny muscle, were tattooed to the wrist with swirly vines and plants and birds. There was an unsavory reek about him, a whiff of the lower echelons of the entertainment industry, of amusement arcade backrooms.

"No," said Rose, "I'd leave them there. They're happy."

"Rose," said Laurie, "believes a lost sock misses its partner and weeps bitter tears for it."

"I do not."

"Yes, you do."

"Of course I don't believe it literally," she said. "Don't try and make me look like an idiot."

"Don't try and make her look like an idiot, Laurie," Adam repeated. He didn't know why. It came out sounding nasty.

"Will you all stop taking the piss?" she said, sitting up and throwing the magazine down onto the rug. "Anyone wants to take the piss has to get out of my room."

"It's OK, Rose," Laurie said, "we all know you're mad, but we forgive you."

Adam picked up the magazine. "Obviously this is where Tattoo should be," he said, looking at the pictures. The dolls were weirdly beautiful. Rose lay back against Laurie, whose large gnarly-knuckled hand slid 'round under her waist and began lazily kneading her stomach under her crumpled blue shirt.

"Catch you later," Adam mumbled, went downstairs and grabbed his ancient Nikon, wandered out into the street and roamed about in the direction of the park. Every now and then he'd stop to take a moody shot of a pigeon or an empty bench. It was a sunny day, dust from the traffic got in his throat. He ambled along, going nowhere in particular, got bored and went back home, lay down with closed eyes listening to the radio still playing the same random pop music it had been playing to his empty room all afternoon. He lived in a mess of squashed paint tubes and discarded rags. Some days he'd get up and dressed and lie back down on his bed, doing nothing fiercely and tremulously till it was time to go to sleep again. After a while he drifted to sleep, drifted out again, drifted back upstairs. Laurie had gone. She was sitting in the middle of all her things. It was getting worse; the stuff was making the room too small.

"Grab yourself a glass," she said. She'd opened a bottle of wine. He lay down on the floor. She fiddled about with some embroidery for one of her frames. A J. J. Cale album played softly. For a long time he stared at the ceiling.

"You don't really like him, do you?" he said.

"Let it go, Ad."

"His breath stinks."

"No, it doesn't."

"He's an ugly fucker."

"Yeah, yeah." Rose put down the embroidery, picked up her glass, took a long drink and poured herself another. Closed her eyes. God, it was tiring. Living. Knocking about the world alone, bloody men, always wanting more. She didn't want an us. Family stuff. Her own was far-flung and had never been demonstrative. She'd spent her teens and twenties falling in and out of love with a series of boys and men. Sometimes she counted them off in her head. They all ended. Feelings changed, nothing was certain, everything was threatened.

"He's got lumps on his face," said Adam.

"Shut up," she said.

"OK, OK, OK." Long-suffering, he got up and walked 'round the room looking at stuff. The whole of the fireplace wall was now covered halfway to the ceiling with shelves she'd made out of bricks and breeze-blocks and planks of wood. You could imagine a little lift man going up and down. First floor: shells, plectrums, combs with missing teeth. Second floor: twigs and branches, random bits of wood. Third floor: odd playing cards, buckles, matchboxes, bobbins of colored cotton. Fourth: things babies throw out of buggies and prams— a little cloth star, a rattle, a mouse with a baby-gnawed nose. Fifth, top: bottles—Tiger Sauce, La Fée Absinthe, Stone's Ginger Wine, blue, green and brown bottles all standing together, a Manhattan of differing heights. Everything had been touched a million times.

"Sit down, Ad," she said. "You're like a kid with worms."

He sat down, picked up the magazine and looked at the pictures of the island. "Look at us, we're wasting time," he said. "Me and you, Rosie. Let's go mad. Let's go to Mexico. Let's go to your weird island."

She looked up and smiled. "One day," she said, "if you're very, very good."

Is This the Ugliest Woman in the World?

Miss Julia Pastrana is surely the most remarkable creature ever to have graced a stage in this city of excess, far surpassing any of the attractions currently on show at Mr. Barnum's American Museum just a couple of blocks away. She has the appearance of an ape but dances like Lola Montez and sings pretty Spanish folk songs in a very pleasant mezzo-soprano while sometimes accompanying herself on the guitar.

The newspaper lay open on a pouf by her feet. It's not that I have a particularly beautiful voice, she thought. It's that they're surprised I have any voice at all that isn't a grunt or a howl.

Wearing scarlet boots, a tight-fitting skirt, and silk panty hose, Pastrana sang an Irish melody—"The Last Rose of Summer"—and danced a bolero, looking every bit like the famed ballerina Fanny Elssler and displaying "a symmetry" that would make the most successful ballet dancers envious.

Three nights on Broadway at the Gothic Hall, a big old palace covered in tarpaulin, the canvas a riotous mishmash of color. Sea monsters, a man with two heads, a boy pierced with pins, serpents and Cyclops and a scorpion with a woman's face. In the corners, scenes from cannibal life. And now her picture was up there too, the head wild and fierce, the body a ballerina.

The front stoop of the rooming house was full all day with people waiting, hoping for a glimpse. She heard them, laughing and fooling around, crossing the road to the coffee booth, but she didn't dare look out. "Think about it, Julia," Rates said. "Who's fool enough to pay good money if he can just run down here and take a look for nothing? Guard your mystery."

When this was over, they were for Philadelphia.

"Or *we* are for Philadelphia," Myrtle said, laying out the cards for solitaire. "I don't know about you, Julia. You know he's had an offer?"

"Delia told me."

They were in the pink parlor on the third floor, a room full of faded brocade and walls crammed with pictures and playbills of all the show people who'd ever stayed there. Julia was at the window, behind the curtain so she couldn't be seen, looking down at the coffee booth across the street. A young man leaned against it with a bored air. Myrtle tossed one of her endless thin cigars into the air with her foot and caught it between her lips. "Look out for yourself," she said.

"I'm not a slave," said Julia. "He can't *sell* me."

Myrtle looked thoughtfully at her, the cigar drooping on her lip. "Can't he?"

"Not unless I want to be sold." Julia turned from the window and sat down opposite Myrtle. "Can I have one of those?" she said.

"Sure." Myrtle gave her a cigar. "Mine's gone out. Pass me a spill."

"I want to travel," Julia said, plucking a spill from a pot on the mantelpiece and lighting it at the fire.

"Well, you'll surely do that. They're all out there, waving their big bucks, you could have your pick of them."

"I don't want to stay with Rates," Julia said. "Do you?" She lit both their cigars.

"For a time, I suppose." Myrtle drew on the cigar, opened her lips and held the smoke in the bowl of her mouth. "He's not too bad," she said, letting it out slowly, "wears thin, travel, believe me. I've been on the road since I was nine," leaning down, passing the cigar to her toes. "Been all over the West, up to Alaska, up in the snows, all over the place."

"I want to go everywhere," Julia said. "I want to go all over the world." She shivered. "I'm cold. I'm getting a shawl. Do you want yours?"

"No."

"I've been in one place," said Julia, "all my life."

"Just look out for yourself, that's all I'm saying." Myrtle shifted a card from one line to the next.

"I'm going to get my shawl." Julia ran down quickly. Coming back with the shawl around her shoulders she saw Rates's door at the end of the passage and thought, I'll go there now and talk to him, no more of this drifting, put her hand in the pocket of her dress and closed it on the gris-gris bag. *Courage and luck,* the Doctor said. *Be brave.*

"Julia!" said Rates, as if delighted, "I was just about to . . ."

"Mr. Rates," she said, with no idea what to say, "what are your plans?"

"My plans, Julia?"

"Someone wants to buy me."

"Everyone wants you!" Rates laughed, came out into the passage and pulled his door behind him. "Barnum! Barnum sent someone! Soon sent *him* packing. Didn't come himself, you note. *Sent* someone."

"So," she said, "am I to come to Philadelphia with the others?"

"Don't you want to?"

"To tell you the truth, Mr. Rates," she said, "I haven't really thought any further ahead than this moment. And now suddenly, I don't know why, but I'm feeling nervous."

"No need for that!" Rates smiled down at her. "No need to rush into anything. Have the girls been talking?" His face took on concern. "I'm sorry, Julia, perhaps I should have mentioned it, but I didn't want to bother you with the details."

"But Mr. Rates," she said, "I need to know what's happening."

"The truth is," said Rates, all business, "I've had three or four offers and I'm weighing them up, settling in my mind which is the best for everybody all 'round. But, more to the point . . ."

"I don't want to go with just anyone," she said.

"Of course not!" Rates was shocked. "What are you worrying about, Julia?"

"Who are they?" she asked.

"Associates. I don't deal with anyone shady, as you know."

"I'd like to know."

"I promise," Rates said firmly. "I'll tell you everything from now on. The truth is there's nothing to tell right now, at least not as far as that's concerned. But," and he bounced eagerly on the balls of his feet, "there is something very interesting, *very* interesting indeed. I've had a request from one of the most distinguished medical men of the age."

Julia's eyes went blank.

"Desperate to see you. *Desperate*."

She'd seen a few medical men as a child. They'd studied her teeth, peered down her throat and down her ears, made her lie down and close her eyes and sing a little song to try and make her forget where they were poking their fingers. But that had been a long time ago. "I suppose I'll have to see him," she said, dully resigned, "him or someone else. I know. They'll say I'm a fake otherwise, won't they?"

"You must realize, Julia," he said. "Oh, it's a bore, I know, but the medical establishment will inevitably take an interest."

"I know."

"Anyway, I've spoken to this Dr. Mott. He's the best. Very top of the tree. Extremely hard to get to see him normally but he's made a space for us. Tomorrow, three sharp."

She must have looked worried because he patted her on the shoulder encouragingly. "Sooner the better!" he said briskly. "Get it over with."

When she returned to the pink parlor, Delia was there, doing Myrtle's hair. "How much is he paying Rates?" she asked when Julia told them about the doctor.

"I've told her," said Myrtle, "time and again. You get something out of it for yourself. You ask how much he's getting for it. You want your cut."

"He's not getting anything," said Julia.

"Ha!" Delia gave a little shriek. "*He* says!"

Myrtle just snorted.

———

They drove from the Bowery to Madison Avenue, where Dr. Mott lived and had his practice. Through the veil, through the coach window, she watched the great show of the streets. New York made New Orleans seem quaint. It was like an ant's nest nudged by a foot, the clanging of the omnibuses endless and deafening, the noise of children, beggars, hawkers. This was really The World, whatever that was. Slap center of the Big Adventure. By night, coming and going between the theater and the rooming house, the city had seemed smaller, enclosed by darkness. Daytime revealed its colors, somber for the most part, slashed with brightness here and there. The farther they traveled, the grander it got. Great buildings rose up like mammoths.

"Shall we walk a little coming back?" she suggested.

Rates raised his eyebrows and pursed his lips. "Oh, I don't think so, Julia."

"It was fine in New Orleans. With my veil."

"This is a rough city," Rates said. "Now, if my memory serves me—yes—it's just along here . . ."

She kept her veil on till she was in the inner room, which was almost filled by the doctor's enormous desk. Dr. Mott, still holding a white towel, emerged from a side room where he'd been washing his hands. "Miss Pastrana," he said, tossing it aside onto a windowsill and coming toward her with his hand outstretched. "I am delighted." He showed no surprise, having seen her twice already on the stage.

"How do you do," said Julia, taking his hand and smiling. Rates returned to the waiting room to read the newspaper he'd brought with him, and Julia took off her coat. She'd rather have seen someone older and plainer. Mott was handsome, young but already distinguished. On his desk was a framed picture of himself with his wife and little boy.

"Come," he said, ushering her deferentially before him into the room next door. There was a high narrow bed, a chair, a screen and a sideboard laid out neatly with medical implements she didn't dare look at.

"You'll find a gown behind the screen," he said.

He was thorough. He got the nasty bits out of the way first. She closed her eyes and did what she always did, what Solana had told her to do. Said a prayer. Sang a song in her head. After that he paid particular attention to her teeth and ears, turned her eyelids inside out, lifted her tongue and looked under it, measured every part of her meticulously from her toes to the circumference of her head, inspected the palms of her hands and the soles of her feet closely, rang bells behind her head and asked if she could hear them.

"I'm told you know your letters," he said.

"I do."

"That's excellent." His eyebrows went up. "Mr. Rates tells me you enjoy reading novels?"

"I do," she said, "very much so."

"Good, very good. Now—starting with the top line, if you please—"

She could read all but the bottom line.

"Very good indeed," Dr. Mott said. "And tell me—what do you like to read?"

"Oh," she said, "whatever I can get hold of. I like *The Linwoods, The Wide, Wide World*. And *The Curse of* . . ."

The doctor smiled and scratched his whiskers. "Very, very good indeed," he said, more to himself than her.

Then it was over and they were back in the carriage, and it was only when she saw the next show pamphlet that she read what Dr. Mott had said about her: "She is a Semi-Human Indian, a perfect woman, a rational creature endowed with speech which no monster has ever possessed, yet she is Hybrid, wherein the nature of woman predominates over the brute—the Ourang Outang."

Ourang-outang? In Mexico?

A long time ago, the big boys talking over her head as if she couldn't understand:

"Jonas Ochoa said she isn't human."

"What does Jonas Ochoa know? Did you tell him?"

"Of course I did. She's Indian, I said. She's a Digger. He says he's never seen a Digger like that before."

"You tell him what Papá says. She's just like us only with hair."

"Then he says that's what I mean, the hair, he says, human beings don't have hair. Not like that, they don't. Monkeys do. Bears do. Wolves do, dogs do. But not human beings. Not like that."

"He has a point."

—◆—

Rates read aloud from a newspaper article to the man sitting across from him in the pink parlor.

" 'This mysterious animal is one of the most extraordinary beings of the present day . . .'—you see, he knows what he's about, the man's a giant in his field," gesturing toward a large folder that lay on the low table between them, "and his examination was completely thorough. I have it here, in writing—" Rates peered down short-sightedly at the newspaper. "His medical opinion is that she is the result of the pairing of a human being with a simian. See! 'She has features in common with the ourang-outang . . .'"

"Better make your mind up," the other man said, a big-boned, yellow-haired showman with a broken nose. "You're calling her the Bear Woman, and he's saying she's a monkey. She can't be both."

"Let's keep it just this side of credibility, shall we?" said Rates with a lofty smile. "There are bears in those mountains but I never heard of an ape in Mexico."

"Of course there are," said the blond man. "There's monkeys."

"But no large apes."

"Not as far as we *know*."

"I've had interest from other quarters, you know, Beach," Rates said. "Barnum's after her. Did you know?" He glanced up. "And here—yes, here it is." Rates slapped the paper. "And don't forget this Mott's at the very top of his—here, says he's never seen anything like her—see, see, something absolutely new, he says, absolutely new, unknown to science." He put the paper aside. *"Science!"* He turned his pale steady gaze onto Beach. "You see my dilemma."

"Not at all," said Beach. "Mine's the better offer, and it's that simple."

Rates pursed his lips and tried to look thoughtful. "Yours may be the better offer, but Mott's working in the interests of knowledge. Science," he said reverently. "Of course I have to take that into account."

"No, you don't." Beach laughed and stood up. "Who cares about science? *She* doesn't. The girl wants a good time." He laughed again. "The girl bit does, who knows about that other thing? Ask her. What's she want?"

"She doesn't know what she wants." Rates drained his glass. "She wants to get around a bit and see the world."

"She'll do that with me. Least she'll see Milwaukee," Beach said.

Rates sighed. "She's a good girl," he said. "Does the very best she can, you know, nice nature. Open to suggestion, you know, very helpful. You say try this, she tries it. No nonsense about the girl. I want her treated right."

"No question about it. Shake then." They stood and shook hands. Beach towered over Rates. "Time of her life's coming," he said. "This time next month she'll be drinking champagne."

They went down to see her straightaway. She was alone. She knew what they'd been talking about. Twice Beach had visited her backstage after the show, filling the dressing room with his bulky self-made air.

"My dear Julia," Rates said, taking small steps toward her and clasping both her hands in his, "I can't tell you how privileged I feel to have been a party to your great success."

Beach smiled over Rates's shoulder, his eyes an eerie pale blue.

"And now," said Rates, "I feel a parting of the ways is nigh."

She looked Beach in the eye.

"Mr. Beach has a proposition," said Rates.

"I thought so," she said.

Her eyes made Beach shiver, she could tell, but he showed no sign of disquiet. What to make of him? Caramel-colored coat. Gold cravat. Carrying his hat. Only thing she could do was trust instinct. He came forward. His cheekbones were shiny ridges, his grin made him look like Punch. "Cleveland," he said. "Buffalo. Chicago. Lenox, Massachusetts. Milwaukee. Cincinnati. I have these lined up for you already."

She laughed nervously. "I don't know where they are."

"Want me to show you a map?" He patted his pockets comically. "Don't have one on me right now, but I sure will next time I see you."

"And the contract?" she said.

The girls would have been proud of her.

On the steps Beach lit a cigar, shaking his head in wonder. A light rain began falling on the steaming pavement, and a breeze blew up from the river. "The strangest thing," he said, gazing down the street to the carriages waiting in line. "The face, the face . . ."

"The face indeed," Rates echoed, scratching his smooth bulby chin.

"Impossible to comprehend." Beach put his collar up and hunched his shoulders. "There's a kind of—no, the word 'wonder' isn't right— she is so—completely—" He shook his head again.

Rates completed the sentence, "inhuman." The rain was turning to sleet. "Went down a charm in New Orleans," he said, "thought she was the loup-garou."

"As if the head of a wolf or a boar——" said Beach.

"I know."

For a moment they stood in silence.

"Beggars belief," said Beach. "I tell you, gives you the shivers. Puts the fear in people. And then she opens her mouth—the mouth of Cerberus!—and this sweet little voice comes out!"

Rates gave a short laugh. "And her English is perfect. She's not at all bad, is she?"

"She's a sensation," said Beach, "that's what she is. She's a good girl, I can work with her."

All gone on the night train. The good-byes said. Good luck, sweetheart, we'll no doubt see you again, that's the way of it. New place, new people. They were going to Cleveland on the train, and after that a long tour. They'd ride in wagons. She'd have one of her own, Beach said. He paid better than Rates. The contract ran till Christmas when they would return to New York, and after that, well . . .

"I plan on making you a famous lady," Beach said, "yes, I do. I will get the best deal going for you every single time, nothing more, nothing less."

And all in writing.

"Before we leave New York," she told Beach, "I want to ride the streetcar. And I want to go to church."

"I don't think there's time, Julia," he said. He was dashing off somewhere.

"Why not? I'm not doing anything."

"Yes, you are," he said. "You're guarding your mystery." He'd picked the phrase up from Rates. "If you go out just any old time people get used to seeing you. They stop paying. Simple as that. Think about it. It's your livelihood, Julia. You'll never want for anything as long as you live, but there's this one overriding rule. Keep 'em hungry."

"I'll wear my veil and gloves," she said.

"You can't go out on your own, Julia." His big red face was worried. "You'll get lost."

"I know where the streetcar stops," she said. "Why would I get lost?"

His face was pained. "It's not that simple. Anything could happen. This is a dangerous city, Julia."

Pointless to talk. That's how it was. Delia and Jonsy had never gone out. Some people just couldn't do as other people did. Even in Culiacán she couldn't.

Only one day more in New York. She sat behind the curtain looking out of the window, thinking of home, wondering if she should send a letter. Who would she send it to? Solana was dead. She couldn't have read it anyway. And the others? What could she say? Perhaps write to Don Pedro. Doing fine. Hope all well. But then after all—after all, she thought, what am I? A servant who moved on. Dear Don Pedro, you were wrong. You said I'd fall flat. My dresses are prettier than Marta's. When she'd told him she was leaving he'd frowned, steepling his fingers and looking at her steadily over the top of them as if deeply disappointed in her, and she'd gabbled about being grateful for all he'd done for her. Then he'd gotten up and walked about the room, staring at the floor. "What do you think it will be like," he'd said, "out there in the world? I am your guardian, you are my responsibility. I mean to continue in that role. Tell me, have you any idea quite how your Mr. Rates intends to present you? Hm?"

"Señor," she'd said, "you know that I can sing and dance, you yourself made sure of it."

"Indeed! That does not answer my question. You're not a fool. Have we kept you prisoner here? There are no bars on the doors or the windows. Why don't you go out then, freely, brazenly? Why?"

She said nothing, because her eyes were filling up and she was realizing that Don Pedro was the one she'd miss the most, even though he hardly ever spoke to her.

"You know why."

Nothing.

"Do you think you'll see any more of the world out there than in this safe home we gave you? Here, where you're known? However far you go, do you think you'll ever be able to walk down the street like any other young woman?"

"Señor," she said, "I can't tell you how grateful I will always be to you."

"You'll sing and you'll dance and you'll play your guitar, and they'll applaud, of course they will. Do you think they care about your talent? Such as it is."

Such as it is, she repeated in her mind. *Such as it is.* Something about the phrase and the way he said it, as if he were throwing it away, hardened her resolve.

"They don't care about your talent, Julia," he'd said, stopping in front of her and speaking gently, "they only want to see the freak."

"Señor," she said, "I know. I want to be independent. Mr. Rates has sent me my fare."

And then of course he'd become sentimental, as was his way, sat down in his chair and gazed at her with moist aching eyes and told her once more how he'd first seen her in the orphanage. "In you came with that old lump of wood in a dress, a little ape but not *quite* an ape, and it was the most curious thing." Shaking his head. *Impossible.* "You were so hideous but you were just like a puppy. You were sucking your fingers. So unaware of what you were. And I tickled you under the chin and scratched behind your ears. I asked you what you liked to eat and you said, 'Porridge, señor,' in the most ordinary little voice. I was surprised you could talk.

"And then the old nun said, 'Oh, she has a voice, señor. Would you like to hear her sing?' And you sang that silly little song, 'Sana Sana, Colita de Rana.'"

Your talent. Such as it is.

It all flooded in, Don Pedro, Solana and her room and the young men coming and going with their friends, calling her out to sing on the patio, and the fig tree and the stone seat and the steps going up to the gallery. Don Pedro the last time she saw him, his sad farewell to the family dog.

The future was as far away as the past. She was frightened, as if time dispersed in all directions, but there was something intoxicating about the moment too. Where was everyone? Beach had gone out. It was half past three in the afternoon. She was on the third floor and could see below a young man holding his head beneath the pump, people walking up and down, flashy long-haired boys in wide trousers, girls strolling about on their own as if it were the most natural thing in the world to do. The window was open and she heard the sound of traffic from the wharves. She went to the mirror, a mottled ailing thing in a tarnished gilt frame, looked at her face and wished that at least her neck could have been a bit longer. Just that. "I'm not a prisoner," she said aloud. He couldn't tell her what to do. "He's a manager," she said, "not a jailer."

She still had some of the money she'd left home with, as well as a fair bit from her earnings.

She put on her cloak and bonnet, her veil and gloves, picked up her purse and went out onto the landing. The house was quiet. She ran lightly down to the front door and out. It was cold, but her cloak was a good one and she huddled down in it. The brownstones all looked the same. Wouldn't do to forget the number. She knew where to go, she'd watched from the carriage window on the way to the theater and seen it all, people clambering on and off the streetcars, carriages in a line waiting for passengers. She kept to the edge of the sidewalk, walking quickly past the row houses and stores to the corner. Down side streets, high tenements went on forever. Kids were everywhere, oblivious to the cold, gangs of them on the roam.

At the corner she stopped and looked about. Nobody took any notice of her. People rushed up and down the street. Two flashy young men were waiting for the streetcar, so she went and stood a little way from them, observing through her veil.

"So I says to him," said one in a high-pitched whine that reminded her of Ezra Porter's voice, "I says, what you wanna do dat for, huh? Looks like you wanna get mowed, dat what you mean, huh?"

At least she thought that's what he said. His hair was brilliant with oil and swept up high on his head.

"Lillian says so," the other replied in a darker voice, "she says he do it all the time, no matter what."

She couldn't take her eyes off them. The cigars wagged up and down on their lips as they spoke, and they wore gold chains across their waistcoats. She felt like a ghost. When the streetcar came she followed them on and offered the driver a handful of money. She had no idea what it cost.

"Broadway," she said. The driver looked at her hand and laughed.

"Lady," he said, "for that you can ride around all day, if you want to."

"Oh," she said, "that's very nice."

He looked at her strangely, then scooped up the cash and gave her some change. The streetcar was crowded but she found a seat halfway down. No one else wore a veil. A fat man in wide trousers stared at her. She sat very still. A squash of girls in black shawls and brightly colored bonnets babbled and laughed as if no one could hear or see them. The streetcar was too close-packed and getting more so, and the noise was crazy. A woman with a kind, worn face stooped to smile at her. She thinks I'm a little girl, thought Julia. A little girl in a veil alone on the streetcar. She coughed genteelly into her gloved hand and nodded, and the woman passed on. Her heart thumped. There were other glances. When the girls swirled down the aisle to get off, she followed.

She stood in the street and trembled, feeling too small. Which way? Which way? This way, that way, nothing she remembered. A fine white sleet began and she pulled her cloak tight. If I didn't have to wear this, she thought, they'd see my figure and know I wasn't a child. She'd never seen so many people up close. A bell chimed from the tower of a church and she looked up. The spire soared above the buildings. A carriage clipped past with a footman in blue livery on the back. Here I am, Julia Pastrana on Broadway, alone. All the swells, she never saw anything like it, strolling along in their shiny shoes. Swaggery men and girls with done-up hair, the women's dresses taking up half the sidewalk. She got a sudden urge to pull off her veil and just walk along and see what happened. Shame. Shame, but so it was and so it always had been. The air was full of a hot peanut smell. Julia felt light-headed and stood still for a moment with the people sweeping past in both directions. The buildings were grand and high, and a few had flags flying on the tops. There was nowhere to sit down, just some wide steps in front of a bank, already taken up by half a dozen or so raggedy little kids holding out their caps for money. Poor little faces. The sleet turned to fine rain, and she walked on and on and after a while the dizziness passed. No one was looking. She must stay hidden, not just for safety, not just to guard the mystery and make them pay, but so as not to frighten the children. You couldn't go around frightening children in the street, it would be too cruel.

She had to keep moving, it was too cold to stop. All the stores were open. A great crush of carriages had tangled up at the crossroads and everyone was shouting and swearing. So this is it, she thought. Here we are, the big life. People playing music on the sidewalk, selling you soda water, hot corn and roasted peanuts. She bought a comb from a booth, one that would build her hair up beautifully at the front, with a clasp made like a treble clef. The woman said it was made of shell. Farther on she came to a long stretch of pavement where men in tights were calling people in to see the freaks: the giants, the midgets, the mermaids and savages and pinheads. Not one of them was like her. One of a kind, Mr. Beach had said. Bearded ladies by the score, he said—oh, yes—but no one like you. Madame Clofullia has a fine beard, but you—

A drunk reeled from a saloon and nearly knocked her over.

"Molly dear!" he boomed, big red beaming face in hers, "I beg your pardon."

She flinched and hurried on.

"Wait a while," he called after her, "I meant nothing . . ."

But she didn't look back. She walked on and on. The stores were bright and the streetcars rattled along, the poor scrawny horses clip-clopping in time. There seemed always to be music coming from somewhere, from windows and doors, and the sounds of singing and glass against glass, the plinking of a pianola. A crowd was surging over the next crossing so she went with them, turned and started walking back down the other side. A child selling papers, a boy no more than nine, bawled loud enough to deafen her. Such a fright he'd get if she drew back the veil. Go on, Julia. Just because you can. But she didn't. Sleet again, small specks falling against a dark gray light.

She must start back. She knew the name of her stop, the name of her street. When she reached the jammed-up crossing again, she slowed down and walked carefully, studying the carriages intently. Why not? She had enough. A well-heeled lady and gent were getting down from one just in front of her, and she ran a few steps in her eagerness. Her boot heel skidded in the wet and she nearly fell, her heart thumping up into her mouth, and for a terrible moment she thought she was going to burst into tears, so strange and dangerous everything seemed. Supposing she knocked her head, and they picked her up and lifted the veil and—it didn't bear thinking about. She righted herself. Ignoring his slightly wary look, she gave the man her address and climbed up into the welcome sanctuary of the musty carriage, still bearing a trace of the musky perfume the well-heeled woman had worn.

F or Christ's sake, Rose, you're gonna have to chuck some of this stuff away."

"Says who?"

"Says me. And I'm the landlord."

She laughed.

At either end of the top shelf, she'd piled books of the same size on top of each other. She laid a plank on top. The stuff underneath was getting kind of squashed, so she'd been moving things up, carefully selecting.

"Seriously though," said Laurie, "it's getting ridiculous. You're turning weird. It's not attractive."

She looked sharply at him. "So I'm not attractive," she said.

"You are," he said, "you're lovely." He was by the door, tying his hair back into a black ponytail that resembled an old frazzled mop. "But you must be able to see that this isn't normal."

"What's normal?"

"Not this."

She sat down on the sofa, saying nothing.

"Now, don't get all funny about it. I'm only trying to help you. I'm beginning to think you've got a problem."

"Not my problem," she said.

Laurie shrugged on a leather jacket that looked a hundred years old. "You know you can get treatment for this sort of thing," he said.

"But I want all my things."

"Don't raise your voice."

"I will if I want to."

"Anyway," he said, "it's just old crap off the streets. Where does it end? You'll be bringing home snotty hankies next. Used condoms."

"Don't be ridiculous!"

"It's no different! You bring home bits of paper and empty lighters, it's just a matter of degree. Haven't you ever thought there might be something just a tad unhealthy about all this?"

He checked his pockets. When he looked 'round, he saw that she was crying.

"What's the matter?" She cried too easily and it got on his nerves. "Oh, for heaven's sake, I'm only saying what any normal person would say."

But she stopped as quickly as she'd started, got up and went to the window. "You get it or you don't get it," she said, looking out into the back garden. "And you don't."

"No," he said, "I don't."

She rubbed absently at a mark on the glass. "Some people just know what I mean," she said. "Some people think I'm mad. What? You know, just total misunderstanding? The other day I put on an old jacket and I put my hand in the pocket and there was this old earring I hadn't seen for years. I don't even know where the other one is. It's like—like their little family was scattered far and wide, like it says in that old Irish song, you wouldn't know it. I just feel for it."

"An old earring in your pocket," he said.

She turned and looked at him. "It's not even a particularly nice one," she said.

"Poor Rose." He smiled. "It must be awful to be you."

She laughed and walked toward him, fluffing out her hair with her hands. "You haven't got the faintest idea what I'm going on about, have you?" she said.

"None whatsoever."

She came close and looked unblinking into his eyes. "Really?" she said regretfully. "Really? You have absolutely no idea what I'm talking about?"

"None at all."

Her kind of eyes gave away nothing at all. "Does that mean I'm mad?" she said.

"Of course, Rose."

"Oh, well!" She laughed and moved away. "Off you go," she said imperiously.

"You know," he said, "it would do you a massive amount of good if you could just let all this go."

"At least it's all clean," she said.

She made a cup of tea when he'd gone. One of her eyes kept watering and she gave it a rub. She liked her place. Who cares, she thought, stirring the pot with one hand and rubbing and rubbing at one eye with the other. Something had got in it, probably an eyelash. So what? Everything belonged. Above the fireplace, the wall was covered with pictures of the dolls of Dolls' Island. She heard Adam clomping up the stairs and stuck her head out. "I've just made tea," she called.

He looked up. His face was thin-nostriled and birdlike. "Hang on," he said.

"I put a shelf up."

"Another?" He went into his flat and came up a few minutes later. She was looking in the mirror, holding her bloodshot eye open with two fingers. The thin black crescent of an eyelash was stuck tight in one corner, and tears ran down her cheek. "I've poured you one," she said. "It's on the table."

"What's up with your eye?" he asked.

"I've got an eyelash in it," she said, poking about in the inflamed corner.

Adam, sitting down and picking up his mug of tea, snickered down his nose.

"*Brief Encounter,*" he said.

"Ah, I've got it. Did I ever show you my eyelash collection?" She turned from the mirror, wiping her face and holding one hand poised as if a butterfly had landed on it.

"Your what?"

"My eyelash collection. I'll show you." The black eyelash was balanced on the tip of her finger. Holding it up carefully in front of her, she went into the other room and returned with a small silver pillbox in the other hand. "There," she said, flipping up the lid. An angel was engraved on the inside of it.

"What the hell," he said.

It was a bed of eyelashes.

"What the hell," he said again, putting the tip of his finger in. A smile came onto his face.

"These," she said, "are all the eyelashes I've ever got out of my eyes or that have fallen out ever in all my whole life."

He sifted. "That's impressive."

"Isn't it?"

"How come your eyelashes fall out?" he said. "Mine don't."

"They don't?"

"No."

"I thought everyone's did."

"Well, I suppose I get the odd eyelash in my eye like everybody else," he said. "But I wouldn't say they were falling like leaves."

"I started collecting them when I was ten," she said. "I remember the moment. I was in a math class and it was really boring and I looked down and saw an eyelash on my hand."

"This is the weirdest thing I've ever seen," he said.

"I used to keep them in a matchbox," she said, "but now I've got them in this nice little pillbox."

"I wonder how many there are."

"Hundreds."

He laughed. "You could get into the Guinness Book of Records with these," he said. "Hundreds of eyelashes. A great pile of—of—eyelashes! Crazy!"

Eyelashes from when she was ten, when she was thirteen, fifteen, nineteen, twenty-two, thirty-six.

"In a way," she said, "this is me."

She flicked the newest lash into the box with the rest.

"You get it, don't you?" she said.

"Yeah," he said. "I get it."

Life ran along to the various rhythms of trains and wagons and carriages. She traveled with a sad contortionist and a fat lady, and the world became a series of windows, with dark streets below where people walked, dime museums, sideshows, the sound of a barker's spiel descending into nonsense, and sheds thrown up fast, with pockmarked mirrors and jugs of cold water and the lingering smell of pomade. She was getting better, playing all the time, practicing in rooms and halls, in warehouses, in backstage lots.

In Cleveland she saw another doctor, who asked about her monthlies. Since she'd been on the road she'd met three very distinguished men, who were all very, very clever, much cleverer than anyone else she'd ever met, but they'd all said different things. One said she was ourang-outang, one that she was neither Negro nor human, another that she was her own species, a species of one. She was HYBRID, SEMI-HUMAN, MUJER OSA, TROGLODYTE OF ANCIENT DAYS, UGLIEST WOMAN IN THE WORLD. The news ran before, everywhere they went, the papers carried it, the newsboys cried it on the corners. Canada sold out before they reached Cincinnati.

She was good with the audiences by now, knew which eyes to meet and which to let go. She didn't blame them for looking. How could they not? Might as well ask the moon not to rise. Occasionally, to one particular pair of eyes in a sea of them, her returning stare had said, think about it, just consider, and they had blushed like maidens. When she came down and walked among them, the bold ones stepped forward to shake her hand and stroke her wonderingly, as if she were an exotic animal. The questions were always the same. Are you happy? Have you ever had a beau? Would you like to get married? Sometimes a young buck flirted with her. On their part, it felt like a perversion, she saw that well enough. No one ever made a real pass but there was intimacy in all that staring, and when Beach put out the news that desperate suitors, all refused, vied for her hand, she smiled and went along with it. She was saving. When I'm rich, she thought, I'll go back home and show them my new clothes. I'll arrive in a carriage. Walk in, equal, independent. How could it be? What was there in that house but the scrubbing of steps and the hauling of water? Where would she be, where would she live, when she was rich and independent? Surely it would be revealed to her. A house where she was not a servant. Something, someone, a friend. Fresh flowers.

They played Chicago, Detroit, Toronto, Montreal. In some small town in Quebec, she met a bearded lady traveling with her husband, a lean frog-mouthed man who hovered watchfully and silently about her at all times. *She's* got a husband. The great Clofullia has a husband. Dr. John Montanee's love potion was in her pocket. Every now and then she took it out, pulled out the cork and sniffed it. It smelled of cinnamon and lemon. Now and again she rubbed a little on her arms, saying: oh St. Jude, I'm still waiting.

On the way down to Boston they played sideshows. After a show in Burlington one night, the contortionist, a worried girl called Zelda, started crying and wouldn't stop. They were in a field outside town, sitting in the fat lady's wagon. Maud Sparrow was like seven or eight people rolled into one. No one chair could accommodate her, so she always sat on a large and splendidly bedecked sofa, a kind of throne. "What's the matter, noodle?" she asked brightly. She was working her way through a dish of marshmallows. Eating was part of the job.

"Just feeling sick for my home," said Zelda.

"Have a good cry," said Maud. "Best thing. Get it out of you, then it's done." Her face was supported by an overlapping progression of four or five rolls of chin. Her features in the middle were pretty, but diminished by the sheer quantity of surrounding flesh.

"I want to eat my aunt's soup," said Zelda. Her eyes were huge, blue and bulgy.

"I know what you mean!" Julia said. "I really miss the food at home."

Zelda glanced at her and looked quickly away, smiling faintly. She didn't know how to act with Julia. She was trying, you could see, but her eyes couldn't get a hold and slid off whenever she tried to look her in the eye. "She put everything in," Zelda said, "beans and peas. Bread."

"It tastes of nothing, the food here," said Julia.

"Too hot for me," said Maud. "Your kinda food."

Zelda blew her nose. "I don't really want to go home, I suppose," she said, sighing. She had a face that neither knew nor cared what it looked like, though it was beautiful. Her eyes were soulful and her dark hair, prematurely graying, curled in tendrils on her wide white forehead. "It's not very nice there. I just miss my aunt's soup."

"It'll still be there when you get back," said Maud, tearing a lump of marshmallow in two with smooth pink fingers.

"I know." But tears kept on leaking out of Zelda's eyes.

Maud sighed, looked at Julia and made a face as if to say, well, we all have our troubles. Nowhere near as much fun as Myrtle and Delia, these two. "You're so clever," Julia told Zelda. "I wish I could do what you do."

"Thanks." Zelda smiled sadly, not meeting her eyes.

"Cheer up, noodle." Maud stuck her legs out from under a thick yellow dressing gown. She was famous for her legs. Her ankles came down in descending layers like thick whipped cream, almost entirely obscuring the tiny feet that carried her about. Permanent lines had been etched into her flesh where her shoes cut. "You'll be through with this little show before you know it," she said.

Beach stuck his head 'round the door. "Hello, girls," he said, "everything all right?" His head had a swollen pink look like cured ham.

"Yes, Mr. Beach," said Julia.

"Good show tonight," he said, looking as he always did, worried and friendly at the same time. "Maud, I've got your pictures." He came in, nudging the door shut behind him with his foot.

"Any good?" Maud reached out a hand.

"Fine."

She took the envelope. "Beach," she said, "this girl's full of misery."

Beach turned a long-suffering face on the contortionist. "What is it, Zelda?" he said. "What is there to cry about?"

"Nothing," she said.

"Didn't you hear them tonight? You're doing great."

"I know I am."

"Get her some bean porridge, Beach," said Maud, licking the ends of her fingers. "Get her some good thick soup."

"She hungry?" Beach's pale blue eyes drooped down at the corners, giving him a look of permanent bewilderment. "Didn't you eat tonight?"

"Of course I did," said Zelda impatiently, strangely twisting her hands together. "I'm not hungry, not at all."

"What's wrong with the food?"

"There's nothing wrong with the food, I'm just . . . oh, never mind."

"She's just homesick, is all," said Maud.

"Girls," said Beach, raising his eyes to the roof of the wagon as if to the hills for deliverance, "girls, girls, girls, you'll be the death of me. If you're not happy, what's keeping you?"

"The money, honey," said Maud.

Beach stared at each of them in turn as if they'd wounded his feelings. "Get a hold of yourself, Zelda," he said. Drops of sweat glistened on his red, contorted forehead. "You make up your mind. Are you doing this or aren't you? If you are, you got to pull yourself together."

"I know." One of her eyes began to blink nervously. She sniffed and dried her eyes. She was leaving them soon, joining up with a circus and traveling west. Julia didn't think she'd miss her.

"Hm," said Maud, spilling pictures out on the table. Variations on a theme: Maud smiling, skipping, left leg bent, right knee raised, dainty toe pointing. Holding out the huge skirt of her short white dress to show off her pins. She picked one up. "Not bad," she said without enthusiasm.

"Christ," he said, "you girls are hard to please."

"Too much dark 'round the edges," Maud said, passing the picture to Julia. "It's a shame to have to write on that nice white lace."

"There's a space at the top," said Julia, "by the curtain. You could sign there."

"I guess."

Beach hulked around for a while looking disgruntled, told them not to stay up late and left without closing the door. A faint grassy smell crept in with the cold night air.

"Here, you two." Maud stood up, parting her legs and letting her stomach fall down between them to hang momentarily visible under the yellow dressing gown, before putting her arms down and with a practiced flounce, manually hauling it along with her as she shuffled sideways to take a cake box out of a corner cupboard. "Take a few with you," she said, sidling back into place and opening the box on her lap. "Spice and lime. Go on, help yourselves."

As Julia and Zelda walked back to their wagons in the dark, Zelda said, "She's meeting her fiancé in Cleveland. Did you know?"

"No."

Five or six other wagons hunched in the dark like beasts and a small campfire crackled in the field.

"Sometimes I just don't understand this world," Zelda said, cupping her hand around a disintegrating crumble of cake. "She's got a fiancé and here's me all on my own." Zelda licked her palm clean and brushed her hands.

Julia looked at her in disbelief. "Oh, *you'll* be all right," she said.

There was an awkward moment.

"What about me?" said Julia. "I'll always be on my own."

Zelda said nothing. The awkwardness rose higher between them like a wall, and they walked the rest of the way in silence till Julia turned aside at her door.

It was cold in the wagon, and she shivered. The cold was in her bones. Stupid girl, she thought, surprised at the tears she felt. Stupid girl can walk down the street, no one looks twice. She lit a candle, then got under the covers just as she was, pulled a blanket into a sort of tent over her head and ate the last two cakes, one lime, one spice. The lime cake had an exploding center of sweet curd, and by the time she'd swallowed the last mouthful she was crying. Even Maud Sparrow was going to have a husband. All the others, the plain girls, the not-so-pretty, the squinty, the flabby, the downright ugly, not one was as ugly as her. I am ugly, ugly, ugly, she said, and reached for bald, blurred, worn-away Yatzi. It got her like this sometimes. Some old song would get her. I'll never have that, she'd think. Love. Never even have it to lose. They love it when I sing those songs, a face like that, like mine, singing a love song. She felt as if a lump in her throat had sprung a leak, and it was draining from her eyes. Tears made long streaks in the hair on her cheeks. She got up, undressed and put on her nightie, got back into bed and blew out the candle.

She could get no sleep. The wind began to blow, and the wagon creaked. They moved on in the morning, and the wind howled all next day and all the day after as they traveled. Loneliness settled in, as sure and steady as snow.

A few days later, Zelda knocked on her door and walked in without waiting for an answer. "So," she said bluntly, as if she'd been building up to it, "how's this kind of life treating you then?"

Julia was sewing ribbons onto one of her stage dresses. "Oh!" she said, surprised. "I'm getting along very well, thank you."

Zelda sat down and leaned forward, staring into Julia's eyes with something like defiance. "I can't imagine what it must be like to be you," she said too quickly.

Julia showed her teeth in what she knew to be a disturbing smile. "Of course you can," she said. "It's easy. But you don't try."

Zelda looked away. Her mouth drooped open and her eyes were dreamy. "You know, I've always thought I had a good imagination," she said. "I do, that's the trouble. I imagine all the terrible things that might happen and all the places I could be that are better than this."

"There's no use at all in that," said Julia, bending her head back to her sewing.

"I know. But I do it anyway. What are you making?"

"Just sewing some ribbons on."

"I'm moving on," Zelda said. "I've come to say good-bye."

"Oh! It's today, is it?"

"Couple of hours. Indianapolis, Louisville—"

"Will you be happier with the circus?"

"I think so. At least I'm heading in the right direction. When we get to St. Louis, I'll see my family."

"That's nice."

"Not really." She smiled faintly. "They're not really very nice."

Now she comes talking, Julia thought, now she comes making friends. This is what it's like. People coming, going.

"You're right," said Zelda, licking her dry lips and looking uneasily away, "I don't try. To imagine what it's like to be you. My thoughts run away from it."

"Just do it," Julia said. "*I* know." She put down her sewing. "We'll change places. Go on. I can easily imagine what it's like to be you. It's easy. Go on, close your eyes."

"Close my eyes?"

"Yes. And I'll close mine."

They did. "Now," said Julia. "I'm a lady with a nice face. I can bend like a snake. You've got hair all over you. Like the dogs and the *burros*."

They sat for a few moments, then both opened their eyes at the same time and laughed, not knowing what to say.

"You're good with a needle," Zelda said.

"I've always made all my own clothes."

Zelda rose with a long sigh. Catching sight of herself in the small square of mirror by the door, she put a finger to the outer corner of either eye and pulled the skin up listlessly. "At least you don't have to worry about getting old," she said.

"Why? Do you?"

Zelda turned from her reflection. "See you again somewhere," she said.

"You take care now, Zelda."

When she'd gone, Julia sat up late sewing by candlelight till her eyes were tired. I'm a lady with a nice face, she was thinking. I'm a baboon. A hog, a dog, a wolf. I'm from a deep hole in the mountains where the *duendes* come out.

———

Long after dark they passed through a little place in Vermont with a billiard hall and a big clock hanging over the town square. There was some kind of trouble with Maud's wagon so they had to stop in the main street while the drivers fixed a wheel. Julia had been dozing on her bed, but she sat up when the wagons stopped and drew back the curtain. She saw a tidy moonlit street, all closed up, and a dozen or so hogsheads standing outside the store. There was a big barn of a place with a sign that said BILLIARDS, and the clock read quarter to eleven. The forest pressed in all around the town. No one was around, but a candle burned in a window high up in a house on the right, and Julia imagined that there was a child up there, a girl who'd gotten out of bed to look down. She was standing there now, wondering about all the freaks down there. She'd love to see the freaks. That could be me, she thought, up there looking down at me. I'm living in that house, sleeping in that room, this is my town. I live with my parents. And someone else is down here. But no matter how much she tried, when she tried to picture the parents, all she could see was her mother's pigtail.

The wheel was fixed, and the wagons lurched on through the woods a couple more miles out of town, pulled up in an open space in the back of a circus midway.

In the morning, up and dressed, opening her tiny window and looking out as she combed her hair, she saw the big circus tent in the distance, and the bright-colored signs along the midway: LOBSTER GIRL. STRONG MAN. ZEO THE WILD HUMAN.

The air smelled of impending rain. Maud was sitting on the steps of her wagon nearby, eating elegantly with her fingers from a plate of fried bread and bacon while an old man in a long blue jacket, a peddler of some kind, laid out his wares before her on the bottom step. Maud's fiancé, a tall man in a rumpled white shirt, loafed around in the doorway behind her, swigging from a bowl of coffee. Shivering a little, Julia closed the window, pulled a shawl 'round her shoulders and sat down to pull on her boots. Good old boots, she thought. Never had any that fit so well.

She heard Maud's voice: "Well, look at *you*. No one ever teach you it's rude to look up a lady's skirt?"

And the fiancé, mildly, "What the hell, kid, run away."

A laugh, chuckleheaded. A throaty gurgling.

Cato. Surely. She looked out. There was Maud like an empress indulging minions, the old peddler bowed over on one side, Cato on the other, grinning and lolloping from foot to foot in a grass skirt that came down to his knees. Oh, quick. Of course it took ages doing up her boot laces because she was hurrying too much, and by the time she'd gotten her veil on and opened the door, there was Ezra Porter, all togged up in a fancy suit with a high white collar that looked as if it were strangling him, coming across the field with a skinny girl trailing after him.

That same nasal voice, "Cato, what are you doing?"

They hadn't seen her.

"He being a nuisance?" Ezra said to Maud. "Sorry, ma'am!"

The skinny girl went up to Cato and took his hand. "What'd 'e do?" she asked in a hard voice.

"Tried to lift up Maud's skirt," said the fiancé, smoothing back his oiled hair till it was as flat as a plowed field.

"Oh, hell, I don't mind." Maud set aside her plate.

"No, no, it isn't right," said Ezra, "you don't do that, Cato! You know you don't do that!"

Cato grinned behind his fingers, swinging back behind the girl.

"Oh, let him look if he wants to." Maud raised her skirt. She was proud of her legs. "There you are, noodle," she said. Maud's thighs were like mottled pink slush. Held together, her legs appeared to run into one another like liquid and it was impossible to see where they met. She parted them and pointed her toes, and they firmed up, bulging like mushrooms. Cato peered over his fingers, crooning in fascination. The old man, arranging to perfection his rings and chains and lockets and bangles on the lid of his basket, looked as if he'd seen it all before.

"That's it," said Maud, dropping her skirt, smoothing it down and picking up her plate once again. "Now you've seen them. Let me eat my breakfast. Any brooches?" To the old man, "You know damn well I'd never get one of those things over my fist."

"These here," he said in a frail but gravelly voice. His bald head was brown and mottled, wispy white strands of hair still straggling out of it around the ears. Too old to be on the road, thought Julia. His long toothless mouth sank a deep ridge across the lower part of his face, as if a knife had scored it across from side to side.

"Cato!" she called.

He remembered her at once, pulled away from the girl and came bobbing over, shoving up Julia's veil unceremoniously and throwing himself at her chest with an excited burbling.

"Damnation!" said the peddler. The girl stared.

"No cussing," the fiancé said.

The man's composure returned immediately and he turned his shoulder against her.

"How much for the yellow one?" asked Maud.

"Miss Pastrana! Julia! Great to see you."

"Hello, Ezra."

"How you doing? We knew you were on the way. It's all anyone around here ever talks about."

"I'm fine, Ezra. And you?"

"Never better." He grinned. His face was fatter than before. "I got married. Berniece?"

The girl had lank brown hair and a serious face. "Hello," she said, unsmiling, holding out a hand. Julia struggled free from Cato's embrace, reaching out. "Pleased to meet you," she said.

"Stop it, Cato," said the girl, "you'll strangle her."

The old man, chomping on his mouth, was stealing sly glances.

"Well, this is nice," said Ezra. "Seems like we'll be keeping company as far as Boston."

"You seem older," Julia said, sitting with Cato on her top step, "more like a businessman."

He laughed. "Ah, well. Sober married man now, you see," he said. "Cato, come talk to Julia later, we have a lot to do."

"Oh, go on then," said Maud, swallowing coffee. "I'll take the yellow one. Give him the money, Harv."

"Up, Cato, come on now."

"Julia now," said Maud, fixing the brooch on the slope of her breast, "she's got tiny little wrists. She'll take a look."

The peddler, rising, stiff-backed, took up his walking stick, turned but did not look at Julia. "Buy the girl a ring," he said to Ezra.

"She's got rings," said Ezra.

"Skinflint."

Berniece took Cato's hand and hauled him up. The old man dropped coins into his can, closed the lid and started hauling his wares across.

"We're right there," Berniece said, leaning in close for a good look, her eyes moving rapidly backward and forward over Julia's face, "on the midway. Halfway along. Zeo. Come see the show." She looked very young, and her voice came out in garbled bursts.

Ezra grabbed Cato's other hand, and he and the girl began hauling him away.

"Nice boots," said the peddler, looking at her feet. "A tiny foot means small wrists and fingers. I have just the thing for you."

"No thank you," she said.

"Quality." He bent forward, leaning on his stick, taking her left foot in his hand and handling it in an overfamiliar way, as if it were something in a shop he was thinking of buying. His eyes were like pebbles, his blue coat just a rag. "Fine leather."

"Yes," she said, "they're nice old boots," trying to withdraw from his hand, but he held on.

"I know quality."

"I'm sure you do."

He let go, delved into his trove and came up with a horrible bracelet.

"It looks cheap," she said.

He shot her a look of dislike.

"There's nothing I want. Really."

"Fair prices. Better than most. Quality."

"These aren't quality."

The man packed up his basket and stood straight. "Good day to you," he said, walking away.

"Pinheads," Maud said, looking down at her new brooch, "I never get used to them."

It rained and worms came up in the field. Covered well, under an umbrella, Julia picked her way carefully across the grass and joined the public meandering up and down the midway. She wasn't on till the evening. The talkers were yelling, the tang of hot cotton candy mingled with the wet green smell of surrounding woodland. She passed by the sword swallower, the skeleton and the frog-eyed girl, stopping at Zeo the Wild Human's banner. Lions and tigers snarled through the giant leaves of a jungle. FROM DARKEST AFRICA, it said. LAST OF HIS TRIBE. CANNIBAL. Zeo himself, painted in his grass skirt, ran on all fours with a bone in his nose. More hung 'round his neck. It was a good likeness but it didn't do him justice. Pictures never did. Ezra was up on the bally, tapping his cane on the ticket box. His high voice carried far. "*Presenting*! The amazing Zeo! Only surviving member of a lost human race, *all* the *way* from deep, deep, *deep* in the Congo jungle, the very darkest of darkest Africa! Zeo! Alive! Alive, right this way! Show's about to begin, folks!"

The crowd shoved forward.

"See it now!" shouted Ezra. "Hurry along! Let the people through."

Julia let herself be carried by the crowd.

"You may never get the chance again! Don't wait, you're just in time! *Right—this—way!*"

She arrived at the booth and Berniece, who must have recognised the veil, waved her through. Inside it was crowded, green and dim, with rain drumming softly on the canvas. Sometimes being small was an advantage. By degrees, she was able to insinuate herself up near the front of the stage. A green and blue curtain, threadbare in patches, hung over it.

"That's it, folks," Ezra yelled. "All for now. Next show in half an hour."

The show began.

"Move in close now, ladies, gentlemen. Move in close. Any second now, I will draw back this curtain and I will reveal— *The* most incredible, *the* most important scientific and an*thro*-pol-ogical wonder of the world! But first let me tell you a little about how this remarkable specimen came to be here in this country. Thank you, thank you, come in at the back there. Move across now, please—"

Ezra certainly had the talker's gift. She'd never have thought it.

"Zeo! The Wild Human! Remnant! Of a lost tribe of early humans, a precursor of Man as we know him today. He was found naked, ladies and gentlemen, scuttling, on all fours like a beast! By intrepid explorers into the many secrets of the Dark Continent."

"Let's see him," someone yelled.

"Patience," said Ezra. "At the time of Zeo's capture, the nails of his hand measured seven inches in length. Can you imagine that? And they were capable of disemboweling a chicken in one movement. The courage of these brave men as they brought to bay this most rare of wild creatures, this lost hominid, this—words fail— Ladies. Gentlemen. I give you—"

The curtain was drawn back. Cato sat against a painted jungle in his grass skirt. He didn't have a bone through his nose but he wore a long necklace of claws. Cato grinned at the audience and a great throaty sigh rose from their throats. "Oh my God!" someone said. He jumped up and darted to the front of the stage, beaming wildly. A few people backed away. A girl reached up to touch him.

"He fought tooth and claw when they threw the net over him, ladies and gentlemen," Ezra said, as Cato capered up and down the front of the stage, throwing his knees high and laughing. "Six months before he could be approached without risk to life. You can see how very well behaved he is now, ladies, gentlemen. Oh, yes, Zeo is harmless now, but believe me when I say this did not happen overnight." Cato was walking along, bending over to shake the hands of the people at the front. "It required endless patience, months and months of careful training. Believe me, ladies, gentlemen—"

After that, they all wanted to shake his hand.

"—only the most humane and enlightened means were used in the taming of Zeo. At first he would eat nothing but raw meat."

Cato giggled.

"Which he tore with his long sharp teeth, ripping it from the bone."

"Let him eat some raw meat!" a boy shouted.

"But no!" Ezra cried. "As I shall very soon demonstrate, he has learned to eat exactly the same things as we do! You love cake, don't you, Zeo?"

Cato nodded sharply, up, down, up, down, laughing hysterically. The audience surged toward him, enraptured, their senses struggling with him. The great V of his smile stretched itself beyond comprehension.

"How can a brain fit in there?" someone asked. "There's no room."

"That's interesting, ladies and gentlemen," Ezra said. "Notice the shape of the head. Notice how similar to the head of the ourang-outang. Zeo lived with the monkeys in the jungle. No one knows how long ago his particular type of the human race branched off. Even the foremost men of science are wonderstruck! What a chance!" Ezra's eyes gleamed fanatically. "To fathom the mystery of these creatures—for there— still—deep in the deepest and darkest of jungles, they live on, these ancient races. Is Zeo a human being? Is that what a human being looks like? No! Human beings don't look like that. Is he an ape then? Some kind of a bald ape? No! He is something older still, ladies and gentlemen." Cato, knowing his cue, stood still, smiling mysteriously up and over their heads. "Older, and far, far stranger—a race as yet unknown to science—notice, as I say, the shape of the head. So close to the monkey! You see how this is perfect for a creature of the wild, a beast suited to swinging from branch to branch, a hunter of prey. Who would like to shake his hand? Come up, lady! You see, he has excellent manners!"

Oh God, the time! Julia had no idea of it. She slipped away as quietly as she could, but when she got out it was strangely dark. She thought for a second that night had come, but it was just the sky that had fallen in a great black roll of cloud to just above the tree line. The gate to the field where the show wagons were was blocked. A cart lay on its side, a man and a woman screaming at one another beside it. She was late. The crowd, which had doubled since she'd gone into the tent, heaved nauseously. Turning down an alley between two tents, she hurried along the midway's back, shuddering as the mud sucked at her red boots. There was another gate. Her heart hammered. She lost herself in a jumble of small tents and tethered horses and emerged somewhere beyond the midway at the far corner of the field. There weren't too many people here, just a bunch of children by the gate, and one or two families heading home from the fair. The old peddler was sitting on the ground by the hedge with his pack and stick by his side, eating a stump of bread.

"That's her I was telling you about," he said. "That's the ape woman."

Everyone looked at her.

"I recognize the boots."

"You're kidding me," a boy said.

"That's her. She's an ape under all that. God's truth."

Rain again, softly pattering down.

"You're not, are you?" The boy stepped toward her. He was ten or eleven, short and round with a pale bulbous face. "You're not the ape woman."

"No, I'm not." Her hands shook as she put up the umbrella.

"God's truth," the old man said, "that's her."

"God's truth?"

"God's truth."

"Go on then," said the boy, "give us a look."

"Yeah, let's have a look," said a cheerful gawky girl, dragging the hand of a whiny toddler.

"Excuse me," said Julia, slanting the umbrella to shield herself from them, "I really am late."

It rained harder.

"You are the ape woman," the boy said, "or you wouldn't be wearing that veil."

A boy appeared in front of her, smiling. Black hair, long face, buck teeth worn with pride. Her height exactly, probably about ten. A knife jumped in and out of its sheath at his belt, hopped from hand to hand.

"Excuse me," she said. Her voice was firm. Inside she shook.

"Why?" he said. "What have you done?"

The girl with the infant laughed.

They're only children, thought Julia. Walk past. She looked 'round. What, eight, nine of them, boys, a girl on the gate, the baby with its long red curls and swollen red cheeks. Still, some of them are big. Rain thundering now on the umbrella. They moved stealthily apart from one another, surrounding her more entirely.

"Can you tell them to let me pass?" she called to the peddler, but all he did was look at her with hard eyes, mashing the bread with his old wreck of a mouth. There were others too, just watching from a distance.

"Can I get past, please?"

A boy with a snub-nosed baby face stepped in from the side, ripped her veil off and tipped the umbrella from her grip so that it landed upside down in the mud. They all ran back.

She went cold. No. Please, no.

"Give it back!" she shouted.

"Oh God, that's horrible!"

"Jesus Christ!"

"What *is* it?"

All aghast, delighted. She was more than anything they'd imagined or dreamed of. The baby screamed in baby terror, wild and pure, and the girl scooped him up into her arms, hugging him to her. He threw back his head and shrieked himself into a fit. The girl ran backward, picking up his fear and shouting, "Get away! Get away!"

The cry was taken up.

"Get away! Get away!"

Julia was stricken by the baby. Always hated that, upsetting some child who doesn't know anything and means no harm, just scared. Can't help it. Just is.

"Get away!"

She shrank. Her great naked head was all wrong.

"Get it away!"

"Horrible thing!"

"I'm sorry," she said to the infant, "I won't hurt you. I'm so sorry." She started to cry, distorting her face. She could no more control it than the rain could stop itself falling. It made things worse, and the rain came harder, bedraggling her hair. "Go back!" ordered the pale puffy-cheeked boy as if she were the devil, and the boy with the knife stepped toward her with his arms made into a cross. "Back!" he said.

"I just want to get past," she said, mustering what she could of her dignity, trying to look the boy in the eye, say, me to you, please, just let me through. His eyes were gray and perplexed. Something sharp bit her cheek. A stone.

"Go back!" he said.

"Let me through."

He uncrossed his arm and made a kind of calligraphy in the air with the tip of his knife, then sheathed and unsheathed it very quickly several times. It was a good sturdy hunting knife about six inches long, and he handled it like a pet ferret.

"It's got tits," someone said.

They giggled. The child was still screaming, choking on himself. His big sister or whatever she was slapped his back.

"Tits!"

They circled slowly, cracking up with laughter.

"You are horrible," said the boy with the bulbous face. "Did you know that? You are the most horrible thing in the whole wide world."

"Stop it," she said.

"Filthy!"

She was faint. The tops of the trees swooped down toward her.

"Stop it," she said.

Another stone hit her shoulder.

The round boy, his face bobbing in front of her, strutting with his old man's pot belly thrust before him; faces, manlike boys, the screaming baby, the girl on the gate, the knife draining the world into its thin shine. The boy with big teeth came close, his lips thick and winsome. She met his eyes, tried to say, boy, please boy, be good, but his eyes were cold and angry. Fear of the knife stopped her throat.

"Get back, filth," he said.

She turned to run back but everything looked different, just dark leaves and shadows in her way. Something hit the middle of her back.

They were on all sides. Faintness came up in a big white cloud and covered her head, dragging her down on her knees in the mud. No one was coming to her rescue. The wet grass in front of her was flecked with drowned fragments of something feathery and pollenish.

She got up, turned and faced them, dirt on her dress. "I have to go into the field," she said.

"Why?" asked a boy with elf ears and a hungry face.

"I have a show."

"A show!" said the round boy. "You're disgusting."

"It's crying," said someone.

The scrawny girl began to laugh uncontrollably.

"Shouldn't be out scaring people," said the babyface boy seriously.

"I just want to pass," she said. "I'm not hurting anyone."

"Can't you shut that brat up?" The boy with the knife turned his head and Julia tried to go 'round him.

"Shut up, John," said the gawky girl, still laughing.

Then they were all at it, cackling away like jackals.

The baby screamed louder than ever.

"Take him home, Alice," said a redheaded boy at the back. "Take him home."

The girl shushed the baby, never taking her eyes off Julia. "I'm not going anywhere," she said.

Now they were stooping, scooping up dirt and stones.

"Let her go past, Bo." A voice, daring himself to speak, she couldn't tell who.

"Shall I?" said Bo, sheathing the knife and standing with his hands on his hips. He wasn't that big. "Shall I let you pass?" He terrified her. He was mad, he might do anything.

"Yes, please, let me pass." Her voice was shaky.

A stone, badly lobbed, hit her just below the knee. The biggest yet, almost a rock.

"*Stop it!*"

It throbbed. She wouldn't be able to dance. She felt sick. Her eyes overflowed. They were behind her now too, circling, staring, daring one another closer and closer with their movements.

"Don't hurt me," she said, putting her hands over her face.

More stones, a shower.

She took her hands from her face. "Stop it!" she yelled.

"You stop it!" they shouted.

"Stop it!"

"Stop it! Stop it! Stop it!" they chanted back.

She ran through them to the gate. The gate wouldn't budge. She shook it.

"Look, it's mad!" someone shouted, and someone else screamed loudly. Then someone else. Then they were all at it, trying to outdo each other, and she turned and the knife was in front of her face. She screamed one pure scream of absolute horror and went down on her knees with her back in the corner of the gate, throwing her arms over her head and waiting for them to kill her.

The power of that scream from that face silenced everything but the baby, whose screams soared to new heights.

"Get him out of here!" snarled Bo.

"Let it go," someone said.

"No!"

Then a man's voice, stern. "Bring that child over here!"

A gathering crowd.

"What's going on?"

Mud on her skirt.

"What is it?"

"One of the freaks."

"Escaped."

"Where?"

Then Beach, his face red to bursting. "For God's sake! You! There! I see you!" Gripping her elbow, pulling her up. He draped a shawl over her head, putting one arm around her and guiding her through the crowd. "Out of the way, please! Nothing to see, ladies and gentlemen!" She trembled as he pulled her along, couldn't stop it. "Just a few young hooligans of the locality preparing themselves for their criminal careers," he announced. "And I know every one of their names." She kept her eyes closed under the blanket and sobbed.

Back in her wagon, she sat down on the bank, covered her face with her hands and rocked. Beach stood gaping.

"What the hell, Julia! What have I told you? If some old peddler hadn't come and found me . . ."

"Not now, not now," she said, "I have to lie down."

"I've been up and down the midway three times, I thought you'd run away."

"I went to see Cato," she said.

"Who?"

"Zeo the Wild Man."

"For God's sake! You're bleeding."

"Where?"

"Can't you feel it? There, on your cheek." He gave her his handkerchief. "Thank Christ, it'll hardly show under the hair. You can black it up a bit."

"I thought they were going to kill me," she said.

Blood on the handkerchief.

"How many times have I told you?"

"I know."

"*Don't* go off on your own. You *know* that. Anything could happen. What did I say?"

"I know."

"There have to be certain rules." He leaned toward her, scowling, the skin across the bridge of his nose tight and shiny. "There has to be trust."

"I thought I'd die," she said.

She was trembling. He looked at his watch. "Lucky it didn't get nasty," he said, patting her shoulder roughly. "Get yourself rested up. Get yourself clean. You won't be so silly again."

"I hurt my knee," she said.

"Can you dance?"

"I'm not sure."

She walked a few paces. "I think so. I feel terrible."

"Rest."

"I don't want to go on. What if they're out front?"

"You kidding? They won't get anywhere near the place."

"I'm not sure I can," she said.

"Of course you can. You don't let those savages stop you." He turned at the door. "You have an hour and a half," he said.

The rain was really coming down now, hammering on the roof. She took off the red boots and flung them away from her, lay down and cried for half an hour. I was careful, she thought. I wore my veil and gloves. I'll go home, should never have left. Horrible. Deceived myself. Why bother? All that hate. To just walk down a street one time. Be the same. Not look up, look up all the time, saying why?

The faces of the children appeared and reappeared.

I'll be honest with you, Solana had said. *You can be as good as anyone, and you can be proud and always stick up for yourself and get respect, but there's one thing you won't get,* nena, *and that's a man. Not with your face so far gone. Don't expect it. Love? With a face that frightens children? What a joke!*

Horrible thing! Filth! Back! She didn't hate them, that was the truly terrible thing. She wanted to, she tried, but instead of hate there was just depthless sadness and a great hurting.

Crying? That's not the way, Solana would have said, with a slap to the back of the head. That's never the way! Santy Anna took my boys. Do you see me crying?

She sat up.

"No," she said out loud, and her heart sank at the enormity of carrying on. I can't do it, said her head. You can, said that other that always pushed her on. Go home, go home, admit defeat. There was nothing out here, never had been. She stood up, dried her eyes, walked to the mirror, cleaned herself up briskly. Nothing's safe. Not even life. Santy Anna takes boys. Mothers have pigtails. Knives cut, and children are cruel. And I'll go my own way and make my own money and no one'll ever stop me.

A small flap of skin had come loose in the middle of her cheek. It wasn't bleeding much anymore, but the whole area around it was thickening up and darkening. They will not stop me. Her eyes watered again but she stopped them, pressing the displaced skin back into place. She remembered that stone. It hadn't hurt that much at the time, but now the wound throbbed and ached. "As if I wasn't ugly enough," she said and laughed. *God loves you,* Solana said, her conviction firm. *And that's all that matters. And don't you forget it.*

"Here's why you will never be free," said her face in the mirror.

Back!

No.

Let them try.

She set about camouflaging the fierce little wound.

That night when she stepped out in front of the crowd, she couldn't shake a funny feeling that she was also out there in the audience, staring at herself. There was a little girl at the front, holding on to her mother's hand. She stared very gravely and thoughtfully at Julia and her eyes never wavered. Some people said you shouldn't bring a child to a show like this. She might be the little girl at the window last night, the light in the square. Last night when everything was peaceful. Maybe she'd come with her mother and that was her out there, looking at the monster.

The monster, smiling, stared straight back at her.

———

Maud Sparrow and her fiancé jumped ship at Boston. Zeo the Wild Human headed out for Albany with Ezra and Berniece, who were talking of going to Europe, and after that, she was on her own again. She thought about giving it all up, going home, but then—suppose she did and they said, oh, no, we replaced you, Julia. You were ungrateful. So much of the past had been tied up with Solana, so much that she'd balked at, the old woman moaning and groaning all the time, propped high on her pillows, pillowlike herself, breathing loudly and dribbling *chucaca* tea, smelling of piss, dying far from home and talking constantly of her little house with the pictures on the wall, and the arroyo out back where the gazelle came down to drink. No. No going back, not now. Not for Solana, not for her.

In Providence one night, Beach said they were through with the circus. Enough of these sideshows. From now on she would only play solo performances. "We'll sell you as a cut above," he explained, "not for the hoi polloi. Quality performer. Soirée. You know? These little folk songs, they're nice enough, but what about these classical things you do? Say we get you some pearls for the front of that dress you've been working on for so long? How's that coming along, by the way?"

"Nearly finished," she said. "Pearls would be nice."

"Pearls it is."

"And I can sing arias," she said. "I like singing arias."

"That sort of thing."

"I can still sing my old songs too though, can't I?"

"If it seems to be the thing. But I think you should go for a kind of— you know. Go like a lady."

Going like a lady was a game that kept away the spectral children who came and laughed at her sometimes when she was trying to get to sleep. So she went like a lady in Philadelphia and Atlantic City, and after a while realized how greatly things had changed since those first days, little more than two years ago and already becoming rose-tinted. Sitting about watching Myrtle painting her eyes with her feet. She got the best quarters now, the best dressing room. Beach made sure of it. He had other artistes, other commitments, but till Christmas he'd build her up. Next, New York, he said. The Stuyvesant. By then the whole place would be agog. And then—who knows? We'll come to that, he said, and a chill of excitement went through her. Change was constant. She saw that she would not stay with Beach. He grew bossier by the day. He wanted to tell her what to sing and how to do her hair, when to come and when to go. So she waited for Christmas and New York, when there would be change. She knew he was getting offers. If he's getting money, I am too, she thought. I'll make him put it in the contract like Myrtle and Delia said. The thought of those two gave her a homesick feeling. Almost like a family she'd never had. Funny, running into Cato like that. When she closed her eyes, she saw Cato in his grass skirt, grinning at the crowd. That's how it was: bumping into people, bumping off them randomly.

This Eastern Seaboard tour was cold and lonely, a jittery meandering filled with rooms where she hid, bored. She kept running out of things to read. He kept saying he'd bring her more and forgetting. The weather out there was foul and those children would creep into her head, evil gargoyles, fallen cherubs picking at her. A phantom knife would slit her skin, a phantom self cringe. She'd swallow hard, banishing them like demons. Begone! Away! She couldn't go out because of them. And even if she could, what was the point in wandering about alone in every strange place you came to?

It was a long stretch of tedium punctuated with shows, from which she bounced one to the other as if jumping from tussock to tussock over uneven ground. And in the middle of all this a special invitation came.

"This is it!" Beach crowed, shaking it in the air, his great crooked-toothed grin ramping over his face. "Listen. Ha ha! We are cordially invited to attend the annual Grand Military Ball. In Baltimore. This is *it*, Julia. *Recognition!*"

The dress was ready. It had pearl buttons on the bodice to match the pearl cross at her throat, a low sweep of silver lace across arms and breasts, ribbons at the waist. She wore it with long white kid gloves, black satin slippers and a tiny silk reticule. In her hair she wore the shell comb she'd bought on Broadway. Best of all, she was not veiled. One whole night without it, from the moment she entered the building.

The portico was stabbingly bright, full of smiling, glaring faces that swam in front of her like great balloons. A silver chandelier flew swan-like overhead. A staircase rose, wrought ironwork painted gold. She ascended on the arm of Beach, who'd had a stiff two or three for his nerves and was breathing out an air of sweaty perfume and brandy, smiling wildly.

Double doors opened inward. A smart man in black called out their names to the assembled terrifying throng of glorious dresses and bright-buttoned and heavily medaled chests. Nothing in her life had prepared her for this. The beautiful dresses, the shine of the chandeliers, the sparkle of drinks through faceted glass. Flowers hung in garlands and swags around the columns. Every eye was on her.

The band played "Hail, Columbia."

She was led along a line of important men and gorgeously gowned ladies, all so clean and scrubbed, so powdered. She felt like a small child hanging on a big man's arm. It wouldn't do, so she let go and pretended she was tall and sophisticated. She met brigadier generals, major generals, this and that officer, and all their ladies so delighted, delighted, delighted, one after the other, so that she had to keep saying the same thing over and over again. How do you do? How do you do? I am very well, thank you. I am so pleased to be here. Delighted. Yes, this is my first time in Baltimore. And they were all eating up her face with their eyes. A smart man with slicked-back hair ushered her courteously along, and she floated away from the end of the line with Beach in her wake and was led to a table where they were to sit with a gaunt old major and his kindly rodenty little wife. The Major bowed. The wife clutched Julia's hand in her cold white paws and stared hard, mouth clenched in a smile that was both genuine and strained.

"I'm so glad you could come," she said. Her plucked, eager face was overwhelmed by the tremendous froth of her costume.

"Thank you," Julia said. "It's lovely to be here."

When everyone sat, the band struck up something jolly, and the waiters poured champagne. The table was beautifully adorned with flowers and silver and starched white linen. Julia was very careful, sipping slowly. The music calmed her down. She didn't know the tune, but it was so spirited that her head began to sway and her ankle to jog, and the Major leaned down toward her.

"You like the music?" he asked.

"It's wonderful," she said.

The Major's eyes were sad and wet and drooped down at the outer corners. He smiled. Leaning across her, he struck up a conversation with Beach about the antiquity of the band and all the great occasions it had graced. Julia drank. The bubbles went up her nose, half stung, half tickled. How terrible if she sneezed. But her control was perfect. Since that horrible time with the children she'd been practicing dignity every day, diligently and persistently as if it were a musical instrument she was learning. The little wife, still eagerly smiling, was nodding at her very quickly like an inquisitive parrot. Tight-corseted, erect, Julia smiled back. The dancers lined up.

"My dear, this Charlotte Russe is simply delicious," said a hawk-nosed officer, "may I help you to some?"

She declined politely. She was too excited to eat.

"I've never seen such beautiful dresses," she blurted out.

"And your own, Miss Pastrana." The Major's wife reached across and laid her hand on Julia's arm. "It's very charming. A little bird told me you made it yourself. Is that so?"

"I've always made my own clothes," Julia said.

"Very skillful! Such lovely embroidery."

"Thank you."

She felt like laughing. It just all seemed so funny, these polished people wanting her as their guest of honor, all wanting to touch her, say they've met her, yes, she actually spoke to them. And all because of her face. But inside her face she felt ordinary, and there was nothing she could tell any of them. She drank. Careful. Not too much. The second cotillion was announced. A young officer with silky hair and smooth face approached the table, saluted smartly and bowed low.

"Miss Pastrana," he said, blushing deeply, "will you honor me with your hand for this dance?"

"I'm so sorry," she said, "I'm afraid I don't know this dance at all. I really must decline." She wasn't going to make a fool of herself getting it wrong. When she danced it would be something she was sure of. The officer bowed and departed. One more glass of champagne, she thought, and she'd be ready. She wouldn't drink after that. She politely refused three more dances, waiting for the waltz, but when it came the old Major got in first, rising gallantly, taking her hand and leading her onto the floor, right out into the center. From the corners of her eyes she was aware of the other couples, so much taller and surer than she was. The band played "Wild Roses," and they swept into the dance. Of course, once they started, she was fine. This she could do as well as any, better than most. So around the floor they swirled and swirled, her dress one more petal among the rest, to the dignified sweep of the waltz. The old boy was a good dancer. He looked into her eyes as they danced, smiling. He was close to death, she thought. Already his eyes were far away, fading out as if they'd been left too long in a window and the sun had bleached them.

"Are you enjoying this evening?" he asked.

"Very much," she replied. And she was.

"You are very graceful, my dear," he said when the dance ended, and he led her back to her seat.

They were queuing up after that. First she danced the schottische with a bright young lieutenant with red hair and a cockeyed grin. When they got on the dance floor she saw him lose his nerve for a second, saw him truly see her for the first time up close, face to face. His own face changed from pink to white to red in the space of a few seconds. Poor boy, she thought. If I smile now so close to his face it'll scare him witless. So she tried to keep the smile to the eyes only, and said gently, "Don't worry. It's not for very long."

"Oh, no. No, no, no, no, no, Miss Pastrana," he stammered, "you are mistaken—"

The music began.

"It's perfectly all right," she said. "I won't bite you."

He plastered a smile across his face, took a deep breath and steeled himself. But as they danced his smile became real, and soon he was laughing as they hopped about. "You can certainly dance!" he called above the noise. "You never miss!"

"Of course not!" She laughed too. It was like being at home dancing with one of the boys on the patio after everyone had had one drink too many.

He brought his face close to hers as they turned. He'll tell this story over and over, she thought. "This is a *real* schottische," he said. "One two three, jump, one two . . ."

"Yes!" she said, keeping time perfectly.

"I enjoyed that so much," he said when it was over, and kissed her hand before he led her back to the table. Bowing, he backed away with a besotted smile as if she were royalty. Another came at once. Another waited. Beach was grinning like a fool.

"I'm having such a good time," she said, and everyone laughed as if she'd said something hilarious and very clever.

Another came. Another. She danced over and over again. Some of the men were young; some were handsome. And there was one, serious and pale, unsure of his feet, who counted under his breath and shot quick awkward smiles at her when he wasn't looking down at the floor. His lips were childish, his hair long, and the touch of his palm against hers was unlike anything she'd known or imagined. The strangest thing, a sensation in her skin and bones, a sweet tearfulness in the breast, the kind she got from the songs she sang. The feeling lingered when the incident had flown.

As they were leaving, a beautiful young girl in a lavender gown ran up to her. "Oh, Miss Pastrana!" she cried, bouncing on the balls of her feet, "I'm so happy you could come—may I kiss you?"

"Of course."

The girl gave a smothered little shriek of delight, stooped and placed a kiss on Julia's cheek. "Oh, my my!" she said, "I am so happy," and danced away back to her admiring friends while the onlookers chuckled and tinkled applause, though for whom was unclear.

Back at the hotel she lay with her head spinning, the memories already taking form. She imagined them old and precious, finding words for the story she'd tell herself again and again the further away they got. The Ball. The Night of the Ball. When she danced again and again, and some of the men were young, and some handsome. And everyone loved her because she made them so glad they were themselves and not her. She held onto Yatzi and smiled in the dark. And that boy, she thought. That boy. When I'm old I'll remember him. In another place he thinks of me. She sees his face clear, not special but somehow wonderful. He waits in the entrance to the hotel, in the shadows, and, when she comes down, steps forward. He sees her soul. That's when her imagination gives way.

Rose liked to sleep in the afternoon when it rained, stretched full out on the red sofa, head on the cushion, whisper of wet leaves just beyond the window, gurgle of a drain. In one hand she clutched a plastic horse, in the other a dirty leopard Beanie Baby. Tattoo was cradled in the nook of her arm under the thin Indian bedspread. She was not really asleep but not awake either. The gas fire hummed.

She was wandering about in that place she went to on rainy afternoons. Under the trees, trying to sustain it till she could reach the castle with the drawbridge, which she knew was there because she'd glimpsed it a couple of times but never got close enough to take a good look. If you pushed on too far, the whole thing just faded away. It was like trying to see seven separate stars in the Pleiades and ending up with just a smudge on the sky. She could, however, stay as long as she wanted in the wood. She always entered by the southern fence, approached across a yellowing field. For a long time she'd had to crawl under the barbed wire, but she'd put a gate in a few years ago, and now just lifted the latch. There were logs lying about on the edge of the wood, fallen branches, usually a few bluebells and some wild garlic. The weather was always still and mild. The trees were not that dense here, and there were two paths, one to the left, the one she always took. The path to the right didn't look any different, but for some reason she never went that way. It wasn't something she gave any thought to, apart from a vague unhurried sense that she'd take it one day. If you followed the usual path the woods soon grew hushed and holy, high-roofed like a cathedral. It was never so wild as to be impenetrable but always lush. Wildflowers scented the air; ivy stormed over trees and rambling roots. The undergrowth was low and moist. As the woods deepened, there was no sense of a world beyond. There were people somewhere in here, she thought, but she'd never met any. She'd glimpsed creatures. Off in a pollen-dusty glade, a fallow deer, poised. She heard birds, a serene echoing, murmurous as water far away. A stag beetle crossed the path. At last she came to the place where she always stopped and rested. Ancient trees stood at respectful distances from one another. Between them, sinuous green clearings rolled out as if shaken, and the roots of the trees were gigantic, cushioned with starry green moss you could lie down on and fall asleep. She usually fell asleep in the end. Only occasionally did she keep her eyes open and, later maybe, move on to the place where the land opened up, and the little bridge crossed to the moated castle, the drawbridge down, welcoming.

Someone banged on the door.

Damn them.

When she opened her eyes the room was unrecognizable, resolved into its shapes with all dimensions removed. *Rap, rap, rap.* Then the shapes reangled themselves into a different perspective, and for a moment a great high-edificed city with thoroughfares and byways spread out in front of her. But it was gone in a moment, leaving only stuff.

Rap, rap. "Rose!"

I'm not in, she thought.

"Rose!"

Bloody Laurie. If you knock on someone's door three times and they don't answer, they're either out or they don't want to open the door. You don't go on banging and shouting.

Rap, rap.

Sod off. She sat up, leaning forward with a frown, slipping her feet into a pair of patchwork slippers. A couple of minutes later she heard him turn and go back downstairs. She had sharp ears and knew all the sounds of this house, the creakings of particular stairs, the sighings of particular doors. When she was sure he was out of the house, she got up and shuffled over to the mantelpiece for her tobacco. Bang goes sleep. Her big toe, the long nail pointed and purple, stuck out of a hole in one of the slippers.

Laurie could go jump. Too many rows lately. If you could call them that, him nagging on about her stuff as if it had anything to do with him, and she endlessly telling him to give her peace. Anyway, whatever happened to that nice casual no-strings thing?

Her face in the mirror was scarily plain and blank, all the makeup rubbed off her eyes. She looked like no one she knew. Once, in madness, she'd thought it could work but of course it couldn't. It was lust only, never meant to last. Touching him used to be an electric thrill, now it was a shudder. Now her flesh crept apologetically when his clumsy great hand brushed the side of her breast. Oh, here we go again, she'd think, and he sensed it. She was glad he was married. He couldn't blame her for backing off now, could he? She'd let him in tomorrow, or tonight if he came back maybe, so long as he didn't moan. But she wasn't giving up this sleepy rainy afternoon.

She opened a cupboard. Halva. Absinthe. Sugar. Some Dunkaroos from her brother in America. Absinthe. Yes. She turned up the gas fire. Listen to it teeming down. Outside the window was a green garden washed with rain.

She'd shaken thousands of hands and spoken to hundreds of people over the past couple of years, since leaving home; most just wanted to stare and ask the same old things. How are you? Are you happy? Unhappy? Do you wish you were like other people? They looked so closely, they didn't really hear what she replied. I'm like others, she'd say. Sometimes happy, sometimes not. What's the point of wishing? Things are as they are. My life is more interesting now. I travel. Meet people. Her real feelings, too hard to describe, were that life was not back there at home but somewhere ahead, so there was no other way, she'd keep moving. Let them look, yes, yes, I'm real and so are you, let's look at each other. Off they'd go, amazed she could talk, having gazed so much they hadn't really seen her at all. And she'd cry at nights, remembering young men she'd danced with and the faces of children throwing stones, quake at her insecurity, the vagueness of time, but still sing and dance and carry on.

When Theo Lent called, she had no idea at first that he was anything other than a regular rube, though one rich enough to afford a private audience. Beach just said it was a gentleman to see her, showed him in, introduced them and withdrew. They were in the upstairs parlor of a house on Broome Street in New York, a place used entirely by show people. Christmas was past. Snow fell softly, drifting past the window, and a good fire billowed in the grate.

"Miss Pastrana," he said, holding her eyes very firmly, smiling in a businesslike yet disarmingly boyish way, "I've been wanting to meet you for a very long time." She wasn't wearing her veil, but he obviously knew what to expect and showed no sign at all of being unsettled.

"Surely not *so* long," she replied as they sat down. Her first impression was of a smug overgrown schoolboy, twinkly-eyed and dressed like a swell but a little shabby.

"Yes," he said, "*so* long."

He leaned toward her, bringing his face so close to hers she could smell his clean eager breath. His neat round face was cheerful, black hair combed high above his forehead. "I saw you at the Stuyvesant last night," he said, "a remarkable performance! Wonderful!"

"I'm glad you enjoyed it," Julia said.

"Miss Pastrana," he said, coming closer still, "*oh,* look at you, Miss Pastrana." His intensity was ridiculous.

She looked away, excited and slightly alarmed, almost thinking he was going to kiss her. There's some madness in him, she thought.

"Outrageous," he said. "Completely outrageous."

"What is?"

"The things they say."

"What things?"

"I can quote." He sat back. So did she, thankfully, a faint quivery sensation growing inside. "'Eyes like the owl. Gifted with speech. The link between mankind and the ourang-outang.'"

"That was Dr. Mott."

"I know."

"But they all say different things. The one in Boston said I was human."

"Your eyes are nothing like the owl," he said. He never stopped smiling. "How many wise men have you seen?"

"Wise men?"

"Doctors. Fellows with fancy education and tripe for brains."

"I lost count."

"I'm a showman, Miss Pastrana." Mr. Lent leaned forward again but this time more casually, swinging one arm over his knee in a movement of practiced ease that managed to be all wrong. "Let's not beat about the bush," he said. "Have you considered Europe?"

She drew back, surprised. "Europe?"

"London. Paris. Rome." He tossed the words like winning cards.

"Did you know Tom Thumb played for the Queen of England? The Emperor Napoleon turned out for Maximo and Bartola. They've dined with every duke and duchess from St. Petersburg to Madrid." He stared fanatically into her eyes. "Why not you, Miss Pastrana?"

"I haven't thought about it," she said.

"Then do, Miss Pastrana. Do."

She looked into the fire. He talked as if he was acting. "Europe," she said softly. Far away, grand, sophisticated, old. Where Cato was going. Where they all came from, the Poles, the Italians, the Irish, the Germans, all the different accents and faces of the cities she dipped in and out of.

"Five times now I've watched you perform," he said. "Five times I've been amazed. You have great talent. *Great* talent."

"I don't," she said. "I do have some talent, it's true, but I wouldn't call it great."

"I would."

She glanced at him. "You're very kind, Mr. Lent."

"No," he said, leaning toward her again, "I'm not a particularly kind man. But I do know my business. Miss Pastrana—"

The future had seemed as far away as the past till now, but somewhere deep in her mind it began to take shape.

"Don't you know how rare you are?" He laughed, a sudden boyish undisciplined giggle. "How wonderful?"

Julia turned away and smiled. She wasn't usually the one who looked away first, but now she'd done it twice. His zeal was embarrassing.

"I was born into this business," he said. "I cut my teeth on it. I promise you, I will make you rich and famous. I *promise* you."

She looked back at him seriously. "Have you spoken to Mr. Beach?" she asked.

"I have." He had the tone of a man for whom everything is simple, worked out like a tricky equation. "I'll pay him whatever he wants."

She looked away.

"I have money, Julia," he said quietly. She was a little taken aback by his easy use of her first name. She'd been saving a bit. She hadn't thought about making more. "Money is no object," he said. "Whatever you're getting now, I'll double it in a year. I'll triple it. The future's not here, it's over there. And I have contacts."

Yes, she thought. This is it. The future. It's over there.

"Julia," he said. "You'll dine with kings."

In a flash, it came back again: home, Solana, her room, the stone seat, the steps. Glowworms hovering in the dark outside the gate, the fig tree dropping fruit on the cobbles. But this time she knew beyond doubt that she'd never go back. Oh, St. Jude, is this your doing? I promise to forever remember your great favor, forever increase devotion to you . . .

"Kings," she said thoughtfully. "I wonder if they're nice?"

Mr. Lent laughed.

PART 2

Old World

It was Theo and Julia, not Mr. Lent and Miss Pastrana. From the very first, he insisted. She was his sole client. She was all he needed, he said.

They toured the East Coast while he made arrangements. First London, he said. Then Paris, Berlin.

He talked. Oh, how he talked. On a train rattling through the night, everything out there peculiar and dreamlike, the dark land. He'd been in the business since he was in the crib. His father and mother had run a house for those of the human curiosity class, the wondrous, the strange, the *nondescript* in every sense of the word. That's what she was, he said. The singularity, the truly one and only. Cursed? Come on! You're a bloody marvel! Blessed, more like. It had all gone, he said, everything he'd had. Father, mother, the house. Let me tell you this, Julia, what I haven't seen doesn't exist, believe me, been broke as it's possible to be, down in a pit but got back up again, up now, nice and steady. Got a good nose, see. Read the market. Up and up and up, and now I am a wealthy man. I have ideas. I've been all over Europe. You'd love it, Julia. There's so much, there's just so much.

"You'll be a rich woman," he said, "because I'll be a rich man."

She began to wonder, as the cities and the miles and the time flew by, if this was what it was like to be married. Of course not. They never touched, apart from her hand on his arm, his cupping her elbow, touching her fingers as he helped her down from a coach. But there was coupledom in all those traveling hours, the daily life of the circuit jog-

ging on, she and he the only constants. She could talk to him, tell him
about it all, home, New Orleans, everything. At first it felt odd to travel
alone with a man, but that soon passed. More and more he took on the
role of lady's maid, bringing hot water first thing, combing her hair out
after a show, the touch of his hand on the back of her neck sharp and
startling. His quick triple rap on her door was familiar. The more he did,
the more he kept the others away. She missed those old days of company,
Myrtle and Delia, Cato, the dancing in the yard, the breakfasts. When
she was not onstage or practicing, she read books and played her guitar. Rooms. Rooms that looked out on streets and streets and yet other
streets, sometimes an alleyway or wall, or rooftops reflecting morning
sun that crept through thin curtains onto her eyelids, waking her early.
But it wouldn't be for long. In Europe, the circuses were bigger and
grander, he said. There the great circus performers were feted, adored.
The ball in Baltimore, he said, was nothing compared to the glittering
evenings that awaited. And anyway, wasn't life good? He had money.
She had new clothes, new boots—she hadn't worn her red ones since
they'd got her into trouble—new kid gloves, new white petticoats, a collection of veils in different colors to match her several outfits, and when
he came back from wherever he went when he was gone, he liked to talk,
on and on, rambling along in the most intimate way, almost as if he were
talking to himself, so that even though she hardly saw a soul apart from
him it didn't seem to matter so much.

"You put the same things in the booklet," she said, "I took a look, and
some of those things are still there, all that about the Diggers eating out
of a trough."

"Ah, yes," he said, raising his thin black eyebrows, "but the whole
thrust is different. It's a matter of emphasis. Look, I make it quite clear
how vastly superior you are to the Digger Indians. And of course I
deliberately leave a question mark over your origins."

"But that whole story . . ." she said.

"See here." He pulled a crumpled copy of the booklet out of his
pocket. "Listen to how I phrase it. I deliberately say— Where is it? Oh,
here— Yes— 'It is generally credited.' Take note of that. 'Generally
credited.' That says nothing about truth." He looked at her and smiled.
"What is truth, after all? We make our own."

"Do we?"

"And see here." He flicked over a page. "I've been extremely careful with the language. Here. 'The statement that is generally credited concerning her is as follows.' That's the way I put it."

"And the baboons," she said, "and the bears."

"Julia," he said, dropping the booklet, leaning forward and taking her hands in both of his, a gesture that both moved and scared her, for no one had ever done it before. "This is a throwaway. This is not the truth. Nobody wants the truth. What they want is a story. A good one. You could be anything. Your 'loup-garou.' Your demon baby. That is a piece of paper. Pah! *This* is you! This!" He turned her hands over in his, staring fiercely down into her palms as if in wonder. "God!" he whispered, then let go of her hands and drew back. "Never forget," he said, "that words on a piece of paper are nothing more than paper. They have nothing to do with your own self."

———

They sailed from New York on a mail ship to Liverpool. She walked covered through the raucous crowds of sailors and nervy passengers in knots and scatters, seeing little of the teeming wharf but aware of incessant noise and a hectic press of bodies. Theo held her tightly by the hand, keeping her close to him as if she were a child, up the gangway and onto the great ship. It was top-notch, he said, the only way to cross. "Look at that, the size of those wheels! Safe as houses. And I got you the best, Julia. The best I could."

Her cabin was small but comfortable. For most of the eleven-day voyage she stayed in it, taking her meals in there alone. It was just easier. "All that gawking," Theo said. "Don't you get sick of it all? Gawk, gawk, gawk." It was hard to be on board ship, to hear the waves and smell the sea and not have freedom of the decks.

He'd knock on the door. "Julia," he'd say, "I brought you some wine."

"Oh, thank you, Theo," she'd say, and with a wink he'd set it down on the tiny table in her tiny cabin, and off he'd go. Other times, he'd cram himself in, sit down with his hands behind his head and laugh, tell her about the lovely dining room and make fun of the other passengers to keep her amused. When the sun was beginning to fade, he'd come for her, and she'd put on her veil and gloves, and they'd go for a walk about the deck. If the sea was calm it was heavenly, a lovely time of day. The moon would come up and make the water oily black, and the stars would remind her of home. There was fog off the Grand Banks, and a few rough days toward the end, but mostly the weather was fine. She enjoyed the rough times, in any case. She never got sick. Theo did. One particularly bad day when the sea threw up walls of water and heaved them creaking in and out of great troughs and valleys, she went up on deck and walked about holding onto things. It was wonderful. They'd told the passengers to stay below and everyone was hunkered down calling for sick bowls, but she went up in her veil, folding it back from her face when she saw the emptiness of the deck, letting the wind whip tears backward from her eyes. The weather scoured her face. She was an ant on a bobbing cork. If she let go, the sky would whip her away like a bit of old paper. She walked about for ten minutes before dropping the veil once more and going down to see how Theo was.

"Do you need more water?" she asked, putting her head 'round the door.

Theo was lying on his side with a white face and his hair greasing up the pillow.

"No, thank you," he said weakly. He'd not been sick for the past two hours but the faint smell of vomit lingered.

"They're saying it'll be better tomorrow," she said.

"Uh." His closed eyelids flickered.

"That pillow needs turning," she said. "Move your head."

"It's all right."

"No, move your head."

"Julia," he said, "I'm trying *not* to move my head."

"Won't take a second. Here. Let's slip this under, there. Better?"

Just like the old days, nursing Solana. He turned onto his back and frowned, swallowing loudly, his throat convulsing, opened his eyes and looked at her, focusing slowly like a child waking up. She had an urge to stroke his high white forehead, could have done so easily, just wiping the sweat away, but she fought it down.

"I've been up on deck," she said quickly.

"In this? Are you mad?"

"It's lovely. There's no one up there. I can walk about without my veil."

"Do be careful, Julia."

"Oh, don't worry. You don't need to tell me."

"Sit down for a minute," he said. "I'm bored stiff."

"Someone recognized me by my boots once," she said, sitting down on the end of the bed.

"There you are." He swiped sweat from his forehead. "You can't be too careful."

"It was horrible." She looked away, suddenly awkward to be this close with him, all sick and tousled as he was in his pajamas.

"What happened?" he asked.

"They threw stones at me. Children."

He waited a moment, and it seemed to her that the air between them charged like a battery. "Go on," he said.

"Beach came and chased them all away." She looked at him and smiled, dispelling the charge. "Have you ever been really scared?"

He thought.

"I mean really scared, like you were going to die or something was going to hurt very badly?"

He thought some more, then said, "I don't think I have. Not like that."

"I was scared then. One boy had a knife and he kept coming really close with it. And I got this scar. From a stone. Look." She leaned a little forward and parted some of the hair on her cheek.

"My God, I never noticed that," he said.

"Oh, you wouldn't. It's a small thing, but at the time . . ."

"Children are cruel," he said. "Here's what you do." He raised himself up a little and put his hands behind his head. "You step outside yourself. Don't react." He put on his half smile of nonconcern. "They don't exist."

"A stone exists when it hits you in the face," she said.

"Well, you could probably debate that with a philosopher."

"Don't think I'll bother."

He smiled.

"Why?" she asked. "When have you had to do that?"

"Do what, chick?"

She softened at the ease of his tone.

"Pretend you didn't care."

"Oh." He sniggered. "Everyone has to do it sometimes."

"Hm!" she said, looking away, slightly annoyed, he thought, for some reason. So he went on talking. "You know, you don't own the monopoly, Julia. I had to stay at my uncle's up in Westchester County. My cousins were pigs."

"What did they do?" She looked back, interested.

"What they . . . it wasn't so much what they *did* as . . ."

He was beginning to look bilious again.

"Are you all right?"

"Yes," he said, "but I think I'll sleep some more."

She left him to rest, closing the door quietly and going back to her cabin, where she lay down on her own bunk and thought about him for a long time, feeling sorry for the poor boy in Westchester County with his horrible cousins, and wondering what it was they'd done to him.

She tried to go on deck again next day but too many of the crew were about, and then it was too late because the sea calmed down, the screaming wind died away to a mumble, and the weather turned to a gray drizzle that accompanied them all the way to Liverpool, where they disembarked in a solid downpour.

———

The docks went on forever, huge piers and basins, massive buildings lining the river. The sky above them was bunched and black, and rain put a gleam and a polish on the stones of the quay. They got a bus straight to the station, through rough old streets, narrow and crowded. Packs of hungry-looking boys roamed and the cobbles shone. At the station the waiting rooms were full. On the platforms the people pushed so close to the edge with their suitcases and trunks it was a wonder they didn't spill over onto the line. They waited two hours for the London train. Babies screamed, one striking up as another subsided. She thought she'd die of weariness. Theo made her a place to sit, next to a wall and shielded from view by a tower of trunks, but she became hot and started sweating under the veil. Her hands itched and she longed to take off her gloves and give them a good scratch.

"Don't worry," he said, "you can have a sleep on the train."

They were traveling first class; they'd be in London by nightfall.

"So soon?" she said.

"This is a small country, Julia." He sat down on an upturned suitcase and smiled. "You'll get used to it."

And after the vast American distances she'd covered, after the Atlantic Ocean, England was indeed tiny. It took them only seven hours to get to London. They reached the hotel in Covent Garden just before eight. It was a beautiful place, Julia thought, much nicer than any she'd stayed in before. The window boxes on the front were full of red geraniums, and there were flowers in the lobby and more in her room, a huge spray of tall spearlike plants in all shades of pink and purple that gave off a heavy, heady scent. The proprietress was a short, round affable woman with carrot-red hair and thin black crescent eyebrows who greeted them personally, introducing herself as Mrs. Dellow, and showed them to their rooms. The staff had been well prepared, she said. The garden at the back was for the use of guests (ha ha, if we ever get a fine day!), though I would suggest that the lady wears her veil if any of our other patrons happen to be there. Oh, of course. Shall you unveil now, madame? Or would you rather wait? It's all the same.

She unveiled.

"Yes," said Mrs. Dellow. "There you are."

Well warned. Julia smiled.

They ate privately in a room downstairs, served by a young waiter who stole discreet glances at Julia as he set down the dishes. The food was bland and needed salt. She had not managed to sleep on the train after all. Things were bigger than they should be, brighter, because she was so tired.

"I'm not sure whether I'm awake or asleep," she said, pushing her plate aside.

Theo smiled, lighting a cigar. "Then you must go to your room and sleep," he said. "And *I* have someone to meet."

"Aren't *you* tired?"

"Never," he said.

It was about the German tour, he said. He saw her to her room, touched her fingers briefly and was gone. She changed into her white nightie. So tired, yet where was sleep? Two comfy chairs were set in the alcove, and in the large bay window overlooking the square was a table, where she placed her books. An hour later she was still looking out of the window, wide awake, Yatzi lying across her knees. London, said her muddled head. The strange square with its moonlit railings, the black outline of the buildings on the other side of the square sharp against the deep blue skyline. I have crossed the sea. With a man. With dark eyes, and hair with a big wave in it licking backward from his brow.

———

Morning brought sunshine and a clean wet smell from the leaves outside the window. A pigeon crooned on the sill. Julia had managed a few hours' sleep but was wide awake again by six, sitting in her nightie on a cane-backed chair watching sunlight through gauzy white curtains, lost in thought. In two days they opened on Regent Street. Her best show dress was hanging on the screen, white, frilly, ribboned. Once, in Cincinnati she thought it might have been, she'd seen a boy and girl perform a sweet pas de deux outside the big tent, so beautiful, their pink costumes fluttering in a growing wet breeze. Neither could have been more than fifteen. The dance she was perfecting now was growing ever more balletic. That's what she wanted—something to give her that feeling she got when she saw those two lovely butterflies dance. The dress was too bulky. Pretty though, a light sea foam froth about the hem. These days the clothes she wore were so much more beautiful than those she'd made and altered for Marta. Remember her? Running in and out every half an hour or less and putting on a new dress, each with its own particular pair of shoes and stockings, its own particular necklace or mantilla. If she could see me now. She'd have been married to young what's his name three or four years now. And the boys? They were becoming dim, receding into the strange fog of memory. Poor Marta. Poor young what's his name. Poor boys. They're not seeing the world.

And look at me.

Her back was to the door, so she didn't notice when the maid opened it and came silently in with a fresh towel over one arm. Their eyes met in the mirror and the girl screamed, a horrible high, curdling sound. The pigeon launched itself from the windowsill with a loud batting of wings. Julia screamed too, jumping up, heart hammering. It was too sudden, the scream nightmarish. The girl had a long white face, oblong, big-chinned. With her staring eyes and weirdly gaping mouth, she seemed like a vision from a fever.

And then because Julia screamed, the girl screamed more, and they both stood with their hands up by their faces, frozen, screeching at each other like demons.

People came running.

"For heaven's sake, girl, there's no need for that!" Mrs. Dellow came strutting in like a hen. "Pull yourself together!" she hissed, then turning to Julia with a look of practiced concern, said, "Miss Pastrana, I do apologize, Marjorie's been away, she didn't know."

Theo's worried face appeared behind Mrs. Dellow's shoulder. "Are you all right, Julia?"

"Yes, yes, I'm perfectly all right," she said too quickly, but her heart was pounding in a sickly way. "I'm sorry, I was just startled."

"Of course you were." Mrs. Dellow gave Marjorie a little push on the arm. "Screaming like that, you stupid girl!"

The girl shook and stuffed a handkerchief into her mouth. "I'm so sorry, ma'am!" Fat tears welled in her eyes. Poor girl was mortified.

"It's all right," said Julia.

"I've been off sick, ma'am," the girl said, stealing a look, "I didn't know . . . nobody told me . . . I thought the room was empty. I'm so sorry."

"Please," Julia said, "it really doesn't matter."

"It would be a good idea to lock the door, I think," said Theo.

"Not at all, Mr. Lent." Mrs. Dellow shooed the girl from the room. "Why on earth should she? Marjorie. Did you go in without knocking?"

"I thought it was empty, ma'am."

"Please," said Julia, "really, it's nothing. This kind of thing happens sometimes."

"Not at all, not at all," Mrs. Dellow fussed, "I can't apologize enough . . ."

Theo took control. "No harm done," he said smoothly, ushering the woman before him toward the dithering girl in the corridor, "none at all. Let's all just calm down, shall we?"

"You *never* enter a room without knocking."

"I'm sorry, ma'am."

Theo closed the door on them but they could still be heard.

"It's your own fault!"

"I know."

"Making such a fuss! She's a guest!"

"Sorry, sorry, sorry—"

They faded away down the stairs.

Julia grabbed a yellow shawl, threw it 'round her shoulders and sat down on the bed. "That's made me feel quite strange," she said. "Shaky."

"You must not, you must not let yourself get upset," he said. "Remember what I told you. Step back. Look on." He sat down beside her, smiling smugly, but she stood up again immediately and paced up and down the room.

"I hate it," she said in a strangled voice, standing by the window. "Hate it!"

"I know."

"You don't! No one knows."

"I'm sorry," he said. "What a stupid thing for me to say."

Her eyes were dry, but she stared at him with a hard look he'd never seen before. Don't you talk down to me, she thought. The long white curtain, sprigged with violets and pansies, was behind her. Very deliberately, hot and shaking with fury, she turned her face into it, opened her mouth, sank her crazy teeth in and tore with all the clenched might of her jaw. It was thin stuff and ripped loudly. A long ragged rent appeared.

"Oh, for God's sake, Julia! Oh, no!"

She burst into tears. "Yes, yes, you always know what to do," she said. "You have no idea what it's like to frighten people."

"Of course not." Theo got up and stood about uselessly. "Damn it, look at this curtain," he said.

"I'm sorry."

"I'll think of something."

"I couldn't help it."

"You were doing some sewing and your scissors fell against it."

"Sometimes I just . . ." She wiped her face and pulled her shawl close. "I feel horrible," she said. "Horrible, horrible."

"I'll have to pay her for it," he said.

"HORRIBLE."

He flinched. "Julia, please, sit down," he said. "Take it easy this morning. Go back to bed, if you like."

"I will," she said shortly, turning her back on him.

"Good."

He worked on his smile.

"I'll tell them to bring you your breakfast."

She brushed her hair, embarrassed now, keeping her face vacant. She didn't know him well enough to lose control.

"Fine," she said.

"You know," he said, "you're not the only one who needs armor sometimes."

She closed her eyes. She didn't know him well enough for this either. "Let me tell you," he said, speaking quietly, as if someone else was in the room. "If it was possible to die of ridicule, I would have died in childhood."

She wanted him to leave. She wanted to go back to bed and have a good long cry, then have breakfast. "It's not the same," she said, laying down her brush, turning and eyeing the slightly tousled bed, calling there like a womb.

"I didn't say it was." Theo was at the door, his hand on the handle. "But think, Julia, if every word that came out of your mouth, every move you made, every time you made a point or ventured an opinion or asked a question, you were greeted with absolute and utter ridicule, with laughter. Would you not need armor?"

"Your cousins," she said, getting sick of waiting for him to go and climbing into bed anyway, still with the yellow shawl wrapped tightly 'round her shoulders.

His smile had not faltered.

"Why were you staying at your uncle's, Theo?" She closed her eyes and all was calming.

"I was at school up there," he said, opening the door, "after my mother died. My uncle thought I needed an education." His smile lost its glibness.

"You're falling asleep," he said. "It's been a long journey."

But as soon as she was alone, the restlessness returned, and she got up and sat down in front of the mirror and looked at herself. Same old face, following her through life. Now that it was over, she was more sorry for the girl than for herself. Hope she doesn't get the sack, she thought. She wasn't like those others, she didn't mean harm. It must have been a shock. First, she'd have seen the back of my head. Pretty white nightie, black hair. Then the eyes, suddenly, so big and black, and the ape jaw. If they saw more of it, no one would notice, no one would stare or scream or faint. When you see it every day it's nothing, you're just Julia, always there, as you were in the Sanchez house. You face them. Hold the head up, meet it all straight on.

He wasn't angry, she thought. Rates and Beach would have gone mad about a thing like this.

She took down the show dress and held it against herself in front of the mirror. Broad brown hairy shoulders. Short thick hairy neck. Full womanly breasts, covered in jet-black down. Why should they not wear pearls?

She got her sewing kit out of the drawer at the bottom of the wardrobe.

"*You* won't stop me," she told the children gathering in the shadows.

"What are you doing?" asked Theo, coming in with her chocolate.

"What I need, Theo," she said, wide awake, cutting away at the hem, "is something to lie just here," touching herself on the chest, "something very graceful, of the same color as the bodice."

"This is the most wonderful chocolate," Theo said. "Where do you want it?" He sat down. "Sorry, you were saying?"

"Just here on the hollow. Something terribly elegant."

"Absolutely," he said, "I'll sniff something out."

"Not just anything," she said, "I know what I want."

"Of course." Theo had a smile in the way that other people had an eye color. "Isn't that your show dress?" he asked, realizing what it was she was cutting.

"I'm making it better."

He frowned and smiled at the same time. "I very much hope so."

"You'll see."

"Will it be ready in time?" He nodded at the heap of cloth on her lap.

"I think so," she said, "and if not, I'll wear the blue."

"Ah, yes, the blue," he said, as if he had the slightest inkling what she was talking about.

London had the best freaks, always had. The Egyptian Hall, the Promenade of Wonders, the Siamese twins, pinheads, midgets, cannibals, giants, living skeletons, the fat, the hairy, the legless, the armless, the noseless, London had seen it all. In the Hall of Ugliness the competition was stiff. But no one had ever seen anything quite like Julia.

She was the Baboon Lady now, appearing apart from the mass in high style, at a gallery. She was the Grand and Novel Attraction, the Nondescript, the Wonder of the World, a scientific marvel. The little book with the drawing of her on the cover, the one done in New York, showed her poised and carefree, her wondrous, wild hairy head adorned with a headdress of feathers and white roses. Inside, Theo had quoted in full from her certificates: " 'Pronounced by the most eminent Naturalists and Physicians to be a true hybrid wherein the nature of woman presides over that of the brute." He had added: "She is a perfect woman—a rational creature, endowed with speech which no monster has ever possessed.' "

He'd done a marvelous job; the place was mobbed. Like a clerk he'd gathered all the information handed on to him by Rates and Beach, pored over dates, questioned her again about her early memories, which were so vague. The papers had blazoned the story he'd put together, and the crowds caused hold-ups on Regent Street to get a glimpse of the mysterious veiled figure, as small as a child, who was rushed from the carriage to a side door by her manager while the bobbing hordes were kept at a distance. She had a small dressing room with oak walls and a smell of polish, where she got herself ready, following a practiced routine. First she stripped down to her corset and jewelry, then lightly dusted the cleavage of her large dusky breasts with orris root, so that the heady iris scent would rise into her nostrils as she danced. She put a drop of lemon juice in each eye for the brightness, then dressed. She'd cut her show dress to just below the knee so that she felt like a ballerina. When she'd showed Theo he'd laughed and clapped his hands.

"Wonderful!" he'd said. "This is exactly what they want. As much of you as possible, Julia." Her pearl cross lay at the hollow of her throat, and pearls twined through her hair, gleaming on the tight bodice. The dress was cut very wide and low, and she wasn't sure if she trembled from nerves or the cold on her shoulders. It didn't matter, because as soon as she stepped out onto the raised platform and the pianist began to play, she knew it would all be fine. A sixth sense told her. She sang "Ah, Perdona al Primo Affetto" and "Voi Che Sapete," and at the end of each, the audience first drew in a tiny collective breath, held it for a silent moment, then exploded in a riot of applause that needed only fireworks to complete the sense of occasion. She danced the solo from

La Sylphide, then went down among them, letting them shake her hand and stroke her whiskers.

"Miss Pastrana," they asked her, "are you happy?"

"I am very happy," she replied.

"Where did you learn to speak English?"

"A long time ago, when I was a child in Mexico. That is also where I learned to speak French."

"Have you ever been in love?"

"I'm waiting for the right man."

That brought a laugh, with which she went along.

"None of them were rich enough," she said.

Another laugh. And she laughed when a toddler stretched out his arm to her, saying, "Dadda!"

"Can I touch your hand?"

"What a beautiful dress!"

"Miss Pastrana, you're a lovely singer."

"Do you mind being different?"

"No. Not at all."

She returned to the platform and sang one more song, this time with her guitar.

Good God, this is it, thought Theo, standing with folded arms at the back because he liked to see things from the audience's perspective, blinking rapidly and smiling like an imbecile. Sweet little thing, a true artiste, the real thing. He could have cried. She was the most extraordinary being that had ever existed on the face of this ridiculous earth. The papers said so. Everyone said so. They wanted to see her, they wanted to meet her, everyone came, the great, the good, the scared, bewitched, bewildered, the willing and unwilling. And they paid.

Please God, now, let this be my golden coach at last, whispered Theo, raising his eyes to heaven as smiling, clutching the flowers they gave her, she took her third bow.

Please, this time.

———

His career had been down snakes, up ladders, all those years on the road, the dwarfs, the strongman, the knife thrower, the magicians and mind readers, the man with the parakeet orchestra. A hazardous life, hanging around on the fringes of the business while the other side of the family made killings as far west as Iowa. God, wouldn't he just love to pass them by now, those Westchester cousins, not bother to call, say, sorry, too busy, far too many important people waiting. Tossing him their crumbs. Uncle Ben put in a word with Barnum, and the upshot was the trip to Europe, where he met the Gatti Twins, two brothers from Swansea who juggled with knives and did ridiculous feats of balancing. Up the ladder he'd gone, his big chance, four years, four European tours, till one morning in Leipzig when he woke up with a splitting hangover and there were no Gatti Twins and no money, and he realized with a start that he had no idea what day it was, only that he must have been drinking for a very long time. A period of dream and illness followed. He was imprisoned as a vagrant. He stuck it for a week, then got a letter to his father in New York, and after another couple of weeks funds had been sent, and he went back to the States in shame on his uncle's money, back to the old house on the Bowery.

This was where he'd been born, in the back room downstairs, where his mother had been alive, and every room had been full of the show people who came to board. It was in a dire state. Dogs still roamed the stairs and yard, but these were leaner and wilder than those old ones he remembered, and the whole place stank of them. He remembered when the house had always smelled of cooking and drying laundry, when the lobster girls and dog boys had come down for breakfast in the parlor. And he remembered it later when the lobster girls and dog boys had given way to card sharps and fortune-tellers, and it was just him and the old man, and everything was going downhill.

Now the rooms were empty, and his father was sitting in his vest in the kitchen drinking alternately from a Knickerbocker soda bottle and a bottle of whisky. He'd been addicted to both for years. A massive collection of empties gathered dust on a shelf above the dresser.

"What the hell have you done to this place?" Theo demanded, summoning all that he'd learned in the years away from home, the voice, the smile, the suave man he'd groomed himself into. "You've let the whole thing go."

"Look who's talking," his father said. "Look at you."

A failure.

Bailed out again. He looked with despair at the filthy walls and the spit in the corners of the old man's mouth and vowed again: I will not go down. He'd vowed before. No more pillar-to-post up and down the West Coast, he'd said, no more being small and slight and looking young and being overlooked and disrespected and always getting the shitty jobs, roustabout, lackey, ticket man. He'd vowed it and look where he'd ended up. In jail. But not this time. He'd worked too hard for that. No more poor Theo. I'm as good as the lot of you. I'll show them.

I showed them, he thought, applauding wildly in the wings. I did, I showed them.

Barnum was in town with Tom Thumb. Theo met him in the lobby of Arthur's, where he'd been buttering up a contact about a possible German tour.

"Theo!" came the moneyed voice, though the money wasn't flowing so well these days, or so he'd heard.

"Hello, Taylor." Looking his age, thought Theo. Jowls resting on his collar.

Barnum lodged his thumbs behind his wide lapels. "Have I or have I not been hearing things about you?"

"I'm damn sure you have," said Theo.

"And the hairy maiden? She's well, I hope?"

"Very well."

"Have you met Van Hare, Lent?"

"I don't believe I've had the pleasure."

Van Hare was a craggy circus man with long hair and a huge mustache. "Horses," he said lugubriously, as if it were his first name. "Are you the Lent who's in the elephant line?"

"That's his namesake," Barnum said. "Damn inconvenient, two Lents in one business. You should change your name, Theo."

Theo scowled. "Damned if *I'm* changing my name," he said.

"It's business," Barnum said, "not a test of family pride. You don't need people confusing you with someone else."

Theo smiled, slightly strained. "I'm not elephants," he told Van Hare. "That's another branch of the family."

"The successful branch," added Barnum with a laugh and a hand placed on Theo's shoulder to show it was all in fun. "Theo was a twig somewhere down the tree. Isn't that so, Lent? But not anymore."

Theo blushed. "I manage Miss Julia Pastrana," he said.

Van Hare was impressed. You could see it in his eyes, that look they got when they had to meet her. But he merely nodded. Jealous. Ha! Theo's smile widened. A feeling of madcap joy rose in his breast. They have nothing I want, he realized. But *they* want to see *her*. They're desperate to. So he asked after General Tom Thumb, and scarcely waiting for an answer, graciously invited both Barnum and Van Hare to call upon Miss Julia the next afternoon at the hotel, and they happily accepted and all parted on good terms.

———

Mrs. Dellow led them to the lounge. "Mr. Lent will be along in a moment," she said, "if you would care to wait. Miss Pastrana will receive you. Oh, sir, she's such a nice lady! Very sweet-natured."

Julia was by the window, a small woman in an elegant gray gown with lace at the throat and wrists, and a lace cap trimmed with pale blue ribbons. Her veil was blue as well, multilayered and shaded and very pretty, covering her entire face so that no more than a hint of eyeshine could be discerned through it. She came forward and offered a small gloved hand.

"Mr. Barnum, I'm delighted," she said.

Barnum beamed, took her hand and held onto it. She has a big head, he thought. "The pleasure is all mine, my dear Miss Pastrana. May I introduce my good friend and colleague, Mr. Van Hare."

"How do you do, Mr. Van Hare."

"I am well, thank you, miss. And you?"

"I'm very well too. Thank you."

Gently, she disengaged her hand from Barnum's hold and gave it to Van Hare, who shook it solemnly. "Do sit down, gentlemen," she said. But then Theo came in all smiles, and there were more pleasantries and the brisk opening of a bottle of bourbon.

"No, no," said Barnum, with a wave of the hand.

"Will you take lemonade, sir?" asked Julia.

"Lemonade would be most welcome."

"Of course!" Theo yanked on the bell pull.

She sat very still and straight in her chair with her hands crossed in her lap studying her visitors from beneath the veil. Barnum was a grand sort of man with an air of gravitas, richly dressed, with curly hair receding from his face. Van Hare looked like an artist. She could see him in a smock in front of an easel. A maid appeared, the one who'd screamed.

"Lemonade please, Marjorie," Theo said. He got on first-name terms with everyone, fast. "Lemonade for Mr. Barnum."

Marjorie bobbed an ill-at-ease curtsy, snatching a look at Julia as she backed out of the door.

"Sherry for you, Julia?" Theo was already pouring.

"Yes. Thank you, Theo."

He set down a small sherry on the table beside her. "My dear," he said softly, stepping back. She lifted the veil, setting it back over her head with a practiced gesture, nodded her head forward gracefully with a gentle smile, then took a sip of sherry. Theo, his high forehead furrowed, looked at Barnum looking at Julia. Then he looked at Julia herself. *Now there's a sight.* Her sipping daintily from a small crystal sherry glass with those huge horrible lips. Even now he could be struck anew with amazement when he looked at her, as if she were a ghost, something walking that should not.

"Tell me, Miss Pastrana," said Barnum, "how are you enjoying the life of an entertainer?"

"It suits me very well for now," she said. "I do like to see all the different places."

"And how do you like England?"

They'd been in London a few days and she'd seen very little but the gallery, her room in the hotel and the streets between Covent Garden and Regent Street from a carriage window. England was porridge and geraniums and bacon and those streets rolling by, there and back, avidly studied from behind the veil and the window. "I like the porridge," she said.

"Excellent, excellent," Barnum chuckled. "Well— I've heard wonderful things about your talent."

"Why don't you come to one of the shows?" she said.

"I for one certainly will," said Van Hare enthusiastically.

"So will I, if I can." Barnum shifted heavily about in his chair, the cuffs of his wide black trousers perfectly pressed, a gold chain straining across his stomach. "We're preparing to leave for Paris very shortly," he said, "but I shall try and make time."

"Oh, I'm looking forward to seeing Paris. We're going to Paris, aren't we, Theo?"

"Of course." Tough year the old boy's had, he was thinking. Money troubles. Wonder if he read the piece in the *Gazette*? Go see Julia Pastrana and wonder at the ways of God. Or some such. Does he know we're sold out every night? "Paris will be pleasant this time of year," he said.

"Do you think so?" Barnum looked doubtful. "Damn hot and scratchy, I would say."

"I like hot weather," said Julia, "reminds me of home."

There was a knock on the door, and Marjorie came in with a huge jug of lemonade and four glasses on a tray.

"We don't need all that," Theo said.

The girl looked confused. "I thought—"

"If you drink all that, Taylor, you'll get hell from your bladder all night."

"I very well might." Barnum appeared unconcerned.

"I'm sorry," said the girl, "I thought—"

"It's such a warm day," said Julia. "I'll have some too. Thank you, Marjorie. Put it down here on this little table and I'll pour."

Marjorie looked even more confused but set down the tray quickly and left. Julia got up, poured lemonade and handed a glass to Barnum.

"Thank you, my dear," he said. "Excellent."

"When we go to Paris," she said, sitting down again, "I want to go to the ballet."

"The ballet?"

"Something *grand*," she said, "something magnificent."

"Paris is the place for the ballet," said Theo. "Paris or Vienna. You'll see both."

"We should whisk you off to Paris!" Barnum smiled paternally. "This very second!"

Theo knocked back his drink. Look at him. All over her with his eyes. And the other one. He poured some more and spoke. "Business has been, I think I can say, pretty damn marvelous—" regretting the sound of his own voice immediately, thinking it high and nervous, but plowing on as if compelled by a man holding a gun to his head, boasting with eyes downcast and nose turning up, how so-and-so had said, and they'd had to turn away, and everyone's saying, and the newspapers, as I'm sure you've seen, have talked of little else . . .

"What you need, Lent, is an elephant," said Van Hare.

"What are you blabbing on about?" Barnum asked, turning ponderously to his friend.

"An elephant." Van Hare accepted another drink. "Walk it 'round town with a sign saying . . ."

"I'm afraid I'm not in the menagerie business," Theo said.

"You should be. Put the lady on a horse." Van Hare winked at Julia. "That'll pull 'em in. A horse or an elephant."

Theo laughed.

"I'm already pulling 'em in," she said.

"Would you like to work with animals?" Barnum asked her.

"I've never thought of it."

"You enjoy traveling, you say?"

"Oh, yes!"

"Wish I could say the same." Barnum's brow was shiny and he took out a large white handkerchief to dab at it. "I have been far too much upon the road in my lifetime. Do you ever think of Mexico?"

"Of course I do," she said. "Sometimes. But, Mr. Barnum, there's something I'd like to ask you. What was Jenny Lind like?"

"Jenny Lind! Oh, a very pleasant woman indeed. Wonderful voice. And shrewd. Very shrewd woman. Nice eyes."

"I'd love to have seen her," Julia said. "I heard she gives a lot away to the poor."

"Remember Jenny?" said Van Hare. "Not Jenny Lind, Jenny the elephant. Walked the tightrope. Beautiful creature."

"That's Lalla," said Barnum.

"Aha, but she started out called Jenny Lind. They changed her name three times." Van Hare turned to Julia. "You ought to have seen that superb elephant walk the tightrope."

She laughed. Her laugh could be alarming, the protruding crooked confusion of teeth suddenly appearing. But Barnum and Van Hare were pros and never flinched. "How does an elephant walk the tightrope?" she asked.

"Very carefully, I should imagine," said Theo.

"She could do anything, old Lalla," Van Hare said. "Stand on her head. Steady as a rock. Marvelous animal and gentle as a babe. Have you ever worked with elephants, Lent?"

"No."

Theo was watching Barnum. He's interested, he thought. If he offers . . . but no, let him want.

"Lent, was it your uncle had a share in Old Bet?" Van Hare persisted. "Or your . . ."

"Uncle," Theo said. "Two uncles, in fact."

"Now," said Van Hare, "Old Bet you can see to this very day, and she looks just as good as new."

"What are you whiffling on about elephants for, Van?" said Barnum, "Miss Pastrana doesn't want to talk about elephants."

"I don't mind," said Julia.

"Now horses," Barnum said. "I could see Miss Pastrana on horse-back."

"Do you ride, Miss Pastrana?" Van Hare asked.

"I have ridden," she said, "but not for a long time."

"Imagine," Barnum said, "Miss Pastrana on a white horse. White plumes, a partner, someone like Tom Neville . . ."

"Oh, but I couldn't do all the clever things," she said. "Standing up, riding two at a time—"

"You wouldn't need to." Barnum drained his glass. "Come and see me in New York when you get back from Europe." She wasn't sure if this last bit was for her or Theo so she said nothing.

"Who knows when we'll be back in New York," said Theo genially. "If business turns out as good elsewhere as it is here . . . Now—gentlemen. Miss Pastrana needs some rest before tonight's event."

I end the viewing, he thought. Not you, Barnum. I do.

When they'd gone, he poured them both another drink.

"Now that I have so much money," she said, "I think I should give some of it away. I'd like to do that, Theo. It's a nice thing to do when you've got such a lot of money. Yes, that's what I'll do."

Hasn't got a clue about money, he thought. Only knows she's got it. No idea. Good thing she's with me. Some of these vultures—

"Can you get me an atlas, Theo?"

"Of course."

"So that I can mark out all the places I've seen."

"Good idea." He was scarcely listening. "Funny Van Hare mentioning Old Bet," he said. "I was just thinking about her only the other day. Did you ever hear of Old Bet, Julia?"

"Not till now."

He stood with his legs apart on the rug, rocking on the balls of his feet. "My uncle Ben took me to see her in the American Theatre. No higher than this." He patted the air. "Can't have been more than six but I've never forgotten it because my uncle Ben burst into tears when he saw her."

"Why?"

"Well, by this time she'd been dead ten years or so, you see."

"Oh!"

"And they'd had her stuffed. And he'd been very fond of her, you see." He smiled. His eyes were far away. " 'Marvelous beast!' he used to say," imitating his uncle: " 'Should've seen Old Bet drink a bottle of beer. Sucked the cork right out and tossed it away, then up with it and down in one. Marvelous!' " He laughed.

"Did she get drunk?"

"I don't think so." He shook his head and focused. "Oh, yes, Old Bet. She was by all accounts a very clever animal."

Clear as day. Standing with his uncle in front of the beautiful stuffed beast. They were all down for his mother's funeral, because he remembered that she'd not been long gone. He didn't know she'd drunk poison then. It's only stuff, he thought, trying to put this dead thing together with the images of his mother so recently here, cooking in the kitchen with his aunt Losey, hiding in corners, giggling behind her hands, asking if he could see the man with purple eyes who stood in the corner.

"Oh, yes," he said, "a legend, Old Bet."

"Let's go out tomorrow night," she said. "Isn't there anything we can go and see?"

"Won't you be tired?"

"Not at all."

"There's a horse show," he said, "as it happens."

"Ooh, a horse show! Oh, let's go!"

"Well, I'll see what I can do. But all the best seats may have gone by now, and I'm not having you down with the mob."

"Of course not. I wouldn't be able to see a thing."

"It's not that, but it can get rough. What if you lost your veil?"

"I wouldn't."

She was trembling very slightly, he thought, but maybe it was his imagination. Not a full shivering, more of an unseen taut humming within the bone. It struck him that he had it too.

"Are you feeling all right?" he asked.

"I feel excited."

"Well, that's good."

"Sometimes," she said, "when you're excited, it feels like fear."

He got them a box for the second performance. Someone he knew. It was always the way; he knew many, many people, mostly on first-name terms, but no one close and no one for very long. She was beginning to see that he had no real friends. But he could usually pull a string, call in a favor. They went to the show, and she wore bangles that jangled up and down and attracted far too much attention, he thought. But no one cottoned on and they had a good time. A man rode four horses at once, standing up as if in a chariot, and a beautiful girl danced and leapt back and forth between eight black stallions as they cantered 'round the ring.

Going home in the carriage, Julia said, "Mr. Barnum thought I should ride."

"So he did." Theo rubbed the window. "It's an idea."

"I need to practice more," she said. "It's important."

He looked at her thoughtfully. "If you really want to ride a horse, I'm sure I could arrange it," he said.

"Really?"

"Why not? Not now, but soon. I know people in Berlin."

"You know people everywhere!"

"Lent the Almighty," he said, smiling. "I'll buy an atlas tomorrow. You know what I'm thinking, Julia? Russia."

"Russia!"

"We'll go east. Your Russians are some of the best horsemen in the world."

"You've been there, haven't you, Theo?"

"Twice."

"Really? What's it like?"

He gazed out of the window. "Spring and summer are beautiful. Winter's freezing."

"Horses," she said happily. "Russia." As if these words were charmed. Again he noticed the barely perceptible trembling. "Get me a nice Russian novel to read," she said, "please."

Theo laughed. "If you like."

When they got back, someone had pushed a copy of a French theater rag under his door, folded open at a particular page, on which someone had circled a particular item. It was accompanied by a note: "Lent—if you are considering Paris, you should be aware of this. Pays to be prepared—Van Hare." He saw Julia's name, but couldn't understand a word so took it to her room and asked her to read it for him.

"'Curiosities from London,'" she read. "It's a review. Let me see. It's—" She frowned and read on. As she read, her face changed.

"What's the matter?"

After a moment she looked up at him but he couldn't read her eyes.

"What's the matter?"

"What a horrible thing to say." She looked away.

"What? What does it say?"

Her strange eyes filled with tears, which made them shine and grow enormous. For a second, he was afraid of her. He'd never seen her cry. All this time. With all that, carrying that face around with her through life, and he'd never seen her cry. But she blinked, one great swipe of those spiky lashes, and glazed over. She looked down and read: "'For one thing is certain—that—*au lieu de*—instead of displaying this—this—this creature, this creature—who is an insult to all *bien* . . . *bien* . . . *bienséance*—to all good standards—and decency—'"

She laughed and shook the paper.

"'—this creature who'—oh, look, Theo, look!—'who creates revulsion in all who see her—'"

"Oh, Julia, don't take this kind of thing to heart."

" 'She should instead be protected from all public view.' "

Shouldn't be allowed out, said a pale unpleasant boy with a bulby face.

"Ha!" Theo snatched the paper from her. "Because *they* say so."

"That's nasty." She sat down.

"Yes," he said, "it is."

"An insult to decency!" she said wonderingly. "Why am I?"

"You're not. Julia . . ."

"Why do they say that?"

"Because they're . . ."

Child scarer.

"*Why* am I an insult to decency?" She got up, grabbed the paper back from him and walked about the room, holding it open. "I know I'm ugly," she said. "Revulsion though? Revulsion! What have I done?"

"You haven't done anything, Julia." He followed her.

"What do they mean?"

"They're stupid. They don't know what they're talking about. Anyway, they don't mean *you.*"

She laughed. "Who *do* they mean?"

"They mean the show, the whole—"

"No, they don't," she said, getting angry. "Weren't you listening? 'This creature who is an insult to all good standards and decency.' That's me. This creature is me."

"Julia, please." Oh God, he wished he'd never shown her the damn thing.

"Ugly, yes," she said. "Looks like a baboon. Yes. Oh, yes, the non-pareil of ugliness, all of that, yes, true, true, but I am *not* indecent."

"Of course you're not."

She deflated visibly, sinking down on the bed. "What's it all for?" she demanded.

"What?"

"This. All this. I work very hard."

"I know you do."

She wanted him to say that she was a talented dancer, a good singer. It doesn't mean a thing to him, she thought. The music. I could be pulling pennies out of people's ears for all he cares. I don't think he's got any musical appreciation at all. I could be telling fortunes or juggling. So what? He's a manager, he doesn't have to appreciate anything, he sees to all the stuff that makes my head ache. And he does it well.

He tapped his forehead. "Good brain, girl," he said. "That's why you can succeed in this business. You could have stayed at home and been a servant forever, couldn't you? But no, you've got more about you than that. You're a performer. A natural. And because of that you'll always make a living. You don't have to worry about the naysayers. The more they see you, the more they'll realize what you are."

"What I am?"

"Yes?"

"What *am* I? I'm the demon baby. The loup-garou."

He smiled. "You are Julia. And I have huge ambition for you. You have no idea. *Huge* ambition. You mustn't let this upset you."

"Oh, don't be ridiculous!" She threw the paper down. "Of course it upsets me! What do you think I am? Stone?" And then she did cry, sitting down in one of the armchairs in the alcove and hiding her face in her hands. "It's like those children all over again," she said.

"Those blasted children! Forget them! What d'you want to carry them around with you for?"

"I don't."

"Yes, you do."

"Oh, shut up." She looked away.

Theo stood looking about awkwardly. Poor girl, of course she'll cry. I would. Don't these idiots think when they write these things there's some poor girl on the other end of it? "Well, that's that," he said. "We don't need the French. Bastards put me in jail."

She fumbled a handkerchief from somewhere and began dabbing at her face.

"Anyway," he said, "it's only one review. The French are like that. It's *their* loss."

She didn't say anything. Her head was bowed, and he was momentarily touched. "Look at you," he said, "you and your dainty little hands."

She muffled a sob. He put his hand lightly on her shoulder.

"Come on, Julia," he said softly, "don't let something as ridiculous as this spoil things for you."

"I won't," she said into the handkerchief.

He went and sat down in the opposite chair. "This is nothing," he said. "Not even a setback. Things are going well for us, and they'll get better and then better again, you'll see. Oh, for heaven's sake! Who cares about the fool who wrote that? Who is he? No one! No one. *You're* the one they want to see. *You're* the special one."

"But I'm not," she said wearily, drying her face. "That's the funny thing. I'm not special at all, I'm just an ordinary person." She stood up and started walking about the room again.

"Listen," he said, "tomorrow we'll go to—"

"Where's Yatzi?" she said sharply.

Theo sighed, suddenly very tired.

"Where's Yatzi?" A rising note of panic had entered her voice.

"Oh God," he whispered and set about finding the thing, and as he searched aimlessly she began crying again and stood biting her fingers like a child. He'd never seen her like this before.

"Oh, please, Julia," he said. "Perhaps the maid put it somewhere."

"Tonight of all nights!" she cried, and started pulling open all the drawers. "Someone's taken him!"

"Julia." Theo closed his eyes. "Why would anyone want to take an old stick of wood with a rag wrapped 'round it?"

"He's not just an old stick of wood!"

She was in a terrible state by the time he found the doll wedged down the back of the bed a few minutes later. "Here," he said. My God, he thought. Look at it, suck marks on, disgusting. It had two large blots for eyes, a line for a nose and an upturned curve for a mouth. A ragged dress of flimsy green and red cloth was bound 'round and 'round it like a loose bandage. She grabbed it and calmed down at once, and he left her rocking in the alcove, holding onto that horrible old lump of wood.

Back in his own room, Theo stared angrily at the stupid incomprehensible French. I won't have it, he thought. Ridiculous. Poor girl's been measured and weighed and fingered and prodded inside and out, and taken it all. Of course she's human. Bloody obvious. He'd been in the business all his life, and he knew. Human. All of them. But the rubes wanted monsters. And the medics, the professors, the scientists, all of them, they were rubes too. Tell you what, I'll get her picture taken. On Piccadilly there's a place, I'll call in tomorrow and have a word.

Discreet. She's just a hairy girl is all, with a weird face and a sticky-out mouth, a mouth you could hang your hat on. Nice eyes. Nice girl. Roll up, roll up. And we'll put the picture in the new booklet, and we'll have new words. They're not getting away with that.

And he sat down and composed a paragraph very quickly in his best florid, high-minded style:

THE NONDESCRIPT, MISS JULIA PASTRANA, from Culia-cán in Mexico. There is nothing in her appearance in the least calculated to offend the sensibilities of the most fastidious, whether viewed socially, morally or physically. A feeling of pity, rather than of repugnance or antipathy, is generally experienced in the bosom of all who pay her a visit. There is sufficient of the characteristics of her womanly nature to dispel anything allied to the revolting or disagreeable, and connected either with her personal appearance, or the manner in which her levees are conducted. Persons who visit her with an idea of seeing a wild beast in the cage of a menagerie will be disappointed. Those who go with the expectation of seeing some frightful monster will have such expectations changed to sentiments allied at once to awe and astonishment at the mysterious ways of Providence, while his philosophy will be puzzled amazingly to account for his share of the milk of human kindness, and the abundant juiciness of his own heart in view of the wonderful phenomenon that will irresistibly for the time being engross his attention.

He read it back to himself. Good God, man, you've got a way with words, he told himself.

O
h, no," she said. "Absolutely not. You will not, you will not." Lying drunk and sleepy on the sofa, slightly tearful, playing about with that awful burned thing, Tattoo, draping chains of silver and narrow thongs of black leather 'round what was left of its neck.

"Never mind," said Adam, sighing and sitting down next to her, gazing around the room so he wouldn't have to look at her. She was in something long and trailing, faded violet, with her hair piled up in a big black bush of tortoiseshell combs on top of her head. Laurie had gone too far this time, she said. Who did he think he was? She'd caught him loading a massive cardboard box into the back of his car.

"Theft," she said, "pure and simple. My things. My property."

"Well," he said, "I suppose he thought . . ."

"I don't care what he thought." She rolled onto her side. "I said, no, you can't do that. It's only things, Rose, he said, the idiot. Only things. As if that meant anything. Oh, he can be a bastard, you know. Roll me a cigarette, lovey. Well, that was that. You will not, I said. And do you know? He refuses to carry them back up for me. Just dumps the box by the back door and the rain's starting. Not even a lid on the box. I made about ten journeys up and down those stairs."

"Oh, well," Adam said, "everything seems to be back to normal now."

She sat up, propped Tattoo comfortably against a cushion and poured more wine. "I've been really sorting things out," she said.

"Have you?" He looked 'round. No sign of it. Things were just a bit rearranged. It's like playing with Lego or building bricks, I suppose, he thought, yet still somehow wonderful, like a seriously overcrowded junk shop. Dried flowers and feathers hung from the ceiling, and the draped and carpeted walls were now scarcely visible as the growth rioted upward and outward. You had to admit she kept it clean, but surely it was a full-time job.

"Poor old Tattoo," she said. "After all he's been through."

"Ah." He swigged his wine. "He was in the box, was he?"

"He most certainly was. Right down at the bottom as well. Must have been the first thing he threw in. And he knows how I feel about that thing. And when I got up here, he'd been tidying up. Putting things away! I couldn't find anything. So I've told him, I've said, look, you're the landlord, you can evict me if you want to, but you don't touch my things. You don't live here, Laurie. I do."

Adam smiled and shook his head, crumbling tobacco. Couldn't live with her, he thought. Not for long. Poor old Laurie, she's gone right off him. She doesn't care. He'd seen Laurie crying on the stairs one night. Just turned the corner and there he was, the big dripping mess, but he tried to hide it, blowing his nose as if he had a cold. She couldn't care less. She was drunk and sentimental now, not for Laurie but because of her poor things so nearly lost.

"Here," he said, twisting the end of the roll-up and handing it to her.

"Ta."

"You know," he said, "we could open this place up as a museum. Charge admission. The Rose Museum."

"Only no one would come."

"They might."

"No," she said. "You have to be famous."

Adam slid down and sat on the floor with his back against the sofa, and they lapsed into silence. After a few minutes he said, "When you think about it—every person's like a museum of their life."

She smiled. "That's nice."

"Only most stay uncurated. Things fade away into old cupboards and drawers that never get opened. Junk stalls. Rubbish on its way to the dump. Then they just vanish."

"You're a poet, Adam," she said.

Adam turned his head. "If ever you die, Rose," he said. "It'll be a hell of a thing for whoever gets to go through all this lot."

She laughed. "And who would that be, I wonder? Probably my mother."

She hardly ever saw her family. She'd liked her father and didn't like her mother, that's all he really knew. Her father was dead, and there was a brother somewhere, and they came from somewhere quite posh that he could never picture, somewhere like Welwyn Garden City or East Grinstead, those places that just looked like nothing on the map.

"She might get my brother to do it, I suppose," she said, reaching for the tobacco.

Adam picked up Tattoo. "Now this"—he held it at arm's length—"I doubt if you'd be able to give this away."

"Oh, don't," she said, "don't make me feel sad."

"He's in an awful state, Rose. Look. He's got a hole in his shoulder. What's that? Moths?"

"I don't have moths."

He put his finger in the hole, wiggled it about and pulled it out. A tuft of dirty white stuffing came out with his finger. "You ought to patch this up," he said.

"You know," she rolled a cigarette, one-handed, "it's kind of like he makes me feel sick now. Laurie."

Adam put his finger in the hole again. Inside was scratchy.

"I don't know what it is," she said. "He always seemed on the edge of being beautiful, but now he's on the edge of repulsive."

"So how did that happen?" He dug deeper. Straw. Fluffy stuff.

"I really don't know."

"So is that it then?" he said. "You and him? What happens now? Will you still live here?"

"Oh, yes!"

"And he doesn't mind?"

"He won't have to, will he? It's all right. He's got his wife."

"I think he's quite upset though," Adam said.

"Well, I don't see why. We'll still be friends. There was never a commitment. That was supposed to be the good thing about it."

"Ha," he said, "if only things were that simple."

Rose shrugged. "You have to face reality."

He laughed. "That from you!"

She licked the edge of the cigarette paper, "What are you doing?"

"Look. A big hole. There's all sorts in here."

"Don't rip him to pieces," she said, hitting him lightly on the head.

"I'm not."

"Stop it. Give him to me."

"Here." He handed her Tattoo, and the matches.

"You can be quite hard, can't you?" he said.

"I'm not hard."

"Yes. You are. You get all sentimental over bits of old paper but you don't give a toss about people. You've got more genuine feeling for that old doll than you have for any human being."

"What rot," she said, striking a match. "You don't know anything about it."

He put his hand on her hip, just to see what she'd do. She ignored it. He saw her frown as her long chipped nail examined the hole in Tattoo's shoulder. "You've made this worse," she said.

"You need to patch him up."

She laid the just-lit cigarette on the edge of an ashtray. "You know, I used to think this was wood," she said, "but it's not."

"What is it?"

"I'm not sure."

He picked up the cigarette and took a drag. "There's all sorts in there," he said.

"Straw. Dust," she said. "Ticking. Paper. Something lumpy."

"You should get some foam and block it up."

"Look at this." Out came a clump of hardened straw. "That's really old." She laid it on the sofa and dug a little farther. "Paper," she said.

He took his hand from her hip, wondering if she'd even noticed.

"Oh, look!" She sat up straight. Leaning forward, she set about smoothing a couple of scraps of screwed-up fragments on the low table.

"What is it?"

"And there's more—" Fishing about inside and drawing out another strip, longer, creased into powdery near-disintegration. "Wow! Look at this."

"Writing," he said.

"It says—"

They put their heads together, poring over the words that survived, the rubbed-out extremities. An old-fashioned leaf pattern, any color long faded, coiled up one torn edge. Three scraggy scraps, soft and wrinkled, the print rubbed to gray by many years. Here and there a few letters or a word or two made it through the gray.

"Look," she said, "this piece fits with that."

—of Provid—

—A feeling of—

—eeing some frig—

—NDESCRIPT, MI—

—he mos—

—and Mis—

—Sanfa—

—little prin—

"It's an old leaflet," she said, "a handbill, playbill, something. Look."

—dmission—doors ope—

"That's 'admission, doors open.'"

—allery, Regent Stre—

—ndon—

Then one whole word: Culiacán.

"Culiacán," said Rose.

"It's in Mexico," said Adam.

Flowers were heaped everywhere in the dressing room. Every show there were flowers, that's how it was now. They'd given Paris a miss and gone straight to Berlin. Germany loved her, and suddenly life was fast and bright and swept her along—theaters, gold brocade, lights, the face of a crowd, hands touching hers, hands that stroked shyly, as if she were very rare and very wild.

When it came to being stared at, Julia was an expert. She could handle them all, the Rapt Bedazzled, the Eyestalk Gawker, the Holy Seeker, the Furious Affronted, the Scared, the Nauseous, the Shyly or Archly Flirtatious, and—most rare—the Frank Equal. Theo was a Rapt Bedazzled but now he was also turning into a Used-to-Me, like the people back home. For so long now her face had been a fascination, a honey for looks. They flew toward her like darting insects, flew away, returned, irresistibly drawn. But she knew what to do. Meet. Read. Drop or hold. Release. Don't challenge unless challenged. Drag them away from the mouth, the whiskers, the breasts, into the eyes, and sometimes smile. You know when. You always know. If they shout, laugh, shoot hate— look away, resist. Pretend.

But never yet, after all the shows, the little towns in England, the rainy villages, the big-city stages, the lowlands of Holland when the rain never stopped; after all the stares of all the people in all those places and all that went before on the far side of the sea—never once had she been more scared than when standing on this balcony, looking through her veil at the obscure mass of faces. Something was different. The crowd was rowdy. She had to act, speak a language she didn't know, remember the cues. Her heart was beating too fast.

It seemed as if the entire city of Leipzig had turned out.

Der Curierte Meyer!

For the first time ever, after her triumphs in America and England, the Remarkable Miss Julia Pastrana in a play written specially for her.

Der Curierte Meyer—*The Milkman Cured*

It wasn't a real play. It was a musical comedy, a silly little piece, but Theo was right—it pulled them in, the high and the low, and the place was bursting at the seams. German wasn't one of her languages, but she'd learned the lines specially and knew the cues. It was really just her doing her usual songs and dances, with a few lines she had to say here and there, no long speeches or anything like that—

It didn't feel right.

Those men. She'd heard them laughing.

Well, it was a funny play.

Better they laugh than be afraid.

When the curtain rose, a hush fell. A drum rolled.

Stage left, paper roses hung over a wall. A rustic seat by a fountain. Stage right, a garlanded balcony, on which she stood sweating under the veil. A single violin played a sweet rising air, and she ran lightly down the steps as the rest of the strings and the woodwinds came in, danced as the music swelled. If it were just the dancing, her arabesque, her plié, she could do that. Or the songs, but laughter was a different thing. She wore white flowers in her hair. She'd rubbed the love potion into her arms and shoulders. Her gris-gris bag was in a secret pocket. Smiling in expectation, the audience settled in. As the dance drew to a close, voices were heard, stage left. She ran back up the steps, white mesh, tiny white slippers, the dress bouncing and frothing around her in dusty pink and gold layers, and sat down at a small table on the balcony, taking up a large fan with gold and red tassels. Two young men entered below and began speaking in loud braying voices. One was tall and handsome, the other shorter and slightly plump, both with a dandyish air. She couldn't understand a word they said but knew they were talking about their friend Stefan, a fool of a milkman who falls in love as easily as he falls asleep.

But wait! Who is that on the balcony!

She rises, taking up her fan.

Why, she is the remarkable Fraulein Lieselotte. In her own country she is considered a great beauty!

So graceful!

Fraulein Lieselotte! Dear lady!

Down she comes.

Up and down in the footlights, skirts swinging, one small gloved hand idling with the fan, she saunters around the stage. They dart playfully before and behind her like circling bees, calling to one another and to her in ridiculous tones, words that draw bursts of expectant laughter and a few whoops from the audience, vying with each other to praise her pretty foot, her figure, her elegance, begging her to *please, for just one moment, please, dearest lady, lift up your veil.*

She waits for the piccolo, and when its plaintive sound rises up from the pit, she stands still, turning fully to face the audience.

For the thousandth time, the reveal.

A great sighing groan of wonder rises from the audience. Same as ever, but the joke's on those two silly men, now following her as she walks, always keeping her back to them and her face to the crowd. The fat one falls over. Laughter pools like smoke in the domed ceiling. She shares a smile with the crowd. We are in this together, it says. When the horns and the drum blare and she turns on the men, there are screams and disbelieving laughter. She's impossible. My God! My *God*! To be that.

The young men, poor actors, step back, open-mouthed. Julia's heart hammers madly. She smiles and they scream some more. She parades, the piccolo playing, up and down the front of the stage with her skirts seductively swaying. Something in this new laughter, a braying quality, an imp of misrule, an ugliness to square up against her own. She feels as if she's in a pit. The uglier the air, the more gracefully she moves, a sweeping implacable presence chasing them across the stage with her face, driving them to the wall, where they stand knock-kneed and quaking, biting their nails.

She turns from them scornfully, walks center stage and speaks. *You see,* she says, raking the audience with her eyes, *the poor creatures are struck dumb by my beauty.*

An explosion. A howling and thumping of feet on the floor. Now the dance, while they're going mad. Slay them. Laugh, dance with the fan, let it draw circles on the air. The more they scream, the bigger the show. She throws up her big proud head with its massive crown of hair and flowers, flexes her shoulders and twitches her hips, lets drop the shawl so that the dark groomed thatch of her arms and shoulders appears, and the smooth down of heavy breasts in a low-cut dress.

A bell rings. The dance ends. With a flourish, she takes up her shawl and retreats to the balcony, seating herself elegantly and composing the thick veil before her face, while the two men gabble below: *She is quite hideous! And yet, and yet . . .*

Theo, in the wings, smiles warmly at her. It's going well. Some knockabout stuff occurs onstage. The two young men are joined by their friend Stefan, the stupidest thing ever, a clod of a dairyman with baggy breeches and an anxious whining voice. They tease and twit him. Gusts of laughter roll in from the audience as he falls headfirst into the orchestra pit and has to be pulled out by the legs.

But wait! Who is she?

The lights dim and a hush falls. She sings into the silence:

. . . Leise flehen meine Lieder . . .

Stefan falls in love that instant, just with her voice and veiled form. She descends to the rustic seat by the fountain, and his friends abandon him, sniggering behind their hands. Confused, he whirls around.

Herr Milchmann! she cries.

He approaches, covered in sweat, breeches growing baggier by the minute, a single rose in his hand, sighing and beseeching. She flicks her fan, looks away, waggles her foot. The audience chuckles and hoots.

Fraulein, ich bitte Sie, nehmen Sie Ihren Schleier!

Oh, please, put up your veil!

She rises scornfully and walks to the front of the stage. *Let him sigh for a glimpse of my face,* she says, looking over their heads, *he'll get none of me.*

And that was it, really. Just more of the same, the men clowning, she singing, dancing, delivering the odd disdainful line. Toward the end came a prolonged and frantic farce, where stupid Stefan follows her about puckering up his mouth and pleading for kisses, fluttering his closed eyelids pathetically. *Oh, sweet lady, one kiss, one kiss is all I ask.* Whenever he looks away or goes offstage, she lifts her veil and grins at the crowd. In and out goes Stefan, up and down goes the veil, faster and faster. The grin becomes painful, she feels her cheeks quiver. Do they know the skill that goes into this? They roll about, baying and shrieking, till she goes into her last big scene.

Alone onstage, she speaks to them directly.

What a fool this milkman is, she declares.

They roar.

What does he know of love? Nothing! What he calls love is nothing more than a few pearls—she twirls them—*a pretty dress*—she spreads the flounces—*a little foot*—she points the toe— *What does he know*— the music begins—*of the true heart within?* Into her final song, about a true simple heart being worth more than gold.

Stefan enters with his giggling friends. They haven't seen her yet.

Such a man, she says, with a careless gesture in his direction, *is a shallow well. I could never give my heart to him.* With a practiced movement, she veils and turns to greet him. *Your patience is rewarded,* she declares, *behold the woman you love!* Peels down the gloves from her hairy brown arms, withdraws them, tosses the veil aside.

Horror!

He runs but she gives chase as the audience roars, then: *Is this what you want?* she cries, kissing him full on the lips. As he faints clean away, she steps center stage, wets her lips—"Her tongue!" someone moaned— and says, *How many of you ladies can say your kiss has that kind of effect on a man?*

The curtain fell.

She took the applause center stage, wave upon wave of thunderous stamping and cheering and whistling. Three curtain calls. Flowers landing on the stage.

Theo met her in the wings with a glass of champagne. "You were spectacular," he said. "Spec*ta*cular, Julia. You must meet Herr Otto, he is smitten."

———

Herr Otto was an elegant, handsomely ageing man, with a raggedly pointed beard and deep lines etched on either side of his face. "I am indeed," he said, bowing low so that she could study his bald spot, grabbing her ungloved hand and kissing the back of it wetly. Straightening, he looked sideways at her.

"How do you do," she said, still breathless from the whole thing.

"Come and have a drink, Hermann," said Theo, who'd clearly had a few himself already. His eyes had a bright, dancing, almost scared look. "Come and have a drink with me and Julia. Wasn't she *wonderful*?"

They walked to the dressing room along an avenue of goggling faces. She didn't know why but she felt like crying. They were still screaming and whistling out there. He had not given her his arm. She wanted it to hang on to. Something mad was in the air. "Theo . . ." she said.

"Extremely talented," Herr Otto said with a smile in his voice. "Fraulein Pastrana, you have a very pretty voice." His English was perfect.

"Thank you."

There was more champagne in the dressing room, more faces. A woman in a blue gown. Huber the manager, who was round and small with a black mustache and a thick black curl of hair carefully arranged above his forehead. The sound, still battering at the door, something wild in it. Theo beaming like a madman.

"And the incomparable Cricket!" he cried, "Here she is!"

Huber, his face in hers, smiling. "A triumph," he said.

"Julia, come here." Theo took her hand. "This is Miss Friederike Gossmann," he said, leading the woman in the blue gown forward, "the great actress."

"Oh, don't be silly," said Miss Gossmann lightly. "I'm so pleased to meet you, Miss Pastrana. What a marvelous performance you gave."

"Thank you."

"Mr. Lent tells me we can expect to see you in Vienna." She was trim and pretty and assured, and spoke perfect English with a faint accent.

"Are we?" Julia turned to Theo. "Are we going to Vienna?"

"I'm sure we will," he said. "Please, please, everybody, sit down. Miss Gossmann, for you?"

"Only one very tiny one," Miss Gossmann said, holding her finger and thumb a half inch apart, and smiling warmly at Julia. "I'm afraid I can't stay. I just wanted to say hello and tell you how much I appreciated your performance. And to say, please, when you are in Vienna, do come and visit me."

"Of course." Theo shoved a drink in Julia's hand. "Miss Gossmann is the Cricket, Julia."

Julia had no idea what he was talking about.

"Why would she know about that?" said Miss Gossmann. "Julia— you don't mind if I call you Julia?—do please call me Friederike—"

"The Cricket," said Theo excitedly. "A sensation in Hamburg. Should've seen the reviews."

"You were born to play that role, Friederike." Herr Otto sprawled back in his chair, looked at Julia and pulled down the skin under one of his eyes in a peculiar, slightly vulgar way.

"Listen to them!" Huber shook his head. He never looked at her for long. Quick little darts. Waves of cheerful savagery faded beyond the walls.

"Stupendous," Otto said.

"It scared me," said Julia.

Miss Gossmann leaned forward and clasped Julia's hand. Her face, close to Julia's, was friendly and concerned, and she betrayed no sign of unease. She might have been looking at something normal. "I can understand that," she said.

"Scared?" Theo, walking about waving a bottle, smiling, irrepressible. "What's there to be scared of? They loved it!"

"The way they laughed," said Julia.

"It's comedy. That's what they're supposed to do."

"The *way* they laugh."

Miss Gossmann went on smiling and stroking Julia's hand, her green eyes full of sympathy. Her face was birdlike, round and bright with a sharp little nose.

"Just—" Julia shrugged.

"It's a vulgar little thing," Friederike said. "In Vienna I hope to see you perform solo."

"Hermann's going to be our man in Vienna," Theo said, circulating continuously with the champagne. The door was open, people wandered in and out. Julia could hear the men in front of their mirrors down the hall, sponging off their makeup. "You'll love Vienna, Julia," Theo said. "You haven't played a really big circus yet. That's where Hermann comes in. What do you say?"

"I don't know," she said. Her heart was calming down. "I'm tired, I'll think about it later. I'd like to go to Vienna. I'd like to go everywhere."

"Everywhere?" Herr Otto smiled, showing many teeth and high gums.

"First Vienna," Theo said. "Then Warsaw. St. Petersburg, of course. Oh, Julia, wait until you see St. Petersburg. The mysterious east! The Golden Road to Samarkand!" He laughed, clinking glasses with Huber, chortling softly in the corner.

"Vienna would suit you, fraulein," Otto said, leaning forward elegantly, crossing his long legs. "There's already talk of you there, do you realize? I can procure you a season. Perhaps at Carltheater."

"When?" asked Theo.

"I go home in a few days." Champagne sparkled in Otto's thick mustache. "Soon, I'm sure, I'll have news for you."

"I'm talking to Renz as well," said Theo.

"Ah!" said Otto, smiling at Julia, "They want to put you on a horse."

"I do believe," said Theo, "that Julia has the talent."

"I'm sure she does."

"I could learn one or two little tricks," Julia said, "but nothing fancy."

"One or two little tricks is all it would take," said Otto.

Miss Gossmann rose. "I wish I could stay longer," she said, "but I have to be at some silly party. You will come to my house in Vienna, Julia, and we'll have time for a lovely talk."

"We certainly will!" Theo, sparkly-eyed, kissed her hand.

Miss Gossmann left on the arm of Huber. Herr Otto and Theo lit cigars and laughed and talked for a long time, till Julia's head spun and she realized she'd nearly fallen asleep in front of the mirror. "Can we go back to the rooms now, Theo?" she asked. "I'm really tired."

Otto set his glass down. "Indeed. You need your rest and I must be off. Fraulein Pastrana—" He shook her hand avidly. "It's been a great pleasure to meet you. I look forward to seeing you in Vienna."

Theo walked Otto to the stage door.

"So—two more weeks," said Otto. "Think she'll hold up?"

"She's tireless," Theo said, "you wouldn't believe. Strong as an ox."

"Strong, of course, but her mind, you know. What about her mind?"

"There's nothing wrong with her mind."

"Of course there isn't. That's not what I meant."

"What *did* you mean?"

"I hardly know." Otto knotted his scarf and coughed. "Be careful, Lent. Someone'll have her out from under your nose before you know it."

"No, they won't." Theo smiled smoothly.

Returning, he heard the talk in the men's dressing room. A door stood open. The clod of a milkman was transforming into a weary-faced man of about forty-five in front of a mirror.

"Whatever they're paying you," said the man next to him, "it's not enough."

"Doesn't bother *me*," Stefan replied.

———

"Did you see this review? 'The daughter of Esau.' I like that. The daughter of Esau. That has a nice ring to it. It's, you know, respectable. Yes, I like that. What do you think, Julia? Daughter of Esau?"

"Where's that Bible?" she said. "Read it to me."

Theo took the brown leather Bible from a drawer in the table. "Let's see," he said, "if I remember my old Sunday School days, and I do—" He looked at her. So sweet and boyish, she thought. "Here it is." He licked his lips, looked down. "Now the first came forth, red all over like a hairy garment; and they named him Esau. And after that came his brother out, and his hand took hold on Esau's heel; and his name was called Jacob."

"I'm not red like Esau," she said.

He snapped the Bible shut and smiled. "You should get some rest."

"Will we really go to Vienna?"

"Of course. We'll take an apartment." He rubbed his hands together, standing at the door. "We can afford it. That's the thing. Whatever we want, Julia, we can have."

Suddenly there was money, a fat fruit low hanging.

She turned away and yawned. "Whatever I want," she said, thinking he was really a bit of a fool. It made her feel strangely protective toward him, as if he were an overexcited child that needed calming down. "What *do* I want?"

He laughed. "Whatever it is, you can have it."

"I'd like a little house," she said. "So I could make it nice. And enough so I don't have to worry and I can buy nice clothes and—" But there she stopped because it didn't seem real, and her eyes grew sad. Full of champagne and excitement, Theo felt sentimental, almost tearful.

"You have nice eyes, Julia," he said.

She thought, does he want to make me cry?

"Get some sleep," he said, and went out, closing the door. Yes, poor girl, a nice house. Nice clothes. Ask for more, girl, why not? He needed to walk. It was cold. He put up his collar and strode through dark windy streets. By the station he came upon a beggar wrapped in a blanket, a tiny thing with small hands like a child and a man's pinched face. "Here, friend," he said.

The man took the money, folding it in his fist, saying nothing. His fingers were ice cold.

"Money," said Theo and laughed, a fond and rueful little snort, as if money were a much-loved and indulged bad child. He walked on. Not a thing in my pockets, he remembered. Should have stopped to talk. I was once like you, my friend. It comes and goes. Oh, how it does. Should have sat right down with him, said, let me tell you a story. A couple of days after my father died—pneumonia, double—I was clearing out the house. Do you know how many Knickerbocker soda bottles I found? You wouldn't believe it. Two hundred and thirty-three. And in every one, screwed up and stuffed in hard, money. Sitting on treasure like a drunk old dragon for years while everything fell apart around him and my uncles doled out charity. Like I said, it comes and goes. Life's a joke.

———

The second night went even better. The cheers, the whistles, the thunder of feet and the storm of applause, everything the same except that when she came offstage, instead of smiles and roses there were just gawping stagehands and stony-faced policemen looking at her with veiled eyes.

And Theo, wild-eyed, looking as if someone had just punched him in the stomach. "They're closing us down," he said, white and furious. "Can you believe it? They're closing us down."

"Why?"

"Because—I don't know—because they're fools!"

The officer in charge was a heavy-jowled, world-weary man. "No need for that at all," he said in English. "We have to act. Simple as that. Nothing I can do."

Everyone gabbled at once. Huber, the manager, pop-eyed and desperate, argued tensely in German with the police and with Theo. The other actors were worried about their pay.

"I don't understand you," Theo enunciated fiercely, as if to an idiot. "I don't speak the language well."

"There have been complaints," the man said, "more than a few. We have to act."

"You see?" said Huber in English, rounding on Theo, "What am I to do?"

"What am *I* to do?"

She didn't like these professionally careful stares. She, the consummate gatherer of stares. She dropped her eyes.

"Please, gentlemen," Huber said, "this way."

Everyone trailed into his office, forgetting her. A rearguard of stony official men remained with her in the corridor. Their eyes never left her, and she wondered if she were under arrest. But why?

"I have permission from the authorities to stage this show," Theo was saying in Huber's office, his voice loud but unsteady. "We've been through all this. It's a play. A play, not a monster show. Miss Pastrana is a legitimate performer. Have you even read the reviews?"

"Don't show me that," the man said, "there's nothing I can do. I have orders to close you down, and I have to do it." The sound of papers unfolding and rustling, then a crack. Theo's hand smacking down on Huber's desk.

"This is outrageous!"

The policeman was unmoved. "I am sorry," he said, "I have to inform you, sir, that this show is accused of obscenity and immorality and has been deemed dangerous."

"Dangerous? *Dangerous?*"

She went to the door. No one stopped her. She could see the back of Theo's head and Huber in profile picking at his lip. The policeman's eyebrows were stoically raised, his eyes downturned. He addressed a long torrent of words in German at Huber, and the manager took out a gray silk handkerchief and dabbed his sweaty brow.

"What's he saying, what's he saying?" Theo sounded near to tears.

"Bestiality," said Huber queasily. "He's saying they're calling it bestiality."

"What!"

Another torrent.

"Also"—Huber glanced quickly sideways, his eyes catching her at the door and sliding away—"there's been some concern—a doctor—doctors."

"Doctors?"

"These are my instructions," the policeman said in English, sitting down behind the desk, "I have no choice."

"They're saying," said Huber, "that her face might be dangerous for any pregnant women in the audience."

"What are you talking about?"

"That her face might—cause some misfortune—to the mother—the baby—"

"What!"

"Miscarriage—"

Theo laughed, a hard cry of a laugh.

"Spoil the baby," Huber went on, as the policeman rambled on in German, scribbling notes on a piece of paper. "Make it like her."

She didn't wait to hear more. She went back to her dressing room, closed the door and sat looking in the mirror. Someone had stuck a colored drawing in the side of the glass. It showed a handsome round building in a grand park, with elegant people strolling about in front. *Dear Miss Pastrana,* the writing said, *here is a picture of one of the many beautiful buildings in the glorious city of Vienna—your friend, Hermann Otto.*

The scent of flowers was thick.

Theo bashed the door open. "Those idiots. Those beasts. They're living in the Middle Ages."

Julia veiled and stood up, began putting on her shawl. "Is it very cold outside?" she asked.

He stalked about, venomous. "Aren't you angry?" He stopped, glaring at her. "Aren't you furious?"

"Is it snowing?"

She wouldn't look at him.

"How can you stand there like that?" he said. "How can you be *calm?*"

"So what now?" She stood by the door.

"How would *I* know?" His hair stuck up greasily. "Damn Huber carrying on as if it's my fault. How was I supposed to know these benighted peasants believe in old wives' tales? Obscene! *They're* obscene! I hate them!"

Someone came to the door and said the carriage was ready.

"I've never liked Leipzig."

The drunker Theo got, the more bullish he became, striding up and down her room with a glass in his hand, spilling pale liquid over his fingers.

"When were you here before, Theo?" She was sitting on the end of the bed, twisting a ribbon between her fingers. A fire blazed in the grate.

"Ten years ago." He stood looking down into the fire, remembering the Gatti Twins, the awful awakening from his first great venture. "I'm done with this place now," he said, "it's bad luck for me. We shouldn't even have come. Stupid." He hit himself on the head. "Fool you are, Theo! Should have gone straight to Vienna. That's what we'll do, that's what's next. I'll get onto old Otto first thing. Vienna!"

He walked over to the window, lifted the curtain and stood looking out at the snow falling fast across the flat white facade of the buildings opposite.

"I wonder," he said, "what's next."

Suddenly afraid, Julia began to cry.

"Huber just standing there, saying, 'yes, sir, no, sir, three bags full, sir.' Looking at me as if everything was my fault."

A formless gloom was on her, and she felt far from home. Certain words had cut. Obscenity. Not ugly, she knew she was that. Fact was fact. Ugly was ugly and beauty was beauty, and nothing anyone could do about that. But obscene? Immoral?

"Bestial," she said.

He turned sharply.

"After all, what am I really?" Her voice was thick.

"Are you crying?"

"What if I am? What am I?" She laughed. "It isn't *who* am I? It isn't who am I? I know who I am, I'm Julia. It's *what* I am."

Oh God, poor creature, poor creature, he thought.

"Julia," he said, striding across the room and falling on his knees in that ridiculous theatrical way she was getting used to, grabbing both her hands. "I will not have you bothered by ignoramuses and bigots. The words that drip out of their mouths are worth less than the spewings of a sewer. They don't matter."

"Don't be silly," she said.

"Julia, forget them."

"How can I? I blight babies in the womb."

Don't, he thought. I can't deal with this. "*They're* the ugly ones," he said hopelessly, but she pulled her hands from his and covered her face. "You're much better than them. Stronger," he said, but she just shook her head and turned away. He got up, sat down beside her, putting one arm around her shoulders. Touching her sent a thrill of excitement up his arm.

"I want to go home," she said, stiffening.

"Home?"

"Mexico. Home. They'd have me back."

"Ssh!"

"At least they didn't hide their babies."

"We'll go to Vienna," he said. His arm felt awkward.

"It'll be the same there."

"No, it won't, I promise you."

She started wiping her face with the ribbons.

"Here." He gave her his handkerchief. "What do fools matter? You can't let this stop you."

He took his arm away.

"You're a wonder," he said. "A fascination. A miracle."

Julia dried her face and composed herself.

"The people who really count adore you," he said. "They go home and tell everyone—when they're old, they'll tell their grandchildren—how they saw the great Julia Pastrana on the stage, how beautifully she danced and sang, and how charming she was afterward when they shook her hand."

"No," she said.

"They'll remember you all their lives."

She turned to look at him. "I don't think so. I think they just go home and say, guess what? I saw a monkey in a dress today."

Theo said nothing. The shine of tears caught in the down on her cheek. Poor soul, he thought. "I'll never put you through that again," he said.

"I know you won't." She sniffed, wiping her face, "Because I won't do it. I'll go home." She was starting to cry again.

After all, he thought, it's only like stroking a dog. It's only hair.

"You don't want to go home," he said, putting his arms 'round her and stroking her big shaggy head. "You don't want to go home, Julia. And be a servant again?"

No one had held her since she was small. Solana probably, it was hard to remember. Maybe even her mother. There had once been arms around her though, she was sure of it. "I wouldn't be a servant," she said, closing her eyes. "I have some money now, I could be independent."

"Of course," he said, "in a few years, but not now. Not while everything is so perfect for you. They want you in Russia. They want you in Warsaw and Prague. In Vienna. Everyone wants you."

The embrace had become stiff.

"We'll throw that stupid play aside and carry on as we were." His voice was strained. "Just you and your talent. There's so much waiting for you, Julia."

"You know, Theo," she said, and her voice was steady again. "I really don't know what I am."

He drew back. This was the moment when in any normal circumstance there would have been a kiss, she even saw the flicker of it in his eyes, but she also saw that he simply couldn't do it.

"It's all right, Theo," she said, and smiled, and a peculiar understanding passed between them.

"Julia, I will never abandon you. Never. I will always look after you, I promise." He smiled and proclaimed with mock solemnity, "I will look after you in this dark, dirty little world," then laughed and kissed her forehead, drew her head down and stroked again. "You have lovely hair," he said.

I t was all off with Laurie. Adam had hung around and hung around, till the right night came, rain, candles, her birthday cards fluttering from the mantelpiece at regular intervals, one from her mother, one from her brother, one from Auntie Irene and Uncle Bob who she hadn't seen since 1962 when they came to her father's funeral. A world beyond this house. He didn't know her, he realized, didn't know her at all. Who are these parents? These people? Oh, they were just parents, she said. You know. They were OK, I suppose. That scar? How d'you get that scar? Wouldn't you like to know? Fought a bear.

She'd teased her hair out in a big bush and wore a red hat on top of it. Bright red lipstick too, a big wide slash of it to match the hat. This room, this house, this whole smoky moment, stuck in time, as every moment surely is. The raw rich smell of burning herb, the thick dope air. Ultrareal. She rolled and licked and lit a cigarette casually, as if her hands had done it a million times.

"Oh, Rosie, my little Rosie, my little Rose," Adam said, then felt a fool and didn't know what to do.

She smiled. Then kissed him.

Ever since, they'd been in bed more or less all the time. The rest of life stopped. Of course lust was in it, but it was love more than anything he'd known. He thought it might kill him.

"I'll go down with you," he said, "if that's what you want."

"Go down where?"

"Wherever you're going. The rabbit hole. Madness. I don't care."

"What?" She was hardly listening. "What are you talking about?"

"Nothing, nothing."

Forget all. Forget and fall. Skyscrapers rise, grand edifices of junk, towers, a wooden cobra, teddy bears and dolls, pictures, ropes, Buddha, a horse, old jigsaws, shells, ashtrays, boxes and bottles, umbrellas, fans, books, books, books. Chewed pencil stubs among the shoelaces and discarded shopping lists, the boxes things came in.

The madness increases. The weeks roll on, four, five, six, more, forever. Getting on for six months, and he'd look at her and wonder what was real, this or some odd remembered thing, far down at the other end of a telescope, a life as unreal as the mother, the brother, the auntie and uncle, all that mysterious stuff she dragged behind her, her backdrop; only this was his backdrop, the piano in the school hall, his uncle Tommy's grayhound, his grandma, his mates, the band he was in, the drawings he did all over the walls in his room. A whole existence she'd never know, just as he'd never know hers.

He started painting her.

Draped, naked, sleeping, bathing, reading, at a window, in shadow, in white like an angel, fully clothed, made up like a forties movie star, full face, close-up, profile, distorted. All in purple. Photorealist, impressionist, in miniature, on a vast canvas or on the wall, in pencil, watercolor, oils, acrylics.

He never painted anything else ever again, just her, and the funny thing was, nothing he ever painted after he met her was ever as good as his old stuff. He knew it wasn't going to last. It was like drinking for the moment, not caring about the hangover. If he'd been wood or sad plastic, torn or fragile, worthless, she'd have put him on her shelf and kept him forever. Now and again her heart would have bled softly for him. People though—people with their mysterious pesky hearts—she couldn't cope with that. The way she'd turned on a dime with poor old Laurie, one day all over him, the next just a friend, surprised and mildly indignant at his grief. It'd be the same with him when his time came. And in the end she'd be alone because it was the only way she could be, and he wondered what it was in that bland otherworld of mother, brother, uncle and auntie that had made her that way.

A HUMAN MONSTER

Readers will recall last week's report concerning the furore at Leipzig's Kroll Theatre. The outcry, which resulted in the immediate closure of *Der Curierte Meyer,* a lively little musical comedy, was a consequence of several impassioned complaints from both citizens and members of the medical establishment concerned about the possible harmful effects of the public's exposure to its lead performer, the remarkable Julia Pastrana. In short, it was decided that the theater's aesthetic frame was harmed by association with this deformed creature.

What are we to make of this? Very little, one imagines. There is nothing new about the display of human oddities. The problem arises when the sideshow is brought into a respectable theater. Yet we learn that Miss Pastrana has graced the stage of the St. Charles in New Orleans, where once the divine Jenny Lind enchanted the cream of society. She has been guest of honor at military balls, converses ably, sings tolerably, dances prettily and speaks three languages. Unfortunately German is not one of them, as I discovered when I interviewed her in her dressing room at Wirth's Circus. Her English, though, is fluent, so we got along remarkably well.

Miss Pastrana is a young woman of 23. By birth a Mexican Indian, she grew up in the Spanish Catholic household of the state governor of Sinaloa. I cannot begin to convey the full horror of her appearance. The accompanying pencil drawing, brilliant as it is, does not do her justice. No mere representation could. For the full effect, you must see the shine in her depthless black eyes. You must hear the voice, low and womanly, emerging from the thick-lipped mouth, catch the occasional glimpse of the lumpy muscle mass of tongue as she speaks, the veritable rampart of coral-like excrescence behind those lips. Her nostrils are vast, her nose wide-bridged and domed. Her head is very large in relation to her body, her shoulders broad, her bosom voluptuous. She is absolutely covered in thick black hair, face and all, except for the palms of her hands, which are dusky rose and delicate. There is a melancholy in the eyes, which causes pity. I do not think she is very intelligent but she does seem to be aware of her situation.

"Miss Pastrana, life must have changed so much for you."

"So much!"

"Is it tiring for you to be so constantly traveling?"

"Of course, sometimes. But there's good and bad in every situation. Sometimes I get tired, but if I wasn't traveling I wouldn't be seeing so many interesting places and meeting so many people."

"Would you describe yourself as a happy person?"

"Sometimes one thing, sometimes another—"

You tell them, Julia. You tell them. You show them. Theo had given her a glass of wine for confidence before he let the man in. *You remember—*

"In fact," she said with that terrible smile, "the entire experience has been wonderful. I have sold out theaters in America and England. This small upset in Leipzig—that is nothing."

She had dressed herself carefully, done her hair, thought herself back into a defiant state of mind, composed herself in dignity and made herself cheerful.

By God, you're a tower of strength, he'd said, his lips brushing her fingertips.

"Does it pain you, Miss Pastrana? Your condition. You are clearly a creature of . . ."

"Sometimes."

. . . I cannot imagine the loneliness of this woman's life. And yet she appears content. The question of course that is never asked but is in every mind is the question of romance. How can such as she aspire to the joys of womankind? One cannot imagine she will ever marry or experience motherhood. And yet she clearly has a mind capable of understanding her situation. I would not have raised the issue had she not mentioned it herself toward the end of our interview, when the artist had done his work and was preparing to show his subject her image.

"They all want to know the same things," she suddenly informed me, and affirmed that the audiences she was used to always asked, have you ever been in love? Do you have a beau? Will you ever get married? At which she laughed and said that so far she had received at least twenty proposals of marriage. When I asked why she had not blessed one of the candidates with her hand, she replied, "They weren't good enough."

Germany sold out. The circuses at Vienna and Budapest sold out.

"You see," said Theo, "now they show some respect."

She would fall only half asleep on a train and all the circuses and stages and sideshows of here, there and everywhere took to spinning in her head, the crowds awestruck, agape, eyes out of control. Robin Adair, Old Zip Coon, redskins, Chinamen with cues, "I Dreamt I Dwelt," real slave darkey slapping on his thigh, ladies, gentlemen, the eighth wonder of the world, the incredible ape woman, ugliest in existence.

In came the money.

The circuits crossed, crisscrossed, faces came, went, reappeared, faded, loomed. She never forgot one. Some of the old ones from America turned up from time to time. She met Ted in Freiberg, Maud Sparrow and her husband in Pizen, but it was never Myrtle Dexter and Delia Mounier, Armless and Legless Dancing Wonders, or Zeo the Wild Human, and at times she still remembered with a pang the feeling of being in Madame Soulie's yard in New Orleans: Delia wanting to comb her hair, Cato hanging 'round the door, Myrtle making a crimson bow of her mouth at the mirror.

I was happy then, she thought. Am I not happy now?

I'm happier, much happier, rattling along with Theo in carriages and trains, all this traveling together, a kind of peace between us. If I didn't look like this, she thought. Theo and Julia. Julia and Theo. Everything changes, everything moves on, he'll be gone too, like Solana, her old face, her boys long gone, turned legend. That's what time does.

Then she'd feel as if a great wave bigger than the world was coming, the whole of the sea rearing up like a living beast, slow but sure, rolling over everything. When she got scared, she'd slip her hand under his arm. It was warm there, and he never seemed to mind. Sometimes he'd smile but go on reading his paper.

One day in Bautzen, waiting for a coach, Theo said, "This looks like your pinhead."

She leaned over his arm and looked at the picture in the paper he was reading. A sawdust ring. Plumed white horses. Circus, Rakovnik. Acrobats, jugglers, rope dancers, magicians, a boy with three legs, clowns, puppets, dancing dogs. And Zeo the Wild Human.

"That sound like him?"

"Oh, Cato, Cato," she said. "That's him. Oh, yes! Oh, Theo, can we go there? Please? Can we go there? I'd love to see Cato again."

"Oh, you know what it's like, Julia," he said. "We'll probably run into him somewhere along the line if he's crossed the herring pond. We can't just go running off willy-nilly though, can we? We're tied up for the next six weeks at least."

Three months later they caught up with the Circus Raniello in Prague. Not a bad idea, Theo said, we should get you on a horse. Wait and see, they'll be glad to have you. And indeed the man's eyes bugged out of his head when she raised her veil. "Oh, *sì*," he said, "*sì, sì, sì, sì, sì* . . ."

His English was poor but Theo could muddle along in Italian and she caught a few words here and there. Money. Zlatkas, escudos, dollars. Laughter. Out came a bottle of wine and two glasses.

"*E per la mia signora . . .*" said Theo, turning and gesturing toward her. A third glass was produced.

"You don't have to do any fancy tricks," Theo said, "just ride into the ring and do a couple of circuits. Maybe just one or two little tricks if you feel you could . . ."

The man had bright eyes in a square brown face. They moved on and off her face as he poured her a drink.

"Oh, I can ride," she said, "I used to ride Marta's pony. Ask him where Cato and Ezra are. Zeo."

More babble. A lot of babble. The man's face was shiny, as if someone had spent all morning polishing it.

"They're in the town," Theo said. "There's a house."

Here in the park, the wagons made a small village along the edge of a meadow, by the trees. But some of the company were in a house nearby, Raniello said. The landlady was very good, very discreet, no trouble at all, and very reasonable. They were taken on for a two-week run till their Vienna season should begin, given two rooms in the old house, a part of a tenement, with a courtyard and many stairs and unexpected passages leading into unknown realms. The landlady lived on the ground floor with her son, and the show people kept to the second floor on the right-hand side of the courtyard.

When Ezra Porter heard from the landlady that his friend Julia Pastrana was here, he came lolloping down the passage like an enthusiastic bear. "What a gift, what a gift!" he kept saying, grinning hard, shaking her vigorously by the hand over and over again. His chin looked bigger, more double. He was trying to grow whiskers but you could see it was a struggle. Apart from his head hair he was smooth like an Indian, even his chest. She knew this from seeing him wash it at the pump in Madame Soulie's yard. Hovering with his smile and raised brows in the background, Theo was thinking, this isn't a bad setup, not bad at all. Wonder if he plays poker. When the girl came out, thin, very dark, sour-mouthed, with her arms folded in front of her, she stared at Julia's heavily veiled face, then looked at him but didn't smile.

"Theo," Julia said, "this is Ezra Porter. This is my manager, Theo, Theo Lent . . . oh, hello, Berniece . . . where's Cato?"

"Asleep," Berniece said.

"Go and wake him," said Ezra.

"You go and wake him."

"Oh, no, don't wake him!" Julia said. "How is he?"

"Oh, fine."

"No, he isn't," said Berniece, "he's been having an earache."

"Yes, but it's on the mend now."

"You're not the one that's up all night with him," Berniece muttered, clicking her nails.

"Look, my room's just here," said Julia.

"Terrific! Mrs. Vels! Mrs. Vels!" Ezra called down to the landlady, a worn-down, kind-faced woman who was halfway up the stairs with a bowl of water. "You don't mind if we change rooms with Angelo, do you?"

"Don't ask me," she said, "ask him."

Ezra rapped on the door of the room next to Julia's, and it opened at once as if the person on the other side had been listening all the time and knew what was going on. Angelo was a beaky Italian with sad eyes. "You wanna move?" he said in a perfect American accent, "fine with me, I gain."

"You do," Ezra agreed, "you get a view over the river and the town."

"Nobody asked me," said Berniece.

"Oh, come on, Niece. You don't mind."

"Suits me," said Angelo. "I got hardly anything to move anyway."

"I have," Berniece told his retreating back.

Mrs. Vels trod heavily across the landing, spilling a little hot water as she went.

"Let me," said Theo.

"For the lady's room," she said patiently, letting him take over.

"Thank you, Mrs. Vels. Julia, you should rest." He smiled his best gracious smile, first at Berniece, then at Ezra. "Don't feel you have to change anything on our account. I wouldn't have anyone inconvenienced."

"Of course," said Ezra. "You must be tired. You been traveling all day? Look—after the show, I'll bring some beer. You come to our room."

Julia left them talking outside, closed the door, took off her boots and looked out of the window, rubbing the toes of one foot wearily against the back of her other leg. The room faced onto the high wall of a farrier's yard, and a narrow alley that ran between one street and another. It was late afternoon. The sky above the rooftops was dove gray. She lay down as she was, under the covers. The fire in the small grate had not yet warmed the room. She was very tired but it was impossible to sleep because of the talking in the passage, the opening and closing of doors, the footsteps on the stairs.

"Ever run into Delia and Myrtle?" Julia asked.

"I did once," said Ezra. "Well, Delia anyway. Myrtle's out of the business. Had a baby. A boy. Got married."

"Delia's on her own?"

"Last I saw."

"You get here now, Cato, I can't stand it." Berniece's lips were set in a straight line. Cato, doing a ridiculous dance, bony knees akimbo, shrieked and squawked in his nightshirt. Wet-eyed with laughter, leaning together like schoolboys giggling at a prank, Theo and Ezra were drunk, and Cato was wild. Since six o'clock he'd been celebrating Julia's reappearance with mad showing off and hysterical dances that grew ever more deranged and frantic.

"He should have been in bed an hour ago," Berniece said.

"Look, Cato," Julia said, "we can have a lovely time tomorrow. We can go and see the horses."

Berniece made a grab for him, but he skipped away and she stumbled.

"Whoa, girl!" Ezra grabbed her elbow.

"*You* do something," she said, pulling away and sitting down. Her face went completely blank, as if someone had just passed a hand in front of it, wiping out sentience.

"Behave, Cato," Ezra said, reaching once more for the vodka.

Cato ran 'round the room drumming on the backs of the chairs, warbling in a reedy falsetto. He stopped, hunchbacked in front of Theo, leaned on his knees and pushed his face up close.

"Hello there," Theo said.

Cato nasaled something.

"Can't understand a word you're saying," said Theo, laughing.

Berniece poured a shot of vodka and knocked it back as if it were poison. "This room's not as nice as our old one," she said.

"It's fine," said Ezra expansively.

"All we've got is a wall." She looked at Julia. "We could see all the people going up and down the street."

"You really didn't have to move on our account," Julia said. "We could have visited just as well in your old room."

"That's what *I* said."

"But this is nice," said Ezra. "I mean, think about it. He gets on so well with Julia. They're great together. Once he's settled down—"

"He means he wants you to babysit," said Berniece, pouring herself another and twisting one leg behind the other awkwardly.

"She don't have to babysit if she don't want to," Ezra said stoutly, "I never said no such thing. But Julia never used to mind watching him now and then, did you, Julia?"

"Not at all."

"It's no big thing," said Ezra.

"Christ, no," said Theo. "We all help each other out."

"See."

Berniece threw back her head and poured the liquor down her throat.

"You know," said Julia, "I don't mind looking after Cato at all. He always behaved quite well for me."

"Ha!" said Berniece.

Cato wheeled away from Theo's knee, landed by Berniece and scrambled messily up onto her lap, pulling up her skirts with his bare feet trampling into her, arms clamping 'round her neck in an urgent stranglehold. "Cato . . ." she said, desperately trying to cover her legs, the white bloomers bunched at the knees. "Oh, please . . ." He kissed her, jumped down, stood in front of the fire doing funny faces, switching between a frown and a smile, on, off, on, off, getting quicker and quicker till all of them, willing or not, were laughing.

"Don't laugh!" Berniece said, laughing herself, "it makes him worse."

On, off, on, off, past funny to scary.

"Stop it."

"How does he *do* that?" Theo offered Ezra a cigar.

Julia got up. "Come on now," she said, "you show me where you sleep."

"Naah!"

"Yes!"

"Do as you're told now," said Ezra.

"Show me your bed, Cato. Come on." Julia took his hand and led him behind the screen to his cot, which had been made up very cozily with an eiderdown and bolster up against the wall.

"Dark!" he said.

"Nice!"

He threw himself backward on the bed, just missing banging the long cone of his head on the wall.

"Well, aren't you lucky to have such a lovely cozy bed. Get under and I'll tuck you in."

"You should give him a dose of cordial," she heard Theo say.

"Can't get it down him," Ezra replied.

Cato got in and lay down, and she tucked him in and gave him a kiss. He was like a bird that chirped away till you put the cover on the cage. Before long, the darkness in his den had put him out.

"Niece," Ezra was saying, as she emerged from behind the screen, "I don't go out that much."

"Yes, you do." Berniece lit a match.

Theo winked at Julia, and she smiled. It was nice, as if they were an "us" like Ezra and Berniece.

"Is he asleep?" asked Ezra.

"Of course he is." Berniece blew smoke and clanked the bottle neck on the rim of her glass. "She's got the golden touch. Haven't you, missy?"

"Come and sit here, Julia," said Theo, patting the seat beside him. "Have a drink. Where's your glass?"

"Only one more. And water please."

"Oh, horrors! Water!" Berniece said, head wreathed in smoke.

The drink flowed. The men guffawed like boys over stupid things, Berniece scrunched herself up small on her chair and bit her nails, swinging her slippered foot. Julia, sipping, smiled and looked around her, bright-eyed, wondering if this could be a new thing of belonging, like Madame Soulie's yard, but the more she thought about it, the more she doubted. She thought of Myrtle married, a mother, and looked at Theo, the way when he giggled his grin made a childish slash in his face, the way the greased hair fell loose across his forehead. She could never have him. What a thing to think, even for a second. When she closed her eyes, she saw New Orleans, the carriage taking her to Bayou Road to see John Montanee, the streets sliding by, the moon full and high, a face in the sky. Her hand went into the pocket of her skirt to the little bottle with its few remaining drops of love potion.

"Shh!" said Berniece to the men. "You'll wake him up."

"He never wakes once he's gone off." Ezra stood up and hovered about with a soft silly look on his face.

"What are you looking for?" Berniece kicked him lightly.

"I thought we had some lemons."

"We did. We do."

"Have you ever had vodka with hot water and lemon juice, Theo?"

"Can't say I have."

"Oh, let me make it." Julia jumped up. "I know how to do that."

She stood by the window watching as Ezra lifted a pan from the stovetop. "Let me squeeze the lemons," she said, and when it was all done and she'd run across and taken Theo's remaining drink from him and poured it into the steaming cup, she turned her back on the room, retrieving the bottle from her pocket and emptying the last three or four drops in with the rest.

"Here, Theo," she said.

"Listen to them," Berniece said, "listen out there." She'd thrown up the window and was leaning over, looking down into the alley. The sound of drunks singing their way home floated up. Suddenly she turned. "You can get out onto the roof," she said, looking at Julia. "Want to see?"

"I'd love to." Julia had poured herself a hot drink too. She lifted the cup and let the sharp aroma swim about her nostrils.

"My God," said Berniece in a low voice.

She's looking at my nose, Julia thought. The way my nostrils move.

"Come on." Berniece stood up, flounced across to the door. "This way, this way." She led along the passage and up to the attic, a long row of rooms with a long dormer window opposite looking out onto a wide flat space between the yard and the street. The tiles were warm, and they sat down side by side looking up at a sky full of stars. The moon was a wide crescent.

"Well," said Berniece, "it's nice to have someone new to talk to. You've been around a bit, hey?"

"All over the place," said Julia.

"Same with us. You think, oh, here we go, the romance, the road, all the strange people . . . you been to Paris?"

"No, not Paris. We were going to, but they wrote horrible things about me so we didn't go."

"Me neither. I want to go there."

"I go to a lot of places," Julia said, "but I don't really see them. I can't go out like other people, so it's . . ."

"I know! You think: oh! I've been to Amsterdam and Cologne and

Berlin and what have I seen? Walls. Stuck in with Cato. It's like having a baby. Not that I'd know."

Berniece blew smoke at the sky.

"Don't you like it on the road?" said Julia. "I do. I like all the new places. Everything new. Voices. Trees. Money."

"But you don't see it," said Berniece.

"Sometimes I go out with my veil on. But I have to be very careful." Julia smiled. "I went for a walk in New York once. I got on a trolleybus."

"I can't even do that with Cato," said Berniece, closing her eyes and leaning her head back against the sloping tiles. "It's really just too much trouble taking him out. Everyone at him all the time. Can't leave him alone, trailing after him like the Pied Piper. He likes it at first, and then he gets upset and some of them are cruel. It's not worth it." She yawned and opened her eyes. "God, it's just so beautiful up here," she said. Down below, the neighborhood cats cried viciously at one another.

"Listen to them," Julia said, thinking of the devil baby. Poor, poor thing.

"I'm run off my feet," said Berniece, "and Ezra's not really very good with him. Just lets him do what he wants. I'm just a nursemaid really."

"I once knew this girl," said Julia. "I don't know how old she was. Her hair was going gray but I don't think she was very old. She was unhappy all the time. She kept wanting to go home, but then she didn't really want to when it came to it. I don't know why she was so unhappy. Always crying, all the time like a leaky faucet. She could sit on her own head and cross her feet under her head like a bow."

Berniece laughed.

"Zelda."

The cats had shut up, and the sudden silence startled them.

"People come and go," said Berniece.

Julia stood up and walked a little way along the tiles. "You don't want to be like her," she said. "Always wanting to be somewhere else. Even if she got to wherever it was she was wanting to get to, she'd still want to be somewhere else."

Across the low wall, Julia saw roofs, slope after slope, all silver.

"You're not stupid, are you?" said Berniece.

"I don't think so." Julia turned her head. "Are you?"

Berniece laughed. "I'll say one thing," she said. "You sure do meet some unusual people in this line of work."

"You should be glad you've got a nice man like Ezra," Julia said, sitting down again. "He's nice, Ezra, don't you think?"

"Of course he's nice." Berniece looked away, and that blank look came over her again. "Know what I liked most about him when I met him? Cato. The way he was with Cato. I thought, here's this poor little freak and isn't he lucky he landed with this kind man and not some other." She leaned her head back against the slope of the roof. "Some of them out there, you know," she said, "they're terrible. You're all right though, aren't you, with Theo? Funny thing, you and him."

"Well," said Julia, and could think of no more to say, wondering what it was that was pressing down on her, some feeling. She got up again and walked to the low wall.

"Certainly wasn't Ezra's looks I went for," Berniece said. "Looked like a cross between a three-year-old and a bear."

There was a clattering and a clumping, and the heads of the men poked through the window.

"Come out," Berniece said. "See how pretty it is."

"Julia?" Theo's voice.

"I'm over here."

"What are you doing?" he asked.

"Looking."

"Looking at what?"

Theo materialized behind her, smelling of liquor. She sensed him swaying slightly and closed her eyes, wondering what was wrong with her. A mood of roaming sadness was on her, the kind she used to get, when Solana would flick her with a cloth and say, never mind, put it behind you, whatever it is, come on, there's all this to be washed. The old kitchen. The tiles. The smell of pepper. The cats in the alley were yowling at the moon again. The devil baby darted among the chimneys. She felt sad for the moment she was in, as if it had already gone, this night, the four of them drunk on this Prague rooftop.

"Julia," said Theo, "we'll try you on a horse tomorrow. Shall we?"

"Wonderful," she said.

"You know, he's not a real showman, Ezra isn't," he said later, saying good night outside her door, "not from way way back like me, he just sort of drifted into it from meeting someone on the line between New Orleans and St. Louis."

Poor Theo, she thought later, lying in bed as the cats wailed, a sound like the devil baby breaking its heart in the alley. Her sadness coalesced around Theo, the pathos of his ridiculous knowing smile that really wasn't sure of very much. All the time building himself up, telling himself he matters, she thought. He knew a million people and none of them really liked him. She saw that now and it made her care all the more for him, because he wasn't a bad man and it wasn't fair.

———

It took less than a week for Julia to become Circus Ranielli's main attraction. Every night she rode into the ring on a white horse called Sister who performed so subtly and smoothly at the merest tightening of a knee that soon the spectacle of this wild, black beast woman on what might as well have been a unicorn was pulling in crowds the like of which Ranielli had never known. He upped the money.

Hermann Otto wrote, Vienna awaited, agog. Miss Gossmann sent her warmest regards, and begged Julia's presence at a dinner party she intended to give upon their arrival.

"Now that," said Theo, "is something. That, I have to say, is not nothing." He stood in her open doorway, leaning sideways, feet crossed. "Do you know how famous that woman is? She knows everyone. If *she's* putting the word about—"

"Friederike," Julia said. "She was nice."

"She loved you."

"She did, didn't she?"

"Mad about you."

"She was nice. She looked at me as if I was—"

"The Cricket," he said. "Never saw it, myself. Wildly successful. Some romantic thing."

"A play?"

"With music. The woman has a voice, but not to match yours."

Ezra came up beside him with Cato. "Seen Berniece?"

"No," said Theo, standing aside. Cato ambled in, mumbling sleepily to himself, attached himself to Julia's skirt with his fists and closed his eyes.

"He's supposed to be asleep," said Ezra. "He won't go off without her."

"I heard her go out about midday," Julia said. She'd heard their voices next door, Ezra's high and complaining, Berniece's faintly mocking. Then Berniece had left, slamming the door behind her and whistling her way downstairs.

It was two o'clock now. The afternoon threatened rain.

"Can I leave him here for a bit?" said Ezra. "He won't stay on his own. I'm going down to the showground, see if she's there."

"Of course," said Julia, prizing Cato's fingers from her skirt and leading him to the bed. "Lie down here now," she said. "Here we are, let me move this pillow."

He lay down, still mumbling. His fingers were wet and had left marks on her skirt. "Close your eyes now," she said. Ezra went to get his boots and Theo followed, talking excitedly about the Cricket, Vienna, opportunity. "Goddamn it, he's moved my boots again," she heard Ezra say. She sighed. "I need my afternoon sleep too," she told Cato. Already he was beginning to snore softly. Someone came running up the stairs, much too light to be Mrs. Vels, and Berniece appeared at the door, flushed and cheery.

"Julia!" she said, leaning in, fanning herself with a couple of letters she was holding. She crossed the room with clumsy, drunken grace. "And here's my little man!"

"He's asleep," said Julia, raising a finger to her lips.

They were drinkers, Ezra and Berniece, but she'd never seen either of them this drunk this early in the day before.

"Oh, sure, sure, I'll take him off your hands." Berniece leaned over the bed, an invisible cloud of ale and orris root wafting out from her. "There's letters for you, Julia."

"Letters?"

She held them out. "Just arrived. Vels gave them to me as I was coming up."

Julia looked at them, surprised. "Who are they from?"

Berniece hiccupped loudly and laughed, squaring her shoulders to lift Cato. "Well, how would I know that, darling? Ez!" Surprisingly strong, she hauled Cato up, and he flopped over her arms, open-mouthed.

"Here," she said when Ezra appeared in the doorway, "take him."

Julia slipped the letters under her pillow quickly.

"Where've you been?" Ezra looked embarrassed. "I was just about to go and look for you."

"Nowhere," said Berniece, sinking down into a chair and swinging her legs over the side. "Ez!" She pulled pins out of her hair. "Fetch me a drink."

"I'm not getting you a drink, Niece," said Ezra, Cato over his shoulder like a sack. "And Julia doesn't want you in her room in that condition."

"What condition?" Berniece threw a hairpin at him, but he grabbed her hand and pulled her to her feet. "Come on," he said, "Give Julia some peace."

She trailed after him, hair half up, half down. "You're a pal for looking after my little beast, Julia," she said.

"My pleasure," said Julia, closing the door gratefully and locking it. She could hear them on the landing with Theo, and knew that Berniece, drunk-silly, would be flirting with Theo. That's what she did. He never responded, except occasionally to meet Julia's eyes and smile and raise his eyebrows as if to say, what can I do? And Julia would feel gratified that he did so, but irritated anyway by the slender grace of Berniece as she flopped tipsily around in front of him.

Julia ripped open the first letter, read it twice in the window's light, ripped open the second and read that too. Then she read them both again slowly. "I believe your career should move away from vaudeville and into the concert hall . . . classical training . . . culture. A more refined audience than perhaps you have been used to." And this other one. Offers. More money. Numbers.

I could leave, she thought. These are good offers. I could live in Vienna. Friederike would introduce me to all her friends.

She closed the shutters and lay down. But I'm with Theo, she thought. What did I sign? I did sign something but it was ages ago. What would Delia and Myrtle say? Got lax, girl. Get it in writing. Know your worth. He's only a manager. Her eyes filled with tears. Only a manager like Rates or Beach. I could leave him. I'm free.

She pulled Yatzi from under the pillow. "What shall I do?" she asked him.

"I've had a couple of offers," she said the next day.

They were at the circus; she'd just finished a show, and she was still veiled. It was easier veiled.

"Offers?" Theo had been packing her costume into a case, but he stopped and looked up.

"Oh, yes," she said, "one looks quite interesting."

"What?" he said. "What offers? Who said? How do you know?"

"I got a couple of letters," she said casually.

"*I* didn't see any letters."

"Why would you, Theo?"

"Can I see?"

"I don't have them on me."

He frowned. "Where are they?"

"Back in my room, of course."

"Why didn't you tell me?" He sounded hurt.

"Didn't seem important. I haven't really thought about them yet."

"But why didn't you tell me?" He snapped the case shut. "Didn't you want me to look them over? I wish you'd tell me these things, Julia."

"Oh, well. Sorry, Theo. I just wanted to think about them for a bit." She turned away, fiddling with her hair. "We'd have to think quite seriously about things if I decide—I mean, I need to see—what was it I signed up to? Am I obliged to work out a certain period of time?"

Theo groaned.

"What's the matter?" she said.

He closed his eyes. "You're not seriously . . ."

He felt as if she'd thumped him in the stomach. A wriggling clot of emotions tightened his gut, too tangled to unknot.

"Of course not," she said as if it were nothing, "Just a possibility, that's all. Don't worry, I won't do anything without a lot of careful thought."

But he stood looking stricken. "Oh my God," he said, and she was sorry, so sorry for him, but turned away.

"Don't be silly, Theo," she said. "You know this business better than anyone. You know everyone moves on all the time. It's something we have to face."

She pushed through a flap into a tented area full of props and ropes and buckets, where Ezra sat playing cards with a couple of men. They looked sideways at her, knowing full well what was under that veil. Berniece was looking on, biting her nails, Cato next to her.

"Damn carriage is late," Berniece said. She'd been drinking.

Julia nodded. They sat in silence for a while.

"I might not stay with Theo much longer," she said. "I'm considering options."

"Really?" Berniece perked up. "You had a fight?"

"Of course not. Why do you say that?"

Berniece stuck out her lower lip. "I don't know. Just seems sudden."

"I've had an offer. Two, actually."

Theo appeared. "Carriage is here," he said sulkily.

"Ez!" Berniece threw down the stub of her cigar and stamped on it, staggering sideways.

Back at the house, Julia watched the other three drink far too much. Cato was in bed. Down the corridor Angelo was entertaining a bunch of raucous acrobats in his room overlooking the street. Berniece lay on the floor.

"Who's for craps?" Ezra shook a couple of dice in his fist.

"Sure," said Theo, sitting down at the table. Look at him sulk, she thought. It's not a marriage, is it? What right has he to sulk?

Ezra said, "Shoot."

Theo looked straight at her, as if he could hear her thoughts.

"Shoot," said Ezra.

She looked away.

"So I hear there may be changes afoot," Berniece said, sitting up to pour herself another drink.

"What?"

"What?" Berniece mimicked Ezra. "Julia is considering her options. Opportunity is knocking."

"Oh," said Ezra, "what's turned up, Julia?"

"Nothing definite."

"Some flash dandy creeping in sideways to take her away," said Theo, smiling as if it were all a great joke. "And she's my bread and butter. What do I do now?"

"Well," said Ezra, "I'm sure you'll make the right decision, Julia. Shoot."

Theo lost heavily.

"If I were you"—Ezra pulled in his winnings—"I'd consider all angles very carefully. I don't know about all this chopping and changing. Enough that you're in this business without you going and changing the faces you know all the time for the ones you don't. That's what I think. I'm not passing Cato 'round like a parcel."

There was a silence.

Theo rolled the dice.

"What happens if we have our own baby, Ezra?" asked Berniece.

"Then we have that too."

Berniece jumped up. "I want to go on the roof. Come on, Ezra," she shook his shoulder, "let's go up on the roof."

"Later."

"You're boring," she said. He was about to roll the dice when she punched him hard on the side of his arm, and he dropped them on the floor.

"Christ!" he yelled, giving her a push that wouldn't have amounted to much under normal circumstances, but she was tottering already and her feet flew out from under her. Down she came, landing awkwardly and catching her back on the sharp edge of a drawer that had been left sticking out. She burst into tears, jerked upright and ran out of the room. They heard her stagger down the corridor, bouncing between the walls.

"She's going to the roof," said Julia. "She's not safe."

Ezra was on his knees, looking for the dice. "One of them's rolled under the wardrobe," he said heavily.

"Aren't you going after her?" asked Theo.

"It's gone right to the back," Ezra said.

"You should go after her, Ezra," said Julia. "She might fall off the roof."

"Let her fall," said Ezra flatly.

"You'd feel terrible now if she did," Theo said.

Ezra stood up, fat lower lip hanging childishly. "I'm not going after her," he said, tossing the dice onto the table.

Theo stood with a sigh and a stoic air. "I'll go," he said, and walked out.

An embarrassed air hung in the room.

"I think she's too young," said Ezra bleakly.

"I'm off to bed," said Julia, tired of them all. She left Ezra sitting forlornly in front of the abandoned craps game. Half an hour later, he tapped on her door, and she answered in her nightgown. She'd been lying awake trying to imagine Vienna, which she imagined like the pictures of Vauxhall Gardens, with nicely dressed people strolling around in a leafy parkland.

"What the hell are they doing up there?" Ezra said. "This isn't fair."

"Are they still on the roof?"

"I'm going up," said Ezra, "this is a bad way to behave. I put up with a lot."

"I know you do."

"Shall I go up?" he asked.

"Oh, I don't know, Ezra. Maybe they'll be down in a minute."

"I'm going up. I'll go quiet and catch them at it."

She closed the door. I don't care, she thought, getting into bed. I'm leaving. He can do whatever he likes. She blew out the candle and closed her eyes but her mind couldn't rest, and a few minutes later she heard voices on the landing. Theo saying, "Don't involve me in this," the sound of his door closing, then Ezra, "It's really feeble, you know, the way you've been throwing yourself at him."

Berniece said, "So?"

Their voices went muffled into their room, and a few minutes later someone knocked on the door. Julia groaned.

It was Berniece, with white face and bloodshot eyes. "Can I stay here tonight?" she said, trying to push her way into the room.

"No," said Julia, pushing back.

"Leave Julia alone." Ezra was there, pulling on Berniece's arm. Julia closed the door but the scuffling about and the voices went on till the sound of someone hammering on Theo's door brought her out again. She saw Theo's face, half scared, half amused, peeping through the crack of his door. He'd been listening, you could tell. "Aren't you making a lot out of very little?" he asked before anything could be said.

"If you want her you can have her," Ezra said. "She can do what she wants."

"Look," said Theo in a shaky voice, "you're jumping to ridiculous conclusions."

Ezra marched back to his door. "Go on," he said, passing Berniece standing tearful on the landing, "there he is."

"Ezra!" Berniece cried.

He started getting all her pathetic things together and putting them out in the passage, stony-faced. Down the hall Angelo's door opened and faces appeared.

"Aren't you overreacting a bit?" asked Theo, trying to sound sensible.

Mrs. Vels came up and stood at the head of the stairs watching with her arms folded. "Is there trouble in my house?" she asked loudly.

"Ezra!" screamed Berniece.

"I'm sorry, Mrs. Vels," said Ezra, "really, really sorry. Shut up, Berniece."

Berniece gave a little scream, put her hands on either side of her face as if she were holding her head on and flew into Theo's room, pushing him in and slamming the door.

"There," said Ezra, "it's all sorted out now, Mrs. Vels. Sorry."

"I will not have trouble in my house," said Mrs. Vels.

"No trouble," said Ezra, in and out of the room with things.

"No trouble, sir," she said, "or you must leave."

"No, no trouble, I promise. All over." Ezra straightened, attempting a smile. Mrs. Vels retreated, Angelo's door closed and everything was quiet again. Cato appeared, standing in his long nightie, holding on to the doorframe.

"It's like having two babies now instead of one," said Ezra. "What'll I do?"

Everything's breaking up, Julia thought.

Cato didn't want to go back to bed. She had to sit with him while Ezra got him a drink. "Tell you what," he said, "if they go off together and leave us high and dry, you could come with me and Cato. We'd do all right. Me and Cato, we're going home when all this is over and you could come with us. You could come anyway, if you wanted to. Berniece wouldn't mind."

The door opened quietly. Berniece came in and sat down on the chair by the abandoned craps game.

"I'll go now," said Julia.

Berniece started to sob.

Cato mewed and ran to Berniece. As Julia left, he was wiping her face with the sleeve of his nightie.

Theo sat alone in a corner of the tavern watching the comings and goings. It wasn't yet midday, but he needed the hair of the dog. Last night was crazy. This Berniece thing. Mad. There'd been a horrible moment there when he'd thought he was going to be stuck with her, when she barged into his room and threw herself down in tears on his bed. Christ, it was only a kiss. What the hell. But she'd only wanted to lie there and moan for a bit.

What now? This morning, with a sense of shame, he'd gotten up and sneaked out without seeing anyone, walked along the banks of the river for an hour to clear his head, stood on a bridge and looked at the sunlight jigging on the water. When he turned away, he'd been near blind and bumbled along blinking till he hit this tavern. He leaned back and smoked, dipping his finger in some spilled beer and making patterns on the surface of the table. Few more shows and they were through here. Julia was leaving him. All this stuff, offers, contracts—all getting out of hand. And if not now, then soon. Off with the highest bidder some starry night, just like he'd said. Or back home to Mexico.

And me, he thought grimly, back where I started.

Oh, for God's sake, come to your senses, Theo. You never had a fortune like her before. Never will again. He thought of himself scrabbling about the Continent looking for the next thing. Wouldn't be as good as her whatever it was. Should've saved more. Oh, come on, what are you thinking? She's got no one. Neither have I. She's only a woman when all's said and done. It wasn't the hair. That was the least of it. It was the lips. The whole of the mouth. Not like a woman's mouth, more like an animal's. Not that he'd looked too closely, but her teeth were appalling. There were too many, almost, it seemed when she smiled, a whole rampart of them crowding in behind the front ones, though it was hard to tell. Who could kiss that mouth? It looked as if it would smell but it didn't. She was always very fastidious.

The night in Leipzig, when she was so upset—he'd felt something. He reddened. God knows what. He couldn't remember well. At the time it was just a fleeting thing he'd pushed down, horrified, as it raised its head. Till now, he'd hardly acknowledged it. But he thought that for a second he'd nearly kissed her. He'd felt sorry for her. A moment, you just want to give something a squeeze. People kiss their dogs. You see that. The moment came back to him with nervous stirrings in his loins, and then he thought of her mouth, the bulbous upper lip, the other receding, closed firmly but with a gentleness that gave her a certain serenity in repose. He pushed his mind. Suppose I'd done it? Suppose I did, suppose I kissed her? What are you thinking? No. And even if I did . . . no. She wouldn't expect it. What *would* she expect? Not that it would make much difference in practical terms. They were almost living together anyway.

He shook himself out of it and finished his drink.

Walking back, steeling himself for any encounter (whatever it was it would not be easy), he followed trails in his mind, all of them running out in fog. A pair of young girls, arms linked, scuttled past him, each casting a glance. He could get a woman anywhere; it was just a matter of paying. That didn't bother him. There'd been girls when he was in his twenties, a couple in particular, but nothing apart from passing encounters for the past eight years. It didn't matter. Women always wanted to make him do things he didn't want to do, like stay in one place or stop drinking or get up early in the morning. Julia didn't. She was a sweet girl. They'd be like, I don't know, he thought, like, not brother and sister exactly, not that, not . . . oh, I don't know. Couldn't leave him then, could she? Don't care how much you offer, you don't take the wife from a man.

But then—

May I introduce my wife?

My wife.

They'd say he did, even if he didn't. He could hear them. Christ, he does it with that. What is he?

When he returned he knocked on her door. She was playing her guitar. "Come in," she called. My God, he must have been drunker than he'd thought. Stupid, stupid drinking so early. Now all he wanted was to go back to bed and lie down. But he went in and sat down.

"That's a pretty tune," he said.

"It's an old one."

She looked nice, with her long hair uncurled, hanging straight to her shoulders. A wave of sympathy swept him.

"Julia," he said, "I'm afraid."

He didn't know where that came from. His head spun, steadily, stupidly.

She stopped playing. He's showing me his weakness, she thought, relief and euphoria dancing inside. It's going to be all right. "Why, Theo?" she asked calmly.

"I don't know." He slouched down, scowling.

"Are you all right, Theo?"

"I'm sorry about last night," he said.

"What *was* all that?"

"I kissed her. I'm so sorry."

She looked blank. "What's that got to do with me?"

"Last night brought me to my senses," he said.

"What do you mean?"

"Do you want to come over here, Julia?"

She didn't move.

"I think we should get married," he said.

She laughed but looked horrified. "Why are you saying that?"

"Why?" he said "Why does anyone say it?"

"All sorts of reasons."

"Oh God," he said, strode across and sat down next to her, but she pulled back and her eyes were scared. "You fascinate me," he said. "You fascinate me more than any other person I've ever met. And I've never had a friend like you." She got up at once and stood with her back to him, looking out of the window at the farrier's wall. From the back with her long black hair hanging, she was just a girl.

What have I done, he thought.

"It's not love though, is it?" she said. "Not like it is with other people. Real humans."

"What are you talking about?"

"Oh, you know," she said, turning. "It's not like loving a human, is it? You'd be lying if you said it was."

"Don't put me through the mincer," he said, "you know I'm bad with words."

"You're not," she said.

"Of course I love you, Julia," he said, desperately awkward, standing up and going close to her. She turned her head. Her black eyes were unreadable. "Why now? Why suddenly?" she said finally.

"Why?" He sighed. "Because you're going to run away and leave me. And I don't want to lose you."

She stared at him for a while, then said, "That's not enough."

"What do you mean?"

"You have to ask? I want what other people want when they get married."

"Julia," he said, "I wouldn't know who I was if you went away."

Still she just looked at him. Oh hell, he thought, and kissed her on the side of the mouth, amazed, aroused and horrified.

Rose, bare, small-breasted, sat smoking on the red sofa while Adam sketched her. He was having trouble with her feet. Feet were harder than hands. He was tempted to leave them off. She was telling this story about the dolls' island as if it were interesting. Not that it wasn't but not in the way she meant, numinous and full of corny significance. To him it was interesting as a piece of accidental art, but for her it was a ghost story. A long time ago a hermit, once a farmer with a wife and family, lived on an island in the canals near Mexico City. A little girl had once drowned off the island. One day a doll came floating down the canal and he fished it out. Then came another, and another, then more, till he thought it was a sign that the little girl wanted dolls. He hung the dolls in the trees for her. But still more came washing up on the island, as if they wanted to be there. When word got around, people started bringing him their old dolls too, and in the end he had hundreds, then thousands.

He lived alone with the dolls for fifty years. They talked to him and sang him to sleep, he said. And after fifty years he was planting pumpkins with his nephew, and when they'd finished they went fishing off the island. He started singing. His nephew went to fetch something and when he returned the old man was floating facedown, dead. Drowned in the exact same place where the little girl died.

"Please try and keep still, love," Adam said.

"Can you imagine that sound?" Rose closed her eyes. "Hundreds of old broken dolls singing in the middle of the night on an island. And you the only one there to hear them!"

"Yes," said Adam, as if he were talking about an ingrown toenail, "I can see that it might drive you mad."

"We should go," she said.

"To the island?"

"Yes. Just go."

"Keep still."

"Mexico," she said. "Signs and wonders. We pull a paper from a doll, it says Mexico."

"OK," he said, "borrow some money from your rich family, and I'll sell the amp and the bike and go laboring for a few months. We'll go."

"I haven't got a rich family."

"Well, compared to mine." He smudged the shadows on the page of his sketchbook. "It's not a ghost story though," he said.

"Oh, I don't know." Rose opened her eyes. "I think it sort of is."

Not since the Baltimore ball had she taken part in a real social occasion where she didn't have to wear her veil. In the old days, at home in the Sanchez house, she'd not gone veiled— or only now and then, if there were particular visitors. And here she was, with these important clever people, sitting up just as she was with the best of them. A fire burned high in the grand fireplace. Lovely rooms, lovely mirrors, silver, chandeliers, all these delicacies she was scared to touch because everyone looked at her covertly while she ate, as if she were a mythical beast who'd appeared at the table.

The crystal sparkled. And impossibly, there sat her husband, Theo, smiling with his cigar and his dark pomaded hair. My husband, mine.

Friederike smiled at her. Her eyebrows were two perfect black curves. "Julia," she said, "have you tried one of these little bonbons?"

"They look delicious," Julia said, "thank you so much, but I really can't eat another thing."

Friederike took one herself, raising her eyebrows as she popped it in her mouth. Every move she made was graceful. Next to her an Italian acrobat, thick-lipped and handsome, sucked sugar from his fingers. Hermann Otto, humorous, his large, heavily bracketed lips smiling automatically every few seconds, was locked in animated debate with an old professor. The conversation was a mishmash of French and English, harder for Theo, who was missing the ease of those drunken nights in Prague. From what he gathered, the professor, an Englishman and long-time resident in Vienna, thought they were spending too much on this new statue for the great composer. "A lot of poor people in this city," the professor said. "Where's the sense in grand statues when they're dropping of cholera in the slums?"

"What are you talking about?" Massimo, the acrobat, was following the conversation with some difficulty.

"Spend money on the living," said Theo, "not the dead."

"We should respect a great man," said Massimo indignantly, "dead or no."

"Of course we should," the professor agreed, lifting his glass tipsily. He was a red-faced, portly man with a well-fed air. "I'm only saying—"

"Have you been out to the country yet, Julia?" Friederike asked.

"Oh, no, we haven't had time."

"We must take a jaunt out one day." She dabbed the corners of her mouth with a white napkin. "When it's a bit warmer. Oh, I'm so pleased you'll be staying a little while in Vienna."

"Grand funerals," the professor said, "and fancy coffins, and fortunes spent on simpering whey-faced angels. If there was one thing the old emperor got right, that was it. Don't see what was wrong with the old way. Tip 'em in and cover them over. Don't matter to them, does it? Should have left it as it was."

Theo had drunk a lot and lolled easily with one arm hooked around the back of his chair. "Absolutely," he said, "spend it on the living." His eyes were sleepy.

"Man cannot live by bread alone," said Hermann.

"Helps though," said Theo. He knew what they were all thinking. And he's married her! Can you believe? Really? The unspoken question: Do they actually, I mean does he, do you think they really, what can it be like?

"I'm not talking about the living," the professor said. "Mozart's dead. He couldn't care less about a statue."

"You're one of these smash-'em-up people," Hermann said. "What about posterity?"

"Oh, posterity looks after itself whatever we do."

Something was bothering the Italian. "Are you saying," he began slowly, "that we should not honor the dead?"

"Of course we should. But why do we have to put money into it?

Granted that resources are limited, I say the money's better spent on the poor."

"Always with us, as the Bible says," said Theo, and laughed.

He'd had too much. Julia watched him refilling his glass, trying to catch his eye.

"No monuments. No churches, no cathedrals. No frescoes, no palaces, no towers, no . . ." Hermann smiled benevolently at Julia from the far end of the table. "What a world of tedium. Don't you think so, Julia?"

"I think the rich should give to the poor," she said. "Jenny Lind gives ever such a lot to charity. That's what you should do if you have lots."

"Hear hear."

"Well, of course," said Theo, "but that's a different matter. It's all right for you to say it would be dull, Hermann, but what if all the blood and money that went into raising those stupendous structures had been spent on the living?"

"They were," said Hermann. "We're the living. *We* enjoy them."

"Oh, tosh!" said Theo, and she was glad he hadn't said anything stronger.

Massimo was with Hermann. "You should respect a great man," he said solemnly, "and you should bury the dead with respect."

"Depends on what you call respect."

"Once a fellow's dead, he's dead. So why fork out . . . once he's gone, his body doesn't matter a jot."

"It may not matter to its owner," Friederike said, "but it matters to others. It's nice to have a grave for people to visit."

"Acknowledged," said Theo, "all I'm saying is a plain wooden cross in the ground would do as well as a monument."

"Tell me," Friederike asked him, "is your mother alive?"

"Indeed she is not."

"And where is she laid to rest?"

Theo accepted a cigar from the professor. "In a cemetery," he replied, smiling, "what did you imagine?"

"Do you visit her?"

"Never." He accepted a light. "It wouldn't occur to me. My mother's been dead for many years, and I never got to know her."

"Your poor mother."

"Why poor?" He blew out a cloud of smoke.

"You should take her some flowers," Friederike said, leaning across and tapping his arm. "She's your mother."

"I'm with you, Lent." The professor was still chewing. "Now, here's a thing." He leaned forward and twisted all his thick red fingers together as if he were torturing them. "Here's the state of things in my country. Medical science needs cadavers. Can't progress without them. But they can't get them. People don't want their bodies messed with." He pulled his fingers apart and reached for a macaroon. "So you have a ridiculous situation, people slinking about in graveyards at night, everyone forced to break the law so the doctors can get on with their work. Look at old Jeremy Bentham! What a man! Left his body to science." He popped the macaroon in his mouth and sucked. "Soon as he died," he said indistinctly, "had himself dissected for the students. Put it in his will. Got himself preserved, and there he sits this moment with his head between his feet. Now, *there's* a sense of humor."

"Can we change the subject please?" Friederike pulled a face.

"You're a dualist, Herr Lent?" asked the professor.

"I'm a realist. Now my wife," he said, smiling at her, "still has her old doll from when she was very small, and she loves it as if it was a child. Do you see? The doll is a piece of wood. Just the same with a body. Any meaning we attach to it, we put there ourselves."

"I know what you mean, Theo," Julia said, taking it in good part, "I know Yatzi's not really real. But I don't care."

"I think that's beautiful," Friederike said, reached across the table and gripped Julia's hand. *But then she speaks,* Hermann had said that day in Leipzig, *and she's just a girl. Like you,* he'd said. *About the same age too.* She smiled quiveringly, holding Julia's gaze, hoping to convey some message of fellowship.

"I don't give a damn what they do with me when I go," Theo said cheerfully, "they can put me on a hillside for the crows to pick at, for all I care."

"Oh, but you'd want your friends to come to your funeral," Julia said. "You'd want the proper thing. The singing, the candles, the wake."

"Respect for the dead is important," the Italian said, inaptly serious.

"For their memory," Theo conceded, "absolutely. But not for the clay. That doesn't matter at all."

"I want all my loved ones standing 'round tossing handfuls of earth and weeping," Otto said. "And the finest coffin available."

"Me too," agreed Friederike.

"You can have everything," Theo said. "But you won't know about it."

"How do you know?" asked Julia.

"I suppose I can see what you mean," Friederike said. "What's the point of a grand state funeral if no one likes you? Better a wooden cross and a cheap casket and people standing around who love you. But I do like to think I'd get a good send-off myself."

"I'm sure you will," said the professor, "the streets will be lined. But all the same . . ."

"Now," the Italian said, suddenly leaning forward, animated, "shall I tell you a story?"

"Oh, do!" said Friederike.

Massimo took a long drink of red wine, cleared his throat. "When the Medici ruled Florence . . ." he began.

Otto beamed. "Ah, a history lesson!"

The Italian paused and glared at him.

"Please, carry on."

"When the Medici ruled Florence," he continued, speaking precisely, in heavily accented English, "there is a conspiracy to kill these brothers, these Medici. But it goes badly. And of course these men, these conspirators, of course they meet terrible ends. But there is one man. One old man. A conspirator. Him, they torture." He spoke fiercely, glaring 'round the table at each of them in turn but avoiding Julia's eyes. He had not been able to make eye contact all evening. "He is dead. They hang him from the window. They dig a grave and put him in. He is buried."

He paused for effect, "So," he said, "what do you think happens next?" Without waiting for an answer he continued, his voice hard and disgusted. "The people in the streets dig him up. Take him home. You understand, they take him to his house, through the streets, like an old sack through the streets. They come to his own house and knock on the door with his head. They shout: 'Open up! Your master knocks!' That is their fun. Then they throw his body in the river and away he goes but down the river there are children, who pull him out. 'What more can we do,' they say. So they hang him up in a tree and thrash him till they grow bored."

"Massimo," Friederike said, "what is this for?"

"Friederike, I am sorry. That is the end. They are bored. They throw him back in the river and off he goes to sea. The end."

"That's a hideous story!" she cried.

"Yes, it is. And every word is true." Massimo sat back, folding his arms. "And that man's name was Jacopo de' Pazzi."

"It may be true," she snapped, "but do we really want to listen to this kind of thing at the table? That was horrible, Massimo."

"Herr Professor, Herr Lent," said Massimo, "what did you think of my story?"

"A vile story," the professor said, "obviously."

Theo's face, which had grown disgusted during the telling, was now detached and amused. "I can see what you're getting at," he said, "but that story is only vile for us. For poor old Jacopo it's neither here nor there."

"But that's horrible," said Julia, sickened. "Massimo, was he a very bad man?"

"Not *so* bad," he said, coloring. "For the times. Not the worst of them."

"Why did they hate him so much?"

"Who knows."

"Now I wish I didn't know that story," she said.

"And yet, Herr Lent, Herr Professor, they will tell you this is not so bad. They will say this corpse is no more than an old sack."

"Oh, but of course this is as old as the hills," the professor said. "It comes down to human nature in the end, and its genius for humiliation. That is why Hector dragged the body of Achilles 'round the walls of Troy. That is why the conquering army defiles the corpses of the conquered, that is why the heads of traitors were displayed on—"

"Enough," said Friederike.

Theo smiled at Julia. "It's grisly and filthy and unpleasant," he said, "but it didn't affect poor Jacopo in any way at all."

"It feels to me as if it did," said Julia. "They should have left his body in peace."

"What's so disgusting," the professor said, "is the intention of the beasts. The enactment."

Massimo smiled for the first time. His face revealed itself to be friendly and wryly cheerful. "But what if I could see the future," he said, looking at Theo, "what if you were Jacopo de' Pazzi? And I say to you: I see this for you. This is what they will do. And what if you knew that I was right and that this was in front of you?"

Theo laughed. "Well, you are a card," he said.

"You make believe that your soul would not recoil."

A filthy thought. The man's got a vile mind.

"Were you laughing at me," she asked when they got home, tossing the veil aside. He still got a shiver seeing her magnificent head, all beast, released from its constraints. He followed her into the bedroom where she pulled out all her flowers and feathers roughly, throwing them down on the dressing table with a carelessly graceful gesture. "For keeping Yatzi?"

"Of course not. Do I ever?"

"You're always laughing at me," she said, taking off her pearl cross, "you tease me all the time."

"Only in a nice way."

"Huh."

He picked up Yatzi, smiling. "Hello, old boy!" he said jovially, "thanks for holding down the fort. Everything fine?"

"See?"

He laughed. "You don't believe me," he said. "I find your medieval mind charming. I wouldn't have it any other way."

"There's nothing wrong with it!" She took off her earrings, her choker, her bangles. "You'd stop children playing with their toys," she said.

"No, I wouldn't." He sat down with his hands behind his head.

"Anyway, you're just as bad. What about your Venetian umbrella?"

"That's not the same at all."

"Yes, it is. You were so miserable when you lost it."

"Because it was a nice umbrella. I don't credit it with a mind." He laughed.

"I don't credit Yatzi with a mind. It's the same thing. People get attached to things." She stood up and walked to the closet. "There's nothing wrong with it."

"Come here," he said, catching her hand as she passed by, pulling her toward himself and kissing the top of her head. "Aah!" he said, "you're so small!"

The truth was, he was no longer repelled. Such a good old stick, Julia, truly brave. If it were him, he'd have cut his wrists at puberty, most like. And in fact, when you got to know her, you saw her in a different way. Not that you could ever forget what she was, of course, just that she came to seem less monstrous, more strangely normal. She was just Julia, and he never got tired of looking at her. Her face at times—a most peculiar thing—almost beautiful. Like the head of a tremendous wild creature, other, unearthly, impossible.

Still couldn't kiss her on the lips though. Not a true all-out kiss on the lips, the real thing. Couldn't do it as if she were just any woman. But she was as strokable as a puppy, as sleek as a pony in places. He could do everything with her but kiss her on the lips. Kiss her face, yes. Play with her hair. Find the sensitive spots where the hair grew sparse at the bend of an arm or knee, tickle them softly—in the dark she was a warm shapely thing, a plush doll, easy to slip inside.

"Theo," she said when they were all snuggled up, frosty moonlight sifting in through the pale curtain at the side window, "you know at first I didn't really believe you loved me, but now I do."

"Of course I do."

"I know you do. You really do, don't you?"

"Of course."

He heard the sound of her smiling.

She fell asleep, and he stayed awake, staring with a half smile and glazed eyes at the shadowy forms of the dressing table and cupboard, the porcelain bowl and jug, all made mysterious in the clear moonlight. Their apartment was on the third floor of what might once have been a palace, the rooms were so high and wide. They'd done well. It was a fine apartment, and a nice part of Vienna. Hermann had found it for them.

They had it till July, then it was more touring: Poland, Czechoslovakia—Russia, if all went well with the contacts there. There was a fellow in Moscow, a theatrical agent, Volkov.

The walls were thin. One o'clock in the morning and the people next door were still talking, two or three earnest male voices burbling steadily on, breaking out once or twice into bursts of high-pitched laughter. Lately Theo had been troubled by a certain mental tic, an irrational tendency whenever there was sudden laughter to think it was directed at him. Didn't matter that it was impossible most of the time, didn't matter that it was a bunch of kids squawking at Punch and Judy oblivious to his existence, still he thought they were laughing at him. Nonsense, of course. Stupid feeling. Since he married her, of course, it was hardly surprising. Who cares? They can think what they want. He turned over in bed, closing his eyes. They're all the same, he thought, everyone, doesn't matter who they are, even Hermann, even that Friederike, all thinking it. It's in their eyes. Do they do it? Do they *really* do it? My God, the man must be mad!

And if I'm a madman, thought Theo, at least I'm a rich one.

Julia loved Vienna. She had money. She wore beautiful dresses. Why should she not wear beautiful dresses? Why not layer on the jewelry she sent him out to buy. He was good at that sort of thing, could usually pick out something nice. She liked the trips to the theater in the carriage, the long streets of pale-colored stone, the high whiteness of the buildings along the boulevard leading to the park, and the people strolling around on a Sunday in their best clothes, she among them, veiled. She liked their apartment, with the shops on the ground floor, a haberdasher's and a baker's and a coffeehouse, the grim gloomy stairs that appeared so dark from under the thick veil that without Theo's arm to guide her she never would have gotten home. It grew lonely under the veil. The people she encountered were indistinct. Some seemed like workmen, some were more genteel. Across the landing lived the mother and pregnant wife of an officer of the regular infantry, respectable, friendly ladies who no doubt speculated upon the condition of the strange, veiled little girl who sometimes walked out on the arm of the fashionable dark-haired gentleman with cocky eyebrows. She liked the intricate looping and scrolling on the wrought-iron balcony outside their rooms, and the way from there she could see mountains and forest rising far away above the high rooflines. She liked hearing all the different accents of the people in the streets, the sense of a million comings and goings.

Most of all she liked the fact that she was staying in one place for a bit. Everything had been fleeting, changing, faces, places, coming and going, fading in and out. Theo had been the only constant. His round boyish face swam up before her eyes whenever she closed them, and she gave thanks to St. Jude and whatever it was she got from John Montanee. She never worried that the powers would fade. They'd given and would not take back. There was a semblance of routine now, church on Sunday (she made him take her), the knowledge when she closed her eyes at night that in the morning she would wake to the familiar aromas rising up from the ground floor, coffee and new-baked bread, that she would not have to clear her head and wonder for a moment where she was. There was a peace to life after the excesses of Prague. Hermann Otto came 'round occasionally and played cards with Theo, but the drinking was not desperate. And now and again, Friederike called in the afternoon, bringing a book from her library for Julia to read. Since she had seen Friederike's library the night of the dinner, a tiny cozy room with nothing but books, an easy chair, a fireplace and a corner table, she wanted one of her own. It would be peaceful and nice to have a room like that where you could just sit. Not have to do anything but read a book and from time to time look at the fire, gaze into it and dally around in your mind. Somewhere a picture began to form, not only of the room, the fire, the way it would smell and look, the color on the walls, deep blue, but around it a house, not terribly big, warm, with soft rugs and bowls of flowers. She lived there with Theo, and whenever they had to go away on tour, no matter how far, they always came back to it. And whenever they got back, she would go into her library and just sit and feel happy.

But the time went too fast.

A week before they left, Friederike called in a carriage and they drove out, through the meaner streets and the factories, past the garden fences and nice houses, through the building works and then the meadows, toward the foothills of the Wienerwald. They drank wine in the garden of a vineyard. Friederike knew the owner, who had clearly been prewarned. His eyes scarcely flickered when Julia raised her veil for the introduction. A polite tall man with a long doglike face, he shook her hand, smiling politely. She lowered her veil, and he led them to a table in a private part of the garden, bowed and withdrew.

"You really don't need to cover up here," Friederike said, putting her hand on Julia's gloved one. "You must be sweltering under there."

"Not at all. I'm used to it."

"There's really no need."

Still, it was a public place, it was a warm summery Sunday and people were out and about, so she kept her veil down. Both of them were highly recognizable. Look, people would say as Friederike glided past, it's the Cricket! Friederike's picture was everywhere, the critics raved, the public flocked.

"I know," said Julia, "but it's better if I keep it on."

"As you wish."

They were quite high up, and from their table they could see the white town in the distance beyond the trees, the high roofs glinting in the sun. There was a blue jug full of overblown yellow roses on the table. The owner brought them a dish of fat black olives and a carafe of wine so red it was almost black. A flock of pigeons rose up from the nearby woods. "I'll miss you when you go," Friederike said, "but I'm sure you'll be back."

"I'll miss you too," Julia said, "you're one of the few."

"The few?"

"Yes. People look but they don't see me. You do."

"I think that's one of the nicest things anyone's ever said to me," said Friederike, turning pink. And yet, thought Julia, she wouldn't miss her anywhere as near as much as she missed Cato. A woman friend, her own age, things to talk about, books, the stage, wine in the Wienerwald, and yet . . .

The way Friederike looked at her, so frank and warm. A cultured woman, bright, quick, sharp, poised.

And yet, she still got a stab in the chest when she thought of that child on the road with good old silly Ezra and poor lost Berniece. Child! He was in his twenties, Ezra reckoned, but he could have been any age. It didn't matter, child he was. Ezra wouldn't let any harm come to him. But how heart-wrenching they seemed now those three, muddling through, fragile, tiny, vanishing into a past that receded like an echo.

No, she wouldn't miss Friederike like that.

Julia sipped, expert at lifting the veil just enough to raise the glass to her lips but not to be seen.

The wine went to her head.

"I'm very lucky," she said suddenly.

Friederike smiled. Wonderful it must be, Julia thought. To look like that and be sure about everything.

"I'm seeing the world!"

"You certainly are." Friederike adjusted her hat, a fine wide affair with a brim that performed a wavelike contour above her eyes. "I'd like to go traveling one day," she said. "I've never been out of Europe. I envy you."

She envies *me*.

Julia looked aside. There was no one in sight, their patch of lawn was hidden away from the other customers behind a small shrubbery. Leaning forward, she lifted her veil. Friederike's smile widened. "I like to travel," Julia said. "I want to see so much more of the world. And then one day when we've saved up a lot of money, we'll settle down, Theo and me. Then I'll go back home and visit, and they'll all be amazed. I'll walk in with Theo and say, 'Here is my husband.'"

There must have been a village nearby because the church bells had started to ring. Julia remembered the time she wore Marta's blue dress and nearly ruined the wedding. There would be no ostentation, she thought, just expensive elegance. Something simple, shot silk, dove gray, palest blue. Touches here and there of a muted shimmering silver. And white lace-up boots, and her hair done simply with just a feather or two, and a few small white flowers. "I know what everybody says," she said. "They think he's in it for the money. They can't believe anyone could really love someone like me. But they're wrong."

"Of course they are," said Friederike.

You could see she wasn't sure. Actress that she was, you could see she didn't believe. Didn't matter what he did, no one ever would.

But Julia did.

"Is Mexico very beautiful?" Friederike asked.

"The mountains are. We could see them from the town. But you know I didn't see as much as you might think. I could never just go out like other people."

Those days. Solana. The boys, Clem, Elisio. The iguana, the moon, the figs squashed on the stones. A world away.

"I think when we settle," Julia said, "Vienna would be a very nice place to consider."

"Oh, do!" said Friederike.

———

"How was it?" Theo asked.

"Lovely."

"And you stayed veiled?"

"Of course."

"Friederike thinks I have real talent," Julia said.

"And why wouldn't she?" He swiveled his collar 'round and pulled out the stud.

"She should know."

"I dare say."

When they finally left Vienna, Friederike gave Julia a copy of the book on which her great success was based.

"Here," she said, "something to read on the journey."

La Petite Fadette. She had signed it: *For dear Julia, from Friederike (The Cricket). Happy Memories!*

It was good, Julia thought. Unusual.

When did you ever get a heroine like Fadette? No one liked her. They all laughed because she was brown and ugly like a cricket, and her little brother had crooked legs. But then it turned out in the end that she wasn't really ugly after all, not once she'd had a wash and put on a nice dress and started talking nicely and behaving like a lady. And she had a beautiful soul. Then everyone fell in love with her, and she married young Landry, the hero.

Y ou know, we're forgetting who we are," she said.

"I'm not."

"Yes, you are, you just don't know it."

"That's a meaningless thing to say."

She could be so fucking annoying.

"So what are you saying? You want to break up?"

"No, of course not. But you're here all the time."

"Well, you've never said anything before."

"Look, Adam, there's no need to fall out or anything. It's no big deal. All I'm saying is—"

"Oh, Christ, she needs her space, she needs her space," said Adam scornfully. "We all know what that means, don't we? I think about what you want all the time."

"I'm sorry, but that's just not true."

"Why are you being like this?"

"Like what? Like myself?"

"You weren't like this last week."

"Of course I was. You just didn't notice. I told you I didn't want that stupid telly in here, and you wouldn't listen. This is my place. I don't want a stupid telly. If I have a telly I watch the news, and then I'm miserable all the time."

"OK, I'll move it back downstairs then."

"It's not just that, Adam. It's the smell of paint too. It's getting to me. You should paint downstairs."

"So you don't want me to paint you anymore."

"You know it's not that. I just want you to do it downstairs. I could sit for you down there instead of here, and then this would still be my own place where I can come, and I can have it how I like."

"You should have told me if I was getting on your nerves."

"You don't get on my nerves. It's just one or two things. It's just things have changed too much. Too quick. I just want some—"

"You should have told me."

"I tried to."

"You're being really unfair. You never said a word. You knew how it was. How I was. I love you to fucking pieces, and you know it."

"Stop it," she said, "I just want you to spend more time in your own place. We never made an arrangement for you to be up here all the time. It doesn't mean you can't come up here at all. That would be ridiculous."

"But you don't love me. Not really."

"Adam," she said, "you're making too much of this."

"Oh, yes, much too much."

He walked out. Didn't slam the door, went down to his own place, didn't slam that door either.

Rose lay down on the red sofa and covered her face. He's gone, he's gone, he's gone. The relief was wonderful and immediate. Oh, God! She sat up, got up, walked around crying. I never made a promise. No way I gave him any expectations. Why do they do this, why do they do this, why do they always do this? The world piled up against her like a freak tide about to break through. Why do they always want to change things? Smother. Stop your breath. This is who you are now. What I say. What I think you are. They change you and change you and change you, and then when you say, hang on a minute, perhaps this isn't me, they come at you with that lost dog look and cry and hang their heads and it's all your fault. Not just a little bit of it, all of it, always your fault.

She stood looking out of the window. Bring on the rain, she thought. Then I can lie down and close my eyes and listen to it and forget everything else. But no, not today, no rain, only a thick gray sky like glue, lumpy like that stuff we had when we were little and pasted pictures in scrapbooks. Gloy. She wanted him back so she could say, hey, do you remember Gloy? It had a red top that always got gummed up? Looked like snotty frogspawn. He'd remember. In the days before they were together you could say a thing like that, and he'd say, Yeah, I remember. It had been nice then. OK, so the sex had to happen. Run its course. But why did people have to make such a big deal of it?

She couldn't bear another second of real life. She took Tattoo down from the mantelpiece. More of his stuffing was falling out. She lit candles all around the room, tall ones, stumps, white, blue, red, then turned the gas fire high, got the heavy eiderdown from off her bed next door and lay down under it on the sofa with Tattoo, needing that feeling, the stillness, the hiss of the fire, the colors in the dark inside her eyelids.

A phone rang downstairs, shrill and peremptory. Attend to me! Now!

No. Won't. The world is not. Call up the deep woods. Walk in among the trees. In the heart of a letter on an illuminated manuscript made long ago, a mystical landscape, wildwood of hart and hound and hare and moon, where she could stay as long as she liked.

Deeper. Deeper.

She lay down there under a tree, fell asleep and dreamed she was in New York with Adam. She'd never been to New York in real life, but it was definitely New York. They were in a bar. They were whiling away the hours till it was time go to the airport to catch a plane back home. Next they were outside and it was raining and nighttime, still New York, lights and cars, wet sidewalks. They'd lost all their money and their passports, everything, and they were just walking along in the rain. It was lovely. It's real, isn't it? Not a dream, she thought. But then it all started to break up. There was a moment, one fraction of a second when she thought that if she looked sideways—right or left, it didn't matter—she'd see a new place. Like Narnia or something.

She'd been in this moment before, many times, and she always wanted to stay, turn her head and see that place. She never did though. Instead she woke up.

Poland, Czechoslovakia. Christmas in Budapest, beautiful city in the snow, lights hung in the trees, the fire in their hotel room banked up high and all the bells suddenly gloriously pealing on Christmas morning. Then the year gone, and another progressing. She turned twenty-five. Warsaw, Krakow, Brest. East, farther and farther, wide plains and lakes and vast forests, and the sense of excitement welling up all over again every day, something new, something more; more world, more life. They traveled in stages through a long white winter, bought furs in Minsk, stopped once in a village, where she heard from below in the inn where they stayed the sound of someone playing a zither, and at night the sound of wolves howling very far away in the woods. Money flowed. Nothing was out of reach. She still liked to sew now and then, but these days she could hire the best seamstresses available and give them precise instructions. Low-cut, skirts short, silks, ribbons. Theo grew his hair and whiskers and looked very distinguished.

———

"You will slay them in Moscow," he said. "They can't wait. How's this for a name, Julia? Ilya Andreyevich Volkov. They all have three names. And they use them too."

Ilya Andreyevich Volkov was the theatrical agent to whose house they were going. Desperate he was, said Theo, desperate to host the marvelous ape woman. Everyone wants you, you know. He's got a big house right in the middle of Moscow.

"Theo, you've been everywhere," she said.

"Not quite." He smiled, took her hand and pulled it under his arm. They were traveling by night in a coach, through snow, blue under a high moon. From the window she could see a tall peaky castle high on a hill. She found the snow enchanting. It was like stepping into a picture in a book, a landscape she was dreaming. And Theo could even speak a fair amount of Russian. He was in a good mood, excited by his return to the East. It must have been twelve years, he thought.

"So again," she said. "How do I say, 'I'm very pleased to meet you?' "

"I'll write it all down for you."

———

March was bitter cold in Moscow, snow hard packed. A sledge pulled by two ill-matched black horses met them from the coach, and a tall big-boned young man came forward and introduced himself politely in French. His name was long and unpronounceable, instantly forgotten.

"Ye gods, it's cold," Theo said. "Yes, this is our trunk, and this bag here is ours. How far?"

"Not very far. Please, this way." The boy was clumsy in his gestures. "We will be there in twenty minutes. Please sit here, madame."

Solicitously, smiling awkwardly, he spread a thick red blanket over Julia's knees. Teeth chattering, nose turning red, Theo tucked it in. It was dark already, and starting to snow again. When she looked up it fell swirling black against the peculiar swollen sky.

"It's all right for you," Theo said, "you've got a fur coat," and laughed.

The veil kept the wind from her face, her eyes were wide but all she saw from the fast-moving sledge were huddled hurrying figures in wide dark streets, high buildings with many windows and steps, and the round-shouldered back of the tall young man, the cap pulled well down over his ears and a collar pulled up over a gray muffler.

"You know, Julia," Theo said, "last time I was here it was spring. Lovely place. I don't recognize a thing yet. Never mind, this surely can't go on for too long." He raised his voice. "When does the weather pick up around here?" But the boy didn't hear.

Julia felt him quivering next to her as if a string inside had been tightened to the limit and was straining not to snap. She took her gloved hands out of her muff and put them over his. He was wearing a pair of gloves she'd bought him for Christmas in Budapest. She'd veiled up and they'd gone to a market, and she'd made him go and stand somewhere else so he wouldn't see what she was getting him. The woman had looked at the veil as if it were a face she was trying to fathom. He'd been wearing the gloves ever since, they were good and warm, and she chafed them as if it could make a difference. He laughed and his breath was white fog. "Twenty minutes," he said. "Twenty minutes. I'm timing it."

It took twenty-three.

Volkov was at the door to greet them, wearing a professional smile. "At last, at last!" he said, running down the steps, a handsome wizened little man with a look of premature age. "My good friend!" He clapped Theo on the shoulder. "Madame! We will speak English. Yes?"

The house was a plush, overblown affair, full of gilt and fat pink satin. Volkov was rich.

"Ilya Andreyevich Volkov," said Theo smoothly, "it has been a very long journey."

"And you are tired. Tolya!" he shouted to the boy who'd driven them in and was now bringing in their luggage. "Show Mr. and Mrs. Lent to their rooms."

Theo hated that. Mr. and Mrs. Lent. Was there something in the way he said it? Behind the smile, the style, the smarm. They're all the same, he thought. You can see the thoughts turning in their heads like cogs. They do it. What's it like? And he's not even seen her yet.

"Shall I send up chocolate? Please, you must rest. And later, when you are rested . . ."

Yes, later, the revealing.

When the boy had left them alone, Julia lay down on the bed at once, scarcely taking time to look at the two large comfortable rooms they had been given. "I might sleep," she said.

Another revealing. One more. One more, one more, and one more and more and on through life.

"I'm so tired."

"No rush," said Theo. "Let them wait. My God, look at this." He was fingering the curtains. "That'll keep the cold out. You could wear that on the Steppe herding your goats or whatever it is they do. That must've cost."

He sat down, pulling off his collar.

"I'm not going down," she said.

"Old money, you see. You can always tell old money from new. He doesn't really need to do this, you know, all this show stuff, he does it because he's got the bug. It gets people like that. Wait until he sees you." He laughed shortly, a huffing of breath. "Bet he lies awake all night."

She didn't go down that night. She went straight to bed. Someone knocked on the door, bringing hot chocolate. Theo carried it in to her and she drank it sitting up against the pillow, watching the snow drift past the window. There's nowhere farther than this, she thought. The other side of the world. She closed her eyes. A dream of heat came, Mexico, drenching sun. Heat came through her palms from the cup she held. When she opened her eyes, she couldn't focus for a moment, and thought the fire that crackled in the grate was the glowing in the brazier when Cayetano was getting ready to shoe a horse. But then she saw the snow sifting down, finer now like flour, and it was still snowing next morning when she woke, dressed carefully and went down to meet the household. There they stood in a line as if she were royalty or the new mistress, all perfectly prepared: Volkov, his ancient mother and the servants. The mother was a tiny shriveled thing with watery lips and pale sore-looking eyes, very bent over, leaning on a stick on one side and the arm of a stout maid on the other. There was a housekeeper, a cook, a couple of girls, and Tolya, the tall young man from the night before. Theo, in personable professional mode, did the introduction. Well-trained, he thought. Not one of them showed a flicker. You'd think they met women who looked like apes every day. He got an urge to laugh. She didn't open for another two weeks. Till then she was under wraps, with only this lot and the Salomansky musicians getting a look. Oh, yes, they may look as cool as cucumbers, but look, they're overjoyed, they're wild, already they're thinking in their minds what they'll say, even though they've been sworn to secrecy. You should see her! It's unbelievable! Just you wait.

She'll slay them.

———

The sledge, driven by Tolya, carried them most days between the house and the rehearsal room at the Circus Salomansky. Tucked in with her furs in a shawl that covered her nose and mouth, she was no different from all the other muffled forms carefully picking their ways along the freezing pavements. Theo, in new checked trousers and with perfume in his lengthening side whiskers, wore a habitual smile by her side. She was practicing new steps, a Russian dance with two handsome booted male dancers who flattered her shamelessly. Now you are happy, he thought, watching her count time with the pianist, because of me. She works hard. God, she's come on! At her peak. And with the new costumes. Poor Theo. Poor, poor Theo. Such a refrain to have always running in your head. Poor, poor Theo, an idiot high voice nagging on the edge of consciousness, as inescapable as the sky, no matter that his face wore its perpetual wry smile and his eyes were soft. Nonsense, nonsense, all is well. But so many voices spoke in his head. What have I done? What woman now would have me, tied to that? If he puts his thing in that he's not putting it in me. The way they look at me, everyone, all with that same question. Does he actually do it with her?

Yes, he does. He does, and it is altogether compelling. He is obsessed. There's no doubt revulsion plays a part in it, he doesn't understand it, why he grows hot and tense and hard even as a shiver of horror shoots along his spine. Everything stands up for her, every hair on his head, every nerve and fiber.

"Are you all right, Theo?"

She was bending down toward him where he sat, a look of concern on her face.

"Yes, love," he said. "Why do you ask?"

"I don't know. I thought you looked, I don't know, sort of serious."

He laughed. "Serious? Me?"

"Watch my new dance," she said, swishing away. "Tolya's been teaching me."

At Volkov's she practiced her new songs, three Russian, one new from America. Polina, a big friendly girl who brought her hot water in the morning, had been drafted in to help with pronunciation.

"That's impossible!"

"Not at all. Try again."

Theo, lounging in a chair, crossed his legs and lit up a fat black cigar. "It doesn't matter," he said, "an accent can be charming."

"And this line?" Julia asked. "This means?"

"By the edge of the lake where you gave me your hand—"

"It doesn't matter," he said again. "You don't have to know what it means, you only have to know the sounds."

"I want to know what it means," Julia said. "How can I give it feeling if I don't know what it means?"

"Well," he said, "happy, sad, whatever the mood. That's all you need to know."

Polina, her back to him, made a face, very slight. Silly man, her face said.

There was a knock on the door.

"Come in!" called Theo.

Tolya entered backward with a tray. "I've brought you some cocoa," he said.

"Oh, lovely!" She clapped her hands. "Just what I want!"

"Not for me." A glass of red wine was on the small table by Theo's side.

"Tolya's a country boy, did you know, Theo? That's where he learned to dance. Didn't you, Tolya?"

No conception of how to treat a servant, Theo thought. You'd have thought this was a family friend dropping by. She was much easier with these two than she was with Volkov and the old lady. The crone kept pretty much to her own quarters with her nursemaid, and Volkov was out at his office a lot of the time, so they didn't see that much of them anyway, apart from at mealtimes, which were awkward and protracted.

"Look! He's been teaching me." She seized the boy and whirled him around, humming some Russian tune he must have taught her.

"You're a marvelous dancer," Tolya said, "such an easy pupil." He looked delighted. Well, of course, imagine, something to tell the grandchildren about, the time I danced with the eighth wonder of the world. Something you'd never forget, as Theo knew, an armful of sweetly smiling animal, a womanly arm around you, little hand, gardenia, furry brow as strokable as a cat's, lips of an ape, thatched black brow.

"I have danced with many men," Theo heard her say. "In Baltimore they were lining up. But you, Tolya, you are the best."

The boy was pretty and beardless with long fair hair and a ring in his ear. She really liked that young man.

"Wait till you see all my costumes," she was saying to him. "How many changes do I have, Theo? Is it five? The kilt, the sailor, the—"

"Four," said Theo.

"But I will not be coming," said Tolya.

"Why not?"

"I will be working," he said and laughed, dancing backward, drawing her after him.

"That's terrible," she said. "You *must* come."

Look at that, Theo thought. What's she doing? Is she flirting with him? The way she lifts her face, the way she turns. Is she making a fool of herself? Surely not. But the boy acts charmed, as if she's a normal girl, and that big lump Polina is clapping her hands and singing along.

"It really isn't difficult," Julia said, growing breathless.

"Not for you," said the boy.

"There," said Theo, standing, "I think it's time you rested, Julia. Thank you, Tolya. Thank you, Polina."

"I'm not tired," said Julia. "Dance with Polina!" And she grabbed his arm and the arm of that silly girl and shoved them together, and the girl began to shriek with laughter as if someone were tickling her. It was like dancing with a heaving overstuffed bolster. Theo didn't want to seem like a misery, so he whirled her twice 'round the room to show he was willing and deposited her by the door. "Madame," he said gallantly, opening the door, "you dance like an angel."

Her face had gone bright red, whether from the exertion or the thrill of being in his arms, he could not tell. But then she looked at him, and her eyes were serious. "No, sir," she said with pathetic dignity, "I dance like an ox, as you well know."

His smile faltered, then reasserted itself. "There's no answer to that," he said cheerfully.

"Thank you for the dance, Miss Julia," Tolya said, following Polina out the door, glancing shyly sideways at Theo, who inclined his head, smiling and formal.

"You *must* come," she said. "Both of you."

"You know, Julia," Theo said when they'd gone, "I wish you showed the same enthusiasm when we dine with Ilya Andreyevich Volkov and his mother."

"They're boring," she said simply. "And I can never remember all their names. It's much easier with Tolya and Polina. They're just Tolya and Polina."

"Oh, you get used to it. And yes, he is a bit of an old bore, and she is practically nonexistent, but don't forget we're in their house. Eating their food. And I don't think you realize quite how much that man has done for us. For *you*. We're all sold out, everywhere. The entire tour is his doing."

"I know. But I don't like his face. It's false."

"False?"

"He's always smiling," she said, "but his eyes never smile. You're like that too sometimes."

"Isn't everyone?"

"Yes, but he's like that all the time. Anyway you're not like that with me, only with other people. But he's like that all the time with everyone. And he laughs too much."

"Poor man!"

———

The ugliest woman in the world, the walking singing, dancing, impossible woman beast opened to a packed house. Watching with Volkov from the wings, Theo was almost tearful with pride and anxiety. Look at her. Just look. If she messes it up now. My God, she's a pit pony, a Trojan, the way she's gone at it. All this new stuff. Over and over again at midnight, the words, the steps, the dancing fingers on the fret board. And look, all they want is to look at her, eat her face. She could just stand there. What a crowd. Not just hoi polloi, this lot, look at those aristocrats. Volkov beside him spoke some Russian thing, the tone was my God, oh my God. Never ceases to impress. Oh my God, my God, just look at her, what is she—is she even human? Look at their mouths hanging open. She paraded along the front of the stage playing her guitar, singing some old song and swaying her skirts. When she went into her dance, she was so practiced she didn't have to think about it. At least that's the way it looked. Oh, she's a good girl, she is. Wait'll she does "Lorena." *Oh, Lorena.* Pure sentiment was a sensation he liked to sniff out, confront and destroy at first stirring, but "Lorena" bashed through all that. "This is all the rage at home," she'd said, in some godforsaken little hole in Poland, singing it for the first time. She played it now on her harmonica, a thin, slow, plaintive tune. To see those huge lips so sensitively draw such yearning from that old harmonica. Terrible. Quite terrible. Such beauty. Such a surfeit of ugliness. Then she sang:

The years creep slowly by, Lorena,
The snow is on the ground again . . .

And it was all he could do to keep the tears from his eyes.

The crowd went mad. Volkov bounced up and down, applauding vigorously. Theo could have crowed. Wouldn't you like to have her? Wouldn't you just love to steal her away? Don't worry, you'll get your cut. Up struck the band. White dress shining in the spotlight, she performed a ballet and a Spanish dance, her old stuff, well perfected, then sang an aria she'd learned specially, one of those Russians. Her voice strained a little at times but recovered itself quickly. "Ah, now we come to the best bit," said Theo. "Here come the boys." Shouting, laughing, they leapt onstage, they've been flattering her and she's basking in it, very good for the performance. She greets them with a massive smile, the audience draws a breath, the boys take her hands and all three dance in line, a quick-footed jaunt that involves a lot of changing places and backward and forward. Here's where it could all go wrong, the timing must be exact, but she's got it to a tee, good girl, God, they're loving it, look at their faces, and those boys, the way they gaze at her. They'll never forget her. Something about these Russian lads, half of them have got the Steppes running in their blood, half wild themselves, I suppose. She does like them. Well, they allow for the costume changes, so necessary, and the crowd likes it. Old Volkov there, she's right, he has greedy eyes. Look at that ridiculous dance, the old Cossack thing, all hup! hup! hup! as she glides off. Grinning, clapping their hands, dancing backward. She reappears as a Scottish lassie in a kilt and throws herself into a wild highland fling, a killer but she handles it. Look at those tiny feet go, slipping against one another like little fishes.

"You can't say this girl doesn't have stamina." Volkov laughed with his cold fish eyes. Next she was a sailor in white bell-bottomed trousers, cross-armed, dancing a hornpipe, and then, by God, in less than a minute, a Russian peasant in a red skirt with a fancy apron and a lot of embroidery, trailing long colored hankies from her fingertips.

The crowd as one stood up and cried, "Bravo! Bravo!"

"Oh, yes, yes," said Volkov. "Oh, yes, bravo, bravo, bravo."

She glided 'round the empty stage as if on wheels, waving the hankies in the air so they coiled and floated lightly with the music, three times 'round, her massive wild face aloft. The boys and their shiny boots returned, handing her gracefully between themselves into the final dance. They are on springs, their legs fly out, their boot heels crack. And Julia center stage, quick stepping, swirling, a butterfly.

Yip! Yip! Yip!

The crowd goes wild.

She finished with a simple Russian folk song, alone with her guitar.

"Julia," Theo said, stepping in front of Volkov to greet her in the wings, "my love, you have conquered Mother Russia."

———

Polina banked up the fire. "There," she said, getting heavily to her feet. "Keep you lovely and warm."

Julia lay sprawled on the big sofa with her head on a cushion. "Thank you, Polina. Look at the snow! It's so beautiful." Her shoes lay askew on the rug. The snow fell strong and steady past the window. Polina didn't even give it a glance. "You must feel the cold so much," she said, stooping to pick up the shoes, "coming from a hot country."

"Yes," said Julia, "but I'm beginning to get used to it. It was cold in New York. It was cold in Europe."

"Polina," said Theo, coming in from the bedroom in his dressing gown and slippers, red wine spilling over his fingers from a tilted glass, "did Julia tell you about the show?" He strode across to the fire and stood grinning before it.

"A great success," said Polina, setting the shoes neatly side by side next to the bedroom door, "I knew it would be."

"It's colder here," said Julia, "but I came in stages so . . ."

"A triumph!" Theo was tight. They'd been drinking downstairs with Volkov and some fat friend of his whose name she couldn't remember, a prince no less—only prince here didn't mean the same as in other places, it seemed. Princes and counts abounded. She'd had only one glass of champagne, but the men had polished off half a bottle of vodka before starting on the wine. It had been so boring. "And I have to say, Polina"—Theo gestured with his glass and more wine sloshed—"your *coaching* was a stunning success!" He laughed. "The voice of the people! Where are you from, Polina?"

"From Meshchanskaia," she said, as if that would mean anything to him. "Careful, sir, don't spill your wine."

"Ah," he said, "where the peasant tongue holds supreme sway. Julia, I think it worked."

"What did?"

"The common accent. They loved it."

"Will there be anything else?" Polina asked.

"Don't think so." Chuckling, he took a swig. A long strand of hair had come adrift and slanted across his left eye. "That's all."

"What I do like about snow," Julia said to Polina, "is being warm inside watching it fall. The fire's magnificent. Theo, please don't block the heat."

He jumped aside. "At once, my lady!" When is that girl going? His head was about to burst. Go on, you silly girl, get out. Thank you.

"Can you believe what we have achieved?" Wide-eyed, he walked about in his new dressing gown, which was exactly the same color as his wine. "There's no limit."

"She reminds me of me."

"Who? Polina?"

"She reminds me of me when I was at home." Julia yawned. My God! The mess of teeth!

"Do you still think of it as home?" he said, a little sadly.

She had to think about that. "I don't know," she said finally. "Home is with you." Her eyes closed. "I'm asleep," she said, smiling.

All of a sudden he felt weepy. Not like him. My diamond mine, my fortune, my millstone, he thought, still amazed at what he'd done. Look at her. He could go out. Send her off to bed, go where no one knows him, a drink, a game of cards, a few discreet questions. He could find them, the girls in their small rooms. Girls who don't know he's married to a freak.

There was a tap on the door.

"Oh, let Tolya in," she said, "he cheers me up."

"Don't *I* cheer you up?"

"Of course you do," she said, sitting up, "but you're here all the time. Come in, Tolya!"

"Tea," said the boy, coming in with a tray. She even knows what his knock on the door sounds like, thought Theo, placing himself once more in front of the heat. The fire jumped when the door opened, and the wind howled. I'm not going out in that, he thought. But still, he knew he'd never be able to sleep, his mind was feverish.

"They went *wild*, Tolya!"

"Of course." He smiled his big-toothed smile, putting the tray down on the small table beside Julia. "I've been listening to them talk. Prince Rudakov wants to invite you to his party."

"Oh, dear," she said, as if it weren't a huge honor, "I'm not sure I'll enjoy that."

"Of course you will," Theo said. "It'll be just what you need. I knew this kind of thing was going to happen. Didn't I tell you? Whats his name. Bartolomeo or whatever and his sister."

"Maximo and Bartola," she said. He was always going on about them.

"They met royalty. Went to the White House, shook hands with the president. And they weren't anywhere near as good as you, they were more akin to your little friend Cato."

"Cato," she said wistfully.

"Anyway," said Theo, looking irritatedly at Tolya as he poured tea for Julia, with a delicate touch for such a clod of a thing, "are you quite sure you're the person who should be telling us this?"

"Sorry, sir," said Tolya, not sounding it at all. "Didn't really think."

If I was Volkov I'd never employ him, thought Theo, sprawling himself into a chair.

"And my dance?" Tolya said. "It went well?"

"Oh, Tolya, you should have been there! It was marvelous! You'd have been proud of me."

"I *am* proud of you."

"No, really, really, the steps you taught me, they made the show. They were the highlight."

"Well, not quite," Theo said dryly.

The stupid boy laughed. "Miss Julia," he said, "you are so nice a person."

"I'll tell you something," she said, "you're easily as good as those other two, those dancers. You should have been up there on that stage with me."

Tolya snorted. "Much better to dance with you here," he said. "I am very privileged."

"You most certainly are," said Theo.

"Anything for you, sir?" The boy straightened, turning with a polite smile. "Tea?"

"I have my wine."

"Ah, but those boys, Tolya!" said Julia, picking up her cup and warming her hands 'round it, "Oh, you should have seen them, the life in them."

"I suppose a dance like that," Theo said, "in a country like this, probably comes from the cold. You have to dance to keep warm."

"There may be something in that," Tolya said, beginning to withdraw.

"Certainly damn freezing, this place." Theo stretched his legs and put his slippered feet on the fireplace screen.

"Yes," she said, "I miss the sun."

"Wait until spring," said Tolya.

———

Spring came suddenly, along with an invitation.

Prince Rudakov sent a carriage to bring them out to his coutry house for a weekend party, and Volkov rode with them. The sun was hot, everywhere was willows, a haze hung over the fields, rolling away into wooded distance. Now and again they passed a church or a wretched huddle of shabby huts and knocked-together barns, and sometimes carts drawn by bony horses, ragged people at the reins. At last the driver pointed with his whip to a red roof among the green slopes, and a few minutes later the house came into view, long and low, with many windows and a balcony running the length of the upstairs story. A sloping lawn ran away at the front and tall trees closed in on three sides. Rudakov was there as soon as the carriage turned into the drive, waiting in a pale linen suit like an eager child about to get a present. *"Enchanté,*

enchanté," he was saying before she'd even gotten out of the carriage, and Theo stood by, beaming like a proud father as the Prince fawned all over her.

"The countryside is very beautiful," she said in Russian, something she'd learned specially.

The house was sumptuous inside. She unveiled in a small parlor. Rudakov had seen her before, of course, but there was his mother and sister, his wife, three stiff little boys on their best behavior. And when they'd all stared their fill and exclaimed their delight, a servant showed them to their room. Julia started fretting about her dress, a flounced crinoline with tiny bows decorating each tier of the skirt and one great bow fanning out at the back, trailing long silver ribbons. It was too fancy, she said. The kind of thing for grand entrances and sweeping down wide curving staircases.

"Nonsense," he said, wandering out onto the landing, standing a little dazedly looking over the balcony rail. A door in one corner opened and a tall young woman in a pale pink dress ran across the atrium with skirts raised. He caught a glimpse of a thin white ankle before she vanished through another door. Well, now, he thought, craning a little over the rail. Maybe cop a dance with her later.

But when evening came, it wasn't a dancing sort of a do, more of a grand soirée, with a piano only, and lots of formal introductions. Julia's entrance was a showpiece. Prince Rudakov was waiting at the foot of the stairs as she tiptoed down on Theo's arm, her dress like the great cup of a flower, lifting and settling as she moved. She'd been getting ready for hours and her hair was a flowery masterpiece. The Prince led her into the big parlor where ornate chairs were artfully arranged around small tables bearing dishes of Turkish delight and bowls of pink and blue flowers. The guests stopped their twittering and turned as one to gaze.

"My dear friends," Rudakov announced in a ringing voice, "I am delighted to introduce to you Madame Julia, the great artiste."

Theo hung back.

The usual sort, he thought, scanning the crowd. A couple of military men, a few distinguished and delighted middle-aged women, lavishly dressed, with their indistinguishable husbands. A tall blond man with a haunted face and thin lips stared with something approaching passion. And there was the beauty he'd seen earlier, now wearing something golden brown and shiny that displayed her fragile shoulders. Rudakov was saying the girl's name. Liliya Grigorievna Levkova, my cousin. She laughed in a self-conscious way when she was introduced, wrinkling her nose and narrowing her eyes. It made her even more beautiful.

Theo drank too much that night and remembered little afterward apart from Liliya Grigorievna Levkova, shimmering always in the corner of his eye, and the intense blond man who scarcely blinked and never took his pale eyes from Julia for a second. At some point, Rudakov crossed over to the man and drew him by the arm to be introduced:

"My very good friend, Professor Sokolov."

Sokolov pushed his furrowed brow at Julia, his staring gray eyes.

"Madame Julia Pastrana," said Rudakov, a flourish in his voice.

"Hello," said Sokolov in English.

"How do you do," said Julia.

"Monsieur Lent," said Rudakov, "her husband."

Sokolov barely glanced at him, but gripped Julia's hand as if he'd never let it go, and stuck his face right in hers so that she drew back a little.

"Professor Sokolov is a very distinguished doctor," Rudakov said.

The professor began to talk to Julia stumblingly, smiling and sweating—had read everything ever written about her, followed her progress, utmost fascination, immensely gratified—and on and on, till Theo drifted away, floating 'round the room with a vague smile on his face and another drink in his hand. Someone was playing something dull on the piano. Old Volkov was getting tight. Then he saw her, Liliya Grigorievna Levkova talking animatedly to the mother of Prince Rudakov, a stern old lady in a pearl cap. And glory, she caught his eye and came running over as if he were an old friend. "Oh, Mr. Lent," she said in perfectly accented English, "what a lucky man you are!" Close to, she was not as young as she'd appeared from the balcony, but none the worse for that.

"Am I?" he said.

"She's so sweet! So lovely!" A delightful voice, low and eager and exciting.

"Oh. Yes, she is."

"It's so romantic," she said. "I can't wait to hear her sing. I've heard *so* much about her!"

"Julia is a very fine singer," he said.

"Everyone's dying to hear her. And will she dance? Oh, she *must* dance! What a pity we have to sit through all the others first. And I hear you are to tour very soon?"

"Yes. And then we are going to St. Petersburg. To the circus. We will make St. Petersburg our home for a while."

"Oh! We'll be so sorry to lose her."

"We'll be back for the Christmas season."

"How wonderful. You'll be in St. Petersburg in the summer."

"Yes."

"She has such an effect on everyone!" said Liliya Grigorievna. "Just look at Professor Sokolov." She giggled. "Poor Julia! Go and rescue her." She turned him, giving him a familiar little nudge in the back before swishing off to talk to someone else. Where she'd touched him, it was as if a little creature had woken up under the skin. He found himself beside Julia. Sokolov was speaking urgently at her, a set smile on his face.

"Theo," she said, taking his arm, "Professor Sokolov has been telling me all about his collection of anatomical Venuses. They sound horrible."

"Horrible but fascinating, no doubt." Theo's smile widened and quavered. "Forgive me, Professor, I must borrow my wife for a moment."

Solokov bowed politely. "Of course," he said.

"Not another doctor," she whispered in Theo's ear, rising on tiptoe as he led her away.

"Don't worry." He lowered his head. "This is purely social."

"I'm sick of the lot of them."

"Not surprised."

"I'm not a piece of meat," she said.

"You most certainly are not."

No more, he'd promised, after the last one. No more poking and pressing and measuring.

"Not *exactly* a doctor anyway," he whispered, "I don't think."

"These Venuses," she said, "they're opened up. You can see what's inside."

"My love, they want you to perform," he said.

She sighed. "Do I have to?"

"I think they'll be very disappointed if you don't. I think they'll never smile again."

"They'll get over it," she said glibly, but she'd been expecting it.

"Not the full show, of course." He leaned close and spoke into her ear. "Just a song or two, and one of your pretty Spanish dances. Nothing too strenuous!"

"I don't mind dancing," she said.

"And a song? That little Russian thing?"

"That's a whole performance, Theo," she said. "Why didn't you say? I haven't got my guitar."

"Yes, you have. It's in the box."

"So you knew?"

"Oh, Julia, you must have realized. You know what these things are like. Lots of other people are going to be doing their turns and none of them are going to be anywhere near as good as you. It'd be peculiar if you didn't perform."

So, after sitting through a great deal of apparently hilarious stuff in Russian and the mediocre warbling of several ladies and a portly baritone, the party was treated to three songs and a Russian dance from the one they had after all come to see. Julia performed as well as she'd ever done, and they applauded wildly, turning their delighted faces to one another.

"Oh, Julia," Theo called out, "one more please."

"Oh, yes, yes!" cried Liliya Grigorievna, bouncing a little.

"Sing 'Lorena,'" he said. "A new American song," he explained to the people, went to take a sip and noticed that his glass was empty.

She didn't want to but smiled obligingly and once more picked up her guitar.

Oh, "Lorena" would slay them. He retreated to the back of the room and refilled his glass. The doors to the veranda stood open. The chandeliers glittered, the crystal glasses glittered, her big black eyes glittered. Big black, wet eyes. He saw Sokolov, his doctor's stare. He looks like a thin white bird, a crane or something. Oh, what a specimen you are, my jewel. No one else has got what I've got, and everyone wants it. Professors want you. *A hundred months have passed, Lorena, since first I held that hand in mine.* She brings tears to the eyes. Look at them. The parted lips. The fixed eyes. Not one of them can look away, not for one second. Don't suppose they all understand the words but even so . . . he slipped out onto the veranda. The air smelled of lilac. Before him, just about still visible through the deepening night, a descent into a steep wooded valley. From out here it was just a woman's voice, a nice voice, not magnificent but sweet and full of feeling. Hard little worker, my Julia, uses what she's got. She's bought you this. This lot, that ridiculously beautiful woman, they wouldn't give you the time of day if it weren't for her. Snobs the lot of them. And that pompous old general. Those awful whiskers and that stupid little beard. Those villages we came through, probably full of cholera. What a world. And that fat fool down there stuffing himself like a goose. Still, the same everywhere. Jesus, he could have gone down the sewers himself one time. Back there. Easy to go under in this business. The sultry evening air carried the drink to his head very quickly. No more going under. Not for me. Not anymore.

She was drawing to a close when he returned to the room, standing by the veranda doors with his glass and his empty grin.

I hardly feel the cold, Lorena.

That's the way, Julia.

An uproar of applause. The beauty was jumping up and down and clapping her hands, turning to the girl next to her, all teeth and lips and perfect little nose. Sokolov applauded sternly. His mouth constricted to a thin short line, perfectly straight. Theo watched his wife engage with the process of acclaim and congratulation, using all the bits of Russian she'd learned, "Yes, thank you, how kind." He watched Liliya Grigorievna cross the room like a fawn and embrace Julia, then he watched them converse. Amazing, those two faces close together, their two mouths side by side. It made his head spin. The world could not contain such strangeness. He found himself next to them. They were talking animatedly.

"Liliya Grigorievna was just telling me that there's this wonderful fortune-teller in St. Petersburg," Julia said. "She lives near the circus."

"And now he's going to laugh at us," Liliya Grigorievna said.

"Indeed," said Theo, smiling, "I am."

"Theo," she said later back in their room, "you knew I was going to perform. You brought my guitar."

"Of course I did, dear."

"How much did they pay us?" she asked.

He laughed.

"Theo! It's not funny. You should tell me these things."

"Come on, Julia, you know you're not interested in all that."

"I thought this was a social visit," she said. "But I find I'm the paid entertainment as usual."

"It's both!" he cried, coming behind her and clapping his hands down on her shoulders. "Haven't you had a nice time?"

"How much did Rudakov pay?"

"Julia," he said, pushing himself down beside her and smiling drunkenly into her face. His hair was in a mess and his cravat was loose and stained with wine. "You know damn well it wouldn't mean a thing to you if I did tell you an amount. We did well out of it. You don't have to worry about a thing. *We—we* did well."

"I'm always the entertainment," she said.

"Of course you are," he said, "because you're so wonderful."

"I like Liliya Grigorievna," she said later, tucking her feet in under his thigh as they lay in bed. "When we get to St. Petersburg, I want to go and see that fortune-teller."

"Don't waste your money," he said, "it's hogwash." Then after a moment, "Anyway, who was this fortune-teller who said you would travel a very, very long way? A thing just about anybody with half a brain could have told you."

"It was in New Orleans," she said.

"Oh, your time in New Orleans."

"I want to see her anyway."

Theo yawned. "Oh, if you want," he said, "as long as you know you're wasting your money. Tearing it all up into tiny pieces and throwing it in the sea. Who cares?"

"Oh, you," she said sleepily, and in a moment had drifted away silently and completely. There one minute, gone the next.

Wide awake and still drunk, tears starting in and out of his glazed eyes for no good reason, Theo stared at the moonlight shadows stealing over the top of the curtain onto the ceiling. These tears made no sense, and he didn't understand them. He only knew he felt terrible. Julia slept by him like a faithful dog. He could feel a pulse beating strongly under the fur in her neck where his hand rested. "It's not fur," she always scolded, "it's hair." As if it made a difference.

After a long tour they arrived in St. Petersburg in a high summer of thick yellow heat and many storms. "Here's where we get you on a horse again," Theo said. Close by their rooms was the grandest circus of them all. She was tired as hell, and it felt as if they'd been on the road forever.

"What's the matter?" he asked.

She'd been getting weepy these past couple of weeks. Sentimental weepy, so that the sight of a dog scrounging 'round a bin or the sound of birds singing in the dark of an early morning would set her off. Now she stood looking out of the window at the gnats dancing in a smoky pollen haze that hovered outside the window overlooking the garden behind their lodgings.

"Why are you crying?" he asked.

"I don't know," she said, and grabbed his hand and kissed it and told him she loved him.

"I love you too."

He could say "I love you" and mean it, at the same time crying out a silent howl of confusion to the heavens. Who is she? Who am I? What am I doing in this strange land?

"Oh, I'm all right," she said, pulling herself together. "I'm perfectly fine," and stepped away and began picking at the garland of small white flowers she was adjusting for tomorrow night's performance.

"Well, you've got a whole day off. What are you going to do?"

"I think I'll read for a bit."

"Good idea. Put your feet up." Theo paced twice about the room. "I think I'll go out," he said.

"Bring me something nice," she said, looking up, "from the pastry shop."

"Not in a hurry, are you? I thought I'd take a stroll around."

"Not in the least."

He went back to the circus, walked about behind the scenes, just strolling with his hands in his pockets, drinking in the smells of the place. Nothing like it. How could he live without this? The circus was in his blood. He'd tried other things, they didn't work. God! Raising his eyes to the glory of the place. Not so much a circus as a huge palace with columns and frescoes and chandeliers. He'd never forget the sight of her in that ring last night, riding in on a white horse, three times 'round, then dismounting, and smoothly into the dance as the horse is led away. Such a small thing, Julia in that great space of red curtains and gilt, the tiers of boxes around the ring going higher and higher, back and back, with the toffs and the swells with their jewels at the front, and everyone else behind. Oh, you have cracked the nut, boy, you've made it, he told himself. One in the eye for the folks back home. From the circus he walked down to the river, over a bridge, back across another, went into a tavern and sat in a corner with his drink, his suave smile imposing itself upon his face as it did more and more these days, even when his insides were quivering. He drank a few more, then walked back, got halfway upstairs before remembering about the pastry shop and went back for a couple of sweet buns.

When he got back, she was gone.

He looked in the other room. "Julia?" he said. "Julia?"

But there was nowhere she could be. She'd gone out.

He broke out in a sweat.

———————

She knew exactly where to go. Behind the circus, Liliya Grigorievna had said. The street with the barber's on the corner, and on the other side a habadasher's shop. A few doors down, red door, number sixteen. And on the way back from yesterday's rehearsal she'd seen it plain, as if it wanted to be found so easily, the barber's corner, the habadasher's opposite, a quick glance down the narrow street as they passed. I'll go now while he's out, she thought. I'll just knock on the door and make an appointment, I'm sure she won't be able to see me straightaway. I'll get back before him, and he'll never know. Ah, but then I'll have to get away again, won't I? One thing at a time.

It was ages since she'd been out alone. Not since the American tour.

She walked past the pastry shop. Her bonnet was deep, the veil very thick and long. A young man was swabbing the steps. He smiled and tipped his head to her, respectful, and she nodded back. It wasn't far.

The door was answered by a very beautiful little girl of eight or nine with long tangled golden ringlets.

"Dobryj dyen," said Julia brightly to assuage the effect of her thoroughly veiled condition. *"Parles tu français, ma chérie?"*

"Oui, madame," the child replied gravely.

Liliya had said the fortune-teller spoke good French but no English.

"I'd like to make an appointment to see Madame Pankova," Julia continued in French.

"Un moment," said the child, withdrawing into the shadowy hall and disappearing into a room at the back. Now that she was here, Julia felt silly. Of course Theo was right. You couldn't be on the road any length of time and remain unaware of the artifice involved in this kind of thing, but still, she thought. Now and again you got an exception. She had no doubt whatsoever that the gift existed and that one or two people had it, you just had to weed them out from the rest. She heard voices, the child's and another that cracked and croaked. In a minute or so the girl came back. "If you can wait twenty minutes or so," she said, "she'll see you now," and showed her into a small sitting room with a cheerful fire, comfortable chairs, a samovar on the sideboard and a tall unlit white candle in the center of a round table. Madame Pankova had just seen another client and needed time to remuster her strength, the girl said with the air of someone much older who'd said the same thing many times. She took Julia's money, asked her to please sit, then poured tea and politely offered the cup, raising her large gray eyes to where Julia's would have been.

"Merci," said Julia, amused by the child's official air.

There was a slight hesitation, a flicker of time when it seemed the girl was going to say something more, perhaps ask a question, but it passed and with a solemn bow she turned and left the room, leaving the door open. The sound of dishes being washed came from somewhere down the hall. A bell rang far away in the city, a steady, listless tolling. There was a poster of Paris on the wall, and the wallpaper had a pattern of coiled ferns.

Madame Pankova entered twenty-five minutes later from an inner room, a short fat woman in a dark blue dress, leaning heavily on a stick. "I have constant pain," she said by way of a greeting, "constant pain. Nothing can be done about it."

"I'm so sorry," said Julia.

"Nothing to be sorry about. Yeva!"

She sat down in a high wing-backed chair, resting her stick by its side. The girl appeared and set about what was obviously a familiar routine of putting a battered footstool under Madame Pankova's black-buttoned boots, which were tied up with indigo ribbons in floppy bows. She lit the tall white candle in the center of the table, placed a worn deck of playing cards next to it, drew the curtains to shut out daylight and withdrew as quietly as she'd come, closing the door behind her.

"Well," croaked Madame Pankova, "*you're* a mystery woman. Are you going to take that veil off?"

"No."

"Why not?"

"I never do."

Madame Pankova sighed heavily. She was a swarthy woman with long white hair hanging down under a red handkerchief. She sighed again, looked away, blew out her cheeks in a rude kind of way and looked back. "What do you want to know?" she asked.

"Can I ask anything?"

"Anything at all."

Julia thought for a few seconds, then said, "Does my husband love me?"

Madame Pankova drank some tea. "Don't you know?"

"I think he does."

Madame Pankova held up her finger for silence, stared expressionlessly for several minutes at the dark shape before her. At last she leaned forward, wincing and gasping softly as she did so, picked up the pack of cards and shoved them across the table.

"Shuffle," she said.

Julia shuffled with thinly gloved fingers.

"You're not taking your gloves off to shuffle? Don't want your palm read?"

"No. Just the cards, please," Julia said.

Madame Pankova nodded.

"Is that enough?" Julia asked.

"Is it?"

"I don't know."

Madame Pankova shrugged and looked away as if she'd lost interest.

"There," said Julia, "that's enough," and laid down three cards as commanded. They meant nothing to her. There was the ace of spades and the kings of spades and clubs.

"One more," said Madame Pankova.

The nine of hearts.

Madame Pankova stared at the cards blankly for a few minutes, then said, "This is a mess," and after a longish pause, "You're having a boy."

Julia started.

Madame Pankova leaned over with her eyes closed and her head in her hands. Her fingernails were violet, long and thin like talons.

"Your boy is a traveler."

She sat back, opened her eyes and drank some tea.

Julia's heart was a distant pounding in her throat and wrists. The blood came and went, not always regular. She hadn't seen it in a while. Why hadn't they thought about this? What, was it too impossible to think about?

"Can you tell me," asked Julia, trying not to seem surprised, "will my baby take after his mother or his father?"

Madame Pankova slopped her tea with a shaky hand. How old the hand was, older than the rest of her, a shriveled, shiny-veined whitening chicken claw. "Both of you," she said. The hand scooped up the cards and shuffled them expertly back into the deck.

"Shuffle again."

The second spread was bigger and mostly diamonds and spades. "Yes," said Madame Pankova. "He does. Your husband." Three or four vague meandering forgettables later—it appeared there was some trouble ahead but this would pass and peace would be restored—she suddenly said, "Your mother is watching over you. She is saying, you are *mine.*"

"My mother?"

"'You are mine. You are *mine.*' She watches."

Dead, then.

Of course.

The room was too hot. The fortune-teller pointedly consulted a small watch on the end of a purple ribbon that she drew from a pocket. "One more question," she said.

"One more," repeated Julia softly, "one more."

"Come, come," said Madame Pankova.

The sound of seagulls passed over the street and settled petulantly somewhere close by.

"Am I human?" Julia asked.

Madame Pankova looked down into her lap and said nothing for a long time.

"Why do you ask?" she said at last.

"Because," said Julia, "I want to know for sure."

Madame Pankova closed her eyes and raised her eyebrows high. "It's possible to be human and not know it," she said, fingering the ribbon in her hands. The minutes stretched, and Julia wondered if the old woman was falling asleep. But then she opened her eyes and stared into the candle flame. Another minute passed.

"You're human," Madame Pankova said, snapped her eyes shut, sighed, snapped them open again and called, "Yeva!"

Immediately the child appeared, hovering through the darkness like an angel in the candlelight, to the window to throw back the curtains. Light flooded the room. Madame Pankova screwed up her face and muttered darkly to herself in Russian, then raised her ravaged face and said loudly for Julia's benefit, "The pain is terrible. No one knows how terrible the pain." Out she hobbled, the stick trembling, and the child blew out the candle.

A boy. All the way back, hurrying, she held one hand against her stomach. Are you in there? But of course it could happen. Never discussed, never considered. She'd thought she couldn't. Why? Because she was so wrong in so many ways, somehow she'd thought that would be wrong too. And he'd never said anything. Never a what-if or when-we, like other couples. It must've been there all the time like an island in the fog and neither of them had seen it. It might not come, the unimaginable boy. Creature-to-be. It would hurt. The thought of Theo made her scared. He never said he wanted a child. Never said he didn't. The show. She couldn't dance, ride horses. Any day the familiar stain, the sense of drain would surely come. The old woman had mostly just rambled, vague—you will make a good friend whose initial will be T, some-thing has been troubling you, your husband thinks about you a very great deal, he is thinking of you this very moment, yes, I'm sure he is. But that thing about Mother. Mamá walking away. Pigtail eternal. Julia's eyes filled. What a fool she'd been. Keeping that so close all her life, the eternal clue she invoked at night before she went to sleep. That was her mother, neither alive nor dead but simply other, gone. A dream, not in life or death but somewhere else. At no time had she ever thought: my mother is dead. And she'd never wondered about a real woman some-where up there in those green and sandy sierras, somewhere you could reach by walking. She'd been a child with a story.

She's dead now. Final. And this boy.

It might all come to nothing.

Theo was there when she got back.

"Where the hell have you been?" he said furiously, stamping over as she came in the door.

"I went to the fortune-teller," she said.

"Oh, for God's sake! You can't do this, Julia! You can't just go out without me whenever you want."

"Well, you know I don't. It's all right, I was covered."

"That's not the point."

Here we go again. "No harm done," she said, "I'm back now."

"It's just not fair, Julia," he said as she unveiled and took off her gloves. "It's not fair to *me*. What if something happened to you?"

"I only went 'round the corner."

"You have got to be honest with me, Julia, this is just not fair. You waited deliberately till I'd gone out, didn't you? Then you sneaked off. I bet you thought you'd get back before me and I'd never know."

It was so true that she couldn't help but smile. I've done it, she thought. I went out and nothing happened.

"It's not funny!"

"Sorry," she said.

He'd sulk for the next couple of days. He was getting it down to a fine art. Here came the first harbingers, the noble suffering face, the down-cast brow. He was spinning a little web of woundedness between them.

"You know damn well I'd have taken you if you'd asked," he said.

"Oh, but you'd have laughed at me."

"Well, yes, but that's understandable. Giving your money to some fraud! Oh, Julia."

"You really do think I'm stupid, don't you?" she said. "Like all those other people who think I must be because I have this." She pulled on her beard.

"I know you're not stupid," he said coldly. "That's why it makes me angry to see you behaving as if you are."

He walked out abruptly. His footsteps echoed in the stairwell. She went to look. No blood.

Instead of a heat haze, there was rain falling softly on willows outside the window.

"I wish we could go to Vienna," she said.

"Don't you like it here?"

"It's getting cold again."

Theo took a match from a silver box and lit a cigar.

"I think," he said, shaking the match with the air of a man with nothing to do, leaning back and blowing smoke upward, "if we give it another two years. Till we have enough for a decent apartment somewhere pleasant—Vienna, by all means if you like, or even . . ."

He broke off and gazed into space.

She picked up that lump of wood, her old doll, and lay down on the bed, turning on her side. "Thank God, nothing for a while," she said.

"Nothing at all unless you want to go to the circus."

"On Friday."

"Why Friday?"

"Darmody's juggling."

"Fine. I'll get tickets."

"I have friends in Vienna, don't I?" she said proudly.

Theo nodded, savoring the tang of his cigar. He'd get them a box, the best he could. She'd walk in on his arm, veiled. Everyone would know who she was but no one would get near. They'd whisper: that's Julia Pastrana. But if they wanted to see her they'd have to pay.

"Vienna is certainly a possibility," he said.

"I can't ride anymore," she said suddenly in an odd tone.

"What do you mean?"

"I can't ride."

"Why not?"

She looked away. "I'm having a baby," she said.

Theo's face didn't change.

"You're not serious," he said.

"I think I am."

Oh God. His face didn't change. A thousand voices murmured in his head.

"I'm sure I am," she said.

It couldn't happen. He was always careful. When? Not always easy getting out in time. When? Oh God, after a few drinks. Who cares then? "What?" he said, screaming inside.

"I've missed twice now."

"Twice." He swallowed, playing for time.

"A baby," she said, meeting his eyes with a wary look.

Time slowed for Theo, his every move, the way his lips formed the shape of an opening to allow smoke to drift from them, the way the smoke seemed alive as it played with the air. He closed his eyes.

"Do you think that's why I've been feeling so tired?" she asked.

"Very likely," he said.

When he opened them again her eyes were glistening. "You don't want it," she said. "You don't want it because you think it'll be like me."

His eyes filled with sympathy. His brain went *tick, tick, tick*, bring another poor freak into the world, *tick tick*, as it is they're all looking at me, *tick, tick, tick*, this is impossible. "Not at all," he said, "not at all." He knew he ought to go to her but was suddenly afraid. "You have to see a doctor," he said. "Make sure."

"You don't want it."

"Don't be silly."

The shine of tears under her eye. "Will you love it, if it's like me?" she said.

"Of course I will!"

"You don't want it to be like me though, do you?"

Tick, tick, tick. Calm. "Listen, Julia," he said, pulling sense on like a cloak, walking over to her, caressing the sides of her arms and smiling reassuringly, "it's mine, it goes without saying I'll love it." A hairy baby monkey, he thought. "But obviously it would be better for him to be born normal."

"Him?"

"Or her."

"But if he isn't?"

"Just—I don't know, Julia, I don't know what to say, it would just be better if it was normal. But I don't suppose—I don't know how these things work. We need to get a good doctor . . ."

Trailing off.

Think, think, think. We have—six, yes, six more shows to February. She'd never get rid of it, not her. Catholic. She can sing anyway, play her guitar. They'll still come. Could she dance? Even if she just stood there, whatever she did, they'd still come, just to see her. "It'll be all right," he said with worried eyes. Doing sums in his head. Oh God. We need to rake in as much as we can before. She'll have to take it easy for a bit. But not for too long. She's a trouper.

"We'll get you to a doctor," he said. "If we were in Moscow we could get Sokolov."

Perhaps she'll miscarry, he thought. No. She's as strong as an ox. He laughed. Strong as a Julia.

"Don't laugh at me," she said.

"I'm not laughing at you."

It was confirmed. She was three months gone. The doctor had shaken Theo's hand and looked him steadily in the eye on parting, and he'd seen it there, the thing he would find in all eyes from now on, the thought: My God, he does! He fucks the ape. Now they'd all know. Looking in the mirror, he practiced the smile he would smile back at them. Calm, proud, defiant.

Three months, four, five, still dancing, hardly showing. The sparkle was back in Theo's eyes, and a weight lifted from Julia's mind.

"After these shows we should settle for a while," she said. "Till the baby's older."

"Sure," he said, smiling. "But not for too long."

While not quite at rest, his mind had settled now. First, the child might be normal. Firstborn. My seed. Blood of my blood and all that. It was a tangle. He'd no idea how he felt. Fatherhood had never been a consideration. But then, he thought, if it's hairy, think about it. If they flock now, imagine. The ape woman and her remarkable offspring. They'll be trampling over one another to get a look. And the science! God, those doctors salivating. How well they lived now—Theo bit the end off a high-class cigar—but this would be nothing. They could live anywhere. A place here, a place there. The best. Sometimes a creature formed in his mind, a baby monkey with human eyes as soft and sweet as a kitten's.

"Our baby will grow up in the most wonderful world imaginable," he said expansively, lying back on the chaise and trying to blow smoke rings, "backstage. Born in a trunk. Town to town. The thrill of it all. The smell of sawdust."

"Face facts, Theo," she said, breaking the thread on something she was sewing. "We can't drag a baby around all over the place. Not when it's tiny."

"Some of the happiest people I've ever known have been born into the business," he said. "Suckled in the wings. Weaned in a circus wagon."

"I think we should go back to Vienna," she said. "After the last show."

"Well," he said, "we'll see."

To Moscow, where the baby would be born. Ilya Andreyevich Volkov had found them a nice little flat near the Arbat, and was lending them Polina to take care of the place. He sent Tolya to pick them up from the posting stage. The familiar face was reassuring, breathing smoke into the frozen air from deep inside a sheepskin collar. We don't go back, she thought. Or hardly ever. We move on. And on and on. At night the names of places paraded through her mind as she fell asleep. Moscow, snow, Tolya, Polina, almost a homecoming.

"My congratulations to you both," Tolya said, grinning widely as he hoisted the trunk onto the carriage. Look at the monkey father, Theo thought, shivering. He could see the thought in the boy's eyes.

"Oh, it's so lovely to see you again," Julia said, ridiculously excited as if the boy were a lost kinsman home from war.

"And you, madame."

"Hurry it up, Tolya," Theo said, "I'm soaking wet out here."

"Of course."

Theo climbed in and huddled himself up, shivering. "What a climate," he said.

Julia laughed. "Look at you, all snowy!"

It was late afternoon, already dark. The shops were open, the streets crowded. She was humming, leaning forward to watch it all go by. It was pelting down, fat flakes falling intently. Tolya carried their trunk up and Polina was there, smiling and flustered, showing them the bread and pies she'd laid out, the rich pickle-y soup simmering at the back of the stove. The fire blazed. "I'll make tea now," she said.

"Heaven," said Julia.

Theo threw himself down in the biggest chair and closed his eyes. Three more months. Oh, well, Moscow. Maybe he'd see Liliya Grigorievna. Julia flittered here and there, opening doors. "Theo," she said, "come and look."

"In a minute."

"Will you eat now or later?" asked Polina.

"Now," said Theo, "I'm starving. Julia!"

"Wait until you see," she said, appearing in the doorway.

The table was already set. Polina served soup and put out the bread. "I'll go now," she said, "if there's nothing else you want. I'll come in early and see to the fire. Tolya can give me a lift now."

"Of course."

"You're looking so well, madame," Polina said as she put on her coat. "We've all been so excited about your news." I bet you have, thought Theo.

"Oh, stop with all the 'madame,'" said Julia. "Call me Julia."

"Oh!" said Polina, pausing with her muffler wound half 'round her neck. "That's so nice."

"And you too, Tolya." Julia broke a piece of bread in half.

"Thank you so much, madame," he said, and the three of them laughed.

"And now," said Theo, "let's eat before we expire."

"Oh, isn't this nice?" she said when they'd finally gone. "Aren't we lucky?"

"Indeed we are."

"And wasn't it nice to see Tolya again? And Polina."

"Absolutely."

A fog of tiredness was making Theo feel stupid. It was four more days till Christmas and he'd arranged for her to see a doctor the day after tomorrow, get it over with before the holiday. She was well enough, but no harm in making sure. He watched her eat. She was fastidiously clean and dainty, as if to compensate for her appearance. She caught him looking and her eyes smiled.

"You have lovely eyes, Julia," he said.

She did. That wasn't a lie.

"He just kicked me," she said.

"The brute."

She'd put his hand there the other night. That peculiar feeling against his palm, something alive under the skin. Her belly was hard and round. She wore loose gowns now except onstage, where she covered the growing mound with a crinoline.

"You don't seem that tired," he said.

"I was," she said, "but now I feel all excited. Hurry up, Theo. There's a cradle." She pushed her bowl away and stood up.

"Aren't you going to eat anymore?"

"Later," she said. "Come and see." She went next door, and he heard her struggling with the catches on the trunk. He finished the soup and ate another slice of bread with butter before following her next door. The room was pleasant but not large. The bed filled most of it. A blue-and-yellow jug filled with dried flowers and grasses stood on the chiffonier. There was a chest of drawers, a pretty armoire painted peasant style, and above the bed a picture of a country lane in a flat landscape of thin spring trees and low sun. She'd changed into her nightgown and was taking all the little dresses and bonnets she'd been making for the baby out of the trunk and laying them on the bed.

"Look," she said. Next to the bed, a hooded cradle with a white blanket.

"If I die," she said in a practical voice, folding things neatly away into the bottom drawer, "don't forget I've put his things in this drawer all ready, in sizes. Look, the smallest at this end, getting bigger over there."

"You won't die."

"I know, but just in case."

"No talk of dying. You'll have Trettenbacher. He's the best."

"I know." She shrugged. "No harm in being prepared."

He lay down on the bed with his hands behind his head watching the snow drifting above the curtain. She closed the drawer. Her nightgown was too long for her and she had to hold it up. "And the coverlet," she said, reaching once more into the trunk and bringing out a tiny quilt embroidered with flowers. "There!" she said, laying it down on top of the white blanket in the cradle, stroking it gently.

"I'm glad it's not Sokolov," she said. "When am I seeing Dr. Trettenbacher?"

"Day after tomorrow." He turned back the covers and started to undress.

"I wonder what he's like." She got into bed and sat with her knees up, watching him.

"Trettenbacher? I told you. The best."

"Yes, but I wonder what he's *like*."

———

Trettenbacher was a brisk, bluff man with a shiny red face and a heavy thatch of gray hair. "She's very healthy," he said, closing the bedroom door after the examination, "apart from the fact that she's coming down with a cold."

"Oh, good," said Theo, standing by the fire, "yes, Julia's always been healthy. Polina!"

Polina appeared.

"Take her some cocoa, would you, Polina," he said. "Get her to lie down."

Trettenbacher waited till she'd left, then said, "That's not to say we might not have a problem."

"Problem?"

"Her size."

"What's wrong with her size?"

"She's narrow," said Trettenbacher, snapping his bag shut.

"Julia? Narrow?"

"It's a big baby."

"But she's quite hefty," said Theo.

"It's what's on the inside that counts." Trettenbacher looked up, smiling in a meaningless, professional way. "But don't worry," he said reassuringly, "she's not the first. Might have a hard time but we'll get her through. Now, I'll see her again after . . ."

"Tell me the truth," Theo said, scared. "Is she in any danger?"

Trettenbacher looked at the fire. "Well . . ." he said, and Polina came in with a tray. "Cocoa was all ready," she said, smiling and bustling through the room. "Any for you, sir?"

"No." Theo glared at her. "I am trying to speak to the doctor."

"Oh, sorry, sir."

Stupid woman.

"Let me," said the doctor, opening the bedroom door for her, ushering her in and closing it sharply behind her. "Now," he said, "where were we?"

"Danger," said Theo sharply.

"Of course. Birth is, of course, always dangerous. She's probably a little more at risk than the average woman but not as much as many."

"What's that supposed to mean?"

"Exactly what it says." Trettenbacher walked to the door. "There's always danger. She'll be fine. Make sure she gets plenty of rest. She's not still dancing, is she?"

She was, not as much, a little, slower. Three more stops on the tour. "Of course not," Theo said.

"Mr. Lent," said Trettenbacher, "I must stress that your wife will have the finest available medical care, the absolute best of modern obstetrics." He buttoned his overcoat. "I can assure you I have no shortage of extremely talented volunteers to assist me." He smiled. "Scientifically," he said, putting on his hat, "this is a fascinating case. A tremendous opportunity."

Theo imagined them all craning to see what came out. She could die, he thought, as the doctor's footsteps faded away in the stairwell.

"I'm off now, Mr. Lent," said Polina, coming out of the bedroom. "I've taken her some cocoa and she's having a nice lie-down."

"Thank you, Polina."

"Are you all right, Mr. Lent?"

Theo blinked. "Of course I am, why do you ask?"

"I don't know, I thought you looked a little—upset."

"No, no, I was just thinking," he said, then realized he was standing, gaping at the girl in a vacuous sort of way. "Good, good," he said, reviving, "we'll expect you on Christmas Eve then, as arranged. Very good. Thank you, Polina."

By Christmas Eve, Julia's cold had settled in, and she had an awful headache and was beginning to wheeze. There was no question of her attending the party at Volkov's, but Theo went anyway. She didn't mind. They'd be together all day tomorrow. Polina came to make hot drinks and see to the fire. She'd brought a cake and some nuts, and after she'd puttered about at the stove for half an hour they sat down and ate the cake while Julia drank some awful milky buttery thing that Polina said would do her good. The slippery texture made her gag but she sipped away obediently.

"You get that down," Polina said, "and you'll be better before you know it. I dare say this must be the coldest winter you've ever seen."

"I wanted to go to Vienna," Julia said, "but the schedule won't allow. Not yet."

"It's a shame you can't go where you please."

"Who can?" said Julia.

"Some can."

"Can you?"

"I'm going to my father's tomorrow," Polina said, as if that answered the question. "My sisters and brother will be there."

"Oh, well, you mustn't stay up late, you know. You'll be wanting to make an early start tomorrow."

"Not that early." Polina took the empty cup from Julia. "They don't live far. Shall I make you some more of that before I go?"

"No, I'm fine. Thank you."

"How's your head?"

"Better, I think."

"You should have a sleep," Polina said. "There's nothing a good sleep doesn't improve." She stood up.

"This creature's kicking me," Julia said. "He doesn't want me to sleep."

"Calm down, you bad baby." Polina leaned over and patted Julia's huge drum of a belly. "Let your poor little mother sleep. Now. I'll just tidy up a bit in there and then I'll be off."

But after she'd gone there was no chance of sleep. A boy. Big boy. Elbowing, kneeing, sticking his feet everywhere. Kicking right where all the milky slop lay and making her feel sick. She put her hands over him. Theo Junior. Don't let him be like me. Make him normal. It would not be so bad, she thought, to live in Moscow. A house here, instead of Vienna. It was quiet, no sound but the snow, placidly falling, kissing the window. "Look at your cradle, little man," she whispered. A baby's smooth head, her dark hairy hand, an indrawn breath. Elisio. Solana holding her hand. Come away. "I'm your mother," she said. "Now go to sleep." But he was restless under her ribs.

Theo came back drunk at midnight, face glowing with cold. "Merry Christmas!" he cried. "It's Christmas Day!" striding to the window and flinging the shutters wide. "Listen to the bells."

"Theo! Don't open the window, we'll freeze."

"Sorry." He knocked against the chiffonier, yanked at his collar. "Did I wake you?"

"I wasn't asleep," she said. "How was it?"

"Oh, wonderful. You know Volkov. Only the best when he puts his mind to it. Everyone dressed up. You know. Games and all that jolly stuff. Plenty to eat. We all sang Christmas carols. Liliya Whats her name was there, and she asked after you. Sends her love. How's your cold?"

"The same."

He sat on the side of the bed, grinning at the floor and chuckling to himself. He had danced with Liliya Grigorievna Levkova, this smooth fragrant creature, her slender waist a thing of beauty. She'd smiled in his face the whole time, chatting brightly. He hadn't got the foggiest idea what she was talking about, her words were floating somewhere in the air above his head. One dance.

"Want anything?" he asked. "Shame you weren't there. A drink?"

She shook her head.

"Poor old Julia," he said, patting her knee, "never mind, it'll pass. You should have gone to sleep."

"Every time I start dropping off, he kicks me."

"Oh, he does, does he? You're that sure it's a boy?"

She smiled, taking his hand. "I have a feeling."

"Give the little bastard some vodka," Theo said, "knock him out."

She settled back on the pillow. "I think he's quieting down a bit now. He doesn't like it when I cough."

"Cough no better?"

"On and off. I'm afraid I'll be tossing and turning."

"I'll sleep in there," he said, "give you some peace."

"You should. You don't want to catch it."

"It's nice in there by the fire," he said, "I'll take this other pillow."

"Look at you," she said fondly, "you're reeling."

"No, I'm not."

"Get yourself another blanket from the chest," she said. "Now that you're back, I think I can sleep."

By the time he'd made the chesterfield comfortable and got ready for bed, she'd fallen asleep. He poured himself one more drink, lit a cigar and stood in his dressing gown looking out of the window. It had stopped snowing. Everything was still, and the moon made the snow-covered street blue. His heart raced. "There's nothing to worry about," he told himself aloud, swaying slightly, "nothing at all to worry about." He drank some more and didn't remember going to bed and falling asleep till the bells woke him. Julia was up making tea, padding about in her nightie, unaware that he was watching her. Her strangeness could still strike him breathless.

Three more months, give or take. Lyublino, Pushkino, Mytisci. Three more months, my little trouper.

———

It was a Tuesday in March, a very cold morning, and she'd just gotten up. She'd woken early, Polina wasn't here yet, and she was stirring the still-glowing embers of last night's fire back into life. Suddenly she was soaking wet. Everything was soaking wet. She took the candle from the mantel, went back in and touched Theo's shoulder. He was frowning in his sleep, mouth open, a faint snore back in his nose.

"Theo." She shook him gently. "I think it's starting."

Theo blinking, scowling at the candlelight, his hair in his face.

"It's early," he said, grunting, sitting up in a groggy fuzz, "are you sure?"

She stood shivering, holding her wet nightdress away from her body. "Look at this."

"It's too soon," he said.

"I know."

Theo groaned. First sign, Trettenbacher had said, bring her in. We won't leave anything to chance, her being so small. He swung his legs out of bed and the cold hit him.

"What time is it?"

"About five."

"Oh God!" He started dressing, semiconscious. Julia stood quietly, holding her stomach with both hands and looking down at it. It felt heavy, ridiculously so, but then it had for ages. She listened for pain within her body, but there wasn't any, just a great cold that made her tremble all over.

"Quick," said Theo, "put a dry nightie on."

She took one from underneath the piles of bibs and booties and neatly folded baby dresses in the chiffonier.

"Right," he said, running out to fetch a carriage with his coat half on, "get yourself all muffled up. Be ready."

She wiped herself clean with a towel and was ready by the time he came back. In the carriage she felt something shift inside. "Theo!" she said, gripping his arm.

"Nearly there," he said. But the first real pain she'd ever known began, and she tightened her grip so much on his arm that he clenched his teeth. The pain soared, made her close her eyes, tense every muscle and hiss. "Nothing at all to worry about," he said with more confidence than he felt. "You're getting the best possible medical attention."

The pain ebbed but came again at the door of the hospital. Trettenbacher himself came out to greet her, flanked by nurses. She was doubled over, Theo holding her up.

"My dear, your teeth are chattering," Trettenbacher said, rubbing her cold hands. "There's nothing to be afraid of."

"I'm not afraid," she gasped. "I'm cold."

"Well, we shall warm you up! This way—"

"You're in good hands now, Julia," Theo said, shifting from foot to foot in the cold. "Trettenbacher, do you need me for anything? Should I wait?"

"Not at all. It won't be for some time."

"You'll keep me informed."

"Of course."

"Brave girl!" Theo said. "You can do it!"

"Of course she can!"

The nurses took her to a room painted white, with a high bed. The pain was gone. They told her to lie down and call them as soon as it came back. A door was open, there were voices. One of the nurses came back with an extra blanket. "Very cold out there this morning," she said pleasantly, "icy. How are you feeling?"

"Scared," said Julia.

"Of course you are."

She was a kind-looking woman with a tired smile and a soft, wrinkled face, deeply hollowed. "Everyone feels scared with their first. Only natural. Don't worry, it'll all be over before you know it." Julia knew her from one of the doctor's visits.

Another came and stood looking over her shoulder. This one knew her only by reputation and had been longing to see her. "Poor strange thing," she said quietly.

The hollow-faced nurse smoothed down the blanket and checked the water jug. "I'd try to get a bit of sleep, if I were you," she said.

Impossible.

It was hideous. The pain beyond words and imagination, a raw black bubble blowing bigger and bigger, unendurable. Surpassing, turning its monstrous back for the fall like a sea beast. In the respites, the nurses came and went, and Trettenbacher with his assistants. All morning. But what was time? She knew it passed because of the window. She'd watched the light come up, watched the snow so cool and lovely a world away, wanted to roll in it, roll away the heat, watched the flakes grow sparse and slow, watched the white unremarkable sky persist in indifference as she burned, till slowly, scarcely perceptibly, it dimmed toward another evening.

"I can't stand it," she said, tears wetting the front of her nightgown.

"Not much longer," a voice said briskly. One of those doctors. There were lots.

The hollow-faced nurse, smiling kindly.

"She's quite the stoic, isn't she?" someone said.

Then it was dark and there were no more respites. In the end it was only pain, and the pain was like fire, greedy for air, greedy for the whole world. Julia put back her head and moaned, a long harsh growl that rose to the pitch of a scream.

"Time to send for the father," someone said.

"Chloroform," said Trettenbacher calmly, calling his students 'round him.

The pain was taking her away. The voice, urbane, whispered in her ear, "There is nothing to worry about. We'll give you something for the pain now, your baby is very large and we'll need to help him along."

She couldn't see or think.

"Take another look, Dr. Chizh, can you feel the head? Breathe. Breathe in very deeply, *very* deeply."

She was lost in the dark.

"Heroldstein, check her pulse."

Chizh cut and Trettenbacher, stern-faced with concentration, reached in with his metal tongs and slowly pulled into the world a big, hairy boy with screwed-up eyes and clenched fists.

Peace. No more pain, or if there was it was ignorable, just ordinary pain, tame pain that would one day die. They were sewing her up. The baby had not cried when they pulled him out, though he took in that first mighty gasp of the world audibly. What is this now, and how should I meet it? Steel yourself. He was quiet when the nurse finally placed him swaddled in his mother's arms, the most beautiful baby in the world. Apart from the soles and palms of his tiny pink feet and hands, he was hairy all over, even the backs of his ears, and his big cone-shaped head bore a great healthy black mop. He was puzzled, perfect.

That's how it was when Theo arrived, their two hairy entranced faces staring each at the other.

"He knows me, Theo," she whispered.

"Of course he does." Theo reached furtively toward the baby's mop of a head. "You're his mother."

"No, I mean he *knows* me. Isn't he beautiful?"

"He is."

"Just look at him. Theo. Theo Junior."

"He won't look at me," said Theo Senior.

"He can't see much yet."

"He sees *you*."

"Yes, he does. He sees me. Do you want to hold him?"

He'd rather not, but couldn't say. Babies were odd. He might drop it. Well, he'd better do this, so he took it and there it lay, it, him, the baby, warm and heavy in his arms. "Hello," he said to it.

"I wanted so much for him to be normal," she said, "but now it doesn't matter. His skin's pale, look. He gets that from you."

"So it is."

Poor child would suffer, Theo thought. Mine. My child. How did it come to this?

She burst into tears. "He's so beautiful and everyone will call him ugly," she said.

"No, they won't."

But of course they would. His path was clear. Ape Boy. Remarkable, Unparalleled, the only Mother-and-Child Ape People in existence.

"He'll be a wonder like you are."

"But *I'm* ugly. The ugliest in the world. But he's not, he's beautiful, but no one will see it. It's not fair."

"Ugly's only a word," Theo said.

"No, it's not."

She wiped her face with one hand.

"We have to look after him, Theo," she said. "We have to make sure nobody's cruel to him."

Theo's own eyes filled up, but he wasn't sure who he was crying for. "Of course we will," he said. "It'll all be fine, *he'll* be fine, *we'll* be fine."

"Don't let anyone throw stones at him," she said, and he picked up her hand and rubbed it firmly between his own till the baby started crying and Julia had to feed him. Theo stared in disbelief at the size to which her breast had swollen. She was very tired and started dozing while she fed, head drooping down toward the baby's puplike face. After a while the nipple slid from the baby's mouth and both were asleep. Theo covered her breast and went to find Trettenbacher.

"They're asleep," he said. "Everything seems to be fine."

"She's had a nasty time," the doctor said. He looked tired. "She needs her sleep."

"What were the odds, I wonder," Theo said, "fifty-fifty, eh, Doctor?"

"What? That the condition would turn out to be hereditary?" He shrugged. "Who knows? We know so very little about it."

"Well." Theo sighed a very deep sigh. There was a flattened look about his eyes. "The world must make a place for these people."

"As it does," said the doctor.

"Does it?"

Trettenbacher offered him a cigar, and the two men were quiet for a while. Trettenbacher was thinking about the medical report he would write and where he was going to publish it. Theo went out for a drink. The night was dark and cold, the stars above sharp as ice. A man in the tavern started talking to him about the price of tobacco.

"I've just become a father," Theo said.

"Hear that?" the man yelled. "This man's just become a father."

The whole room, glad of a diversion, began drinking his health.

"What is it? Boy or girl."

"Boy," he said proudly.

"Congratulations! A man needs a son. Strong boy, is he?"

"Very."

Round after round to the new son.

He was misty-eyed when he got back to the hospital. Thank God I've got a sense of humor, he thought, bursting into laughter standing on the snow-covered steps. There we all are drinking the health of a fine, decent-looking child, son and heir, the sort any man would be proud to own, and little do they know. Boy. Child. Well, it's true, isn't it?

He went in to find Julia crying, and the nurses running about tight-lipped. Not a doctor to be seen.

"They've taken him away!" she said.

"What's going on?"

"I don't know. The doctors took him. I was feeding him, and he started coughing."

"I'll find out. Don't worry, I'm sure it's nothing."

The corridor was empty. He walked about till he found a nurse to waylay. "What's going on?" he said. "Why isn't anyone looking after my wife? She's very upset. Why have they taken her baby?"

The nurse was a small strict creature. "Oh, Mr. Lent," she said, "we didn't know where to find you. It's all under control. The baby was having a little trouble breathing, but the doctors are taking care of things. Please go and sit with your wife."

"He was all right a minute ago," said Theo.

"I'm sorry, Mr. Lent, you've been gone a couple of hours. He had a little choking fit while he was feeding, and it seems to have set something off. But the doctors are taking care of it."

Oh Jesus, he's gone.

Theo walked to the end of the corridor. He'd seen it before with puppies. When he was a kid, the one that didn't thrive, always thinking, yeah, sure, it'll make it, but it never does. Not once all this starts. Poor bloody creature. What was that all for? Eh? She'll go mad. The way she looked at it.

He turned and walked back, preparing his face.

"What's happening?" she asked, twisting a useless wet handkerchief in her hands.

"I don't think it's anything serious," he lied jovially. "This often happens, I think."

"They said he stopped breathing."

"Yes, but they know what they're doing, these doctors." He smiled reassuringly. "It's quite amazing the things they can do these days."

He said all the right things, but she still cried.

"When are they bringing him back?"

"I don't know."

"Go and see. Please go and see, Theo. Ask them how long."

But then the hollow-faced nurse came in and took over, plumping up the pillows, filling the water jug, wiping Julia's face with a cool cloth. "Now, now, no more crying," she said. "This happens sometimes. Dr. Chizh knows what to do."

"Is he breathing?"

"Of course he's breathing."

Theo tried to read her face. Good poker players, these nurses would make.

"Where's Trettenbacher?" he asked.

"Dr. Trettenbacher's gone home. He'll be here first thing in the morning. Shall I bring you some tea? Mr. Lent? You look done in."

Theo wasn't a tea man but said he'd take some with lemon and sugar. He'd forgotten he was drunk. The tea scalded his throat. Good, he thought, concentrating on the burn. Good. Julia sipped some too, her hand shaking a little as she raised the cup. The nurse went away and returned almost immediately. It was all looking very good, she said. They would be bringing the baby back in about a quarter of an hour. "In fact," she held up one finger and tilted her head, "listen . . ."

The newborn cry.

"It's him!"

"Of course it's him."

Julia laughed. "He's all right."

"See," said Theo.

Round spins the wheel. Round spins your head, your life, your future. To be or not to be. Theo was not convinced. Long, long ago, when he was a child, his aunt Losey lost three in a row.

This baby, when it returned, was as good as gold, feeding steadily then falling asleep. A quiet baby. That's the way with some ill babies, he knew that. *She* didn't though. She was happy.

"You go home, Theo," she said, touching his arm. "You're so tired."

"Go home, Mr. Lent," the nurse said. "She'll go to sleep now. God knows she needs it and so do you. Get some rest."

When he got home, Polina had been in and cleaned up and left bread and cheese and pickles. He did nothing for a while, just gazed into space. Don't think of him. He never even was. What a thing! What a terrible thing! His head felt light. It would've been all right. They could have made him part of the show. It was the only real life for them, after all, people like her, people like him. At least he'd never have had to want for anything.

Theo put his hand over his eyes.

Already he was hardening himself to the boy. Terrible thing, terrible, but you just had to get on with life. People got over things. His aunt Losey did. Best thing all 'round. Bring another poor freak into the world to suffer. They'd go back to how it was, and he'd take her to Vienna for a holiday. She could see that Friederike she likes so much, go to a few shows. No need to work yet.

He slept restlessly and went back to the hospital late morning the next day. Julia was very tired.

"I feel sick," she said.

Theo touched the baby's hand. It was just like any baby's hand, the grip, the softness of the palm. He smiled faintly. "Are you all right? Do you want a sick bowl? Shall I get a nurse?"

"No," she said, "it'll pass, I think."

"Look, he's sleeping now," Theo said. "I'll put him in his crib."

"Would you?" She yawned and turned onto her side. "He's a very sleepy boy, isn't he?" she said.

"He is."

Then she was asleep too and there wasn't much point in hanging 'round. That day a thaw had began. The sweepers were driving slush along the sides of the roads when Theo went home for the soup Polina had left on the stove, buying himself a pie on the way and eating it before he even reached the door. There was a note from Volkov inviting him to dinner tomorrow night. After he'd eaten, he lay down and fell into a sleep much deeper than any the night had allowed, and it was dark when he woke. Polina had left a bunch of pansies in a jug on the table and they caught his eye as he was leaving. She'd like those, he thought, pulling them dripping from the jug and looking 'round for something to wrap them in. He couldn't find anything so let them drip as he trudged blearily back through the slush to the hospital. Trettenbacher took him into his office as soon as he arrived. "She's taken a fever," he said, leaning back behind his desk. "Dr. Chizh has given her a sedative, and we've managed to get her temperature down. She's asleep now, best thing for her. A good night's rest can work wonders." All under control, his manner said. "You might as well leave it till morning now."

"I brought her some pansies," Theo said blankly.

"Wonderful. Give them to one of the nurses, and she'll make sure they're taken care of. Now, Mr. Lent, I'm afraid I have to tell you that the child's chances aren't good."

He wasn't surprised.

"How is he?"

Trettenbacher sighed. "He doesn't seem to want to breathe for himself," he said. "That may change. We're doing everything we can, naturally."

"What about her? Does she know?"

"We had to take him from her when the fever came on. She was upset, of course. But she has no idea how ill he is."

"I'm afraid of how she'll take it." Theo looked down at the water drops from the flowers gathering into a small puddle by his foot.

"Well, it will be hard," said Trettenbacher. "You know that." He stood up. "Still, it may not come to that, we'll have to see."

Of course it will come to that. He realized halfway back that he hadn't left the flowers. "Look at that," he said to them. "I took you out for a walk," and laughed. He thought how pretty they'd look scattered in the street and wanted to cry.

In the morning he was met by Trettenbacher again. "He went less than half an hour ago," Trettenbacher said. "She doesn't know yet."

"How is she?"

"She's not feeling well. But we're doing our best to bring the fever down."

"Someone's got to tell her."

"We thought perhaps you would want to."

"Oh God," said Theo.

He wasn't surprised the baby was gone, but he was shocked at how ill Julia looked. "What's the matter with her?" he asked, and the sound of fear in his own voice scared him.

She was breathing as if it hurt, staring strangely. A new nurse was on duty, a raw-boned masculine woman with a clean sick bowl in her hand. "A fever," she said stoically, setting the bowl down on the table by Julia's head. "The doctor's treating it."

"Theo," Julia said, "they won't let me see him. Tell them they've got to let me see him."

"Not now," said the nurse calmly, mixing a drink. "You need to rest."

"I want to see him," she said.

"Look what I brought you," Theo said, the pansies, on their second outing, drooping a little in his hand. Her breath was rank when he leaned over.

"I want to *see* him," she said.

"Now, you just calm yourself," the nurse said, placing a cold cloth on her forehead.

"Will you take these and put them in water, please, nurse," Theo said. When she'd gone he sat down beside the bed. The corners of her eyes were sore and red, and she looked at him as if she knew.

"Has he gone?" she asked.

"Yes, Julia," he said, "he's gone."

Her eyes welled up. "Why?" she asked.

"I don't know."

"Has he gone?"

"Yes."

"What have they done with him?"

"I don't know. Shall I go and find out?"

"Has he gone?"

"Now, Julia, don't you worry. He's . . ." What? In a better place. At peace now. He said nothing. The nurse came in with the flowers in a jug and put them down on the table next to the sick bowl.

"I've told her," Theo said.

"I want to see him," Julia said, and her throat began to convulse. The nurse grabbed the sick bowl and supported her shoulders. He watched in fascinated horror as Julia's mouth, cavernous, complicated, reshaped itself and spewed forth bright yellow bile. She retched emptily for a few more minutes before the nurse lowered her head back down onto the pillow.

"There, you'll feel better now," Theo said uselessly, "now that's up."

"Tell them to bring him," she said.

"The little one's gone to the good God, who knows best what to do," the nurse said, "and it's your job now to get better. Drink this." She slipped a pill between Julia's lips, pushed it quickly back on her tongue, poured in a little water and stroked her throat as if she were a dog. "Probably best if you leave, Mr. Lent," the nurse said. "We'll send for you if there's any change."

There was no change that day. He walked about for a bit, then went back to the tavern where they'd drunk the baby's health. There was no one there that he recognized, and he sat by the wall drinking and wondering what to do. It occurred to him that she might die, and his mind went blank, then started turning over and over. The end. The end of backstage, the lights, the crowds, the smell of sawdust. His savings wouldn't last forever. He should have made good investments but speculation had never been his strong point. He calculated the cost of travel back to the States. His eyes burned. How could he live? He'd go back, find another fortune. Out there somewhere, another. Another.

How could there be another Julia? His heart felt sick.

He drank, pushed the thoughts away, pushed the baby away, tried to push *her* away. Push away the whole strange interlude in his life. If she was going to die, he couldn't risk emotion. He remembered he was supposed to be going to Volkov's tonight for dinner. "God damn," he whispered. One more, and home to the quiet apartment. I'll go mad in here, he thought, but there was nowhere else to go and he couldn't go in the bedroom because all the baby's things were there. So he passed the time trying to read one of her books but couldn't keep his eyes on the page. At seven he changed and set off for Volkov's.

It wasn't a big affair, just Volkov and his mother and the professor, Sokolov, with his bright, fierce bird's stare. Somehow they'd all heard the news, and of course everyone asked after her.

"They've taken blood," he said.

"The little one," the old mother said, "he's in a better place."

That was all she said all night. The atmosphere was restrained. These fevers killed, everyone knew.

"She's a strong girl," Volkov said, "she'll pull through."

"She's strong," Theo replied, sounding more hostile than he'd intended, "but she's grieving. That weakens one."

As he crossed the hall after dinner, Tolya came up to him. "Can she have visitors?" he asked.

"She's nowhere near well enough," Theo replied. Sokolov was walking behind him.

"Do let me know when she *is* well enough," Tolya said solemnly as they passed into the drawing room.

Theo nodded.

Sokolov leaned close enough for Theo to smell a sourness on his breath. "A word, Lent, if I may?"

"Of course."

They sat down. "I believe you said you were returning to the hospital later this evening?"

"That's right."

"Please," said Sokolov, "allow me to put my carriage at your disposal."

"There's really no need. Thank you for the offer, but the walk does me good."

"No, no, I insist. It's going to be a very cold night."

The evening dragged on. When the time came, Theo, dreading whatever he'd find at the hospital, found himself rattling through the streets in Sokolov's carriage, the professor beside him. The day had been long, and he'd drunk a lot. Now I am coping very well with this, he was saying to himself in his mind. The baby, poor little nothing, he didn't even exist. Couldn't call that an existence. Julia now, strong as an ox, she'll pull through. Back to how we were before. Odd, yes, but we were getting by. It was working. Never before stayed in places like we did, those grand beds and expensive rooms. Everyone wanted to know us. She'll get over it. They do. Look at Aunt Losey. Three in a row. Lots of women do.

"I would like to be very frank and I hope you will not take it amiss," said Sokolov. "I would like to put a proposition to you."

"Fire away," said Theo.

"Are you familiar with my work, Mr. Lent?"

"To some extent.

"Perhaps not with my most recent studies. Are you aware of the work being done at the Anatomical Museum at the university?"

"No."

"Some fascinating progress, Lent. Quite staggering. Lent, I realize this is an inopportune moment, but I must stress the importance of time."

"Time?"

Theo had no idea what the man was talking about.

"Mr. Lent, I will be frank and ask you to consider the possibility of offering your son's remains to our Anatomical Museum at the university."

My son. How peculiar.

"Time?" said Theo, a look of profound bemusement on his face.

"The scientific benefits would be enormous."

"What are you suggesting, Doctor?"

Sokolov took a deep breath. "Your son is a medical curiosity. This you know. I repeat: the scientific benefits would be enormous."

"And I repeat: what exactly are you suggesting?"

"We have perfected a method of embalmment more sophisticated, I believe, than any that has gone before. This is new territory, of course."

"You want," said Theo, turning away from the misty window and looking at Sokolov, a pair of anguished eyes, a thin forehead, all muffled up against the cold, "to embalm my—son."

"Forgive me," said Sokolov. "A very bad time."

"Yes, indeed. A very bad time."

They didn't speak again until they reached the door of the hospital. Sokolov leaned over and shook Theo's hand. "I am so very sorry for all your trouble, Mr. Lent," he said. "I do appreciate your loss, and I would hesitate to bring this up at such a difficult time, but I am aware of the importance of time in this case."

Theo's face didn't alter. "Not now," he said.

"Of course. I am so sorry."

The cold air bit as he got out of the carriage. Snow beginning, slowly swirling. He didn't want to go in, wanted to run far away, a time before, once, before, anytime. But he went in, idiot-blank, and they said she was a bit better and he could go in and see her, but she was absolutely worn-out so best not to stay too long. Someone had given her a rosary, and she was lying with her eyes open, slipping the beads between her fingers. The look in them cut him.

"What is it?" he said, taking her hand, "what's the matter? You've been very sick but you're getting better now. Soon be home."

Her breathing was shallow. Though they'd cleaned her up, she still smelled faintly of vomit and diarrhea.

"What have they done with him?" she asked. "Have they thrown him away? They do that, don't they?"

"Of course they don't."

"I want him buried nicely."

"Of course. Thrown him away! Where do you get your ideas from?"

"Where is he?"

"He's in the morgue."

That set her off crying again. "A terrible place," she said. "Why do they put the dead in such terrible places?"

To grieve so deeply for someone she'd never known. Not like a person you've known for years, Theo thought, that's understandable. But a baby, it never lived, never knew you, never got the time to be a person. So where does it come from, all that grief?

"Good God," he said, "you're still burning up. Would you like some water?"

The fever seemed to radiate out from her into the room.

"We have to look after him, Theo."

"Of course we do."

She turned her head on the pillow and looked at the wilting pansies. "Aren't they lovely?" she said. "Did you bring them?"

"Yes."

"You're sweet, Theo. He still needs someone to look after him."

"Here. Drink some water."

"My stomach hurts," she said.

"Yes. Don't worry. It'll go away."

She lifted her head to sip. Her hair was lank and straight.

"There," he said, "that's better."

"I think I'm going to die."

"What? Ridiculous. Of course you're not. You're going to get better and better, and we'll go to Vienna. Don't talk like that."

"I wouldn't mind if it wasn't for you," she said, "but I'll really miss you, Theo."

I can't take it, he thought. Two, three days ago, everything was normal.

"I want Yatzi," she said. "Will you go and get Yatzi for me?"

Oh God, this'll kill me. "Yatzi!" he said indulgently. "Oh Julia, you are so funny. You and your old stick of wood." He leapt up, glad to get out of this awful sick room and back out in the cold. "Of course I'll get him."

He'd walk. It would be good for him. As he walked, he sang under his breath to stop himself from thinking. No point in thinking while the wheel was still spinning. They were good doctors, they'd pull her through. A letter on the rug. He ripped it open. Nothing good for sure. The name. Sokolov. He read: ". . . hope you will give it careful consideration . . . a very fair remuneration for your valued co-operation." Oh, hell, it never lived. Just dead matter. ". . . when she feels well enough . . . many would dearly love to see her . . . so much concern . . . a privilege . . . to see her . . . for which many will pay . . ."

He ventured into the bedroom, avoiding looking at the cradle. There it was under her pillow. This old Yatzi thing. She hadn't given it a thought since the baby started, and now look—back in favor.

"There, my dear," he said to it, "you're wanted again."

He was back at the hospital within the hour and gave her that old lump of wood. She fell asleep immediately, holding on to it.

———

Some time in the very early morning, she woke and lay for a while remembering where she was and why she was alone. She didn't feel sick anymore. She wasn't shivering. It was warm in bed and a curious sensation crept over her, as if she were back in the mountains. She'd never been away. Mamá was there, and Yatzi. They were happy. Mamá made Yatzi out of wood. She put something in him, something invisible that came from the mountains with us when we came down. "That thing's filthy," Solana said. "At least let me give that bit of old cloth a good wash." *Todos me dicen el negro . . .* "Little girl," said John Montanee, "you still a little girl." How old? Dancing. The snake dancing. She was in her bed in the Sanchez house. Sunlight on the wall. Don Pedro came in. "Look," she said. "My baby."

"She's better," Theo said to Trettenbacher.

"No," the doctor said quietly but firmly, "I'm afraid that's not true."

"She *seems* a lot better."

"It's the nature of the illness. This is puerperal fever. It follows a pattern."

"How can you be sure?"

"Nothing's ever sure," said Trettenbacher.

"Would now be a good time?"

"There's never a good time."

"Perhaps it would cheer her up to see people."

"She may well relapse before night. If she is to have visitors, best it were soon," Trettenbacher said shortly and walked away.

Theo sat down at the bedside and leaned over. "Julia," he said softly, "Julia," whispering, "my dear, there are some people who would very much like to see you."

She lay on her side. Her eyes were open but vague and gummy. Her breathing was steady but slow, and a hot, sickly smell rose from the sheets. She said something in Spanish.

"I don't understand," he said.

More Spanish. Her voice had deepened.

"So many are praying for you, love," he said. "Some friends who want to wish you well and a speedy recovery."

All waiting on benches.

"As they always did, my love," he said, "like old times."

She smiled. "Has Cato come?"

"He's on his way."

What harm?

"Would you like to sit up a little?"

He settled her against the pillows, spread her hair out across her shoulders.

"There," he said. "I'll just bring them in."

And oh God, but they'll pay.

Sokolov had come from the museum. He sat first by the door. A line of faces looked expectantly, solemnly, toward Theo. Sokolov stood up. Theo leaned close and spoke rapidly into his ear. "I don't see a problem with your plans for the child," he said. "As long as his mother doesn't find out."

Sokolov smiled, almost boyish in his unconcealed delight. "I think that's the wise decision," he said. "I'm very grateful. We shall talk soon."

Theo glanced along the row. A couple of learned doctors. Some dandy young buck. His girl. Couple of ladies. Old man in black fur. All rich.

"Ten minutes," he said.

She saw faces looking at her.

"Theo." He could scarcely hear her.

"Yes, Julia."

Her mouth was dry. "Give me a drink."

He held the glass to her lips, and she wet them and spoke.

"Do they want me to sing?"

"No, no, you don't have to do anything."

"Don't cry," she said.

"I'm not. Don't worry about anything, Julia, it's all going to be fine. It's just some friends come to say hello."

"Has Cato come?"

"Soon."

The faces blurred in front of her eyes. She didn't recognize any. Voices murmured. Someone wanted to shake her hand. A face, close up. Faces. It was hot. Too hot in here, she wanted to say, but couldn't remember how to say it. Her hands were touched. The faces melted into one another and the mess made her feel sick. It swirled about then re-formed into a mass of spiteful child faces.

"Take them away," she said.

She turned to look at Theo but all she saw was the fig tree dropping its fruits onto the stones on the patio and Federico the iguana stretched along the lower branch. His eye swiveled and fixed on her. The stones burned. Fiery, they rose up around her. Solana would come soon and take her back to bed, because she was sick. So sick.

The hollow-faced nurse came in softly, walked over to Theo and said, "There's another young man for Miss Julia. He says his name is Tolya."

Theo looked up, surprised. Julia's eyes had closed, but she opened them now and it made him jump, as if she were dead already and her corpse had opened its eyes.

"Tolya," she said.

He looked about at all the serious faces, feeling as if he'd just woken up. The old man in black fur was staring at him intently. "Lent," he said, "can I ask her a question?"

"I don't think so," Theo said.

"Tolya," said Julia, lifting her head a fraction from the pillow.

"In a minute, dear," said Theo, "we mustn't overcrowd the room."

She sank back, tossed her head and started speaking in Spanish again, a note of panic entering her voice.

"Mamá," she said, "my belly's sore."

"Julia," said Theo.

"Time to leave," the hollow-faced nurse told the assembly 'round the bed, smiling as she began to usher them toward the door.

"There," he said, "they've gone. Here's Tolya."

But she was burning up again.

"Only for a minute," said the nurse, leaving the room and closing the door quietly.

Poor clod sat there gawking. Theo felt himself dislocate. We are getting there, he thought with almost a sense of wonder. That far-off place 'round every corner. This is it. Tolya reached out and took her hand, sat holding it silently, stroking the back of it with his thick fingers. She probably didn't know he was there. "The fur is very soft," he said.

"Not fur," said Theo. "Hair. She doesn't like you to call it fur."

"I'm sorry."

"I don't think she'll mind if it's you," said Theo.

When her head began to toss upon the pillow, Tolya left in tears. I won't cry, Theo told himself. I'm not here. The nurse came by and gave her something that put her into a restless sleep, and he went out into the corridor, down to the front door and stood gratefully gulping cold air.

"Here, Lent," said a slightly aggrieved voice, "was that entirely fair?"
The old man in black fur stood on the steps smoking a pipe.

"What are you talking about?"

"In there," the old fool said. "That was nowhere near ten minutes."

"What!"

"I know it's special circumstances," he went on, "but that wasn't cheap. And then you go and let that other fellow in for nothing."

Theo stared at him for a moment, turned and walked back inside. Sokolov was coming out of Trettenbacher's office. "My dear Lent," he said, busying himself with his gloves, "I am so sorry."

A year ago, we'd never have imagined. A year ago—a theater opening, pink flowers in her headdress. "Yes, yes," said Theo impatiently. He returned to her bedside. How long had he been gone? He'd only been gone a minute but it was all changed again, sleep gone, two nurses, Julia doubled over on her side, Trettenbacher striding importantly in. Her nightie was up, her stomach swollen up hard like a coconut. Her eyes squeezed tight. Trettenbacher laid his hand on her stomach and she screamed.

"Wait outside, please, Mr. Lent," said the hollow-faced nurse.

He could hear her screams in the corridor. He couldn't bear it. He ran outside, stood on the steps, covered his face. She wouldn't want it. Him remembering her like that. No good. He walked backward and forward on the steps for several minutes, punching the side of his head from time to time. He could not carry it, this death, this end, it should not have happened. "It's all over," he said aloud. No more on the road. No shows. No rush of it all. Her in the spotlight, taking a bow, the applause, the smell of perfume. He went back inside, found a nurse and said he was going home, it seemed there was no use in his presence here and could someone please let him know as soon as there was any news. Then he almost ran home through the dark empty streets.

She didn't even know I was there, he told himself. What's the difference, here or there? There was another letter from Sokolov on the rug. He skimmed it. Money. Let us talk. The remains of your son. I would not raise such a delicate issue were it not for the pressures of time.

He poured a long drink.

The museum, he read, I'm sure you realize, would pay very handsomely indeed for two such specimens.

Around midnight they called him, but she was dead by the time he arrived, her hands crossed on the coverlet, hair combed, eyes closed. All gone, that sickness, pain, everything. He should do something, say something. The nurses were there. "So, was it . . . ?" he said, "Did she . . . ?"

"We helped her all we could," said the hollow-faced nurse.

"I'm very grateful to you."

"Mr. Lent," said the big nurse, touching his arm, "here are her things."

He didn't remember getting home, but there he was, sitting on the bed looking at the baby clothes he'd taken from the chiffonier. All in sizes, as she'd said. The poor could have them. Her guitar. The harmonica. A pair of small white dancing shoes standing neatly together at the side of the bed. And this ridiculous thing in his hands. Ye Gods. Yatzi. What do I do with you? He walked into the other room where the fire still burned in the big fireplace. I looked after her, got her a living, kept her company, he thought. And she certainly looked after me. Wouldn't hear a word against me. Always on my side. He stood looking down into the flames. Tears came into his eyes. What now? Can't have this around. Reminding me, reminding me.

He dropped Yatzi into the fire. The old bit of dress was so faded and rotten that it just curled up and died. The wood beneath caught quickly and burned with a dark green flame. Just a piece of burning wood.

PART 3

Next World

"You know she's fucked-up, don't you?"

Laurie was halfway up a ladder on the landing, a paint-brush in his hand. His black hair, grown longer and wilder, tumbled in dusty waves halfway down his back and there were flecks of green paint in it here and there. He was wearing a pink T-shirt so old and limp and torn it formed a kind of mesh on his torso.

"Yeah, I suppose," said Adam.

"Those things," said Laurie. "That room. That horrible thing there." He indicated Tattoo, dangling head down from Adam's hand. Adam looked down at it, bashed it lightly against his knee.

"What you doing with that anyway?"

"Said I'd fix this hole for her," said Adam.

Laurie looked down from the ladder as one wiser, an old soldier dispensing hard-won knowledge. He rested the paintbrush on the rim of the tin and it sat there looking precarious. "Chuck it away!" he said passionately.

Adam was watching the paintbrush, wondering if it would fall. If it did, it would make a right old mess. "I might just," he said.

Serve her right.

"I mean, what does it all really mean to her?" Laurie, upright on the ladder, somehow gave the impression he was sitting back on his heels. He dragged bits from his jeans pocket and started rolling a cigarette. "It's infantile. Arrested development. Like a kid with a dummy. Those things are a security blanket."

"Yeah." The brush wasn't going to fall. Boring. Too stuck there in its wallow of sticky gunk.

"Stuck up there with all that shit because she can't face reality. Reality. Know what I think? She's trying to stave off death. That's all it is, attachment to the physical world." Laurie put the roll-up between his lips, clicked his lighter. "I say go with the Buddhists. You know, no attachment, face death every day, every minute, and all that. Every second. Look it in the face. She can't do that."

"No, she can't."

True. Like a child.

"It's all crap." Laurie rubbed his nose with the back of his hand and sucked. She did it with him, thought Adam. A year or more. Longer than me. I know. They were at it all the time. God, that ugly fucker, I used to say. How can you, Rose? I think he's beautiful, she'd say. Laurie up there on the ladder, aging crags, rough, tough-eyed.

"So anyway," said Laurie, "has she chucked you out?"

"Pretty much."

Laurie, the roll-up stuck to his lower lip, picked up the paintbrush and wiped it on the rim of the tin. "Yeah," he said. "That's what she does. She chucks people away but she can't chuck out a pile of old crap." He slapped paint on the wall. A fine spray jumped back in his face but he didn't take any notice.

Adam went back to his room.

Poor old room had been neglected all that time he was up there making believe. Got cold and unloved, the air unused. Hello, Room, back again. That first night, two months ago, first night in six months he'd slept alone. Like sleeping in a hotel. Waking up wondering where you were. Give me a couple of days, she'd said. Couple of days indeed. The second night he'd gone up and tried the door, but she'd locked it. Well, of course. Third, he knocked and she got up eventually, and he walked in as if everything was normal and he was just late coming home, and started getting into bed. It was warm, full of her shape. Oh, Ad, she'd said sadly, and got in beside him but only wanted to go straight to sleep again. Well, OK. He could cope with that. A week or so of just that, sleeping like buddies, no sex. Then: really, Adam, you've got to start getting used to your own room, as if he were an infant she was weaning from her bed. I don't know what people make

such a fuss about, she'd said one day when they were having a terrible row—sex, what's the big deal? We can still be the same, you in
your place, me in mine, it's not as if we have to break up or stop seeing
each other anymore, Jesus, Ad, we've lived alongside each other long
enough. Nothing's changed. OK, we had sex for a while.

So that's the big deal, he'd said, and she'd said: not for me.

———

He'd been sitting there for half an hour doing nothing, gawping into
space. There in his hands was Tattoo. He looked where the eyes had
been. "Hello, old thing," he said.

Chuck it away.

Go back, say: ha ha, I couldn't be bothered fussing with tape and
stuff. He's only going to fall to pieces somewhere else next week.
Chucked him in the bin. It was bin day, they took him away. In a land-
fill by now.

She'd go mad.

You did what? Oh, how could you be so cruel!

And he'd say, yeah, see, that's exactly what you did to me. You took
away my Tattoo.

Now two months had gone by. Next week was Christmas. He lived
in his room, she lived in hers, and she acted as if everything was fine
and they were just old friends, and it was killing him. It wasn't as if
he could stop it. Her face swimming up in his mind all the time, these
snapshots. These feelings, illusion or not, that when he looked at her
there was something there of himself, a thing he recognized as if from
old, old days, days so far back they didn't even exist in any known
reality. Made no sense. Didn't matter what you called it. And last night
she'd come swanning in and said, "I don't like turkey. Shall I get us a
big chicken for Christmas?" What the fuck? Like they'd be together.
Like he didn't even get consulted, it was taken for granted. What was
he supposed to do?

Laurie was right. She was fucked-up, missing some normality gene
that makes people do what they do, sleep with the same person for
years, all that, live together, kids.

"Can you fix that hole in Tattoo for me?" she'd said. "You said you
had some duct tape."

"Not now. Tomorrow."

"OK." And she'd swanned out again.

————

She'd been sleeping on the red sofa when he knocked on her door at four o'clock. The room was stifling and perfumed. She'd made it Christmassy, with holly and paper chains. All her crap was clean and tidy, a dozen or so Christmas cards lined the mantelpiece. In the center she'd put a very small tree she'd made out of twisted wood and pipe cleaners covered in gold foil. Tiny silver baubles hung from its branches and on top was a star. Through the branches peered the cracked, crazed and sightless faces of the dolls of Dolls' Island.

"Oh, thank you," she said, handing him Tattoo. "Thank you, thank you, you good, good boy."

My best friend.

Right, he thought, shaking himself back here, now. Get started on this thing. Where's the duct tape?

The two bodies were embalmed (I have used the word "embalmed" because it is one which is usually employed in such cases; but it does not convey a correct impression of the nature of the substances which I used in order to arrest the progress of decomposition, and to preserve the body in its entirety) by me with a view to their being permanently preserved in the Anatomical Museum of the University of Moscow. Both of the bodies were embalmed in the space of six months. During that time—from the beginning of April to the end of September—they were exposed to different atmospheric influences and different temperatures—to 15 degrees, 18 degrees, 20 degrees, 25 degrees, and even 30 degrees (centigrade) of heat. The body of the mother is now quite free from smell. The parts which had already begun to decompose exhibit a gray colour, deepening into a bronze hue. The lower part of the forearm, the hands, and the feet, have become mummified and of a whitish color. The breasts have diminished, and are wrinkled in some parts; they have also assumed a bronzed appearance. The shoulders, the back, and the sides preserve their dusky-yellow hue. It is wonderful to see how little change the face has undergone, having remained all but unaltered; the only difference is, that the eyes have sunk in, the lips are slightly thinner than they were, and there is a trifling diminution in the morbid process of the gum, which has grown hard and white. The body of the child exhibited very slight traces of decay at the period of embalming, and has undergone little perceptible change up to the present time; it has shrunk very little. The colour of the skin remains what it was during its lifetime, and the pliancy of its limbs is still preserved. The fingers and toes, however, have become mummified.

The bodies of these two individuals—one of whom has been the subject of general curiosity—well deserved a place amongst the rarities in this museum, and wherever they may be they have a claim upon the scientific world.

(Sokolov, *The Lancet,* May 3, 1862)

"Do you want to know what he did? You won't believe it. He's had her stuffed, her and the baby."

"What kind of a man would do that? Puts them in a glass case and carts them around in a big box and charges a nice price to look at them. They're flocking in. Got it made, he has. Not one embalmed freak but two. Mother and child."

"Good God!—I saw her. It was her, Julia Pastrana, it really was. Standing there like a tart with her hands on her hips in a red dress. Can you believe?"

"You know, I saw her in Munich once. Good little singer, and she had some lovely dance steps. But the face though! Meet that in a back alley of a dark night and you'd know it—"

"Buckland saw him in London. Cool as a cucumber, the man walks up to him and says, d'you want a private view? Costs him, of course. Well, it would. Said he never saw anything like it. Had this cove from the museum with him, one that stuffs the animals, says he couldn't work out how they'd done it. Stupendous job! But what kind of a man does that? Got to ask yourself."

"Kind of man that marries someone like that in the first place, I s'pose."

"Still. Not her fault, is it?"

"No, but you can't say it's natural, can you? I mean, would *you?* Thought not."

"Nice girl, by all accounts."

"I knew her—"

"Poor Julia—"

"There's something totally abhorrent about the man. There was always something suspect, looking back, but we gave him the benefit of the doubt. More fool us for being fooled, and she was charming. Really. Liliya took to her tremendously. You know Liliya, ever the romantic. Why can't they be truly in love? That's what she said. But when he did that—well, she couldn't see how he could do it, I think it made us all uneasy. She wouldn't go and see them when they were here. None of us did. Oh, yes, my girl Polina went. Didn't say much. That he could do a thing like that—"

"He's made."

"A rich man."

"She signed my picture. She was quite shy—"

"But that's just gruesome, that is! Having that poor baby nailed up there on its perch like a bloody monkey on a stick. Such a funny little face. You expect it to turn its head."

"The embalmed Female Nondescript—"

"You can see the handouts blowing up and down Piccadilly. The most lifelike embalming anyone's ever seen. A Moscow doctor, some sort of secret formula, you'd think she was alive—to be honest, it's scary. I don't like it."

"I don't suppose any normal woman would look at him."

"No fool actually. Got himself covered. Sells the bodies, then gets them back. Sees how good a job they'd done on them so wants them back—oh sure, knows a mother lode when he sees it. All of a sudden he's asserting his rights. Goes down to the American consul, crafty beggar, shows them the marriage certificate and all. My wife and son. Didn't think of that the first time, when the money changed hands, did he? Made a loss, mind you, getting them back—but who cares? Makes it up in a week. All that work, thinking they're getting two nice prime specimens for their museum, and up he comes and waltzes her off to somewhere, Vienna, I think—"

"But of course she's from Mexico, isn't she? They do all that sort of thing there, so I suppose it's not as bad as if they did it to one of ours—"

"You know, in a funny sort of way, she's strangely beautiful. Something to do with her expression. I don't know—she's very hard to forget. I will say—you should go, go see her."

"I mean, she was something in life."

"That is not Julia," Theo explained to the reporter. "That is not the boy. That is mere matter. It doesn't matter. There is no significance. It's just words in the head, that's all it is, words in the head."

"Mr. Lent, I'm not quite sure what you mean."

"Why not? It's absolutely clear."

"Perhaps not to our readers. Of course, they are all fascinated by the exhibition, but you must admit there's a personal side to this story."

"Of course. What has that to do with anything?"

"Some may find it strange that you travel with the embalmed bodies of your wife and son."

"Would you find it strange if I traveled with a portrait of them?" Theo had practiced all this. There was no flaw in the logic. "A keepsake? Perhaps a strand of hair in a locket. What's the difference?"

"The difference," said the man, who was smarmy and impish, a little like himself, "is that these are actual—corpses."

"Actually, no," said Theo smoothly. "They're mummies. Just as I said—that is not Julia. That is not the boy. That is mere *matter* and it doesn't *matter*. There is no significance." He leaned forward, eager to make his point. "Is it wrong for people to look at the mummies in the museum? Go to Italy. The churches are full of relics. Corpses, mummies, dead bodies, cadavers—"

Theo realized he was gesturing too extravagantly. "Just words in the head," he concluded. "That's all it is, words in the head."

"Tell me, Mr. Lent." The man addressed his notepad. His eyes were amused. "How long have you been touring with your wife and child?"

Theo sat back and smiled, scratched his ear. "Oh, now, let me think. Seven years—let me think. Yes, getting on for eight possibly."

"Remarkable. And you've shown them all over Europe."

"Oh, all over. First in London, that must have been, yes, seven years ago, but we've been all over Europe and Scandinavia. The Swedes love her. And now here we are again."

"And they're still pulling the crowds!"

"They're still pulling the crowds."

"And where to after this, Mr. Lent? What does the future hold?"

"We're going back to Vienna," Theo said. "She always liked Vienna."

Once more to the elegant white town.

Julia stood among the show booths at Prauscher's Volksmuseum, her baby in a sailor suit by her side. In life Theo Junior had never stood, but now he did, sturdy on two booted legs, nailed to the stand.

Before the doors opened, Theo Senior stood in front of his exhibit and gazed into its wide sightless eyes. Glass, of course, but so real. People said they followed you about the room. The doors opened and in came the floods. She was making as much as she ever had. He slipped behind a screen, walked down a dim passageway and pushed open the door of a room at the end. It had the look of an abandoned office that someone had shoved a pile of boxes into, along with an old broken-down piano with gaping teeth and a soft saggy chair covered in a brown blanket. A bottle of whisky, three empty glasses and his silver cigar box were neatly arranged on a small table next to the chair, which sank as he lowered himself into it so that he felt as if he were sitting on the floor.

"Ridiculous," he muttered to himself, pulling himself forward and out of it, pouring himself a drink. He knocked it back, poured another, knocked that back, poured another, lit a cigar and lay back with his eyes closed. For a good ten minutes he lay perfectly still, stirring only to raise the cigar to his lips from time to time. The stiller he lay, the more his mind tumbled like an acrobat. The thoughts seemed not to be his own. It was as if inside his head was air as big as the air surrounding him, an echo chamber reaching as far in as the heavens reached out. In that air, the broken off and wandering fragments of the thoughts of millions twined and twined in and around each other in passage. Some meandered by. Others were comets or bright shooting stars. None of them lasted.

The door was open. Prauscher rapped on it and Theo's eyes opened at once.

"You've got a countess come a-calling," he said.

"What?" He stood awkwardly. The chair didn't want him to go.

Prauscher was a florid man with a look of bursting about him. "A countess, no less," he said with the hint of a sneer. "The Countess Prokesch-Osten."

"A countess," said Theo. That was good. "Well, show her in, I suppose. Or is there somewhere more—"

But she appeared in the doorway. "You don't remember me, do you?" she said.

"Friederike." He nodded.

She came in, Prauscher hovered, Theo closed the door on him. "I'm sorry," Theo said, "there's only this thing here to sit on, but if you—"

"How can you?" she said.

Theo sighed, smiling his mild smile, a man wronged. "You too," he said softly. "I'm sorry, Countess, but I no longer feel the need to explain myself. I've already done that, many, many times."

"I know you have," she said.

The years had been kinder to her than to him. She had light crow's feet at the corners of her eyes and her lips were thinner, but her hair and eyes shone and she was still in her prime and elegant. Theo still looked younger than his age, but these days he was beginning to notice an aging look when he glanced at a mirror, the skin of his throat looser, his hair turning gray and receding. In a few weeks he'd be forty-five. "I don't understand," she said. "I never will."

"Then I can't make you."

"How can you smile? How can you stand there completely unmoved? I knew her for only a few weeks, and I hate to see her like that. And the baby! The poor baby!" Her eyes filled with tears.

"Friederike," he said, "please. If I may still call you Friederike. Or is it Countess Prokesch-Osten now?"

"Call me whatever you like," she said. "I don't understand. You have taken away every last shred of dignity she had."

"No." A flicker of anger, which he tried to hide. "Any dignity a person has exists while they're alive. Once you're dead it can't be touched."

"Rubbish," she said, "you know that's not true."

"Friederike! That is not Julia. That is an image of Julia."

But she shook her head. "If you can't see how grotesque this is, I'm sorry for you."

"Grotesque? Grotesque?" Now he really was angry. "No. I will not have that. She got enough of that when she was alive."

She listened, said nothing, just looked at him seriously for a long moment.

"Why did you come, Friederike? You must have known it would upset you, and yet you came anyway. Of course you did, you had to.

Because you can't help yourself. No one can. She was unique, born for looking at. What's so terrible about that?"

She blinked rapidly, licked her lips and shook her shoulders. "She should have had a decent burial, like everyone else," she said, turning to leave.

Theo smiled. "It's only the body, Friederike," he said. "It's not *her*."

Countess Prokesch-Osten took a small handkerchief out of her glove and swiped it briskly over the end of her nose, then sniffed loudly. "Nevertheless," she said, "it produces the most—profound—sadness." She folded the handkerchief and put it back inside her glove. "Well," she said, "it's been many years. My memories of her are very fond."

"As are mine," said Theo quietly, then smiled brightly. "So!" he said. "A countess!"

He knew she'd not appeared on a stage for years, but he'd had no idea she'd married so grandly.

She smiled coldly. "Yes" was all she said, then turned and walked out of the room without saying good-bye.

The road wound on for seven more years.

Sometimes, fresh from the dim room of a whore with its sad trappings of drapes and shades, he'd stumble along the midway into the wagon where he'd placed her in her case next to his bunk, and he'd lie in bed and talk to her.

"You know," he'd say, "you'll never believe what they said in the *Figaro*. Been talking to Buckland, I bet. *You* don't think I'm a monster, do you? Of course you don't."

He never had truck with all these idiots who said he was mad. What were they moaning about? For God's sake, what are they, pagans who worship graven images? Insane. Whatever came after death—and he had no idea what that might be, though he wouldn't rule out the possibility of there being *something*—it had nothing to do with that mummy. Julia was gone, fully and finally. What remained was no more than a portrait. Call it a keepsake. About the boy, he scarcely thought.

Sometimes the night would close in, become nothing less than the sum of everything. In the stillness, the pounding of his blood was an approaching army. Silence vibrated behind it. Her glass eyes looked away, past him. It had been a long time since that face had lived, but still, on nights like these, he would fall into a reverie of communication with it.

"*You* know, don't you," he'd say. "*You* understand."

And the years marched on around him, hustling him along by the shoulders like a man in a crowd.

———

He was in Bremen when he got word of a hairy girl in Karlsbad. His pulse jumped. It reminded him of the first time he'd heard about Julia, and known, just known that this was something of importance in his life. Here was another, clearly signposted by circumstance. Things conspired. He was in certain places, certain times, to hear by chance a conversation, a mention, until one night he met a man in a sideshow who was running three pinheads and a skeleton woman who looked as if she were on death's doorstep. "'Eard about that girl in Karlsbad?" the man said, a small weaselly Cockney who spoke as if he were offering stolen goods.

"Yes," said Theo, "I have."

"'Airy as this one. Easy." He'd been hanging around Julia's case all day, couldn't get enough of her and her boy. Stood gazing and gazing. If he'd had the money he'd have offered, Theo could tell, but he knew she was way beyond him.

"This girl," said Theo. "You seen her?"

"You kiddin'?" The man snorted. "Guards 'er like the crown jewels, the old man."

"So," Theo offered him a smoke, "how do you know what she's like?"

"I was down there." The man accepted a light. "Everyone knows about 'er. I was talking to this fella knows the family. Covered 'ead to foot, 'e said. Old man's filthy rich and keeps her in."

"Hm," said Theo. They stood smoking quietly for a while, looking at Julia and the boy. "Did you try?"

"Oh, yeah! Tried, all right. Couldn't get near."

You couldn't, Theo thought. I bet I could.

A couple of months later he made a nice deal with Prauscher, and left Julia and the boy with the museum while he went off to Bohemia. Strangely freeing to be away from her glass eyes, the boy's vacant stare.

He spent a few days hanging 'round getting the lie of the land, talking to people in taverns, discovering that the girl's name was Marie, her father a linen merchant with a big house near the cathedral. He laughed when he saw it. The garden wall was ten feet high. "Rapunzel, Rapunzel," he said, "let down your hair."

First he left his card. When that didn't work, he sent 'round a crate of first-class port wine and two dozen red roses. Let them just think about how much that cost, he thought. Two days later, receiving a note of thanks and a brusque invitation to call at four o'clock on Friday, he celebrated by getting drunk. By Friday he'd recovered from the hangover and gotten himself shaved and spruced up by a barber, and by the time he stood on the steps of the big white house, on the dot of four, he'd persuaded himself to feel fettlesome and fine. The old man received him in a slightly shabby sitting room filled with things that looked costly but used: bowls, dishes, a glass-fronted bookcase and several tables bearing the scratch marks and stains of generations. The sound of children running through the house penetrated the walls, the voice of a woman; French, it sounded.

"Let me get straight to the point," said Theo. "I know you must be sick of people taking a mercenary interest in your daughter, but I want to reassure you that my proposition is wholly different from any other you may have received."

"No," said the old man. "The answer is no."

That's what you think.

It took less than an hour and came down to money in the end. The old man wasn't as bad as all that, just a businessman to the core who knew a good deal when he saw it. He'd just never had a good enough offer for her before. Prim-faced, worn-out, tragic-eyed, he sat there, talking about how dear his daughter was to him, what a good education he'd given her, how dignified, charming and refined she was. He couldn't possibly consider anything but the very best for her.

"Of course." Theo accepted a second glass of fine port wine. "And that is why, in spite of the fact that I intend to ameliorate your inevitable anguish at the loss of a daughter with a very considerable financial settlement, I come not as a businessman but as a suitor."

It was the marriage proposal that clinched it, even though initially the old man objected to the age difference. Thirty years, but Theo knew he didn't look his age and managed to trim a few years off without being specific. He spoke movingly of his first marriage and sad bereavement. The success of that union, he stressed, a bond so strong, so misunderstood by some of lesser sensitivity, must speak for him. He of all people could truly understand a woman like Marie. He of all people could give her wealth, security, respectability, marriage, children. He didn't mention the mummies.

"You are talking about public display," her father said.

"Not at all. I am talking of artistry. She has a fine voice, I'm told."

"Who told you that?"

No one had, but it was a good stab.

"Oh, it's well known. I don't remember where I heard it."

"She sings," her father said, as if stating the obvious. "And of course she plays the piano. I gave her a good musical education."

"Excellent."

"Singing and playing the piano at home for the family is one thing," said her father, "I'm sure she has no inclination for anything more."

"One step at a time," said Theo. "First the young lady must be consulted. Her happiness in the matter is the only thing that counts."

The old man sat sucking his teeth thoughtfully for a while, but Theo could see he'd gotten him. "Come tomorrow," he said. "Let me talk to her." He smiled faintly but none of the tragedy lifted from his eyes, which strayed to the window, the garden. "She's a very strong-willed girl," he said, "she won't do anything she doesn't want to."

"Oh, absolutely!"

Out in the sun, Theo strolled along by the garden wall, looking up. "Rapunzel, Rapunzel," he said. A man cleaning the windows of a house a little down the road had stopped for a break and was sitting in the shade of a side alley eating a hunk of bread. Theo couldn't resist it.

"Borrow your ladder for a minute," he said, taking it from where it leaned up against the house.

"Hoy!" the man cried as he bore it away, but Theo had already propped it against the high wall and was up there peering over into the garden. There she was. Nothing like Julia, that was his first thought. Thinner, paler, more nose, less mouth. Fine beard and mustache though, and her jet-black eyebrows were gloriously bushy. She was lying on her stomach on a blanket on the lawn, twenty feet or so away, reading a book. A white dress. Trees and bushes billowed 'round the edges of the lawn, and he got an impression of small children by the back of the house.

"Marie!" he called. She looked up and met his eyes at once, seeming unsurprised. Perhaps strange men looked over her wall every day. "Marie," he said, "I'm Theo."

She stared back at him, unperturbed. More mannish than Julia.

He smiled.

"Hoy," said the man, standing at the foot of the ladder.

Marie looked back to her book as if he were of no interest to her whatsoever.

"See you tomorrow, Rapunzel," he said, kissing his fingers to her, and climbed down.

"Quite finished, have you?" said the man.

She was in the garden when he called next day. A small table and two chairs had been placed in the shade of a lime tree, and she was sitting demurely in a pale blue dress with lace at the neck and elbows. Her book lay open facedown in front of her. Her father, who was giving nothing away, introduced them formally, then left them alone, but Theo knew they were being watched. Two small girls looked out of a high window in the back of the house, and he sensed other eyes.

He opened his mouth to speak but she cut him off. "Well," she said, not smiling, though her eyes seemed amused, "you're the desperate suitor." Her voice was edged with sarcasm.

He laughed. "I am."

Up close, she was impressive, eyes piercing and intelligent, lips full and soft. Her nose spread wider than her mouth, wider than its own length, so flat it seemed to be melting, sinking back into her face.

"Let's be frank," she said. "I never saw you in my life till your head appeared above my garden wall yesterday. You never saw me. And yet you want to marry me. This is pure business."

"I wouldn't put it like that, but . . ."

"I would. Certainly from my point of view. Just because I'm like your first wife in one respect doesn't mean we could make a good marriage."

"Of course not."

"And you're old enough to be my father."

"Just about," he said. "I'm sorry about that. Not a thing I can do about it."

"What would be expected of me? You want me to sing? Suppose I can't?"

"You can."

"Where would we live?"

"Vienna. St. Petersburg. Anywhere we fancy. Money's not a problem."

"You're talking about a nomad's life," she said matter-of-factly.

"To some extent."

"I won't do that forever," she said. "For a while, perhaps, but not forever."

"Of course. Thank you for your honesty," he said. "Let me try to explain something."

She raised one of those magnificent eyebrows and quirked one side of her mouth.

"I have hunches," he said.

"Hunches?"

It wasn't what he'd meant to say, but on the spur of the moment he was inspired to meet honesty with honesty. She'd like that.

"Yes," he said, "it was a hunch. Don't misunderstand. I'm nothing if not rational, but experience has taught me to respect certain apparently inexplicable reactions to circumstance. I don't believe in precognition, obviously. But the mind responds to things picked up by the senses . . ."

"Yes, yes," she said. "You have hunches."

"Only very rarely." He shrugged, a considered gesture intended to be endearingly awkward. "If they were not rare, they'd be meaningless. And as soon as I heard your name, I knew."

"So you want to get married on a hunch?"

"Yes. I am convinced this is the right thing to do."

She drew in a long breath, put her head on one side and just looked at him. When he began to speak, she put her hand up. "Ssh," she said, "I'm thinking."

It was a little unnerving. She didn't take her eyes off him and hardly blinked for several long minutes.

"The others just wanted to show me," she said finally. "Why do you have to bring marriage into it?"

"To protect my assets." Suddenly the businessman, leaning forward. Then he smiled. "So you don't go running off with the first smooth talker who offers a better deal."

"I could do that anyway," she said. "Marriage wouldn't stop me."

"Of course." A half shrug, less sure of itself.

They sat in mutual contemplation after that, till the moment had grown intimately peculiar. She was nowhere near as hairy as Julia, he realized. Her throat and chest, what he could see of it, were smooth and white but the back of the hand fiddling with a strand of her hair was covered in a dark down, as was the arm revealed by the falling back of her sleeve.

"I'll take you," she said suddenly. "Shall I tell you why?"

So easy!

"Oh, please, do." *It starts again. Glory be.* He felt a smile wrap itself across his face.

"Because," she said, "I would stand on my head singing nursery rhymes if it got me out of here."

Impulsively, he reached across and took her hand. It was tiny and hairy, like Julia's, and the feel of it gave him a jolt in the chest. "I'll take you away," he said earnestly. "You'll travel. See things."

"I'd have gone with the others too," she said. "You're not the first. But I never got the chance."

She was dying of boredom, the old man never let her out.

"Let me make one thing clear," she said. "I'm nobody's monkey."

———

The wedding took place discreetly in the large parlor of Marie's father's house. Her mother, a pale scrawny woman, wept silently throughout, glancing nervously at him from time to time as if he were death himself come to bear her child away. A gaggle of children smirked and nudged each other. The priest, hearty and florid, did his best to pretend this was a wedding like any other, while her father was positively elated. After all, thought Theo, noting the gleam in the old man's rheumy eyes, he couldn't wait to get rid of her. When it was all over and the carriage drew up in front of the house, her little brothers and sisters—there seemed to be many—finally realizing that she was going away, burst into a caterwaul of grief, gathered 'round her and clung to her skirts. Her mother mournfully embraced her. Marie smiled indulgently, casting a quick, shrewd sideways glance at Theo, returned the embrace briskly, kissed each child in turn, then turned to her father.

"Good-bye, Papi," she said.

"*Liebling,*" he said, hugging her closely but briefly, then kissing her on both cheeks. "Be happy."

"I will."

She smiled as she veiled, then ran down the steps and into the carriage.

"I don't want her put on display like an object," the old man said, following Theo down the steps.

"Of course not," said Theo. The old man would be mad not to realize she'd end up on a stage. Of course he knew. You don't marry your bearded daughter to a showman and expect her to live a normal life. "Anyway." Theo turned to shake the old man's hand before joining her in the carriage. "Do you really imagine anyone could make Marie do anything she didn't want to?"

The old man smiled. And when all the waving was done and they were on their way, Marie put back her veil and laughed. "I'm free!" she said. After that she was glued to the window, a smile on her face, watching the new world roll by. They'd make easy stages from Stuttgart to Munich, from there on to Lake Mondsee for a month-long honeymoon. Then Vienna. You can have dance lessons there, he said. The first night in Pforzheim, he took the best room in the hotel and ordered a lavish meal to be sent up with two bottles of champagne. She ate steadily, calmly. If she was sad about leaving her family it didn't show.

"Do you like the chicken?" he asked.

"Very nice." She looked up. "The broth's delicious."

"See how good life can be, Marie," he said, "how much you've been missing."

She put down her spoon. "Do you think I didn't eat well at home?"

"Not at all. I'm not just talking about the food. You're going to see the world. Meet people. Wait until Munich, we'll go to the theater. You'll love it." He remembered saying all these things to Julia. "Have you ever been to the theater?"

She laughed without humor. "Me? A prisoner?"

He felt sorry for her. "Didn't he let you go out at all?"

She looked away. "Once or twice."

God!

"It must have been very dull for you—locked in your high tower."

"Oh, believe me," she said, "it was. Thank God you came along, that's all I can say. My prince on horseback." She looked at him and laughed suddenly. "Not that you look it."

He felt slightly insulted. Count yourself lucky, he wanted to say.

"Our plans then?" she said. "We sail on the lake. We walk in the hills. We go to Vienna, I learn to dance. And then?"

"We taste liberty, Marie," he said, judging the moment ripe for a touch of romance, "we become as Gypsies, not a care in the world. Oh, you have no idea! The music, the crowds, the call of the new, the magic of the next bend in the road. The rain on the roof of a wagon, the neighing of horses, the—"

"And I sing and dance?"

"Yes. But not till you're ready. You'll be wonderful."

"You haven't heard me sing," she said. "Listen," and launched into a spirited soprano "Wanderlied." Her voice was ragged 'round the edges but easily passable.

"Oh, you'll do fine, didn't I know it." He laughed, applauding. "Wonderful!"

She broke off. "Your hunch," she said.

"My hunch."

"Look," she said, "I want to make a lot of money. Then I'll quit. I'm only going to do it for a few years, then I'm going to settle down and have a nice comfortable life."

"A perfect plan," he replied. "If you want to make a lot of money, there's something you must do."

She raised an eyebrow.

"The name Pastrana is known all over Europe. All over Russia. No one knows Marie Bartel."

"And?"

"The name is the draw. You are Marie Pastrana, sister of the renowned Julia."

She frowned, then laughed. "I don't care," she said. "They can call me anything they like, so long as they come."

Theo stood, fetched the second bottle of champagne, his nerves fizzing up like the bubbles as he popped the cork. Oh, this was going to be easy! It was all coming back, that feeling, possibility, excitement, the sound of the wheels of his golden coach approaching over long hard roads.

"Not Marie," she said. "Something more exotic."

"Yes!" He poured. Her glass overflowed, and she held it away from herself.

"Zenora," she said. "I'll be Zenora."

———

Two weeks by the lake had a soothing effect. Marie liked to linger on their balcony, half sitting, half lying, reading a book, or leaning forward with her arms on the rail and her head on her arms, a dreamy smile on her face, watching the people walk up and down by the lakeside far below. She was so pleased to be out in the world that she could be perfectly content to stay like this for hours, and the view was beautiful. Sometimes, veiled, she walked out with him, and it was like walking with a ghost, Theo thought, this small veiled thing on his arm, just like the good old days. Once, they hired a boat and he rowed out very far from shore, and she sang, old things he didn't know. Not bad. Not bad at all. Give her six months, she'd be ready. It would be easy to pass her off to the rubes. She was covered with hair and that was all that mattered to them. But she was nothing like Julia. She didn't have that same great maw. In bed, she was curious and frank and unnervingly preoccupied with herself, her body more feminine than Julia's, her face more masculine. It was better with Julia.

"There's something I have to tell you," he said one night when they had just made love. She was lounging in bed; he was up, wandering about in his dressing gown smoking a cigar and stopping every now and then to look out of the window at a far mountain against the dark sky. How to tell?

"Then tell," she said.

"You need to understand. The show we'll put together must consist of more than your performance." He swung 'round and looked at her. She was plaiting her long, straight hair. "It must have a historical dimension. You are the sister of Julia Pastrana, don't forget."

"I've been thinking," she said, "if I'm her sister, won't it seem funny that I don't speak Spanish?"

"Oh, you can learn a few words. Enough. The point is the show must tell a story. They need to see her. They need to *see* the real Julia, her child, they need a story. They see her and wonder, then see—you, the living, breathing continuation of her presence and talent . . ."

"I don't quite see . . ."

"Marie, when she died . . ." He stopped, and she saw that he was struggling. His manner alarmed her.

"What's the matter?"

"There was a doctor," he said. "Sokolov. At the university. A scientist. I'll give you something to read about it, you'll see how important it was. They were working on a new method of preservation, it was very important, a huge leap forward—"

He had crossed the room and was sitting on the bed staring at her. His eyes were uncertain, slightly beseeching, but as he continued to speak they toughened and steadied. "I really need you to understand this, Marie. She was embalmed. And the baby. It was some—some method—something incredible, and the university was so delighted to have them. It wasn't . . ."

"They were embalmed?" she said flatly. She'd stopped playing with her hair and the plait, slowly loosening, looked as if it were exhaling.

"Yes."

There was a silence.

"What are you saying?"

"Marie," he said. "You're going to hear people say bad things about me. *Some* people. Oh, you know me, you know I'm not a monster, just read these—"

He jumped up, went to the drawer where he kept his papers, his correspondence with theater people, agents, that sort of thing, and pulled out a handful of journals and playbills. "Here," he said, thrusting them at her, "just read them. I'm going for a walk."

When he got back two hours later she was up, sitting on the balcony in her gown. The papers lay scattered on the bed, the *Lancet,* the reviews, the advertisements. Big blue letters. The Embalmed Female Nondescript. She came in when she heard him, closing the balcony door. "Give me one of your cigars," she said.

He tried to read her face. "Here." He passed her one and she looked at it, frowning.

"Mummies," she said.

"Yes."

She met his eyes with a strong intelligent look that never wavered. "Did you love her?" she asked.

"Yes." He said it in a suave, clipped way.

She didn't blink for a long time and looked at him with an unreadable expression.

"Let us talk," she said.

"Let us," he agreed, lighting their cigars.

"Where are they?"

"Vienna."

"Ah, I see."

"Marie," he said, "there's nothing distasteful about it, I promise you. The mummies are displayed in a glass case very respectably. You wouldn't have anything to do with them, they'll really just be a backdrop to your show. The people will come to see *them*, then they'll see you and your talent, and you'll . . ."

Nothing fazed her.

"Tell me," she said. "Why are we married?"

"I told you. So you can't go running off with any old fly-by-night that takes your fancy. This business is full of crooks. Secondly, because your old man would never have let you go otherwise. And thirdly, why do you think?"

She stepped back and said wryly, "Oh, my dear, don't tell me. You peeped over my garden wall and fell in love with me at first sight."

I have her. Another hurdle flown over, whoosh, there it goes.

"I understand completely," he said, "if you find this disturbing. I realize I'm at fault for not telling you straightaway, but I was a coward, I didn't want to scare you away. You're a free woman, Marie. If you want me to take you back home, I will."

Of course she didn't.

"Oh, I'm not going back there," she said decisively. "I might visit sometimes, but I'm not going to live there ever again."

Relief flooded him. He started babbling about how wonderful she was, how mature, enlightened, understanding, but she cut him off. "If you stuff me," she said, "I swear to God, I'll come back and haunt you."

———

When she first saw the mummies, she was just like everyone else, transfixed. 'Round and 'round them she went, 'round and 'round, saying nothing, then stood still with her attention fixed on the baby.

"He has the sweetest little chin," she said.

After that she took charge of them. First thing she did was demand new boots for Julia. Those ankle boots were all wrong apparently. "Look at her dumpy little legs," she said, "those boots make her look like a washerwoman." She veiled up and insisted on him accompanying her at once to Scheers, where she picked out a pair of knee-high lace-ups that he had to admit did look much better.

Of course a woman knew more about that sort of thing. He watched, oddly moved, as Marie brushed and combed Julia's hair, rearranged the paper flowers, the pearls, the feathers.

"There now," she said, standing back and admiring her handiwork. "You look lovely. Sister."

———

"And how does it feel to be back in St. Petersburg, Mr. Lent?"

"Wonderful. Julia was very fond of St. Petersburg."

Theo had been out drinking with a bunch of hardened old circus cronies, and the reporter was drunk too, though neither would have admitted it. They were in a corner of the vast parlor of the hotel, beneath a pompous portrait of some bewigged nobleman, and the sound of revelry drifted in from the lobby whenever someone opened the door.

"Twenty-one years," Theo said, "maybe a little more, since she last performed in this city. Hard to believe." To be honest, he was losing track. Years, years, many, many, many.

"And yet the memory of those spectacular shows remains strong." The reporter squiggled in his book. He was a big bull of a man who looked as if he should be digging a road.

"Of course," said Theo. "Who could ever forget Julia? Many of those coming through the doors now weren't even born when we last played St. Petersburg, but they grew up hearing stories from their parents about the time the most remarkable woman in the world sang and danced for them. She has become a legend."

"And your wife, Mr. Lent?" The reporter looked up. "The equally remarkable Zenora. One can't help but wonder how she feels performing nightly alongside her predecessor. Particularly as that predecessor is her own sister."

"My wife and I are of one mind," Theo replied smoothly. "Five years we've been together as a family—the four of us—my wife and I, Julia and, of course, her son. And a very happy family at that. In a sense Julia is still with us. We feel that our show is a tribute to a wonderful woman."

The reporter smiled. Skeptically, Theo thought. "I'm sure you realize—many women who marry a widower shy away from any mention of their husband's previous spouse."

"That's true." Theo nodded. "But my wife is a woman of sound good sense. Perhaps the fact that she is Julia's sister makes a difference. They were very close."

"I've heard," said the reporter, "that some people think Zenora *is* Julia."

Theo smiled. Let them think it. Never hurts to keep the rubes guessing.

"It's unusual," the reporter said, "for a man to marry his deceased wife's sister."

"It is." Out with the spiel. "But as soon as she arrived in Europe to attend the commemoration service, I think we both realized it had to be. Our grief united us, and in time that feeling changed to something more profound. We feel that our arrangement, unusual as it may seem to other people, is a source of constant joy."

The reporter didn't look convinced. "It would be wonderful," he said, without hope, "if we could speak with your wife, Mr. Lent."

"I'm sorry." Apologetic smile. "She never gives interviews."

"That's a pity."

"Yes, it is, but I'm afraid she's adamant on that point." He stood up, brushed down his knees.

"Thank you for your time, Mr. Lent."

"It's been a pleasure."

Theo shook hands with the man, checked the front desk for messages and walked heavily back upstairs to their suite. He'd always been a thin man, a slight man, the years had never put any weight on him. There was no need to feel so heavy, yet he did.

Marie was sitting at the writing desk with a pile of playbills in front of her and a large sheet of paper on which she was scribbling rapidly.

"No—no—no," she said as he came in, "this has all got to go. We really have got to update these, Theo, they're terrible."

She was always doing this. He was tired. "What's the matter with them now?"

"You know exactly what's the matter with them. They're old-fashioned." She was thirty years younger than him and was always telling him he had no idea what people wanted these days. Got to move with the times.

"The way you write!" she said. "It's appalling. Listen to this—'this uniquely singular wonder of the natural world'—uniquely singular! Uniquely singular! That's terrible."

"So change it."

"That's what I'm doing."

One side of his head felt funny. Another migraine.

"I'm going for a lie-down," he said, stumbling slightly against the glass cabinet wedged in between the bedroom door and the writing desk.

"Theo!" said Marie. "Careful!"

"Stupid place to put them," he mumbled.

Julia and Theo Junior had just gotten back from another stint in Vienna. Good. It was always nice when they came home. He went into the bedroom and got under the purple silk coverlet with all his clothes on, closed his eyes and tried to shut down his brain, but it wouldn't stop. The door was slightly ajar, and he could hear Marie in the other room talking to herself in a semiwhisper as she crossed things out and jotted down phrases.

Deep down in his bones was an ache. Marie came bustling into the room. "I've got it all worked out," she said, ignoring the fact that he was trying to sleep.

He pretended he'd already nodded off.

"Doesn't do you any good lying about in bed all day," she said. "Best to get up. You'd feel better."

He opened his eyes. "Marie. I'm getting a migraine." He closed them again. "I'm just going to lie here for a while."

"Suit yourself," she said, but carried on irritatingly doing things in the room, opening drawers and rearranging things, messing about with her hair.

"Marie!" he said. "I'm trying to sleep."

"Won't be a moment."

He flounced over petulantly in the bed and pounded the pillow.

"Misery guts," she said without malice, walking out of the room and closing the door behind her. Pain stabbed him in one eye. He could still hear her, singing to herself as she puttered about next door.

When he eventually emerged from the bedroom later that day in search of tea, the migraine having settled slightly, Marie had the cabinet open and was hauling out Theo Junior on his pole. "Look at the state of him," she said, "they've let moths get in. We're not leaving them there again."

"Really? Moths?"

"Look."

"They do pay well," Theo said, "Is there any tea?"

"There's a pot of coffee. There."

Theo shambled over and started pouring. He'd gotten into his slippers and dressing gown.

"Good thing we didn't leave them there," Marie said. "Wish we *could* leave them there. You know the market's slipping, don't you?"

Here we go again.

"Of course it isn't."

"Of course it is."

"You're always crying doom," he said.

"I'm just realistic." She sat down, picking at the side of the small mummy with her dainty, long-nailed hands. He saw that the table was littered with pieces of old playbills and there were more in the bin. "Why are you tearing these up?" he asked.

"I'm throwing them away. I can't stand them any longer."

He put the fingers of one hand through the front of his hair and pushed it back, and was again surprised at how far it had receded. "They're all right for now," he grumbled, "we don't want to run out before the end of the season."

"Don't worry," she said cheerfully, "it's all under control. I've already sent a boy to the printer's."

"Without showing me first?"

"Oh, for goodness sake, Theo, you know I'm better at this sort of thing than you."

"Marie," he said, "how do you think I managed all these years without you? I did all the playbills myself."

"Yes, and they were terrible. Mine are better."

He stood drinking his coffee and sifting through the fragments on the table. He caught words and phrases, some of it in blue curly writing, some plain. Wonder of. Root-Digger. Culiacán where. Broadway and. Many an eminent.

"We need to talk," she said.

"Do we indeed?" He flopped into a chair. "I'm rather tired, Marie."

"Yes," she said, "but you always are, so we might as well talk now. Give me those scraps." She held out her hand without looking up from her minute examination of the baby's hide. Theo gathered up a few bits of paper and handed them to her. "There's an actual hole here," she said.

He yawned, put down his coffee and searched about for his cigars.

"You left them on the dressing table," she said.

When he returned from the bedroom with a lit cigar in his mouth she was stuffing the bits of torn up playbill into a hole in Theo Junior's side. "So much for the wonderful new method of embalming," she said, "it's just sawdust in there."

"Is it?" He leaned over, squinting down at her repair.

"Look." She sounded indignant.

"That's probably just the top layer," he said. "What's underneath is the real stuff. Obviously it's a complicated process."

He watched her tamp the paper inside with the tip of her little finger. "Now you know what we have to talk about, don't you?"

"I suppose so." He flopped down again.

"Look at you," she said. "You're not a well man. You've been on the road for forty years; it takes its toll. Go and see that doctor again."

Briskly, she set about closing the hole in Theo Junior's side with rapid, tiny stitches that she drew ever more tightly together. "You're pushing sixty, face reality. You've earned your retirement."

"Retirement!" he said, as if it were a curse.

"You know what I said, right back at the beginning." She sewed diligently. "I said I'd do it for a few years and then settle somewhere nice."

"I know. That was always the plan."

"You know," she said, "we could afford somewhere really nice."

"Well, yes, that's always been our plan," he repeated, "but it's a matter of timing. The time has to be right."

"It's never right with you," she said. She got up and fetched a saucer, took it to the fireplace and scraped a little soot into it.

"What are you doing?" he said.

"Aha!" She poured a drop of water from the jug onto the soot and started mixing it with her finger.

"To be truthful," Marie said, "the thought of living with these two for the rest of my life is weighing me down. I never thought it would be years like this, you know I didn't. Theo, you can't say I haven't been patient living with them all these years. How many women do you think would do that? Waking up and seeing her standing there. I've grown used to them, but . . ." She started rubbing soot and water over the bundle of stitches with her finger, shading it all in carefully. He stopped listening.

"And it's not been easy," she was saying when her voice filtered back in again.

"You want to get rid of them," he said.

"Not completely." She propped the baby against the side of the cabinet. "But maybe a long-term hire. Nice returns. Not Vienna obviously, maybe Munich. They'd still be ours, of course, but we wouldn't have to keep lugging them 'round with us. Think of how much lighter we could travel."

"Why do we need to travel lighter?"

"Oh, Theo, I wish you'd open your eyes. They're not coming to see her anymore. We've been all over the place and everybody's seen her already. You can't keep it going."

"I think you're being terribly pessimistic," he said, sounding hurt.

"It's me they come for now," she said, "Zenora Pastrana. You know, the one that actually does all the hard work after all, all the singing and the dancing, all that silly stuff, you know. All *she* does, when all's said and done, is stand there."

"If everyone here's seen her," Theo said, "there are other places. We'll take her to Scandinavia. We'll go and see the Northern Lights."

"But Theo," she said, "what if I don't want to go? It's not fair. This is now. That was then." She pulled up Theo Junior's white drawers. "There, that covers it pretty well," she said, and started putting him back in his place. "I know it's hard to let them go," she said, "but I honestly don't see myself staying on the road very much longer."

"You really do want to get rid of them, don't you?" he said listlessly.

"His arm should keep it covered," she said, brushing Theo Junior down with her hands. "There you are, Baby, good as new. I don't think anyone will notice. Theo, you check Julia."

He went and sat in the cane chair in front of the open case, leaned back and crossed his legs, smoking his cigar. "Hello, Julia," he said. Three or four times they'd hired out the mummies, once for a whole two months. Occasionally he thought about them, rattling on trains between cities. Whenever the mummies came home he'd get a certain feeling, as if an old friend had returned. Not that he'd ever really had an old friend to feel that way about. She's been gone . . . she's back. Things are in place. About the baby he didn't think so much. Most of the time it was just a prop. He'd never gotten as far as thinking what his son might have been. But once, putting the mummies away late one night, he'd touched the boy's cold hand, and a shaft of excruciating sadness had pierced him. It was nothing like the warm baby fist he remembered.

Funny. After all this time he could still get lost in looking, just looking at her. Marie didn't have that. Her face, though hairy enough, was completely human. With Julia, you did wonder. Sometimes still, he wondered. But he didn't care. These days he was sentimental in his mind, though not to outward appearance. After a few drinks, reminiscing, he allowed it, sinking into a reverie of the glory days when theater fronts heaved with masses desperate for a glimpse, and she'd tiptoe into the spotlight and strike them dumb.

"She looks all right to me," he said.

"You don't know," she said, "she could be all fleas under that dress."

"We'd know if she had fleas."

He went to bed. Later she came in. "I know you think you can't live in one place, Theo," she said, "but how about this?"

"What?" he said unenthusiastically.

"What about a little fixed concern? Something in the business, then you wouldn't be bored. What about something like a wax museum? Wax museums are very popular. And we could use Julia and Baby. That's something no one else would have. We'd be unique."

"It's an idea," he said with no interest whatsoever.

* * *

No fool, Marie.

Gets what she wants, he reflected, thinking back. First it's, oh, yes, we'll get a wax museum, then we can keep the mummies at home and we'll all be happy. Chip, chip, chip, every day, like a patient woodcarver. Then she's pregnant. Oh, well, that's it, I'm not performing when the baby's born. Then it's, oh, well I'm not taking any chances, look at poor Julia, working up to the last minute and look what happened to her. Face it, Theo. Be sensible. We need to look around. Then—what about this, Theo, a wax museum. Perfect! Prime location. We both like Petersburg. Poor old Theo, you deserve a rest. A lovely apartment upstairs. Plenty of room. A nursery. And all the exhibits included, to which we add—tada!—our Julia, our Baby. A home for them, downstairs with the waxworks, pride of place.

Oh, if it's what you want.

He was ill. Sick stomachs, sore throats, splitting headaches, one thing after another. His sleeping had gone all to hell. Hip baths and purges didn't help. He wondered if it was the pox. He still visited those girls in their rooms, more so since the pregnancy, she wasn't interested anymore. Could be, he thought distantly, could be. Then suddenly they were living above the museum and Oscar was all over the place, as fair and normal as a little Apollo, a squalling being that punched red fists in the air and tried out faces. Theo kept looking at Marie nursing the baby and wondering if she'd got the pox too. Probably not. Pox wouldn't stand a chance with her. She'd just clap her hands and send it on its way. She was right, of course, she was always right. The museum was doing well. It was just off the Nevsky Prospect and pulled in a good mixed crowd. She loved it. Humming and smiling about the place while he wandered like a ghost from room to room feeling unreal, wandered like a visitor among his own exhibits, stopping every time in front of Julia's cabinet. Till one day she said, "We've had an offer."

Munich. Long-term.

"Get her back anytime you want," she said. "No trouble at all. Just think. Know what they're paying? And we can get more if we push."

"Did you open my letter?" he asked.

"It was addressed to both of us."

"We need her here," he said. "She's our pièce de résistance."

"No, she isn't. Peter the First is."

"Peter the First!" he said disgustedly. "He can't hold a candle to her."

"Look, Theo," she said, pushing him gently down into a chair, "I'm going to make you a nice hot tonic, and you're going to drink it all down and then you'll feel better. I wouldn't send her anywhere else but they always look after her well in Munich."

"I still don't see," he said grumpily. "It's not as if we're desperate for the money."

"Theo," she said, "you've got to let the past go. It's not good for you."

"Well, Marie," he said with a losing sense, "if we send them to Munich, I think you'll notice a sudden decline in trade."

"Want a bet?" She bustled about him, making him comfortable. "I don't know when you'll start to listen to me. Times have changed. People just aren't as interested in that sort of thing anymore. They find it distasteful. I don't like people standing there in our museum whispering nasty things behind their hands about you."

"Oh, people are stupid," he said. "I don't care what people say."

"Well, I do, Theo. We've got Oscar now."

"What's that got to do with it?"

Oh, she's right, she's right, he thought now, loitering in the lobby of his wax museum, too tired to be bitter, too unsettled to be at ease. Trade was still brisk six months after the mummies left for Munich. Peter the First was the pièce de résistance. There he stood, dominating the foyer in all his glory. Retire! thought Theo. I'll bring her back. Who's going to stop me? If I could get my health back, know what I'd do? I'd be back on that road. It's the only life. I'm not old, look at Otto, look at Van Hare, look at Barnum. Just get my health back.

Two women came up to him. "Are you the proprietor?"

"I am." He bowed graciously.

"Have you got Cleopatra?"

"Room number three, ladies," he said, twinkling at them but turning it off as soon as they'd gone. He walked to the door and stood blinking out at the cold bright St. Petersburg sunshine. The girl in the ticket booth was worrying her nails.

"I wish you wouldn't do that," he said tetchily.

"Oh. Sorry, sir," she said, turning bright red and looking as if she were going to cry.

"It's all right," he snapped. "Just don't do it, that's all. Puts people off. Don't forget you're in the public eye."

"Yes," she whispered, dropping her eyes.

He stepped out and strolled down Nevsky Prospect. She's still mine, he thought, I can bring her back whenever I like. On the corner of Nevsky Prospect and Sadovaya Street he saw Liliya Grigorievka Levkova hurrying along on the other side of the street with her hands in a muff and her head down. Surely not. Can't be her, she'd be—what?— surely getting on for fifty now. Is it her? What's she doing in Petersburg? God, my eyes. Hardly looks a day older. Before he'd had a chance to think, he found himself attempting to jog in a sprightly manner across the road and intercept her. It made his legs ache. "Liliya Grigorievka," he said brightly, "what a surprise!" She glanced up once, startled, saw him, appeared about to speak but immediately blanked her eyes and hurried past, drawing herself imperceptibly away from him as she did so, as if he were something slimy. And then he wasn't even sure that it was her. He went down to the river and walked along as far as Tuchkov Bridge. It was her. Danced with her once. Oh, Mr. Lent. Wrinkling her nose. Well, that was nice, wasn't it? Running away like that. Snob. Who does she think she is? Full of snobs, this country. He stood shivering, looking down into the Neva's melting ice. The river was choppy, a sharp breeze gusting from the Gulf of Finland. What was wrong with her? Listening to the things people said, that's what. Monster. Vile. Easy to talk. He felt a quivering, a funny feeling in the nerve ends.

Sometimes, in the middle of an ordinary day, a dark flame of terror licked 'round his gut. The water was black but full of light. The sky was dirty. His head was about to burst.

He turned and walked back, needing a drink. The sounds in his head, the eternal inner babble swishing around like the flux of waves, mingled with the sounds in the street. He kept an eye out for Liliya Grigorievka Levkova but she was nowhere to be seen. If he saw her, he'd go up to her and say—he didn't know what. It didn't matter as long as it was honest. That was the trouble, no one was honest. From now on, he thought, what if I never said another word that was not the honest truth? They'd think he was mad, but he'd be sane for the first time. He smiled as he walked. When he reached the museum, he passed the same two women coming out.

"I saw a much better Cleopatra than that," one of them said. "It moved. You saw the snake bite her."

"Yes, madame," he said, "some displays are more vulgar than this one."

He went upstairs and started getting undressed, caught sight of himself in the mirror: a small insignificant man with a double chin. He'd always been pleased with his looks, but not anymore. He got into bed. Marie was out with the boy somewhere. She had friends he didn't even know. He didn't sleep but closed his eyes and pretended. After about half an hour, he realized he had no idea what time of the day it was. It could have been the middle of the afternoon, the dead of night or a fine spring morning. At that moment Marie came swanning into the room with Oscar in her arms. "Oh, no," she said, "you're not ill again, are you?"

Theo bolted upright and screamed, "Get out!"

She flinched. The baby started crying.

"Don't you dare speak to me like that!" she said, shushing the baby.

"Don't you dare speak to *me* like that." He threw his head back down on the pillow so hard it bounced.

She'd had her hair done. All frizzed out. "What's the matter with you?" she said, jogging the child up and down. "Aren't you well?"

"I'm just very, *very* tired."

"Go back to that doctor," she said and walked out.

The doctor couldn't be sure but gave him mercury and potassium iodide to be on the safe side. He got a twitch in his left eye, which started driving him mad. Oscar started imitating it. By the time he was eighteen months old, the child showed signs of being a brilliant mimic. He was a sturdy, smiley boy, not given to tantrums. Most of the time he ran about the place chuckling and chatting amiably to himself, and Theo, often in his chair by the fire, vaguely unwell, sulking but not sure why, felt a kinship with him he'd never known with Theo Junior on his perch. The way Marie bossed them about as if they were equal in status forged a bond between them, and sometimes when she walked out of the room they would smile conspiratorially at one another. Sometimes the boy would sit on the floor by his chair and lean against his legs. Once, he fell asleep there. Theo wondered why the feel of the boy against his legs caused a feeling of sadness to rise up inside him. Something to do with the picture that kept coming into his mind, Theo Junior's stiff unnatural stance on his pole, a stance impossible for any real baby.

"I'm bringing them back," he said, unsure whether Marie was in the room with him or not.

"Yes," she said, proving her existence, "soon."

Soon.

A rash came and went on Theo's back and sides. For six months it raged and itched, and Oscar mimicked his scratching.

"Stop it, you two," Marie would say. "You're driving me mad."

Sometimes he stayed in bed or mooched about at home in a foul mood for days on end, unable to see the point in doing anything else. Marie told him to make an effort. "Look at you," she said, "in your dressing gown. Do you know what time it is?"

"No."

"Do you want some soup?"

"I don't know. Yes."

She pulled a small table up to his knee, set down a bowl of soup and a spoon. "Do you good," she said. "Eat it."

"Any bread?"

"Here, precious one." Marie ripped off a hunk from the loaf and gave it to Oscar. "Give Daddy this bread."

Oscar trotted over and solemnly handed it over. Theo took it listlessly and dipped it in his soup.

"Say 'thank you!' " she ordered.

"Thank you," Theo said.

"Silly Daddy forgot to say thank you!"

"For God's sake," she said a little later, "at least go out for a walk or something. Clear your head."

"Can't," he said, "my legs hurt."

"That's because you don't use them enough."

"Can't."

And this went on like fog, till one day he awoke at noon and felt different.

The sun slanted in across the rug. Pigeons purred on the window-sill. It was high summer. He lay for a while trying to place the feeling, then realized it was vigor and excitement, a peculiar elation that felt like childhood, though it was no childhood he could ever remember having. He sat up. His head was clear. He knew from the quietness that the flat was empty. He couldn't remember when he'd gone to sleep but he was wearing all his clothes, so he got up and walked straight out and down to the street. He put his hand in his pocket and found notes and coins. Plenty. He couldn't remember putting it there. A drink, he thought, heading for the river.

The sunlight on the water hurt his eyes. It was incredibly beautiful, a million small ice-white fishes winking frantically in and out of existence. He tried fixing his eyes on one spot without blinking, but it was no use. Everything moved.

He crossed a couple of canals, rambled this way and that, slid into a tavern, ordered a beer and closed his eyes. His heart was beating hard and fast as if he'd just done something very brave and dangerous. The room was full of babble and laughter, and he began to feel afraid because his mind was full to bursting, not with thoughts or ideas so much as impressions and currents of sound. One hand was in his pocket, in amongst the notes and coins.

Someone jogged his elbow. A long-haired whiskery vagabond of a character, someone he'd drunk with. "You know what you look like, old man," this fellow said, "like you've reached that seen-better-days point in life. I know it well."

"There are no better days," Theo said, "they're all one."

"All one, are they?"

"And all mine."

"All yours?"

"Mine."

He downed his beer and ordered another.

"All one and all mine."

"But look," said the man, "what about me? I have my moments too."

"The same. All the same."

"Ah, well," the man said, "if you say so."

"I do."

He wasn't sure. This was curiously dreamlike. The tavern glowed. The people, the eternal frightened kindergarten of mankind, trembled outside in the dark. His mind was quick and fluid.

"I am an articulate man," he said.

"What?"

He laughed.

"You are what?"

Theo went on laughing.

"If I were an articulated man," he said.

"A what?"

"Artic-articulate man."

"Oh."

"An articulated man!" he shouted, clapping his hands loudly and suddenly bellowing with laughter. As one, the people on the other side of the room stopped what they were doing and looked at him. What's the matter with them all? What are they looking at? "If I were an articulated man," he said, still laughing, "I would tell you what my bones know."

He stood up, and felt as if he was on a stage. He was young again, the old Theo, with the charm and the quickness. Then he realized tears were dripping from the end of his chin and his nose was beginning to run. "Only what's known in the bones is true," he almost shouted at the room in general.

"Sit down, old man," said his vagabond friend. "No need to get so upset. It's only life."

Theo sat down, wiping his nose on his sleeve. The tears confused him. He had no idea where they'd come from, he wasn't even feeling upset.

"Give us a song," someone said.

"I will," said Theo.

"Go on then," his friend said.

He tried to sing "Lorena," but it came out wrong.

"What a miserable dirge," some old woman said. There was a piano over by the door, and she waddled over to it and sat down and started playing some jolly, bawdy old rubbish that everyone joined in with. The tavern keeper, expressionless, wiped a glass behind the bar. Theo felt like dancing, so he got up and set about the fandango, the one Julia used to do. There was a cheer and someone shouted, "Bravo!" Then he went to the piano and sat next to the old woman and started hammering away alongside her, drowning her out and making a horrible racket.

They began to boo and he turned, laughing. The old lady gave him a push.

"To hell with you all," he said.

Out in the bright sunshine, he forgot where he was. There was money in his pockets, he was drunk, his energy had returned and it was good to be alive.

Slowly, he meandered home, breaking into snatches of song every now and then, stopping here and there to buy things, sweets and pies, whatever he saw, for himself, Marie, Oscar. Some stupid friend of Marie's was there when he got home, an awful woman called Marfa Nicolevnya who looked like an old witch and never stopped moaning, yak, yak, yak all the time. Marie gave him a strange look. This awful Marfa Nicolevnya didn't even pause to say hello when he came in, not that he wanted to say hello to her, stupid woman, stupid, stupid woman. She just raised her eyebrows as if he were a fly buzzing into the room, then on and on about nothing, while Marie walked about straightening things in the room, nodding patiently, saying, yes, yes, I see, and oh, really, and oh, dear, a charade of patience and sympathy he knew she didn't really feel. Stupid woman kept saying she was going. "Ooh, I must be on my way in a minute," she says, then fills up her coffee cup and yak, yak, yak, on she goes. Theo wanted to kill her. Scream. Leap from his chair and hurl her out of the window or down the stairs.

He stood up. "Go away," he said.

Marfa Nicolevnya looked at him as if he were mad.

"Stupid droning woman," he said. "Go. Just go."

"Theo!"

Marie stood holding the poker, about to prod the fire, a look of mortal embarrassment on her face.

"Stupid woman," he said, hovering in a vaguely threatening way toward Marfa Nicolevnya. "Why aren't you going away?"

"Theo! Stop it!" Marie advanced on him, still holding the poker as if she were about to bash his brains out with it.

"I'm sorry, Marie," he said, "I just can't stand to listen to that voice or look at her hideous face a second longer."

Marfa Nicolevnya was gathering up her things, a look of stunned misery on her already miserable face. Marie threw the poker into the hearth and ran over to her. "Oh, I'm so sorry, Marfa Nicolevnya, I'm so sorry, please don't feel you have to go, he's been drinking."

"Oh, good, good, good," Theo said, rubbing his hands together. "She's leaving, the old witch is leaving."

Marie turned on him. "Are you mad?" she yelled. "How dare you!"

"I dare!" He laughed.

"No, no, it's not you, Marie," said the wronged woman quietly, at the door. "I don't blame you." She stared at him mournfully, and he grinned back at her.

"I told you the truth," he said, savoring the moment. It was full of gall, grim delight and bitter shame at the sight of the stupid woman's pale, desolate face.

As her footsteps died away down the stairs, Marie advanced upon him. "How dare you!" She was trembling with rage. "How dare you speak to my friend like that!"

"She's an idiot," he said. "And you're an idiot for having her as a friend."

His head was hurting. He tried to hug her.

"Get off me!" She pushed him away. "What's got into you? If you wake Oscar, I'll kill you. You can't speak to people like that! Poor woman, nobody likes her. And you say a thing like that! You've got cruelty in you. Cruelty."

He swaggered. "How can the truth be cruel?"

"Don't be stupid! The truth *is* cruel. Any fool knows that."

"I'll show you truth," he said, and began hauling all the things he'd bought that afternoon out of the sack and spreading them about the room, a fancy parasol, spoons, a Mongolian cushion and a wooden Noah's Ark with half the animals missing.

"What's all this?" she said.

"The stuff of life." He laughed, covering the table and the bureau with more and more things they didn't need, china ornaments broken from their journey, cakes crumbling in his hands, drawing trails of fluff with them as he dragged them from his pockets.

Her face grew sharp. "How much have you spent?"

"Oh, I don't know."

"For God's sake, Theo!"

"Look," he said, swinging his arms, "I got you all this."

"I don't want it."

"You have no gratitude," he said. "Whatever I do, it's never right for you, is it?"

"Calm down, Theo. Stop it."

"You don't care. You don't care. She cared about me. She loved me, she did. You don't."

"Shut up, Theo. You're making yourself ridiculous."

"*She* never thought I was ridiculous."

"Are you sure?" she said, and walked away into the other room where the boy was sleeping. She closed the door.

He walked into the bedroom, got into bed and closed the curtains. His bones ached. He began to grin, then laugh into the pillow.

For the next three months, he drank in the taverns around the old Hay Market. He told people he owned the biggest circus in New York City and owned a troupe of pure-bred white Arabian horses. He described the red plush, the chandeliers, the gilt boxes, the bobbing plumes on the horses. Every time he lay down to sleep, the circus he owned played in front of his eyes in the dark. Other days he woke up feeling obscurely oppressed and walked about all day in a state of mortal fear. Marie made him sleep on the sofa because he muttered in his sleep. He let his beard grow. He stopped washing and started to smell. She nagged him to go to the doctor, shouted at him, jollied him along, pleaded with him to pull himself together. "You're scaring me," she said.

Oscar still leaned against him and it still made him sad. Sometimes every little thing touched a nerve and he wanted to cry. Sometimes he wanted to kick things. Then a mood of defiant joy would burst up from somewhere, and he'd spend all his money and go down Nevsky Prospect singing out loud, *a hundred months have passed, Lorena*, not caring a monkey's toss what anybody thought of him. At last he let her drag him to the doctor, and the doctor gave him morphine for the pain in his bones, along with some kind of pills he kept forgetting to take. He couldn't follow a thought along its track for more than a few seconds without losing it. The lost thoughts writhed around each other like a mass of bisected worms looking for their other halves. And when that happened he was nothing, only the irrational beat of each moment passing.

Knowledge, he explained to his vagabond-faced friend in the tavern, resides with pain in the bones. Jesus knew that. Bones. Flesh. Pain. Beauty. Truth. Words in the head.

Just words in the head.

Then one night he came home in the early white night of a Petersburg summer, and Julia was waiting for him in the foyer of his wax museum. She was sitting on the bench in front of the magnificent figure of Peter the First, resplendent in his furs and finery. Her eyes gleamed at him. Theo Junior was asleep on her knee with his thumb in his mouth and his hand cupped over his nose. She was real. Both of them were real. His heart melted and he ran to her, but she vanished; there one minute, gone the next, she and her baby.

Marie came down in her nightgown to see what all the noise was about and found him dressed up in Peter the First's clothes, carrying the naked emperor out into the street where snow was beginning to settle.

"What the hell are you doing!" she cried.

"Taking him to the river to see if he can swim."

"Get back in here!"

Half out of the door, Theo looked over his shoulder at her with a grin.

"You've got that twitch again," she said. "You're not well. I'm calling the doctor first thing, you come in now and go to bed."

"I'm bringing them back," he said.

"What are you talking about?"

"I need his space. I'm bringing Julia and the boy back, and I need that space."

"That's the best spot in the whole place, Theo," she said. "Don't be ridiculous."

"I can do what I like," he said, hoisting the emperor higher. "It's my museum. I can throw them all out if I want to."

"Oh, please, Theo, stop all this. You're driving me mad."

"Am I? Am I really, Marie? Driving you mad, am I? Try this!" He shrieked, a short ear-splitting yowl like a cat's. It scared her, so she slapped his face.

"Shut up!" she hissed, grabbing his arm and dragging him back across the threshold with the dummy. When she turned from locking the door, he'd thrown the dummy aside and was crouching at the foot of the stairs with his arms over his head, weeping harshly.

"What did you do that for?" she said sternly. "Why did you scream like that? Horrible sound!"

"Why not scream?" He looked up, his face contorted.

She walked toward him. "Stop it! Stop it, Theo. Stop this right now. I can't stand it."

"Scream then," he said and jumped up, grabbing her by the shoulders and staring intently into her eyes. "We should all scream." He looked terrible, ridiculous in Peter the Great's clothes, wasted and wet-eyed, and the look of trouble in his eyes was painful.

Marie put her hands up and wiped his eyes. "Come on now," she said, "you come on upstairs and I'll make you some tea. You need to lie down."

He pulled away, rubbed his face and ran upstairs with his patchy ermine flowing behind him. Marie swore, gathering up the clothes he'd discarded for the emperor's. As for the emperor, she got him to his feet and leaned him naked against the wall. He'd have to wait for tomorrow for his clothes.

When she went upstairs, he'd gone to bed on the sofa and lay with his back to her.

"That's not the way, Theo," she said quietly to his back. "Giving in to these mad kind of feelings. Resist them. Just stop. You don't have to go mad."

He said nothing.

"I'm warning you, Theo. You're getting too much for me to handle. If it carries on, I don't think I can live with it."

She returned to her own bed in the next room.

Next day the doctor gave him a powder, and left some more for him to take. He drooped nervily about the flat for a few days, till one night the sound of the people in one of the houses in the street tipped him over the edge. Snow fell lazily past the window. Marie was giving Oscar his supper, and there was peace in the air till those idiots started. It sounded to him as if a regiment of soldiers were getting very drunk.

"What in God's name are they doing in there?" He started up and went to the window.

"What?" Marie asked, wiping off the spoon on the edge of Oscar's dish.

"That god-awful racket!"

She listened, poised. "What?" she said again.

"Are you deaf?"

"I can't hear anything."

"You can't hear that?" He threw open the window and stuck his head out. He could hear them, a couple of houses down, continual bursts of brash, deafening laughter.

"Don't shout," she said.

"Me? What about them?"

She put down the spoon, went over and stood beside him. "What is it?" she asked patiently.

"Listen!"

"Yes," she said, "it's only those people with the dog. They've got some friends in."

"But that's ridiculous! They can have their friends in but why should the whole street have to put up with them?"

"It's not that loud." She took him by the arm and closed the window firmly. "See. If we close the window you can't hear it."

"Completely inconsiderate!"

He wouldn't sit down. Backward and forward he went with a murderous look, to the window, in and out of the bedroom. He kicked the fireplace screen.

"Now," said Marie to Oscar, whose full attention was on his pacing father, "just finish this last little bit and we'll have a story."

Theo cursed like a man being dragged to the gallows.

"Theo!"

"If you can't hear that, you're mad," he said.

"Ssh! Voice down!"

"Me? Voice down? *Me?*" He laughed horribly, and she thought he might be about to burst into tears. "Why don't you go and tell *them*! Voice down!"

"Calm down, Theo, please."

Another burst of laughter broke over his head, stupid, mocking and viciously indifferent. He screamed harshly, covering his ears and slamming his eyes closed.

"Theo! Please!"

He wanted to storm over there and beat them all to death. He roared. Oscar laughed.

"It's not even that bad," she said, "I can just about hear it if I stand really still and . . ."

"Are you deaf?"

"No, Theo," she said, raising her eyes to heaven, "I am not deaf."

He put his head down and ran toward the wall as if he were going to butt it, but stopped short and swept all the things off the writing table instead. Then he swung around and dashed the samovar across the floor. Oscar started to cry. Marie swept him up in her arms.

"Get out!" she shouted. "Get out if you can't behave like a respectable person."

He ran out, down through the museum and into the street. He started shouting up at the house next door but one, cursing and screaming and damning them all to death, then ran away.

"Oh my God," Marie whispered, and went to call on a neighbor to watch the child.

———

The police were called because there was a madman on Tuchkov Bridge, pulling money out of his pockets, tearing it up into little pieces and throwing it into the black water of the Little Neva. After that, out came handfuls of copper. That went over too. Then he took off his clothes down to his socks and drawers and tossed each item separately out into the void, cheering and laughing as each one landed on the water and was carried away. A large crowd had gathered at the entrance to the bridge. Two policemen approached. "Enough now, old man," one of them said.

"Shut your trap," said Theo.

He ran from them, and a chase began. He laughed and leapt in the air, shrieking his cat yowl, raving. "Hypocrites," he roared, as the first policeman gripped his arm. "I'm a bad man." They pulled him through the crowd. The cold was getting to him now. "You make such a fuss about all this," he said through chattering teeth, "but what about you? You wouldn't want her, would you?" He was slurring his words as if drunk, but curiously, for once, he wasn't. "Marry her, would you? Give her proper love like a man should? No, you wouldn't, so you shut your trap."

The crowd doubled and a carriage appeared on the far side of the bridge. Three men emerged from it.

"Off to the madhouse," someone said.

They put him in a straitjacket and took him to the police station, where Marie waited, veiled, statuesque, forbidding. She had been waiting to see what state he was in, wondering what she should do. But when she heard the hysteria in his laugh as he looked at her, and saw the wild look in his eyes, she knew she couldn't cope anymore.

"You may as well keep him in that," she said, "I've done all I can. It's not fair on the child. He must be committed."

The paper chains had come as several packs of red and gold paper strips half an inch wide. Licking the sticky ends to make links had made the insides of Rose's cheeks feel sour, but it was worth it for the way they looked, hanging in U shapes all 'round the tops of the walls, above the mirror, around the doors and windows. Tattoo, away being fixed, had given up his place in the center of the mantelpiece to the tree. The crinkled gold paper of its pipe cleaners shone in the fire and candlelight. High above the fireplace, red and gold links also shone. Half asleep, Rose was still in some way aware of a gentle festive peace enfolding the room.

Eyes closed, once more adrift in the magic wood, going deeper. Deeper.

She was never more complete, more sane, than when she was here, every little dropped discarded thing around her also sleeping. The flickering of light from two half-burned-down pink candles, one on either side of the tree, played on her closed lids and she opened her eyes. Half seeing, they misted over with affection. Who cares for these lost things? Things once touched. The touch, still there. Someone was alive and loved them once. Somewhere. How they pull at the heart, and yet they tell me I have no heart. I'm not clever, the world runs rings 'round me. But I'm thickening out now, going somewhere bigger than the world and all its cleverness. Music afar, a thrill in the air.

Closed lids.

The woods. One day instead of falling asleep, she'd get there—

the opening of the trees, the castle across the moat, the drawbridge. Welcome, long awaited. She'd walk across the bridge and go inside. Nothing was more sure. But first she'd fly to the island. No one else around, the waters stirring with the wading feet of a ghost girl, the moon throwing light on smiling mouths, pink and soft, on little feet, little hands, on the eyes of the dolls, some closed, some wide, some gone. And if in some imagining, some fever, the dolls, called by the moon, suddenly opened their mouths in unison and sang together, and she, wherever she may be—very, very far away, glancing sideways— if she should hear even the smallest flicker on the edge of hearing, the edge of sleep, what would it sound like?

Fast asleep now, beyond the woods and the island, unaware that the rain had begun, that it gently flecked her window and set off a sweet singsong in the gutters and drains.

With no sound at all a gold link gave way in one of the paper chains. The chain whispered as it dropped down the wall, bunching on top of the tree but also pulling at some Blu-Tack holding up the next drape, so that that fell too, and the gold link at its end touched the top of the straight gold flame of the candle on the right-hand end of the mantel- piece. The flame reached up, welcoming.

It was free, and ran all over the room, so ripe and lush and ready for the taking, carrying the whole thing and everything in it out of the world.

A few years later Hermann Otto ran into Julia in Munich. He'd been standing for a long time in front of the large glass cabinet, falling into a melancholy state as the rain teemed down on the canvas, remembering the living Julia while gazing at what remained.

The Anthropological Exhibition had been set up under the awning of a big marquee, so that you had to pass it on the way into the circus. Gassner, the owner of the place and an old acquaintance, approached. "Marvelous, isn't she?" he said.

"Indeed." Otto spoke gruffly. "And the poor little chap."

"No matter how much you look at her," Gassner said, "she never becomes more believable."

Otto smiled. "She'd have made a good mother," he said.

"Well," said Gassner, a short dapper man with an oiled goatee, "they're mine now."

"You've bought them?"

"Acquired," said Gassner. "You could say they're donations. I think she just wants to be rid of them. Have you met La Nouvelle Pastrana?"

Otto hadn't. Gassner conducted him through a red curtain, along a draped passageway, and through another curtain decorated with yellow moons on a deep blue background. A small, comfortable grass-floored area was laid out with sofas and easy chairs and low tables set with pastries and wine. Zenora Pastrana sat veiled on one of the sofas but rose to greet Otto.

"I've heard about you," she said.

She was wearing a black straw hat, highly feathered. The voluminous veil of spotted lace, pulled tight 'round her throat, obscured but did not completely hide her features. When she loosened the ribbon and unveiled, the effect was so much less startling than with Julia. Her face, broad-featured and masculine, was immaculately groomed and very friendly. She shook his hand firmly, and they sat down and drank wine. She was in town to offload the mummies en route from St. Petersburg to Karlsbad, she said.

"Ah, yes, to Karlsbad," said Otto. "And what do you intend to do there?"

"Oh, I'm not staying there." She straightened the veil above her thick black brows. "I'm just going to see the old place and then—well, I'll take my son to Paris. It's a place I've always wanted to see. I'd like to buy a house and retire." She reached for her wine. "My husband left me very comfortable, you know. We had a successful business in the center of Petersburg. You knew him quite well, I believe?"

"Reasonably. So very sorry to hear of his misfortune."

"His death, you mean," she said. "Yes, a tragedy. Five years now! My goodness. Time!"

A brain fever, he'd heard.

"Will you miss them?" he asked.

"Julia? Baby?" She looked down, considering. "I will," she said after a while, "but I won't be sorry to see them go. It's time." She smiled. "And I certainly won't miss those long Petersburg winters."

Otto wished her luck and went on his way. In the main display area the rain was a tattoo on the canvas. The flap was open. The grass shone, the lights were yellow. She'd thrive, he thought. Probably get another man. She could. Fine figure of a woman in her way. Poor old Lent. Always something fishy about the man. That simpering smile.

Marie sat on for half an hour making small talk with Gassner, picking with her long manicured nails at a pastry and nibbling delicately. Then she had a carriage brought to the side entrance. But first, she took a last farewell of Julia and the boy. She could hardly look at Baby, the sight of his pretty chin made her too sentimental. So she looked at Julia, grand old thing, still standing proud and defiant. They're not keeping up very well with her hair, she thought, and was almost tempted to pop in and give it a quick brush-up, a little readjustment here and there. But no, all that was past.

"'Bye, sister," she said and marched away straight-backed to where her cab was waiting.

———

The grinding of carriage wheels on a million roads. The man with the money, first one man then the next, and the next; the men who stand at the entrance and call in the crowds that jog by in a choppy ever-changing sea, all grinning and gazing and wondering, avid for mysteries, drifting from the glass cabinet to the two-headed baby floating in a jar, to the waxwork of Robespierre losing his head. Germany, Holland, Belgium, Vienna, where life had been good, where one night when the show was just about over and everyone was getting ready to close up, three last-minute people came in through the open tent flap. A well-preserved woman of about fifty held the hand of an aging pinhead in a long blue raincoat.

"There," said the portly older man with a fine shock of curly gray hair. "Over there, Niece."

"Cato, don't pull," said Berniece, dragged unceremoniously across the grass to stand in front of Julia's cabinet. "God, Ezra," she said, "now I wish I hadn't come."

Ezra came to loom behind them, gazing solemnly, remembering seeing Julia for the first time across the yard in New Orleans, how he'd thought, God, God, impossible, even though he'd been warned.

"Hoo-hah," said Cato in a soft, puzzled tone.

Berniece put her arm 'round his shoulder and pulled him close.

"Yes," said Ezra, "it's Julia."

"He remembers," said Berniece.

"Of course he does."

"I liked her, you know," said Berniece.

"Baby," said Cato, pointing.

They stood in silence.

"Oh! He's crying," said Berniece.

Tears were pouring down Cato's old face. She got out her hankie and wiped his eyes. "Oh, those eyes of yours, Cato," she said.

Budapest.

Krakow.

East and east again to skirt the Russian border. Twenty years, and somewhere along the line Julia and Theo Junior acquired a grand Russian carriage, with velvet and ruching. Back and back and back it carried them, very far, though time of course no longer existed. Years, no more than circles in water. There were oceans and the roaring of waves and weather. Over and over, light, dark, high summer, bitter skies, snow, rain dripping on a puddle, circles, a dark rattling community of pickled curiosities, abnormalities, fakes, freaks, things of no provenance. More years, more roads. The shriek of a train. Ten years of Norwegian byways. Darkness moving on, progressing through something. Could have been a swamp, a birth canal, a long dream. Wars, rumors of wars. And the men and women, their faces changing like the faces on the closed canvas of a half-awake eye. A banner over the entrance to the tent read: HUMANITY, KNOW THYSELF.

The business had been falling off for years. A couple of times they opened up and no one came. Blame it on the war. Her glass eyes stared at the wall in a loft in Sweden as the war passed.

Years, creeping slowly by, nibbled by moths, her hair straight and lank, the flowers and feathers long gone. The boy tipped sideways. Someone dusted her off, set the boy straight, rattled them back to Norway on a diesel train and hauled them 'round on tour again. In a garage in Oslo a spider made its home in the boy's hair. Someone somewhere took Julia's pearl cross and replaced it with a cheaper version, because it made no sense for such a pretty thing to languish on the neck of a corpse. Once in the far frozen north they were delayed for a few days by weather, and the young daughter of the woman who kept the showground came in every day and talked to the boy as if he were a doll. He did look like a doll. His eyes were always open, his face always surprised. In Malmo, the cabinet was dropped as it was being moved and a big crack appeared up the back of it. No one fixed it, and they were on the road again but the crowds were thin. A trickle.

Ten more years of fabric fading, of varnish chipping, seams fraying, fabric fading.

Ten more in storage.

There's no call for it anymore. Really, in this day and age.

Try America. But the ocean changed nothing, it was just the same there, roads, trains, midways, boardwalks. And back across the ocean, third time, to the north, the snow.

There was a warehouse in Oslo full of old fairground stuff. She ended up there with her baby and her Russian carriage, with half a dozen go-karts, a few tarnished bumper cars and all the crew: the phrenological heads, the Anatomical Venus, the piglet Cyclops, the pregnant, hairless six-footed rat and a dusty jar with two sleeping faces at peace, side by side, scarcely discernible these days through the yellowish glaze of grime.

One night, four boys came up to the old industrial estate from the high-rise flats nearby. They fooled about for a while, riding their bikes 'round the padlocked units, chucking cans of Coke into the weeds growing thickly between them, till one of them, taking a piss in front of an old lockup with boarded-up windows, saw that the corrugated metal that covered the door had rusted away at the bottom where it met the grass. He zipped up, hunkered down and pulled at it. Rust fell into the grass and the strip of metal started coming away from the rotting wood behind.

"We can get in!" he called out.

His friends leaned their bikes up against the concrete wall and gathered 'round. It only took a few minutes to rip the metal away and expose the old doors, which weren't even locked but only tied together with a bit of wire. The darkness inside made them pause on the threshold, daring themselves silently to go in. One of them took a flashlight from his saddlebag and bravely led the way in, the others keeping close. The light shone on boxes and closed crates, hulking shapes. Farther in—

"Go-karts!"

"Must have been a fair. Look. Bumper cars."

The light wandered.

"Let's take them out."

"What? The karts?"

"Yeah. Give us a hand."

They dragged two out. They were hauling another two when someone yelled (afterward, no one could say who), and they gagged on fear, freezing in their tracks. The light shot up to the blank ceiling, bounced off shapes suddenly monstrous and unearthly, quavered about queasily till it came once more to rest on the ghastly face of an ape thing with big staring eyes.

After the shock, they laughed.

"It's a waxwork!"

Hearts still thumping, they approached.

"Must be from the House of Horrors."

It stood in front of a fancy carriage in a big glass case, an ape with a great jutting mouth, an ape in a dress. A baby one stood next to it.

"Does it open?"

It did, with a long slow creak so classically scary it made them laugh some more.

"Get her out."

It wasn't heavy. The little one came off its stand. It was rotten underneath and all its hair was gone.

"Put her by the door! Scare the shit out of someone."

"This is falling to pieces."

"What is it?"

"Look—if I put her arm up like this—"

It came off.

A great guffaw.

"Woo-woo, it's coming to get you!"

The arm, bent at the elbow, still wearing a gold bracelet, waving about, chasing faces.

Someone must have seen the light.

When the police car came winking up from Rommen, they fled on their bikes. The one with the flashlight still had the severed limb, tucked under his arm as he skimmed his bike one-handed down the hill. When he got home, he laid it down on the kitchen table and started examining it. His older brother came in to get something from the fridge.

"What the hell's that?"

"Wood. Wool," said the boy, poking the gaping wound where it had ripped from the body. "It's from a waxwork."

"Where'd you get that? Where've you been?" His brother bent down, a look of concentration on his face.

"Sorry, kid," he said when he looked up again, "this is no waxwork. I have to ring the police," and went out to make the call.

There was not too much of a fuss. The police put the big mummy along with its arm in their basement. The identity was established without much difficulty; after all, this thing had a history. No one claimed it and no one seemed to want it. And there was, of course, no crime to answer for so the police had no need to hang on to it. The university took it and put it in the vaults. The rats had been at the baby and he was in such bad shape they stuck him in a bin at the back of police headquarters. Sometime in the early hours a cat nosed the bin open. Later, a stray dog on the scavenge took him in her mouth and ran away. She chewed on him enthusiastically, tearing bits off, then dropped him in a stairwell, where a young man picked him up and, taking him for some sort of voodoo fetish, hung him over the door of his room, which was painted purple and black and decorated with animal skulls and esoteric symbols. A year later, one of his friends, drunk, removed it. It was thrown over the wall of an empty house and lay in the yard till the clearance people turned up and dumped it with a load of other bits and pieces into one of several boxes that ended up in the back room of a junk shop. A dealer, seeing that the wheat and chaff was hopelessly mixed, bought the boxes as a job lot, stuck them in the back of a van, drove them onto a ferry, crossed the North Sea, and hauled them down to London to his bric-a-brac shop in Camberwell. He cleaned up the good stuff. The rest he chucked in a big yellow garbage bin down the road.

Theo Junior lay on top of a pile of rubble in the bin, legless, armless, one-eyed, till a woman called Rose came along, felt sorry for him and took him home.

D reamlike, silent, the island drifted into view like an absurdist painting, a profusion of small faces, blind eyes, sweet lips, smiles, serenity, blight. The roots of the willows reached out, clutching the bank like dragon claws, seeming to anchor it in its place. Cane grew high. The soil was alive, growth was lush. Apart from oak and horse chestnut and silver birch, Adam knew nothing at all about trees, but there was an abundance of type and shade, a richness of sap and leaves and bark, and the water smelled of green darkness.

A man in a snow-white shirt and straw hat met them on the ramshackle landing stage, accepted their money and gave them a small talk in Spanish. Adam didn't understand a word. Anyway, he knew the story. The quiet middle-aged Spanish couple who'd shared his trajinera on the long drift from the city listened intently, laughing once or twice when the guide made a joke. Adam laughed too to be polite, but his eyes, irresistibly drawn to the dolls, would not stay on the man. Faces emerged from the foliage wherever the eye rested, revealing themselves in greater and greater numbers. Even though he'd known exactly what to expect, the whole island disoriented him, and it had nothing to do with fear or superstition. It was the sheer defiance of the place. I am mad and pointless, it said. Here I am.

The guide led them to a scattering of wooden shacks and shelters with corrugated roofs, most of them broken-down and half open to the elements. One had the word MUSEO in large colored letters painted

above the door. They went in. The shrine was tacky. The hermit's smil-
ing face beamed out from a framed color photograph. The doll in the
center had the pretty bespectacled face of a plain schoolmarm in an old
Hollywood film, the kind revealed to be a beauty by the time the credits
roll. Her eyes looked down on the heap of gifts in front of her, the tour-
isty junk people leave, the sad appeasements and compassionate offer-
ings. To comply with the custom, Adam had bought a couple of candy
bars before getting on the boat, and these he added to the mix, wonder-
ing if the guide would take them home later for his kids. Walls, ceiling,
beams crowded in, a fly-buzzing bazaar of misshapes and mutations.
And oh, how time had feasted on the old ones, cobwebs rampant, dirt
triumphant. Young, shiny new ones hung side by side with their own
future selves. He reached up to touch the face of a friendly little girl
with plump sweet cheeks, missing an eye and a leg. The holes that had
once held the knots of her hair made dotted lines that zigzagged back
and forth across the graying pink of her bald skull. Small, crossed pink
feet nestled beside her ear. He looked up. A baby face smiled back.

The guide had gone outside to give them more room. Adam and the
Spanish couple, quiet, almost reverential, stood, looked, walked about.
He was glad he didn't have to talk to anyone. When their eyes met, he
and the Spanish couple smiled at one another. The husband, a small
fat man with a handsome face and flat gray hair, said something to his
wife in Spanish, half whispering, and she said something back, half
irritated, half laughing. Adam went out and wandered in and out of
the other shacks. All were doll-strung. One had an old bed with a rotten
mattress. Was that where he'd slept, the hermit? Imagine the old guy,
living here alone all those years, the dolls becoming more and more each
year. Crazy. He played with them, she said. They didn't scare him.

She'd have loved this.

The Spanish couple had wandered away, seeming disinclined to
explore much farther than the immediate area around the shacks and
wooden shelters. The guide had gone down to the landing stage and
was talking to the boatman. Adam wandered alone around the island,
looking for a place to leave Tattoo. Wildflowers grew here and there.
The high thin shriek of a bird cut the air. The sun was hot and high,
and where the foliage thinned, it made the clear places almost blinding.
Under the trees, the interplay of black shade and bleached-out white

stung the eyes. Sun and rain had worked on the dolls, and worked still. Adam's progress was slow and random, and he stopped constantly, compelled to study at length. Each hand, each limb, each face, ravaged as though with a terrible illness. But there were too many. Had anyone ever counted? Probably not. You could have a competition, like guessing the number of sweets in a jar.

Thousands, he thought.

By the stream he sat down on an old stump and took a bottle of water from the side pocket of his backpack. Duckweed quivered on the water. He looked up at the sky, tipped back his head and drank, then rolled a cigarette one-handed, sliding down to the ground to lean his back against the stump and contemplate the great display. So many hanging heads. A chubby baby in a blue romper suit, heavily inhabited with insect life, looked down at him. Who broke your neck? So hard not to humanize. It was an impulse, the brain just did it. They've got it wrong, those people who think this is a horror show, he thought. It has power, but it's not that kind. It's just dolls being creepy, because that's what they do. Each once loved, now hanging broken. They belong here. They have company. The experience was strangely tranquil, like the feeling in an ancient graveyard when you've worked your way down to the forgotten overgrown heel of it and all the names have long disappeared from the tipsy old stones. The perfect place for old Tattoo. I said I'd do this. Adam lit up and sucked in hard. Rose is gone, and I'm here. She isn't coming back. He stood up. Even if she touched him on the shoulder now, a touch so light it was scarcely there. Even if you believed in ghosts, she'd never be anything more than that, a shadow, a scent, even a fleeting glimpse perhaps. But she wasn't coming back here, not to this life. Some other maybe, out there on another island, a planet not yet formed. Adam opened his backpack and drew from it the truncated mess that had lived for years on Rose's windowsill. "Here we are, Tattoo," he said. He could hear the distant voices of the Spanish couple talking to the guide. Adam had been drinking on the trajinera, and the beauty and strangeness of the place increased a sense that had been creeping closer and closer since Rose died, more than two years ago now. It had made him humble in the face of the great singularity of her disappearance, yet playful also, and more willing to indulge the meanderings of his own thoughts or mind or whatever it was that yammered on.

Yes, she was a mess, but she'd known what it was to love the clay and there'd been some wisdom of a kind there, he thought, looking 'round at the eerie and companionable horde. Anyway everyone was a mess.

She'd love this, he thought. She'd get it completely, this letting go, this final ritual, as sacred in its own way as a full requiem Mass or Viking ship burial. There was a bush near the stream, home to a doll in a long blue dress. She was big, maybe a foot and a half tall if she'd been standing upright, and she was wedged in a cleft between two branches, with her legs stretched out in front and her arms wide open. She was a bit of a hippie, with beads and a floppy hat, and shaggy red hair hanging in a wild tangle to her shoulders. Above her, thin spearlike leaves reached high.

Adam placed Tattoo against the doll's chest and folded her arms in to keep him in place. A bell rang at the landing stage. "There you are," he said. "You'll be fine here."

He stood for a while, just looking, took a picture, and felt it would be something brilliant and beautiful, the little doll in the mother doll's arms, and everything, every last soul whose name had rubbed away, everything unsung, unkept, unrecorded, all running together with them into the grandeur of their ineffable disappearance. He stood a while longer, head slightly bowed as if he were in a cathedral. The bell rang again.

"Catch you later, Tattoo," said Adam.

It was two hours back to the city, the boatman plying his long wooden pole, the boat with its carnival colors and painted arches sliding smoothly over glassy water. The low wetlands were beautiful. Wading birds stalked among water lilies in the shallows, and the trees' reflections rippled. When they found themselves passing other boats, he came out of his dream. Small craft selling cold drinks and burritos drew alongside and soon they were surrounded. After such strange peace, how fine and gaudy—the flower boats, the strident guitars of mariachi bands, the growing throngs of late afternoon.

Afterword

Julia lived between 1834 and 1860. The parts of this book that deal with her life are fictional, but the basic facts are true. She traveled, performed, married, bore a child, died and after death was exhibited along with her child.

Theo Lent (not to be confused with Lewis B. Lent) died insane in St. Petersburg.

Marie Bartel survived her husband and remarried.

The mummies were found in a warehouse in Norway in 1976. The fate of the child's remains is unknown. Julia's body was kept for many years at the Department of Anatomy, Oslo University. After a campaign by transdisciplinary artist Laura Anderson Barbata and Mario Lopez, governor of Sinaloa state, it was repatriated to Mexico, and in February 2013, after a Roman Catholic funeral attended by hundreds, was finally laid to rest in the cemetery of Sinaloa de Leyva.

Acknowledgments

Thanks to Melissa Danaczko, Octavia Reeve, Jo Dingley and especially Francis Bickmore, whose sensitive, insightful and relentless editing was invaluable.

ABOUT THE AUTHOR

Carol Birch is the author of eleven previous novels, including *Turn Again Home,* which was long-listed for the Man Booker Prize, and *Jamrach's Menagerie,* which was a Man Booker Prize finalist and long-listed for the Orange Prize for Fiction and the London Book Award.